P9-CDE-298

PRAISE FOR THE WORKS OF *NEW YORK TIMES*
BESTSELLING AUTHOR DON BENTLEY

WITHOUT SANCTION

"You can smell the cordite, hear the explosions, and feel the fight in this one. Action jumps from every page."

—Steve Berry, *New York Times* bestselling author of
The Malta Exchange

"Weaves adrenaline and angst, intrigue and insight, onto every page. In a crowded field, Bentley just raised the bar and vaulted over it."

—Andrews & Wilson, US Navy veterans and authors of
the *Wall Street Journal* bestselling Tier One series

"Destined to be the best debut of the year. Bentley writes with the precision of Lee Child and the wit of Nelson DeMille."

—Brigadier General Anthony J. Tata, US Army (ret.),
national bestselling author of *Dark Winter*

"Matt Drake has to fight two wars, maybe more, and he has to save himself before he can save everyone else. An intense, deeply personal story written by someone who has been there."

—Larry Bond, bestselling author of *Arctic Gambit*

"Don Bentley has lived this life, and he writes with deep authenticity. This is one hell of a book."

—Nick Petrie, national bestselling author of *Tear It Down*

"A fresh and worthy entrant into the top tier of military-political thriller authors."   —BookTrib

"Another super-charged, action-packed adventure that's tailor-made for fans of Mark Greaney and Brad Taylor. . . . Gritty, timely, and packed with nonstop, heart-thumping action, Don Bentley's *The Outside Man* is a must-read for fans of propulsive, unputdownable thrillers."

—Ryan Steck, The Real Book Spy

HOSTILE INTENT

"The intricate level of who's-doing-what-to-whom adds twists. Readers who enjoy the world of special ops should add Bentley to their reading pile."   —*Library Journal*

"An excellent, fast-paced plot will keep readers engaged."
—*Mystery & Suspense Magazine*

TOM CLANCY TARGET ACQUIRED

"Exciting. . . . The action builds to a terrific, multiple-point-of-view battle scene. . . . Bentley proves himself a worthy successor to Tom Clancy."   —*Publishers Weekly*

"Bentley is at his best with witty inner dialogue and edge-of-your-seat action scenes that feel creative and authentic."
—BookTrib

TOM CLANCY ZERO HOUR

"There's more than enough deadly action to satisfy any military adventure fan."
—*Publishers Weekly*

"A taut, fast-moving tale in the hands of a skillful writer who knows his stuff."
—BookTrib

"Layered with technical details and riveting action scenes, Don Bentley's latest Jack Ryan Jr. thriller represents a new era for Clancy's readers, one geared more toward action and fast-paced plots that put Jack Junior in unthinkable situations readers will devour."
—Ryan Steck, The Real Book Spy

TITLES BY DON BENTLEY

The Matt Drake Novels
Without Sanction
The Outside Man
Hostile Intent

Tom Clancy Target Acquired
Tom Clancy Zero Hour

HOSTILE INTENT

DON BENTLEY

BERKLEY
New York

BERKLEY
An imprint of Penguin Random House LLC
penguinrandomhouse.com

Copyright © 2022 by Donald Burton Bentley II
Excerpt from *Forgotten War* by Don Bentley
copyright © 2023 by Donald Burton Bentley II
Penguin Random House supports copyright. Copyright fuels creativity, encourages
diverse voices, promotes free speech, and creates a vibrant culture. Thank you for buying
an authorized edition of this book and for complying with copyright laws by not
reproducing, scanning, or distributing any part of it in any form without permission.
You are supporting writers and allowing Penguin Random House to continue to
publish books for every reader.

BERKLEY and the BERKLEY & B colophon are registered trademarks of
Penguin Random House LLC.

ISBN: 9780593333549

Berkley hardcover edition / May 2022
Berkley premium edition / March 2023

Printed in the United States of America
1 3 5 7 9 10 8 6 4 2

Book design by Kristen del Rosario

This is a work of fiction. Names, characters, places, and incidents either are the product
of the author's imagination or are used fictitiously, and any resemblance to actual persons,
living or dead, business establishments, events, or locales is entirely coincidental.

If you purchased this book without a cover, you should be aware that this book is stolen
property. It was reported as "unsold and destroyed" to the publisher, and neither the author
nor the publisher has received any payment for this "stripped book."

To Captain Mark A. Garner and Nickayla Myers-Garner.

Mark personified his alma mater's creed of
"Duty, Honor, Country" both in life and in death.

Nickayla's resilience, grace, and poise in the face of
unspeakable tragedy is a true-life story of heroism
more compelling than any novel I could write.

May their sacrifice never be forgotten.

Si vis pacem, para bellum.

(If you want peace, prepare for war.)

ONE

AUSTIN, TEXAS

Four shots rang out in quick succession, the retort thunderously loud even through my Peltor hearing protection. I detested indoor shooting ranges with their close confines and dingy interiors. Some jackass with a hand cannon always seemed to be in the lane next to mine, and today was no exception. Whatever. Shooting under crappy conditions was still shooting, and that beat the alternative.

Usually.

"What's he hitting?"

"Air," I said, eyeing the target adjacent to mine.

The crisp white paper overlaid with a bad-guy silhouette swung merrily beneath its metal hanger without a care in the world. I could see why. A scattering of holes graced the paper's edges, but the black target lines spiraling outward from the center were completely unbroken.

"You're kicking butt," I said, turning back to my own

lane and the woman sharing it. "Put another couple pairs center mass, and we'll call it a day."

"Already?" the woman said. "You must have other plans. Or something."

As a matter of fact, I did have other plans.

Or something.

But I knew better than to take the bait.

"Less talking. More shooting."

I gave the instructions in my no-nonsense firearms-instructor's voice, and the woman responded accordingly. Settling into a shooter's stance, she adjusted her balance and extended a 9mm Glock away from her chest in a two-handed grip. Her hips shifted as she transferred weight to the balls of her feet. The movement was slight but noticeable.

At least to me.

Then again, I do love my wife's hips.

I reached forward, touching Laila's back. "Remember to square your shoulders," I said, fingertips pressing against her smooth, silky skin.

My wife was an exquisitely beautiful woman. With a Pakistani father and an Afghan mother, Laila was a melting pot of genes from one of the world's most ethnically diverse territories. Modern-day Afghanistan and Pakistan had hosted countless foreign conquerors, and Laila's appearance reflected the region's collective influence. Her dark complexion and waves of midnight hair framed emerald eyes that left me speechless.

This morning, she was wearing a simple white tank top paired with tight faded jeans and a ballcap embroidered with the Texas Gonzales flag. But there was nothing simple about the way the cream-colored shirt highlighted her almond skin or the thick black ponytail tumbling down her back. On a normal day, my wife was distracting.

Today, she was intoxicating.

"More coaching," Laila said. "Less touching."

She adjusted her stance again, snugging her hips against mine. Laila squeezed off a pair of shots before I could reply, but that didn't matter.

I'd lost the capacity for speech.

Laila followed up her first aimed pair with a second and then a third. The silhouette sported six new holes, all within the ten ring. The paper target was only five meters distant, but there was no doubt that Laila was getting the hang of this. I was a good coach, but she was a highly motivated student.

For good reason.

Her Glock's slide locked to the rear after the final shot. Laila ejected the spent magazine and placed it and the pistol on the tray in front of her. Just like she'd been taught.

"How'd I do?" Laila said, facing me.

I could tell by the way her green eyes sparkled that she already knew the answer. Even so, she'd more than earned a compliment or two. As her instructor, it was my job to give them.

"You did—"

The hand cannon erupted.

Again.

I jumped, and Laila shrieked.

A peal of male laughter greeted Laila's decidedly feminine exclamation, followed by an admonishment to grow a pair.

Charming.

"Just a sec," I said. "I've got to take care of something."

"Where are you going?" Laila said, grabbing my biceps.

"Only be a minute," I said, smiling the smile that had melted the hearts of interrogators the world over.

"Matthew," Laila said.

Her green eyes were no longer sparkling. They were shimmering. This was a very important distinction. Sparkling eyes meant a happy wife. Shimmering ones were akin to the buzzing of a rattlesnake's rattle.

"Quick chat with our neighbors," I said. "Nothing more."

"You're a spy," Laila said. "You lie for a living."

She had me there.

"But never to you," I said. "Besides, lying's only a small part of the job. I mostly build bridges of cultural understanding."

"Bridges to nowhere," Laila said.

Her tone was still less than pleased, but her eyes were no longer shimmering. Good. A pissed-off wife meant that my other plans were dead on arrival. On the other hand, a happy wife raised my chances of getting lucky a second time to at least fifty percent.

I'd toppled governments with less.

"Right back," I said.

This time my smile wasn't forced.

I'd been operational for the last six weeks and had just flown back into country the previous evening. We were at the shooting range this morning because Laila wanted to practice, but I had plans to help her out of her tank top once we got home. No way was I going to let a couple of redneck jackwads interfere.

Laila frowned, but she didn't ask me to stay.

Progress.

Sliding around the length of sheet metal dividing our lane from the hand cannon, I introduced myself to the gentlemen on the other side.

"Y'all need help?" I said, smiling my second-best smile.

My first-best smile was reserved for Laila.

And sometimes men who wanted to kill me.

My sudden appearance caught the shooters by surprise. They jumped at the sound of my voice. I thought that was funny.

They did not.

"Help with what?" the one on the left said.

He had the thick build of a former athlete whose frame now sported more fat than muscle. The smedium shirt he wore stretched Saran Wrap–tight across his pudgy chest jiggled as he spoke.

"Great question," I said, still grinning ear to ear. "From the looks of your target, you probably think I'm offering shooting pointers. I'm not. I'm just wondering if you need help with anatomy."

"Anatomy?"

This time the question came from the gentleman on the right. He looked as if he'd stepped from the pages of *Soldier of Fortune* magazine. Asolo boots, 5.11 pants, and a PFG shirt.

A regular tactical ninja.

"Yep," I said. "You geniuses just asked my wife to do something anatomically impossible. That means you're either idiots or rude. I'm hoping for idiots, because acting rude to my wife carries consequences. Or maybe this is all just a big misunderstanding and y'all want to apologize. What's it gonna be?"

The men sized me up before sharing a look. I understood. At six feet and one hundred eighty-five pounds, I wasn't physically insignificant. But neither was I Arnold Schwarzenegger. The 1980s Arnold Schwarzenegger, that is. Today's Arnold was still fit, but I could take him.

Probably.

In any case, I was sporting what Laila playfully termed my ragamuffin look. At least I hoped it was playful. My hair was long and my beard scruffy, but the Wrangler pearly-snap shirt I was wearing framed the wide shoulders and broad back of a person for whom physical fitness was more than just a passing fancy. Put that all together, and I don't know what you get. But whatever it was didn't seem to be enough to convince Beefcake and Mr. Ninja to back down.

"Who the hell are you?" Beefcake said, folding his arms across his chest.

Now we were getting somewhere.

"Great question," I said, my smile widening. "I'm—"

"Drake? Is there a Matt Drake here?"

The question came from behind me. I turned to see the man from the gun range's check-in counter holding open the door to the shooting lanes.

"I'm Drake," I said.

"Phone," the man said, "inside. Says he's your boss."

"I'm on vacation," I said.

"He said you'd say that. He also said to tell you that people who hunt terrorists don't take vacations. Pick up the phone or he'll send the FBI. Again. Sorry—his words."

"I'm coming," I said.

I waited a beat for the man to leave and the heavy soundproof door to close behind him. Then I turned back to Beefcake and Mr. Ninja.

"We're short on time, so I'll cut to the chase," I said. "Apologize to my wife, and we can all leave happy. Refuse, and I'll be forced to come find you *after* I finish putting another jihadi in the dirt. So what's it gonna be? Now or later?"

They chose now.

Bridges to nowhere, my ass.

TWO

Matthew? Is that you?"

"Yep," I said, holding the phone between my ear and shoulder as I packed my shooting gear into my range bag.

Even though our range time had been nearly complete before the interrupting phone call, Laila had been less than thrilled with our abrupt departure. She was now in the gun store attached to the range, expressing her annoyance in a manner designed to get my attention.

Shopping.

Shopping for a baby Glock to carry in her purse.

What a woman.

"Then use your man voice. I can barely hear you over this racket."

I paused in the middle of zipping the bag closed. The check-in guy had been kind, or terrified, enough to let me take the call in his office. The soundproofing in the door and walls rendered a silence absolute enough to hear my heartbeat.

"Where are you, Chief?" I said, dreading the answer.

"At a slam-poetry reading. At least, that's what the sign says. But none of it even rhymes. And don't get me started on the audience full of hipster jackasses. Cups of fufu coffee are the only thing slamming in this joint."

I could hear the disappointment in his voice even as I took a seat in the flimsy chair opposite the metal desk. Defense Intelligence Agency Branch Chief James Scott Glass, former Army Special Forces team sergeant and current night terror to jihadis everywhere, was attending a slam-poetry reading.

If this wasn't a sign of the apocalypse, I wasn't sure what was.

"Can you hear me now?" I said, shouting into the phone.

"No," James said. "Between the screaming from the stage and the yapping audience, I've been in firefights that were quieter. Wait one. QUIET."

The silence that greeted James's outburst made my soundproof room seem loud.

My boss certainly knew how to work a room.

"Speak, Matthew," James said, coming back on the line.

"Still here, Chief," I said.

I debated barking, but didn't. Mostly because I was an adult and whatever had James desperate enough to call me from a slam-poetry session probably wasn't a laughing matter. But also because even ten years into forced medical retirement, my boss was not a man to be trifled with.

"Good," James said. "I need you to come in. Now."

"I just landed last night. I haven't even been home for twelve hours. I'd remind you that I'm on vacation, but I suspect you're not familiar with the term. It's Sunday. Give me twenty-four hours with my wife, and I'll grab the direct to Washington Reagan tomorrow. I'll be in the office before lunch. The world's not gonna end today."

I thought it was a pretty good argument.

James didn't agree.

"You're not going to DC," James said. "Our embassy in Vienna had a walk-in."

Walk-in was slang for someone who came in off the street purporting to have information of interest to the US government. The vast majority of these folks were people hoping to trade something of minimal value for the ultimate prize—US citizenship. As such, walk-ins were normally relegated to the most junior CIA or DIA officer. But occasionally something of value did stroll in the door. If James was calling, I had to think the Vienna walk-in fell into this category.

"Can you give me any specifics?"

"Not over an open line. But I will say this—the walk-in asked for you. By name."

That was interesting, but not entirely unexpected. As an officer for the Defense Intelligence Agency, I ran and recruited assets the world over. While the goal of every recruitment was to snare an asset who produced meaningful intelligence for the duration of their career, this wasn't always the case. Sometimes an asset transitioned to a job without the requisite access. Sometimes they just stopped producing. When this happened, the asset was formally closed, but I always tried to part ways on good terms.

Every now and then, dormant assets found themselves in a position where they could again become useful. This was why I always provided mine with an email address and a phrase to employ if they needed to reestablish contact. These instructions didn't include plans to visit the American embassy, but the assets I ran were, by and large, intelligent men and women. If they believed that a crash meeting at the embassy was necessary, I wasn't going to second-guess them.

As embassies went, Vienna was one of the most crucial. Although the Cold War had ended more than thirty years ago, Vienna was still a city of spies. Its central European location made the Austrian capital a geographical crossroads between East and West. Vienna would be an ideal venue for a spy on the run to contact an old handler.

"Which of my aliases did the walk-in use?" I said.

"You're not listening, Matthew," James said. "He asked for you by name. Your true name."

I sucked in a breath, contemplating James's answer. Like any sane handler, I never operated under true name. If this man knew my identity, he merited my attention.

"What's his name?" I said.

"Wouldn't give one. Just a message. He said to tell you the Irishman was calling in a favor. Ring a bell?"

It did.

"I'm booking a ticket to Vienna," I said.

"No need. A Gulfstream's sitting on the tarmac at Austin-Bergstrom. Get moving."

THREE

The fading orange light streaming through the cabin window caressed Laila's sleeping face with gentle fingers as we hurtled east. Though the converted futon in the Gulfstream's conference room comfortably fit two, half the bed was empty. My wife was curled against me, head pillowed in my lap, midnight hair spilling across my legs.

I wasn't complaining.

After hanging up with James, I'd gone to tell Laila the bad news with more than a little trepidation. We'd both agreed that DIA, even with its long absences, was still the best place for me. For now. But to mitigate some of the strain the frequent separations placed on our marriage, I'd worked out an arrangement with James. Laila and I could live in the city we'd both come to love—Austin. In exchange, I'd deploy when needed. But when I was home, I worked from Austin with the mutual understanding that this "work" consisted mainly of being available should James need me.

I'd spent the last several weeks traveling, conducting asset validations both stateside and internationally. This meant that I was due for some downtime. In anticipation, Laila had already taken a vacation from her demanding job. Laila was a forensic accountant on the path to partnership, so her absences had to be delicately managed. Knowing what it took for her to coordinate an absence, I didn't think she'd be thrilled about me jetting back to Europe so soon.

Once again, my wife surprised me.

"I'm going with you," Laila said, flashing green eyes daring me to say otherwise.

"Baby, this is a work trip," I said, "not a boondoggle. Besides, I have to head straight to the airport. You don't even have your passport."

"I didn't say I was staying in Vienna," Laila said. "But I am going with you. You're flying private, right?"

I nodded.

"For twelve hours?"

I nodded again.

Laila leaned closer, the intoxicating scent of vanilla and jasmine following her. "Want company?"

I did.

Now we were midway across the Atlantic, winging our way toward God knew what. I tried to concentrate on the Irishman waiting for me in Vienna, but my thoughts kept returning to the beauty stretched across my lap.

True to form, James had ensured the Gulfstream came equipped with my go bags packed with an assortment of clothes and equipment. This meant that while I had something to change into, Laila did not. She'd improvised with one of my T-shirts. The fabric was soft, but overstretched from countless wears. It hugged her curves, but kept slipping off her shoulders.

I wasn't complaining.

Laila shifted as I watched, and the T-shirt fell scandalously lower. Though there was quite a bit to enjoy about the view, a length of toned brown arm demanded my attention. Or, more specifically, the band of puckered white scar tissue that encircled her triceps muscle just above Laila's brachial artery.

For the first six years of our marriage, I'd kept the two worlds I inhabited starkly separate. When I was home, I was Laila's husband—a guy who played guitar and sporadically filled out applications for graduate school. When I was operational, I was Matt Drake—former Army Ranger and Defense Intelligence Agency officer.

But four months ago, a former Iraqi general turned criminal mastermind known as the Devil had caused my two worlds to collide with devastating consequences. Laila had nearly died in my arms.

She'd been the lucky one.

To get my attention, the Devil had put his pistol to the head of my DIA teammate, a sassy scientist named Virginia Kenyon, and pulled the trigger.

Laila had dealt with the trauma in the same way my driven wife faced every challenge—head-on. She'd registered for a concealed-carry class while still lying in her hospital bed. Her doctor signed her release paperwork a week later, and she'd demanded we stop by the gun range on the way home. In the weeks that followed, she'd become a shooting fanatic, determined to never again be easy prey.

As with anything else Laila put her mind to, my wife had become quite the shooter. Her gun-handling skills still needed smoothing, but that was just a matter of time. My accountant wife could now draw her pistol from concealment and accurately put rounds on target.

She was no longer a victim.

This newfound self-reliance did much to ease her mind, but little to assuage my guilt. Virginia was still dead, and my wife had come much too close to joining her. I closed my eyes, two horrific images competing for space in my brain. In one, a curtain of auburn hair spilled across a dirty cement floor as Virginia lay in a crumpled, lifeless heap. In the other, my hands were soaked with arterial blood as I frantically tried to stop Laila's hemorrhaging before she bled out in my arms.

As the scenes warred for prominence, flashing back and forth like still frames from a snuff film, my right index finger began to tremble. Balling my fingers into a fist, I breathed in through my nose and out through my mouth, trying to relax the rebellious muscles before the spasms spread. My condition was still not fully understood, but the symptoms seemed to worsen under periods of extreme stress.

Like now.

"Hey," Laila said.

I opened my eyes to see her staring at me.

The trembling ceased.

"What are you thinking about?" Laila said, tracing the length of my jaw with her index finger.

As always, her touch made me shiver, and as always, my reaction made her laugh.

"You," I replied honestly.

"Me in this T-shirt or me in Iraq?" Laila said.

"That T-shirt is pretty distracting," I said, inching the fabric over Laila's stomach.

"You didn't answer the question," Laila said, swatting my fingers away, "which means Iraq. Baby, for the hundredth time, it wasn't your fault. We live in a fallen world, home to both great beauty and unspeakable evil. You can't blame yourself for one any more than you can take credit for the other."

"I know," I said, giving up the battle for the T-shirt in favor of linking my fingers through hers. "But my work is a magnet for men like the one who hurt you. I signed up for that. You didn't."

"I signed up for you," Laila said, reaching up to run her fingers through my hair, "and everything that comes with you. That's what marriage means, Matthew Drake. Besides, if I'd wanted safe, I would have dated that nice doctor Mom had her eye on."

"You chose me over a doctor?"

"A surgeon, actually."

"Why?"

"I can't seem to remember right now. Maybe you could help me."

This time the T-shirt slid off just fine.

FOUR

A nother coffee, sir?"

"*Nein, bitte*," I said, handing the bow-tie-wearing waiter a twenty-euro note.

Jet lag was hitting me hard, but I knew from experience there was a finite amount of caffeine I could ingest before I turned into a twitching tweaker. After downing three of Café Central's famous Viennese-style coffees in a little over an hour, I was dangerously close to reaching critical mass. Caffeine jitters were fine for a casual day at the office.

This wasn't that.

I used the tiny silver spoon that had accompanied my equally tiny ceramic cup of *kaffee* to stir the last bit of *gupf* into the brew, trying not to gawk at my surroundings. The vaulted ceilings were tied together in intricate arches supported by marble columns. Lamps hung in ornate clusters while glass display cases filled with pastries of every description dominated the far end of the shop.

Though I'd been on the ground for less than two hours, I could already see why the old Cold War hands still raved about assignments to Vienna. For a guy used to recruiting assets in Middle East back alleys that smelled of equal parts sewage and rotting trash, this was a nice change of pace.

"American?" the waiter said, returning with my change.

"Canadian," I said. "Is my German really that bad?"

"Not at all," the waiter said with a gracious smile. "I like to practice my English."

He was kind, but I knew that my German really was that bad. My assigned area of operation was a bit less genteel than old Europe, and my linguistic repertoire reflected my assignments. I spoke pretty good Arabic, got by with Pashtu, and could curse in Farsi. My German was a product of the two years I took in high school. Still, after years of globe-trotting, I found that most people responded graciously to attempts to speak their language.

The waiter was no exception.

"Your English is very good," I said, leaving a sizable tip before pocketing the rest of the coins.

"Thank you," the waiter said, scooping up the bills. "Are you sure you're not American?"

"Very much so," I said with a laugh. "Why?"

"This morning someone gave me twenty euros to pass a message to an American with your description."

"Sorry, friend," I said, my smile still plastered on. "You're not looking for me."

"Okay," the waiter said with a shrug. "Enjoy my city."

I politely nodded and went back to studying my sight-seeing map of Vienna as the waiter made his way to another table. I kept my face frozen in my best perplexed-tourist expression while my thoughts raced. Posing as Canadian was standard practice on the odd occasion I needed to travel in Europe. Simply being an American could be a polarizing endeavor, even amid our supposed Western allies.

A person's reaction really was a coin toss, and rather than take the chance, I'd become pretty good at impersonating a Canuck. Say what you want about stereotypes, everyone really did seem to love Canadians. That aside, the waiter's interest went beyond casual conversation. If he did have a message for me, it might be worth hearing.

Or it might be a setup.

Based on how my trip was progressing so far, I was betting on the latter.

After landing hours earlier, I'd taken the metro to the US embassy. Okay, not directly to the embassy. I wasn't traveling under a diplomatic passport, so I had none of the protections offered by official cover. Jet-lagged or not, I needed to approach this operation with the same focus on tradecraft I would have employed had the city been Aleppo instead of Vienna. So instead of just schlepping to the embassy, I'd embarked on a ninety-minute surveillance-detection run composed of trains, cabs, and finally hoofing it. Only after I was certain that my tail was clear did I make my way to American soil on Boltzmanngasse, where I expected to find Nolan Burke, former member of the Real IRA.

Aka the Irishman.

But Nolan wasn't there. As the pretentious CIA case officer who'd met me inside the embassy explained, the Irishman was a walk-in, not a renditioned terrorist. If he wanted to leave the embassy, the CIA officer couldn't stop him.

Or hadn't, anyway.

In a miracle rivaling Lazarus's resurrection, I didn't point out that the contingent of armed Marines a floor away could have helped him do just that. Nor did I explain that if the underwhelming agency employee would have fed the footage from the embassy security cameras into the Agency's facial-recognition program, he would have discovered that Nolan was very much a terrorist.

And a wanted one at that.

Instead, I'd put on my most pleasant face and asked if perchance the mysterious visitor had left me anything. He had. A piece of paper with *Café Central* and *1100* scribbled in a doctor's handwriting. After taking the paper, I'd thanked the CIA employee and beat feet out of the embassy before the sloth-inducing malaise infecting the building's occupants somehow spread to me.

Okay, that wasn't entirely fair. Technically speaking, any activity occurring on the City of Music's cobble-stoned streets had to be coordinated through our embassy in Vienna. This meant that the CIA officer who'd met with Nolan was operating on home turf, while I was the outsider. As with any two governmental agencies, the DIA and CIA often viewed each other through a competitive lens. With this in mind, I was lucky the Agency officer had seen fit to pass me Nolan's note at all. I'd been waiting for the Irishman for more than an hour with nothing to show but jittery nerves and an air-travel-induced hangover. Now Nolan had decided to get cute by leaving a message with the waiter.

Or maybe he hadn't.

Either way, I was done drinking coffee.

Gathering my tourist map, I waved to the waiter and headed for the door. Nolan Burke was a terrorist, but he'd saved my life and Laila's at great risk to his own. He was also no stranger to the art of espionage. He'd disappeared after the murder of two policemen in Northern Ireland. A man with the highly tuned survival instincts necessary to evade MI6 and Interpol for decades wouldn't have staked his entire contingency-contact plan on a single waiter who liked to practice his English.

I'd done my part by flying fourteen hours at the drop of a hat.

The next move was up to Nolan.

I paused at the curb, watching Vienna traffic crawl down Strauchgasse. I waited for a break in the cars and then darted across the street, turning right toward Herrengasse. The route I was following meandered past hotels, coffeehouses, and bars. All were well-known landmarks and full of pedestrians.

Perfect for a crash meeting.

Turning down the street, I walked on the right side so that I could face oncoming traffic. The unfolded tourist map in my hand provided me with an excuse to amble aimlessly, pausing frequently to look in store windows and scrutinize street signs. I didn't see any overt surveillance, but that just meant that if I had watchers, they weren't amateurs.

A triggering event was one of the surest ways to spot a surveillance team. Seemingly nonrelated incidents like car engines starting or the movement of people or vehicles that coincided with something you did. For instance, a car engine that turned over the moment you stepped out of your apartment could be a triggering event.

Or it might just be your neighbor leaving for work.

This was the maddening part about espionage. Depending on your vantage point, everything or nothing could be significant. I preserved my sanity by adopting a single rule—coincidences don't exist. Sure, this meant that sometimes I ascribed intent when there wasn't any. But I was also still alive. Case in point, a black Audi station wagon was making a U-turn against traffic on the opposite side of the street. It might just have been a frazzled driver trying to avoid the warren of one-way streets that crisscrossed Vienna.

I didn't think so.

I paused in midstride as the Audi cut off an approaching Mercedes construction truck, tires squealing. The truck driver blasted his horn, but I barely noticed the sound. I was too focused on the shiny black hood rushing toward my side of the street. That and the painfully empty void on my right hip normally occupied by my concealed Glock 23. Carrying a pistol in Austria without the backstop of official cover risked the wrath of the Austrian Federal Police. A simple embassy meet wasn't worth the headache.

At least that had been my reasoning up until about three seconds ago.

The Audi whipped across the street and bumped against the curb before skidding to a halt. The shimmering passenger door missed my knees by inches.

"Are ye getting in or standing there?" a familiar voice called through the open window. "I'd recommend getting in. The Russians are right behind me."

A smart man might have asked a question or two first.

I've never been mistaken for a smart man.

I opened the door and slid onto the leather seat next to the man who'd saved my life. Nolan Burke—former member of the Real IRA and current international fugitive. A terrorist who'd taken a step on the path to redemption.

Here's to hoping his feet were still treading on the straight and narrow.

FIVE

Nolan floored the accelerator before I'd even fully shut the door.

The Audi's turbo responded with a throaty growl.

Driving on the autobahn was both an exciting and humbling experience. Exciting because the stretches of unregulated road were made for testing your vehicle's performance limits or your own—whichever came first. Humbling because the cars that most often chased you from the fast lane were unassuming black station wagons.

Just like this one.

The Audi A4 allroad shot through a slot between two parked cars with about a millimeter's worth of clearance. I tried not to duck below the dashboard.

Nolan never flinched.

"So how have ye been?" Nolan said.

From his casual tone, we could have been sitting

across from each other at Café Central instead of screaming down a Vienna side street. Nolan's appearance suggested otherwise. His unkept hair hung limp around his face, and his bloodshot eyes were framed by dark, puffy bags. His chin was covered in reddish stubble, and his shirt was wrinkled and untucked.

The Irishman was on the run.

"Great," I said, slamming the seat belt buckle home. "Thanks for asking."

"And your wife, how is she?"

Nolan spooled through gears as he spoke, shifting with a Formula One driver's precision. The acceleration crushed me into the bucket seat as he poured on the gas.

"Fine as well," I said. "Thanks to you."

"I heard about her injury," Nolan said, shaking his head. "Bad bit of business, that."

A woman and man strolling hand in hand had the audacity to consider stepping into the crosswalk. Nolan politely tapped the horn and downshifted, the engine screaming as he redlined the rpms.

The happy couple wisely stayed on the sidewalk.

The Audi's speedometer edged back past one hundred kilometers as Nolan clutched back into fourth gear, rocketing through the intersection.

"It was," I said, picturing the puckered skin on Laila's shoulder. "Nolan, why am I here?"

"Cutting to the chase, are we?" Nolan said, careening around another corner. "Fine. I need help, and I have information to trade for it."

"What kind of information?"

"The Russian kind. The KGB is up to their old tricks."

"Don't you mean SVR?" I said. "The KGB dissolved with the Soviet Union back in the nineties."

"Bah. New name. Same men."

Nolan spun the wheel violently to the left, turning off the main drag into a narrow alley. "Now be a good lad and grab the hardware beneath your seat. We're in a spot of trouble."

By *spot of trouble*, Nolan seemed to be indicating the two cars parked nose-to-nose in a makeshift roadblock fifty meters in front of us. A pair of plainclothesmen stood in front of the cars. Even if they hadn't been carrying the collapsible-stock version of the AK-74 in the loose, easy grip of men accustomed to pointing guns at others for a living, their affiliation was plain. If you knew what to look for, that is. Slavic features and cheap suits bunched across thick shoulders and arms. Not to mention the twin looks of disdain for which their kind was famous. Whether they were in the employ of a billionaire oligarch or the nation-state that bequeathed them mattered little.

The gunmen were Russian hoods through and through.

As we careened toward them, the Russians raised the short-barreled rifles to their shoulders and settled into shooting stances. Unlike the happy Viennese couple we'd scared back onto the sidewalk two streets ago, these men weren't intimidated by the 3,726-pound car barreling down on them.

Lounging around in the Café Central suddenly didn't seem like such an imposition.

"What's the play?" I said, reaching under my seat.

Though our tactical situation was not ideal, I assumed that Nolan had a plan.

But I would never know.

Just as my fingers touched a hard plastic buttstock, motion registered in my peripheral vision. I turned to see a silver Mercedes symbol mounted on an enormous bumper. A bumper seemingly hovering outside Nolan's window.

Then steel met steel.

I pinballed between the door and dashboard, my head bouncing off the doorframe even as the airbag blasted me in the face. Nolan, who hadn't been wearing a seat belt, collided with me, his shoulder catching me in the chin like a well-thrown uppercut.

The lights didn't completely go out in Georgia, but they dimmed.

Significantly.

Rough hands dragged me from the car. I tried to resist, but my major muscle groups weren't cooperating. The Russians yanked me from my seat and dumped me on the ground like a pile of wet laundry. I tried to sit up, but my brain had other plans.

The world spun.

I slid into darkness.

A slamming car door roused me the second time. Opening my eyes, I saw two gunmen dragging Nolan's limp body toward one of the roadblock cars. Though his face was a mess of cuts, and blood streamed from his broken nose, Nolan's eyelids fluttered open. He offered me a weak smile before his captors tossed him into the backseat and climbed in behind him.

I pushed myself upright, trying to stand, but flopped onto my side instead. My legs were wobbly, and while the world was no longer spinning, it was still badly listing. Gritting my teeth, I closed my eyes, pressed both palms flat against the cobblestones, and pushed. Ignoring the gonging in my head, I struggled to my knees, swaying like a drunken sailor.

This kidnapping wasn't going down in a Karachi back alley. It was happening in broad daylight in a major European city known for its effective police force and almost nonexistent crime. To get away with this, the snatch team needed to minimize the information a potential witness could pass to the police.

So they needed to minimize me.

Heavy-soled shoes crunching on broken glass lent a sense of urgency to my effort. In my current state, I wouldn't survive a round with Tinker Bell, let alone Russian killers. But firearms were the great equalizer. The Audi and the weapon secreted under my seat were just feet away. The violent crash sequence surely would have shaken it loose, but I'd take scrounging in the car for a gun over waiting for death in the middle of the street.

Since the world was off axis, I kept my eyes closed to neutralize the vertigo and stumbled toward the car. After three lurching steps, my outstretched fingers found the Audi's cool metal frame. Wrapping my hand around the car's doorjamb, I tumbled into the inviting interior.

Or tried to.

Someone grabbed a handful of my shoulder and spun me around. My arms were wet noodles, but I threw an elbow as I turned, hoping to bury the pointy end into a Russian jaw or temple.

I missed.

My attacker ducked beneath the clumsy strike, hammering me with a body blow to the stomach, followed by a hook to the kidney. I'd taken a punch or two in my life, but nothing like this. The Russian had fists of concrete. Lightning sparked across my abdomen.

I doubled over, gasping, powerless to avoid the inevitable knee to my jaw.

It didn't come.

Instead, the Russian drew a pistol from the holster at his waist and pressed the barrel into my forehead. But rather than the thunderclap I was expecting, I heard two Russian words instead.

"Moskva rulit."

Then he swung the pistol in a vicious arc.

I tried to get an arm up, but my nervous system wasn't taking calls. Steel bit into my skin and pain rocketed through my skull.

Then I felt nothing.

SIX

"You look like shit."

"Thanks, Chief," I said, adjusting the bag of ice I was holding against my throbbing head. His assessment, while accurate, was becoming all too common.

Maybe I needed to start ducking.

"Don't get all sensitive," James said, his gravelly voice booming from the speakers hanging from the ceiling. "I'm just saying that maybe you should start ducking."

As a Green Beret who'd spent eighteen years kicking in doors and shooting bad guys in the face until a Taliban RPG had robbed him of his right eye and ended his operational career, James spoke with a certain bluntness. Though he'd traded his multicams for office attire, James had refused to adopt the Brooks Brothers dress code expected of Senior Executive Service–level civilians. Instead, he wore his dress shirts open at the collar and rolled at the cuffs, exposing tattooed forearms. He didn't own a tie, and when the occasion mandated a sport coat, the fabric strained to contain his wide back and massive chest. A black eye patch, which sharply contrasted with the gray stubble that remained of his hair, completed his wardrobe.

When James offered tactical advice, he wasn't speaking metaphorically.

I dropped the soggy Ziploc bag onto the white oak conference table in front of me, careful to aim for the towel my CIA counterpart had so thoughtfully provided.

Or at least I mostly aimed.

I'd managed to flee the site of Nolan's kidnapping before Vienna's finest had arrived, but my CIA escort had been less than thrilled to see me once I returned to the embassy. This was probably because my unexpected presence interrupted something important, like his afternoon solitaire game. In any case, after a not-insubstantial amount of grumbling on his part, he'd arranged for medical attention and a secure communications link to DIA headquarters in Washington, DC. Now I was repaying his less-than-stellar interagency cooperation with a cantaloupe-sized wet spot on the CIA's polished hardwood table.

Petty?

Perhaps.

But it'd been that kind of day.

"Didn't your mama ever tell you that if you can't say something nice, don't say anything at all?" I said.

"Come on, Matty," a baritone voice answered. "You gotta be human to have a mom. Besides, the chief's right. You don't look so good. You seen a doctor?"

"Yes, Mom," I said, placing the ice pack back on my face. "Mild concussion and some bruising. Nothing that a couple of ibuprofens won't fix."

That wasn't entirely true. The embassy's resident Navy corpsman had done a pretty thorough evaluation, but he'd recommended an MRI to rule out any swelling of the brain or unseen hematomas. He'd also wanted me on bed rest for the next twenty-four hours, since the onset of symptoms from a concussion were often delayed.

I'd overruled him on both counts.

I'd had my bell rung enough times to know when an injury was serious. My head throbbed, but in a day or two I'd be fine.

Mostly.

"Don't get all pissy, brother," the man said. "This is what happens when you decide to go jaunting off on missions without me."

I grimaced as I adjusted the ice pack, but I didn't argue.

The thing about good friends is that they tell you the truth. A best friend does so without the obligatory sugarcoating that passes for conversation in polite society. The man who was speaking was a former Delta Force sniper whose call sign was Frodo. He was also my best friend. When I'd first shown up to Iraq as a baby-faced DIA officer straight from training, Frodo had been on loan to the Agency from the Unit. The chief of base had tasked Frodo to be my bodyguard. Neither of us had been thrilled with the arrangement.

At first.

But it didn't take long for Frodo to prove his worth as I began recruiting assets from the multitude of Sunni militias duking it out with the Iranian-sponsored Shias. Back then Iraq really had been the Wild West. I'd run a couple of high-placed agents who helped us to bag an al-Qaeda bomb-making cell. The bomb maker's terrorist friends had expressed their displeasure at this turn of events by trying to bag yours truly. Frodo convinced them of the error of their ways with a little 7.62mm diplomacy.

Nothing says de-escalation like a well-placed head shot.

After smoothing out some rough spots in our relationship, we began to jibe.

At the end of the tour, Frodo had requested a leave of absence from the Unit, and we took our show on the road. Six years later, we were doing our thing in Syria when an explosively formed penetrator, or EFP, amputated Frodo's left arm at the elbow and ruined his left leg. In the two years since, we'd had to relearn our roles. We were still partners after a fashion, but Frodo's days as my shadow were over, as my steadily increasing number of concussions could attest.

"You two about done with the ass grabbing?" James said. "If so, I'd like to get down to business."

"Almost," I said. "Where you calling from, Frodo?"

Unlike the familiar view of James's conference room on the left side of the split video screen, Frodo's portion was dark.

"Home," Frodo said. "I've got the stomach bug. Trust me—you don't want to see this."

"And here I thought commandos were tough," I said. "Well, if you want to stop feeling sorry for yourself and come to Vienna, I'd be happy to have you. My CIA brethren aren't offering much in the way of assistance, and I've got shit to do."

"Like what?" James said, reaching beneath the conference table for his ever-present white Styrofoam cup. "Your walk-in is in the wind. Hell, by now he's probably in a ditch with a bullet in his skull. Not to mention that your description is all over the Austrian news, and your fingerprints are on the Irishman's car. Sloppy, Matthew. Very sloppy."

James punctuated my impromptu performance review by noisily spitting a brown stream of tobacco juice into the cup. My boss was living proof that you might take the man out of operations, but you'd never take operator out of the man.

"You'll have to pardon my poor tradecraft, Chief," I said, blood beginning to boil. "I didn't exactly have time to sanitize the car. You know, with the SVR hit team trying to kill me and all."

"Not SVR," Frodo said. "Directorate V."

"Who?" I said.

"You need to brush up on your Russian operatives," James said.

"Give me a break, boss," I said, my head pulsing in time with my heartbeat. "I don't work the Russian threat."

"You do now," Frodo said. "Directorate V, or Vympel, as it's also known, is part of the Russian FSB. They specialize in dissidents and defectors. Our intel analysts have been comparing visas against known aliases and scrubbing airport video feeds. Nothing solid yet, but the digital bread crumbs are pointing toward that way."

"They the ones who whacked that dissident in London?" I said.

"No way," James said, shaking his head. "That was GRU shit. Way too flashy and sloppy to be Directorate V. Your walk-in got snatched off the street, while in a vehicle no less. What's more, the Austrians have nothing. After they broke contact with you, both the shooters and your Irishman evaporated. Only Directorate V could pull off something that slick. Either way, your boy's long dead."

"No, he's not," I said.

"You trying to be ornery?" James said.

The spit-stained Styrofoam cup was hovering midway to his thick lips.

A prisoner awaiting execution.

"Think about it, Chief," I said. "The Russians staged a picture-perfect ambush. No *Polizei*, no pedestrians, and no cameras. For a good five minutes, we were completely isolated. If they'd wanted the Irishman dead, they could have done it there. He's not in a ditch. Not yet."

"Why not?" James said.

I shook my head. "Don't know. Nolan and I didn't get much time together."

"Did he say anything?"

"Nothing real specific," I said, trying to remember the Irishman's words around the throbbing of my head. "Something about the KGB being up to their old tricks."

"What's that mean?" Frodo said.

"Hell if I know," I said.

"Anything we can use on the kidnappers?" Frodo said. "Descriptions? Distinguishing features?"

I shook my head. "They were professionals. It went down fast, dirty, and hard. Chief would have been proud. I can work with the facial-sketch program, but I don't think it's gonna help. I cracked my noggin during the crash sequence, so everything was kind of blurry. But one of them did say something in Russian to me. Sounded like *musket roulette* or some shit."

"Moskva rulit?" James said.

"That's it," I said.

"You speak Russian?" Frodo said.

"I was a Tenth Group guy," James said. "Russian was our mission set."

"Swell," I said. "What does it mean?"

"Verbatim it translates to *Moscow rules*," James said. "But that doesn't really capture the spirit of the phrase. The saying goes back to the Cold War days. It meant that the norms usually observed between competing intelligence services didn't apply. The KGB played by big-boy rules."

"The Chicago way," Frodo said.

"The what?" James said, even as I smiled.

"That's some *Tinker, Tailor, Soldier, Spy* bullshit right there," I said.

"Bullshit or not, the Russian was telling you to mind your own business," James said.

"Which I'm not gonna do," I said.

"Matthew, your boy is gone," James said. "Even if he's not dead, he's on a one-way trip to the motherland."

"I don't agree," I said. "The Austrian BVT isn't the Mossad, but they certainly know how to lock down their country. Amateurs would try to smuggle the Irishman out now. Professionals would lie low and do the interrogation on Austrian soil. Much less risky. Once they get what they need from Nolan, the SVR can either ditch the body or exfil him back to Mother Russia when the heat dies down. He's still in-country, and I'm gonna find him."

"Son," James said, "I love your tenacity, but we don't have time for that."

"From where I'm sitting, I've got nothing but time," I said. "You pulled me from my vacation to meet a walk-in. Now I'm here. I'm not getting on a plane with my tail between my legs just because a Moscow thug smacked me around."

"Nobody's talking about getting on a plane," James said. "There's something else I need you to do, since you're already in Vienna."

I stared at James, trying to make sense of what he was saying.

Then it hit me.

"Son of a bitch," I said, slamming the Ziploc bag on the table. The seal burst, sending ice cubes scattering across the polished wood.

"CIA's not going to like that," Frodo said. "That table looks expensive."

"You set me up," I said, pointing my index finger at

James. "The walk-in was just an excuse. You had something else in the works the entire time."

"I wouldn't put it quite like that," James said.

"Chief," Frodo said.

"Okay, fine," James said. "I might have had an errand in mind."

"Seriously?" I said.

"Matthew," James said, "I actually am your boss. The Defense Intelligence Agency exists to do more than just fulfill your homicidal urges."

"Chief," Frodo said again.

"What?" James said. "It's true. When that boy gets rolling, bodies start dropping."

"Really?" I said.

"Don't get all sensitive," James said. "Lord knows I've met more than my share of men who needed killing. But do you know the amount of paperwork I get saddled with every time you put someone in the dirt?"

"We're done," I said, getting to my feet. "I don't have time for this shit. Nolan saved my life. He called in a debt. I'm going to honor it."

"By doing what exactly?" James said. "Going house to house looking for a half-dead Irishman? If he's alive, he doesn't have much time. You gonna burn it by dicking around by yourself? Or would you rather have the full weight and power of the Defense Intelligence Agency behind you?"

I stared at James, considering. He was right. I could make things happen in my neighborhood. From Syria to Iran, I had a string of assets who could shake the proverbial trees on my behalf. But in Vienna, I was just another American who spoke bad German. I needed access to the DIA's resources, which meant agreeing to James's bargain.

With a sigh, I sat back down.

"This is a shitty thing to pull, Chief," I said.

James shrugged his massive shoulders. "It's a shitty world, Matthew."

"Frodo—you'll ride herd on finding Nolan?" I said.

"I got you, brother," Frodo said. "Just like always. Every operation leaves a trail. The Russians might be good, but they're not perfect. I'll start by tapping the in-country DIA officers and work it from there. And for the record, I had no idea Chief was planning a bait and switch."

"I'm right here, jackasses," James said.

"Never doubted you for a minute," I said to Frodo, ignoring James.

Which was true. But it was also good to hear that cubicle life hadn't transformed my best friend into a bureaucrat. His days of punching a bad guy's ticket might be over, but I still needed Frodo to think like a warrior.

"We gonna hold hands and sing 'Kumbaya' or can we get down to business?" James said.

"Business," I said. "Nolan's clock is ticking. What's the errand?"

"I need you to bump a scientist," James said.

"A cold approach?" I said. "That doesn't seem like a great idea."

"Don't be a nervous Nellie," James said. "This isn't

Iraq or Syria. It's Vienna. Music City. The European equivalent of Nashville. Nothing bad happens in Vienna."

"Except for Russian hit teams," I said.

"And Hitler," Frodo said.

"The Russians were an anomaly," James said, "and Hitler was born in Braunau am Inn."

"True," Frodo said, "but he got his start in Vienna."

"Could you two focus?" I said.

"I'm focused like a goddamn laser," James said. "You should be too. Nolan's clock is ticking."

"That's what I said," I said.

"Good," James said. "Then get to work. Your target is in Vienna to present a paper at an academic conference. He's a late addition, so he just popped up on our radar."

"Before or after you stuck me on a plane to Austria?" I said.

"Okay," James said, "so maybe we thought he was going to attend the conference. But thinking isn't the same as knowing."

James's explanation aggravated me, but I didn't push it. Scientist or not, I still would have climbed aboard that plane for Nolan. That my debt of honor parlayed nicely into an operational need for James was beside the point.

"Where's the conference?" I said.

"Vienna University of Technology," James said. "Presentations will be followed by a poster-board session. Find our boy, bump him, and get a second date for DIA's Vienna Station. Simple."

On the surface, what James was asking did sound simple. My job was to recruit assets or, in layman's terms, spies. Volumes have been written about the psychological aspects of this process, but at its heart the steps were fairly simple: Meet someone, develop rapport, and secure a second meeting, or "date." This is what intelligence officers did.

But like most things in the shadowy world of espionage, the devil was in the details.

"Will he have minders?" I said.

"Yep," James said. "He's Chinese and a computer scientist. That the PRC is even allowing him to attend, let alone present, is nothing short of amazing. That's probably why he was a late addition. I expect he'll have two government minders. Maybe more."

James was good. I had to give him that. Talking about the minders had me focusing on the mechanics of the approach—how to separate the scientist from his guardians. People who were there to protect him from spies like me. My operational wheels were already spinning fast enough that I almost missed a key bit of information.

"Wait," I said, the suspicious part of my mind finally catching up with the tactical portion. "You said *late addition*. How long before the start of the conference was the scientist announced?"

"About thirty minutes," James said, fidgeting.

"Thirty minutes?" I said. "That means that the conference has already started."

"Which was why I said the time for ass grabbing was over," James said.

"You want me to plan and execute an approach on the fly with less than twenty-four hours of prep?" I said.

"More like four," Frodo said. "The poster-board session happens this afternoon."

"Seriously, Chief?" I said.

"It's Vienna, Matthew," James said. "Nothing bad ever happens in Vienna."

"I feel like I've heard that somewhere before," I said.

"Matty, I know you're pissed, but the chief is right about one thing. This scientist is important. I used the last couple of hours to come up with a targeting package and some suggested angles for your approach. The info's waiting in your secure email. It's not ideal, but you're good at this shit. The best, actually. What James isn't saying is that he trampled the CIA's Chief of Station to make sure you got the approach instead of one of her guys. Give it a go. If the scientist doesn't bite, no loss. If he does, we'll pass him off to a DIA officer for the second date. Either way, I'll be working Nolan while you take care of this. Good?"

It was not good, but once Frodo explained the rationale behind the ad hoc operation, it sounded feasible. And my best friend was right—this was what I did. For better or worse, I was good at convincing people to betray their country.

Time to put my talents to work.

"Okay," I said. "What can you tell me about the scientist?"

"What am I," James said, "Bill Nye the Science Guy? He does computer shit."

"I've put a summary in the targeting package," Frodo said, "along with a copy of his academic paper. It's nerd stuff, so I'm not sure how much it will help. Here's the high-level summary: Our boy specializes in inserting artificial intelligence into tactical platforms."

"Great," I said, "so I'm supposed to pitch the dude that invented Skynet?"

"I'll be back," Frodo said in his best Austrian accent.

"You two need help," James said.

"Culture, Chief," I said. "Get some."

"Speaking of culture," James said, "you might want to buy a new suit before the poster-board session. You look like shit."

So I'd been told.

SEVEN

After I'd finished my call with James and Frodo, the CIA officer assigned as my handler offered me a ride to Margaretenstrasse in the fourth district, home to a number of high-end fashion stores. As much as I hated to admit it, James was probably right. My pearly snaps, jeans, and cowboy boots did me right most of the time, but I'd stick out like a sore thumb at a button-down academic conference. I needed a new set of duds, but I didn't want to be chauffeured by a CIA lackey.

This was fine, because the junior officer seemed to be about as thrilled with idea as I was. Partly because, like most CIA employees, he didn't think much of his DIA counterparts. We were the redheaded stepchildren no one knew about, and they were the stuff of movies and legends. Left to his own devices, I'm sure he would have been quite content to collect my abused bag of ice and show me the door.

But interservice rivalries weren't the only reason he wanted to part ways.

Vienna was a genteel assignment. No CIA Ground Branch guys with operator beards and hulking shoulders prowled the halls, and the distinctive *whump* of rockets did not send everyone scrambling for the bomb shelters. This wasn't Iraq, Afghanistan, or Syria.

Hell, this wasn't even Pakistan.

This was Vienna. Home of Mozart, chocolate, and the type of highbrow espionage favored by English novelists. Each of Vienna Station's CIA officers probably thought they were Smiley from a le Carré novel. Civilized old Vienna was a place to match wits with your adversary, not dodge bullets.

And then there was me.

I was covered in Nolan's blood and sporting a knot on my forehead.

No, if I were a betting man, I'd say my dapper young CIA officer wanted to be nowhere near the blast radius of whatever was coming down the pike next. I'd attracted the wrong kind of attention. The last thing he wanted to do was play chauffeur for a DIA knuckle dragger with a Russian bull's-eye pinned to his back.

That was fine.

I'd had about all I could take of what passed for hospitality from the Central Intelligence Agency. Instead, I surrendered my ice bag and towel, walked a couple of blocks, ordered an Uber, and settled in for a pleasant crosstown trip.

But, judging by the flashing blue lights behind me, pleasant wasn't in my future.

"We must stop," my driver said, flashing me a smile in the rearview mirror.

"Bullshit," I said. "What do you have under the hood?"

"Sorry?" the driver said.

"Don't be sorry. Just answer the question. This is a six series, right? You've got three hundred fifteen caged-up horses waiting to be set free. Floor it."

"*Vhat?*"

"Put your foot on the gas and push it down," I said. "Five hundred euros if you lose the fuzz *Smokey and the Bandit*–style."

"*Nein. Nein.* We must pull over."

"Come on, son. Y'all really aren't German. You don't have to follow the rules *all* the time."

"We're pulling over. Now."

"Damn shame," I said. "After you drop me off, make sure you turn in your man card. While you're at it, exchange this fine piece of German engineering for a Vespa or something."

The driver was no longer smiling. In fact, he wasn't looking at me at all. I couldn't blame him. Not really. I'd been the one who'd been too proud to take the CIA officer up on his offer.

Now I'd have to pay the price.

Two *Polizei* climbed from an emasculated four-door sedan. They were beefy fellows, and the way they approached the car was telling. One positioned himself behind the trunk but offset to the left, about the seven o'clock position. The second came even with my door. But he didn't tap on the window like his American counterpart might have. Instead, he motioned for me to get out, maintaining a good five feet between my door and his person.

Interesting.

If these had been normal cops on a normal traffic stop, they would have stood on either side of the car within fisticuffs range. All the better to teach me a lesson in Austrian hospitality if I made the misguided decision to cause trouble. But their current positioning didn't lend itself to apprehending a fleeing man.

Then again, I'd yet to see someone outrun a bullet.

Opening my door, I eased out of the car.

"Hiya, fellas," I said. "I told the driver to slow down, but he didn't listen."

I was smiling my widest aw-shucks smile, but the bruiser nearest me wasn't biting.

"Halt, bitte."

He'd used the word *please*, so I was inclined to acquiesce. Still, the famous Viennese hospitality didn't quite reach his cold blue eyes. I stopped, hands at shoulder level, palms facing the policeman.

Might as well get this over with.

Without turning from me, Bruiser 1 directed a stream of rapid-fire *Deutsche* at the driver, who suddenly discovered the raw power his BMW had been hiding. While he didn't spin tires, he came as close as a well-heeled Austrian could. The midnight black car rocketed away to the purr of eight well-tuned pistons.

Then it was just me and the fuzz.

"Arms apart. Spread your legs."

All the *bitte*s seemed to have vanished along with my non-man-card-holding Uber driver. I complied, keeping any further smart-ass comments to myself. Austrians, like their German cousins, were not known for their senses of humor. Also, now that we no longer had an audience, Bruiser 2 had produced an HK MP5 from beneath his blue windbreaker.

The submachine gun was pointed at me.

I've been frisked a time or two, and I had to admit that Bruiser 1 knew what he was doing. His search was quick, professional, and not overly intrusive. Without being a jackass, he exerted enough pressure to let me know what was in store if I decided to become uncooperative. Which made me sincerely hope that I wouldn't have to return the favor by breaking his nose and appropriating the Glock holstered at this waist. I'm all about maintaining good relationships with our sort of European allies, but I have a thing about jails.

I don't go.

"Gut," Bruiser 1 said. "Now face me."

I turned to see that Bruiser 1 now held a small electronic device about the size of a deck of cards. I looked at the ground, giving the camera in the center of the device a view of my forehead.

"Look at me, *bitte*."

In addition to my staunch opposition to jails, I also have a thing about biometrics. Especially mine. I keep them to myself. No way was I allowing a foreign country, even one as hospitable as Austria, to enroll my identifiers into their national database. My livelihood depended on my ability to anonymously slip into and out of countries. This became exponentially harder when the country had your fingerprints, DNA, or a close-up shot of your face. At some point, I might be forced to give up my biometrics.

Today was not that day.

"Look at me."

No *please* this time.

Bruiser 1 was learning.

"No," I said, still looking at the ground.

"Scheisse," Bruiser 1 said.

He stepped closer.

That was a mistake.

Because I was looking at the ground, I could see his feet. Which meant I knew exactly how far away he was standing. I rotated my left arm up in a tight arc, knocking the enrollment device from his hands.

It fell to the ground.

I stomped on the case and plastic crackled.

That solved that.

Bruiser 1 didn't agree. With another curse, he lunged at me, obscuring his partner's gun line in the process.

Mistake.

Then again, anger makes people do stupid things.

Or so I've heard.

Bruiser 1 was a big dude, and big dudes have big-dude strength. They don't usually bother with elegant joint locks or submission holds, because their muscle means they don't have to.

Usually.

Rather than working an arm bar or a front choke, Bruiser 1 simply reached for the part of my body closest to him—my shoulder. His thick fingers grabbed the fabric of my shirt, digging past the muscle and finding a handhold on bone.

That was going to leave a mark.

Instead of pulling away, I dropped my shoulder, extending his arm. Then I swept my left hand alongside his meaty forearm until I found his elbow. Shifting my grip, I locked his extended arm and applied pressure at the joint. Bruiser 1 now had a choice. He could bend forward at the waist to relieve the pressure on his elbow or allow the bone to break.

He chose to bend.

I kept tension on his extended arm while stepping behind him, careful to put his body between my vital organs and his potentially trigger-happy partner.

This was where things got tricky.

"Easy now, fellas," I said, converting the arm bar into a shoulder lock by twisting Bruiser 1's arm outward and upward. "Let's take a nice deep breath before one of us does something stupid."

The thing about catching a tiger by the tail is that you can't just hold on to a five-hundred-pound predator and hope for the best. You need a plan. Ideally, that plan would have been settled on long before I had one of Vienna's finest in a joint lock while his partner screamed obscenities and looked for a clean shot with his MP5. But sometimes life just wasn't ideal. Besides, I was pretty sure I could talk my way out of this. Dad said I could sell snow to the pope.

Or something like that.

"All right, Mr. Drake. I've seen enough. Please release the policeman."

The new voice surprised me for two reasons. One, it was coming from behind me. Two, it was distinctively feminine. While still maintaining the shoulder lock on Bruiser 1, I pivoted so that I could glance over my shoulder.

A woman stood with her arms across her chest.

I caught only a glimpse before Bruiser 1 decided to see if the woman's presence distracted me. I gently persuaded him otherwise by ratcheting up the pressure on his shoulder joint. To be fair, a glimpse was enough for me to understand why Bruiser 1 might think that.

The woman was classic Austrian—shoulder-length blond hair, fair skin, and blue eyes. Her sleek dress and heels should have been out of place on the cobblestoned street, but somehow they weren't. She looked elegant and radiated the confident sexiness of a woman in her forties. A man stood to the right and slightly behind her. He was also dressed in a suit, but his broad shoulders and short hair screamed *Muscle*.

"I'd love to let my friend here go," I said, "but there's the little matter of the submachine gun his partner is pointing at me."

The mystery woman laughed.

It was a good sound.

Silvery and full of genuine amusement.

"What's wrong, Mr. Drake? Don't trust me? I guess I wouldn't either in your place. One moment, please."

She switched to German and gave instructions to the

second policeman in the no-nonsense manner of a person who expected to be obeyed. The policeman with the MP5 didn't reply, but his angry frown spoke volumes. He eased the submachine gun's barrel downward until the muzzle was pointing at the pavement.

"Happy?" the woman said.

"Very," I said. "But if he would be so kind as remove his hands from the weapon, I'd be downright ecstatic."

Another musical laugh followed by another stream of German. The policeman's frown turned into a scowl, but he took his hands off the MP5 and raised them to chest level, allowing the sling to carry the weapon's weight.

"Fantastic," I said, releasing Bruiser 1 from the shoulder lock. "I knew we could all be friends."

"We are far from that, Mr. Drake," the woman said. "But perhaps we can at least become acquaintances. Now, if you don't mind, let's continue this conversation in my car. Your demonstration, while effective, has wounded the pride of these otherwise fine officers. I'm sure you know how silly men with wounded pride can be."

Did I ever.

Who are you exactly?" I said to the blonde.

We were seated side by side in a BMW X7 with her driver-bodyguard at the wheel.

True to her word, after I'd freed Bruiser 1, neither *Polizei* had attempted to take me into custody. This was probably fortunate for us both. But that didn't mean we were bosom buddies either. Bruiser 1 got to his feet and turned toward me, his face flushed and his breath coming in quick, uneven gasps. He was both pissed and embarrassed.

A lethal combination in a man.

He took a step closer.

I'd brought my hands up to chest level, ready for round two, when the blonde's voice cut through the air.

"Nein."

She followed that up with a string of German I didn't understand, but grasped the meaning of all the same. He looked from me to her, as if weighing his options. Fortunately, his partner grabbed him by the shoulder and nodded toward the car. Bruiser 1 went, but the parting look he gave me needed no interpretation.

This wasn't over.

Not by a long shot.

The blonde was smart enough to know that whatever truce she'd brokered was precarious, to say the least. Looping her arm through mine, she'd guided me toward her waiting car as her muscle pulled rear guard in the event that Bruiser 1 had less-than-noble intentions. Two minutes later we were belted into the BMW's plush interior, accelerating with the casual indifference of those for whom posted speed limits are merely suggestions.

Who are you?" I said after fastening my seat belt. Call me a sissy, but I had a one-car-crash limit for European vacations.

"Come, come, Mr. Drake," the blonde said with a smile. "Surely you can do better than that. Just like a gentleman never asks a lady her age, people in our line of work don't just give away our names."

"But you know mine," I said.

The woman's smile grew wider. "Of course I do, Matthew. The Cold War ended decades ago, but espionage practitioners of all nationalities still love my country. It's said that on any given day more than seven thousand spies call Vienna home."

Her answer, while not exactly specific, did much to confirm my suspicions. The woman's authority over the *Polizei* was unmistakable, but I'd known more than my fair share of cops.

She wasn't one.

Which meant that she was something else.

BVT if I had to guess.

"If you know who I am, why the games?" I said.

"Excellent question, Matthew," the blonde said, settling into the black leather seat. "Knowing someone's identity is not the same as knowing who they are."

"And who am I?"

"A man with grit. And perhaps a man with whom I share common interests."

"That's quite a lot to deduce from just one interaction."

"Matthew, please. You insult me. I told you before—this is my country. Just because this is the first time you've seen me doesn't mean it's the first I've seen you."

"Fair enough," I said. "What common interests do we share?"

Her smile vanished.

"The interest in seeing the Russian operatives who kidnapped your friend receive their just dues. Agents of a foreign government committed a violent crime on my streets. Mine, Matthew. This cannot stand. There is an accepted way of doing things. A natural order. If violations go unpunished, chaos will ensue. Understand?"

"Sure," I said. "Kidnappings are bad for tourism. I get it. But what does this have to do with me. The Russian *rezidentura* is on Reisnerstrasse. Why not express your government's concerns to your counterpart in person? Or, better yet, find an SVR officer or two in a dark corner of your beautiful city and state your displeasure more forcefully."

"I'd love nothing more than to do just that," the woman said. "But Austria is in a tenuous position. During the Cold War, we served as a buffer between the United States and the Soviet Union. Neutral ground, as it were. But for the last two decades, your country has become ever more focused on never-ending wars in the Middle East. This has left a vacuum. A vacuum that the Russian Federation has been only too happy to fill. My intelligence service isn't strong enough to push back against the Russians. At least, not overtly."

The blonde let the last sentence hang in the air, watching me from the far side of the car like a hawk eyeing a mouse. Like any good intelligence officer, she was waiting for me to make the first move. To take the bait she was dangling. My reaction would set the stage for the rest of our relationship.

It would determine who was running whom.

Once again, I was back in the dark corridor, outnumbered four to one. A madman had my wife, and a onetime Irish terrorist was the only hope I had of getting her back. I'd offered Nolan a chance at redemption. A way to atone for his sins by helping me escape from the Devil's henchmen. He'd taken the deal and fulfilled his part of the bargain.

Now it was my turn.

"I understand your predicament," I said, choosing my words with the care of a blind man traversing a minefield. "But what if someone was willing to carry a message to the Russians on your behalf? Someone with grit. Someone without ties to your intelligence service. What could you offer such a person?"

"I can think of two things," the blonde said with a smile. "The first is this superb piece of Austrian engineering."

Reaching into the Luis Vuitton handbag at her feet, the blonde withdrew a Glock 23. She handed me the pistol, butt first, along with two spare magazines and a Don Hume in the belt holster.

The exact rig I carried.

Huh.

I press-checked the pistol, confirmed a round was in the chamber, and holstered it in the supple brown leather. Then I slid the rig inside my jeans and the two spare magazines into my pockets.

"What's the second?" I said.

"The address where the Russians are staying," the blonde said, reciting a series of digits and a street name. "It's a flat about two blocks from here."

The BMW slowed to a stop near a crowded intersection as the blonde spoke. The implication was obvious, but I'm a fan of getting things out in the open.

"Just so I'm clear," I said, unbuckling my seat belt, "what do you expect me to do with this information?"

"Give the Russians my regards, of course," the blonde said, her smile now more predatory than pleasant. "On a completely unrelated note, the *Polizei* are currently running a citywide exercise. A rehearsal for a possible bioterrorism incident, I believe. In any case, for the next thirty minutes, the officers charged with responding to disturbances on this side of town will be indisposed."

"Thirty minutes?" I said, checking my watch.

"Exactly," the blonde said, reaching across me to open my door. "We Austrians are nothing if not punctual."

I wanted to press for more information, but didn't. She'd clearly said all she intended to say. The rest was up to me. Fine. I had an address, a Glock, two spare magazines, and a thirty-minute window.

I'd gone to war with far less.

Climbing out of the BMW, I shut the door and began to walk.

It was time to pick a fight.

EIGHT

"Peter—is everything all right?"

Peter Redman looked from his yellow notepad to the kind brown eyes of the most powerful man on the planet and considered his answer. The question shouldn't have been difficult. Peter was chief of staff to the president of the United States. A president who had won reelection by a substantial margin, thanks to the election strategy Peter had engineered. Along the way, Peter's fellow Democrats had recaptured the House while keeping the Senate in friendly hands. Even better, the Republicans hailing from the states that the president had carried had lined up to cosponsor several pieces of legislation that Peter had shepherded into existence.

It wouldn't be too far of a stretch to say that everything was coming up roses.

Or at least it had been.

"Sorry, sir," Peter said. "Just thinking about tonight's address."

"Ah, yes," President Jorge Gonzales said, a smile warming his face, "the speech that will remind everyone why they elected me in the first place. The one that puts the storm we've weathered firmly behind us. Feeling good about the current draft?"

"Yes, sir," Peter said.

The son of Mexican immigrants and the first Hispanic to hold the nation's highest office, Jorge Gonzales didn't have an impressive political pedigree tied to generations of family wealth. What he did have was charisma, a work ethic second to none, and a generally sunny disposition.

"Then for God sakes, smile, friend. We're through this. The Charles situation is reprehensible, but not your fault. As I've told you countless times, he stole money from under the nose of the world's premier intelligence organization. If he fooled them, he could certainly fool you. It's long past time we shook this off and got back in the fight. And by *we*, I mean *you*."

The Charles situation, as the president had so casually termed it, was a dumpster fire of epic proportions. Charles Sinclair Robinson IV had been the administration's pick to fill the void at the head of the Central Intelligence Agency after the previous director's resignation. Because Charles was a career CIA officer who'd deployed to Syria and several other Middle East garden spots, Peter had believed that he was uniquely qualified to take over leadership of the nation's most prestigious intelligence entity. Peter had lobbied heavily for his college friend's appointment, and President Gonzales had concurred with his chief of staff's recommendation.

Unfortunately, Charles's résumé also boasted a couple of less savory qualifications—embezzlement and accessory to murder.

Charles had been apprehended in the middle of his confirmation hearings, and the scandal had hit the Beltway press like a cluster bomb. In the time since Charles's arrest, Republicans had been making hay of the situation while the president's cabinet was still on war footing. No one had tried to pin the blame on Peter yet, but he'd been in politics long enough to recognize a brewing coup when he saw one.

His brand was damaged, and the long knives were out.

It was only a matter of time before someone drew first blood.

"You're right, sir," Peter said, forcing a smile. "You're right. I'm just disappointed in myself and disgusted with the damage it's caused your presidency."

President Gonzales's smile shifted to a look of concern. Standing, he put his hand on Peter's shoulder. "You can't allow the grind of this place to make you lose track of why we're really here. We're happy warriors, Peter. No matter how good or bad things go, less than four years from now we'll be turning this office over to new occupants. Until then, we must take joy where and when we find it. Tonight will be joyful. You'll see. Now, get out of here for a couple of hours."

"Sir, I'm fine," Peter said, waving away the president's concern.

"That wasn't a suggestion. For the rest of the morning, you're persona non grata in these offices. Go for a walk. Buy an ice-cream cone on the Mall. Talk to a pretty girl. Do something that has nothing to do with politics. I mean it, Peter. Go find fulfillment elsewhere. The place won't burn down without you."

Peter wanted to argue, but he knew better than to try. Jorge Gonzales was a good president and an even better friend. But once he set his mind to something, there was no changing it.

"Okay," Peter said, "you're the boss, but for only a couple of hours. After that, I want us to go through the speech once more."

"Yes, yes," the president said, making shooing motions with his hands, "I'd be happy to review the address we've already edited half a dozen times. But only if you promise to actually have fun. I want smiles, Peter. Real ones. Don't make me send a Secret Service agent to babysit."

"Never that, sir," Peter said. This time his smile was genuine as he got up from the conference table. "See you in a bit."

The president gave a final acknowledgment in the form of a wave, but his attention was already elsewhere. Peter paused at the door to the Oval Office, drinking in the image of his friend hunched over the *Resolute* Desk, rereading the words that Peter had spent most of the previous night writing and then rewriting.

The stress inherent in the world's most sought-after job had already transformed the president's wavy black hair to a startling shade of gray. He hadn't carried much extra weight when he'd taken office, but now the president's frame seemed almost desiccated. The blistering pace and grueling hours of the last four years had been a blast furnace, consuming every superfluous pound. Leading the greatest nation in the history of the world wasn't for the faint of heart, but Jorge Gonzales had refused to let the office remake who he was as a man.

Peter wished he could say the same.

For a moment, Peter thought about confessing the real reason he couldn't smile.

But he didn't.

Instead, Peter closed the door softly behind him. In the last four years, Jorge Gonzales had aged at least ten. The fine lines that had once creased his forehead had deepened into furrows, and his intelligent brown eyes now required reading glasses. He'd quietly borne the American people's hopes and dreams on his narrow shoulders without complaint.

Peter would carry his own cross.

He owed his friend that much.

Summer in Washington, DC, tended to be a miserable affair. Stifling heat, thick humidity, and tourists everywhere. Not exactly a ringing endorsement for those thinking of making their homes in the nation's most self-important city. Still, today was a welcome deviation from the season's norm, and Peter found himself enjoying the walk across the National Mall. Temperatures hovered in the low eighties, a breeze was blowing, and the sun shone brilliantly from a cloudless blue sky.

Compared to the West Wing's stiflingly claustrophobic atmosphere, the air felt refreshing. The Mall's many paved paths were full of people enjoying summer's détente. Pedestrians ambled to and fro, spanning the range from well-dressed office workers to kids in shorts and T-shirts and runners in tech gear.

Though he was the president's chief of staff, Peter had never sought the spotlight. Countless hours spent pounding the pavement along the Potomac had allowed Peter to maintain his trim runner's build, and good genetics had kept his flyaway blond hair mostly in place. Even so, he didn't have a politician's memorable looks. Nor did he write editorials or defend the administration on the Sunday shows.

Instead, Peter concentrated on what he did best: laboring behind the scenes to bridge the gap between Jorge's grand ambitions and the political drudgery required to get there. As such, Peter still wasn't a readily recognizable face, even after four years as a member of the president's staff. In a town full of important people, Peter was one of the rarest of breeds—a staffer focused solely on helping his boss fulfill campaign promises without political ambitions or delusions of grandeur of his own. With this in mind, Peter wasn't worried about being interrupted as he ambled down the broad pathway leading from the Washington Monument on the east side of the Mall to the Lincoln Memorial on the west.

But an interruption came all the same.

One moment he was mentally cataloging the list of revisions he wanted to make to the president's speech.

The next he was sprawled on concrete.

"Oh, God," a female voice said. "I'm so sorry. Are you okay?"

Peter was okay, but he wasn't happy. The unexpected collision had caught him in midstride, knocking him to the ground. The hard pavement had been both unforgiving and a detriment to his freshly dry-cleaned pants. Standing up, Peter brushed away the dirt and grit from his knees, his face twisting in anger.

He turned, intending to give the careless woman a piece of his mind.

But the words evaporated.

She looked different today, to be sure—just another jogger in formfitting tights, a pink sports bra, and a matching hat—but he recognized her face all the same. How could he not? He saw those same features every time he closed his eyes.

"You," Peter said.

The woman nodded. "Good," she said. "You remember."

Of course he remembered. Peter had a gift for faces. It was one of the attributes that made him such a savvy political operative. But her face wasn't one he'd ever have to work to recall.

She'd made sure of that.

"What do you want?" Peter said, staring into the woman's caramel eyes.

"I want you to repay your debt," the woman said, touching Peter on the arm as if to steady him. "You remember your debt, don't you?"

As before, her accent was subtle, lurking just below the surface and just as hard to place. But this time, unlike their first meeting, Peter didn't need to guess her nationality. She'd made that detail abundantly clear.

"Of course," Peter said, stepping backward so that the woman's fingers fell away from his sleeve.

"Excellent," the woman said, her bright smile at odds with her hard eyes. "Because it's come due."

"What do you want?" Peter said.

"Not here," the woman said.

"Then where?"

"The Broken Arrow," the woman said. "Tonight, late. After the address."

"Tonight is impossible," Peter said. "I have—"

"Tonight," the woman said, her tone brooking no disagreement. "Call before you leave. Tell the hostess that you need a table for Johnson. The bar's open until four a.m. Walk. I'll meet you there."

"Walk?" Peter said. "It'll take me twenty-five minutes."

"More like fifteen," the woman said. "Good exercise. Okay?"

"Sure," Peter said.

"Excellent," the woman said, her smile widening. "Oh, and, Peter, don't stand me up."

The woman turned and jogged away before he could reply.

Peter stood rooted to the sidewalk long after her lithe form had disappeared from sight. For the first time in his adult life, he literally had no idea what to do next. His indecision was understandable. Politics, Peter could handle.

Encounters with Russian intelligence operatives were a different matter.

NINE

A man being beaten has a very particular sound. A dull, almost rubbery *thunk* that can't be mistaken for anything else. This was what I heard from the other side of the apartment door. That cries for help didn't accompany the *thunk*s didn't count for much. The Directorate V wet-work team had snatched Nolan without firing a shot.

That took skill.

Operatives who displayed this level of competence would have made provisions for the touchy-feely portion of the operation. The part where men screamed and blood spilled. Case in point, if I hadn't pressed my ear against the metal door and known what to listen for, I would have missed the telltale signs of an interrogation in progress.

But I had.

Now I knew that someone was getting the shit kicked out of them inside that apartment.

Unfortunately, that's about all I knew.

Much to my dismay, the blonde hadn't stuck around to offer support, moral or otherwise, for what she'd so aptly termed the unpleasant part of the operation. As soon as I'd climbed from the backseat, she'd pulled the door closed and the BMW had shot away from the curb. Though it hadn't been stated outright, the context behind her SUV's disappearance was easy enough to understand.

I was on my own.

This wasn't in itself a problem. Ever since an IED had ended Frodo's career as a commando, I'd been operating alone. Don't get me wrong. I wasn't some sort of masked crusader. I typically had help in the form of an asset or two or potentially some other wayward soul I'd recruited to my cause. But generally I faced down the bad guys alone and unafraid.

Or alone, anyway.

That said, though I had a tendency to stroll into the lion's den, I never did so unprepared. While I didn't always have the luxury of entering a target building with a stack of Unit assaulters leading the way or a contingent of Rangers in overwatch, I was not suicidal.

At least, not intentionally.

But this particular operation was beginning to feel that way.

Vienna might not have no-go areas like Paris, but there were still parts of the city in which the *Polizei* were less than welcome. Like her Western cousins, Austria had the pleasure of experiencing what it meant to be part of an organization in which one member set the immigration policy that the others reaped.

During the height of the Syrian civil war, the German chancellor had decided to throw open EU's floodgates for refugees. Accordingly, millions of people had poured in from the Middle East, many never getting as far as Germany. Setting aside the health challenges that masses of largely unscreened refugees represented, there was also the very real concern that a nation simply could not assimilate such a vast number of people so quickly.

I'd spent most of my operational career in the Middle East, first as a Ranger on combat tours to Afghanistan and Iraq, then as a DIA officer operating across the Islamic Crescent. At first blush, the street where the blonde had deposited me could have been lifted from Mosul or Aleppo. Arabic writing dominated the storefronts. Most women wore hijabs, with some going so far as to don niqabs. Hookah bars and coffee shops competed for space with halal butchers and hawala money-transfer storefronts. Groups of idle unemployed young men gathered on street corners.

Keeping my head down, I'd entered the building matching the address the blonde had rattled off and tailgated through the front door behind a mother carrying groceries, and her three children. While I certainly wouldn't pass for a native, my dark hair and eyes and scruffy beard looked more at home here than in Café Central.

Hopefully that would be enough.

Thankfully, the mother continued down the dimly lit hallway past a dingy upward-spiraling stairwell. The apartment I was looking for was on the second floor. Even so, I paused by a bulletin board filled with tattered paper slips hanging over the communal mailboxes. Once I was sure that the mother wasn't coming back, I headed upstairs, my shoes squelching against the sticky tile. I passed the second-floor landing, continued to the third, and ducked down the hall.

Waiting.

Listening.

If someone was following me, this was when they'd make their entrance.

But after several long moments, I heard nothing beyond the apartment building's ambient noises. Taking a calming breath, I crept back down the staircase, this time staying as close to the wall as possible in hopes of minimizing the squeaking sounds.

I made it to the second floor uneventfully and started down the hall. It was darker here—a kind of perpetual twilight that the flickering naked bulbs hanging from the ceiling did little to pierce. The doors weren't well insulated and the smell of cooking food permeated the air as the indecipherable mumble of untold voices provided a soundtrack. The flat I was looking for was the third door on the right, but I walked past without pausing, retreating farther into the darkness.

I didn't stop until I'd reached the fire escape at the end of the hall.

From the looks of it, the grimy door hadn't been opened in a long time. If ever. Indecipherable German words covered the greasy surface, but the accompanying stick-figure pictures helped fill in the blanks.

Emergency door only.

Alarm will sound if opened.

Retracing my steps, I stopped in front of the target door. I crouched to the left side of the entrance, out of the peephole's field of view, but close enough for my spider senses to start tingling. At first, I didn't understand why my lizard brain was so amped up.

Then I got it.

The door to this apartment was different from its neighbors. Thicker. Newer. Light didn't stream from cracks where the steel met the floor, and wafts of cooking meat didn't float from the edges. Someone had gone the extra mile to make sure that this door fit the frame exactly.

I placed my ear against the cool metal and that was when I heard the unmistakable *thunk*. The good news was that I'd come to the right place. The bad news was that Nolan was in trouble and I was alone.

Easing away from the door, I leaned against the wall, thinking. The Russians who'd kidnapped Nolan had numbered at least three—two in the blocking vehicles and one in the ramming truck. Was that all? Probably not. The snatch had been executed with a smooth precision that spoke to more participants. A hidden surveillance team and some backup shooters. I was betting on a minimum of four additional bodies.

But maybe the Russians had beaconed Nolan's car, allowing them to monitor his comings and goings from a distance. A GPS tracker or perhaps even a handheld drone would provide real-time situational awareness without the requisite personnel. This was good news after a fashion, but still pointed toward a higher body count. Someone had to monitor the GPS positioning info or pilot the drone. Figure one operator and a backup. That still brought the number of potential adversaries behind the door to five.

Plus one man to watch the safe house while the others were operational.

Call it an even six.

I was a fan of even numbers.

Six highly trained Russian assassins on the other side of the door interrogating a single Irishman. Nolan was former Real IRA. I'd studied enough of the back-and-forth between the British SAS and the Irish Republicans during the Troubles to know that one did not become an operational member of the IRA without a significant amount of training. During their heyday, IRA operatives honed their craft alongside Hamas, Hezbollah, and others in terrorist academies located in Libya and other unsavory Middle East locations. Judging by the way he'd handled himself in that dark Iraqi hallway, I believed Nolan could give as good as he got.

But not if he'd been worked over by Russian goons for the last several hours.

Six Russians operatives against a single American and a beat-up Irishman. Not the best of odds. I needed to even things out. A way to negate the undoubtedly over-whelming amount of firepower and muscle in the apartment. In fact, I needed the Russians out of the apartment altogether. Glancing down the darkened hallway, I felt the beginnings of a plan come together. The thirty-minute window of relief from the *Polizei* was steadily closing, but I still had ten or so minutes.

It would have to be enough.

Retreating toward the staircase, I drew my Glock and shattered the light bulb hanging from the ceiling with the pistol's barrel. I did the same thing to the light bulb closest to the fire escape, while leaving the one in front of the target apartment intact.

Any direct action team worth their salt would recognize the significance of a lighting change on their front stoop. The bulb in front of the apartment door would have to stay, but in the ensuing commotion, I was hoping the Russians wouldn't notice the darker hallway until too late. With the mood lighting set, I just needed to add some chaos and confusion to the mix.

Fortunately, chaos and confusion were kind of my thing.

TEN

I eyed the fire escape a final time as the blonde's clock ticked down in my head. Seven minutes. Eight tops. Not a lot of time. I holstered the Glock and snapped a kick into the door's crash handle, putting all of my weight behind the blow. The door swung outward on rusty hinges before rebounding back into place with a thunderous crash.

Nothing happened.

Cursing, I shouldered the door, holding it open at its widest arc.

Still nothing.

Grabbing hold of the grimy frame with both hands, I rocked the door against its hinges, slamming metal against metal. White paint flecks floated down, filling the air with metallic snow as the joints shrieked. Just about the time I was ready to concede defeat, the fire alarm sounded.

At first, the throbbing tone was tentative, as if finding

its voice. But as I jiggled the door back and forth, a full-on electronic scream pierced the air. The earsplitting squeal demanded attention, but I wasn't leaving anything to chance. Running down the hall, I banged on the first apartment door and screamed the one word that seemed to translate regardless of the language—*fire*. Doors opened and heads began to pop out like prairie dogs emerging from their burrows.

The downside to my scheme was that the air didn't smell smoky. I had a plan for that too—the power of suggestion. I began coughing uncontrollably as I pounded my fist against each doorframe. As people made their way into the hallway in clusters, I continued coughing while waving nonexistent smoke from my face.

For a terrifying moment, I thought my plan was dead in the water.

Then someone else began to cough.

It was a hesitant sound at first, but much like the still-ringing Klaxon, it found its footing. That cough was joined by a second and then a third as imaginary smoke began to foul otherwise fine bronchial tubes.

Human beings are social animals, and social animals survive through mimicry. Whether it's a herd of deer raising white tails as they flee an unseen threat or a thousand cattle stampeding across an open plain, social animals instinctively react to danger by mimicking the response of fellow creatures. So while the air might have been perfectly breathable, the shock of coming into a dark hall accompanied by a blaring fire alarm and a coughing maniac did the trick.

The trickle of people became a flood as men, women, and children streamed toward the staircase. So far, the doorway with the Russians behind it was proving the exception to the rule. No head emerged to take stock of things. Instead, the reenforced steel barrier remained ominously shut.

Time for a change.

Easing through the mass of people, I positioned myself in front of the apartment and beat against the metal with one hand. With the other, I drew the Glock, keeping the pistol pressed against the length of my leg. I pounded harder and harder, still screaming *fire* in Arabic.

Nothing.

Then the door swung open.

I didn't recognize the man answering the door. This was good and bad. Good because he had no reason to suspect that I was anything more than what I appeared to be—a Good Samaritan clearing the building of occupants during a fire. Bad because the Russians in the apartment numbered more than just the three-man snatch squad.

"Da," the man said, his eyes narrowing.

He was a big 'un. At least three inches taller than me and probably forty pounds heavier. Either the product of good Russian cooking or, more likely, the cocktail of performance-enhancing drugs the Russians had perfected through experimentation with their Olympic athletes.

"Fire," I said again, indicating the hallway with my non-Glock hand.

I bladed my body to block his view of the pistol, but this man wasn't a terrified mother or father with children to protect. He was a trained killer and therefore naturally suspicious of the human race. He took a half a step from the door's threshold, leaning into the darkness, eyes squinting, nose sniffing.

There was no fire, and he knew it.

A child gave a shriek from somewhere behind me. The killer instinctively turned toward the sound, and I caught him behind the ear with the Glock's barrel, swinging for the fences. Advanced polycarbonates are all well and good, but nothing beats an honest length of 187mm forged steel when it comes to an old-fashioned pistol-whipping. The strike opened a gouge on his skull and should have dropped the Russian to his knees.

It didn't.

Instead, he mumbled something incoherent and shook his head like a dog flinging water from its coat.

Not good.

I put my entire body weight into the next swing, using both hands like I was holding an ax handle. The Glock smacked into his noggin with a dull *thud*. The giant wobbled and then slid down the doorframe before pitching headlong across the floor.

David might have made do with five smooth stones and a sling, but I'd take a Glock 23 any day.

I hadn't used the pistol as a club because I was reluctant to kill the men who'd taken Nolan. The Russians might have spared my life, but that decision was undoubtedly driven by expediency rather than morality. If

Frodo was right, and he usually was, these operatives hailed from an organization within the FSB solely devoted to murdering defectors and dissidents.

In other words, the Russians weren't exactly innocent noncombatants.

No, I hadn't fired the Glock for a much more practical reason. I didn't want the operatives in the apartment to know what they were up against until the very last second. Unfortunately, the man who materialized out of the dimly lit hallway behind me had other ideas.

"Quickly, brother," he said, shouldering past me into the apartment. "We must get them out."

The man screamed as he barged into the apartment. "Fire, fire, fire."

I tried to grab his arm as he rushed past me, but missed. Now he was eyeball-to-eyeball with the five or more killers who'd been torturing Nolan.

Things were not proceeding according to plan.

With me, they seldom did.

ELEVEN

Sprinting behind the innocent bystander, I lunged, putting my shoulder into his lower back. This illegal block had been a mainstay during my time playing football for the notorious Coach Nick Petrie. But instead of the star cornerback from our high school rival, I laid out a middle-aged man with a pudgy dad body. Also, unlike the episode with that cocky cornerback, this time my unsportsmanlike hit saved someone's life.

The do-gooder bounced off the refrigerator and tumbled to the ground, thereby missing the high-velocity metal projectiles passing through the space where he'd just been standing. The sounds of multiple pistols discharging were eardrum bursting inside the apartment's narrow confines.

On the bright side, the fact that I could hear meant that I was still alive.

I'd take ringing in my ears over a slug in the chest any day.

My Glock came up to eye level without conscious thought as I surveyed the room, leading with the pistol's front sight post. The narrow passageway I was occupying emptied into a common area that must have passed for a living room. Nolan sat in a single chair situated in the center, his hands and legs secured with duct tape.

Two Russians were standing in front of him, evidently taking turns working him over, judging by their bloody fists. Another thug sat reclining on the couch. A fourth and a fifth were loitering by a card table littered with half-full ashtrays.

Their weapons were drawn, so they would die first.

The Glock's thin front sight post found the closest Russian seemingly of its own accord. I pressed the trigger to the rear twice and then shifted my sight picture to his compatriot, putting another aimed pair center mass. I didn't stop to check the accuracy of my work.

There wasn't time.

Drawing from a seated position was a bitch, and the man on the couch was having a hell of a time with it. I caught his movement as he fumbled with his belt. Swinging the Glock three inches to the left, I put two rounds in his chest.

So far, so good.

I transitioned to the two Russians with bloody fists.

Then Murphy entered the equation.

Just as I was beginning my trigger press on thug number one, the dad body I'd knocked to the ground decided to stand up.

Right into my gun line.

If this had been a room full of combatants, I would have pulled the trigger anyway, confident that the Glock's .40-caliber slug would still have had plenty of stopping power after tearing through Dad-bod's chest. But Dad-bod wasn't an enemy combatant. He was a good man in the wrong place at the wrong time.

And I wasn't a murderer.

Releasing the Glock with my left hand, I grabbed Dad-bod by the rounded shoulder and tried to jerk him out of the way.

I was too late.

The nearest Russian vaulted the distance between us, landing on top of me.

Now I was in a different kind of fight altogether.

TWELVE

Close-quarters combat is visceral. When engaging someone from a distance, you can trick your mind into believing that the human-shaped target in your sight picture isn't really a human at all. This isn't the case when you can smell what the man you're trying to kill ate for lunch.

Or in this case, drank.

The scent of vodka would have been overpowering were it not for the fetid stench of cabbage and onions. His breath made me want to puke. I might have actually given in to that urge if I hadn't been so busy trying to stay alive.

Alcohol induced or not, the Russian had no shortage of courage. Rather than trying to maintain a standoff, he'd hurtled the distance between us, belly flopping onto Dad-bod. The three of us collapsed in a squirming mess of limbs and curses. Because I'd been trying to pull Dad-bod clear at the time, my hand with the Glock was at the bottom of the pile.

Where it was doing no good.

Time to change strategies.

Swimming past Dad-bod's shoulder, I snapped a left hook at the Russian's temple, even as I tried to rip the Glock clear. Neither effort was successful. The Russian shrugged, tucking his head between roided shoulders like a turtle retreating into its shell. My fist bounced off a biceps that felt like a cinder block, even as Dad-bod tried to roll away from the Russian, putting more weight on my gun hand in the process.

This wasn't going well.

Choosing to abandon a gun in the middle of a fight wasn't easy. Fortunately, the Russian helped my decision-making process. As I was hammering him with ineffective left hooks while still trying to free the Glock, he changed the fight's calculus. With the practiced ease of a man who'd done this a time or two, he dipped his hand into his pocket and pulled out a knife.

When you're fighting for your life, there are two sounds that demand your attention. The first is the *ca-chunk* of a shotgun racking. The second is the steel-on-steel *whisk* of a knife opening. Both sounds are terrifying, especially when you're close enough to your opponent to see that he hasn't flossed for a week.

I tore my right hand loose from Dad-bod's butt cheek, abandoning the Glock in time to catch the Russian's downward strike. Six inches now separated his serrated blade and my throat. That was the good news. The not-so-good news was that he outweighed me by at least forty pounds and was hopped up on equal parts roids and anger.

And he had friends.

I needed to end this.

Fast.

Pivoting on my right hip, I pushed the Russian away and drove the knife into Dad-bod's shoulder. Jerk move? Maybe. But even though he didn't know it, I was Dad-bod's best chance of surviving. If the Russian killed me, Dad-bod was next on the chopping block. So, if given the choice between a painful stab wound or a lethal one, I was pretty certain Dad-bod would have chosen the former. Either way, the Russian's knife was out of play for an instant. Rolling right, I shifted onto my hips and scissored my legs, pinning the Russian's throat between my right calf and left shin. A true ninja could have turned this into a triangle submission.

I am not a ninja.

So instead of doing some Bruce Lee shit, I torqued my hips back to the left, driving my legs into the ground along with the Russian's head. As my combatives instructor in Ranger School used to say, where the head goes, the body follows. The Russian might have been able to bench-press a refrigerator, but I had control of his head.

Which meant I had control of him.

Rocking forward, I grabbed my left ankle and yanked upward, pinning his neck in the crook of my leg as I rolled onto my knee. Still not Bruce Lee quality, but judging by the gurgling noise the Russian was making, not too shabby for a farm boy from Utah.

I was pretty proud of myself.

Until Dad-bod's head exploded.

I looked toward the deafening report to see the business end of a Glock pointed at my face. I raised my hands in surrender, but one look at the gunman's face told me the gesture was futile. He'd just watched three teammates die.

There would be no quarter.

The gunman's forearm muscles clenched as he pulled the trigger.

The pistol fired.

But not at me.

Still secured to the chair, Nolan had somehow rocked to his feet, launched himself forward, and tangled the gunman's legs.

The round meant for my head shattered the oven beside me instead.

Rolling to my right, I shot both arms under Dad-bod's corpse, freeing the Glock and releasing my choke hold on the Russian I'd been fighting. The gunman's pistol fired again, but I was focused on my Glock. I shot instinctively, finding his center mass with the front sight post and pressing the trigger three times. Without pausing, I rotated left, pushed the pistol into the Russian's forehead, and fired a contact shot.

Then I remembered to breathe.

Extricating myself from the pile of bodies, I stumbled toward Nolan, who was still strapped to the overturned chair. Now I knew where the gunman's second shot had gone. The linoleum floor was sticky with blood.

Nolan's blood.

Grabbing the chair, I flipped the Irishman onto his back. His head lolled to the side, but his glassy eyes found mine.

"Hold still," I said, going into triage mode. "I've got to stop the bleeding."

"No need, old son," Nolan said, his Irish brogue thickening. "I'm through."

Blood misted from his lips, scattering crimson flecks across his chin. His eyes were nearly swollen shut and his nose was clearly broken. But it wa the rapidly expanding red stain beneath his left armpit that spelled trouble. The gunman's bullet had passed through one lung.

Maybe both.

Nolan had minutes.

"It's bad," I said, compressing the wound. "But if I can slow the hemorrhaging, you've got a chance. Grit your teeth—this is gonna hurt."

"Stop. Just stop!"

The forcefulness of Nolan's words surprised me. I looked from the horrific wound to his face.

"It's not me that needs saving. It's her."

Nolan paused, licking his lips. His skin was pale and growing lighter. His eyelids closed before fluttering back open.

"Find her," Nolan whispered. "Before they do."

He recited a series of digits that I memorized.

"Who?" I said, putting my ear to his lips. "Who do I need to find?"

"My daughter. Call her. She'll answer."

"I will," I said, "but you've got to stay with me. Do you hear me?"

He didn't.

Nolan was gone.

THIRTEEN

I stumbled down the back steps of the apartment building, keeping my head slanted downward. This was partly to maintain my footing on the rusted, skeletal fire escape and partly to obscure my face from the legion of cameras dotting the neighborhood.

Vienna, like its European cousins, had begun to rely more and more on a network of closed-circuit television cameras to replace old-fashioned police work. Fortunately for me, the cameras were expensive and neighborhoods like this one weren't high on the Austrian Federal Police's list. At this point I was more worried about the warbling of distant sirens than about CCTV.

I doubled my pace, hurtling the last several stairs in a jump that landed me on the rough concrete. A crowd of people had gathered on the street in front of the apartment building, and I angled away from them, heading toward a beckoning alley as the sirens grew closer. Either the blonde's thirty-minute window had expired, or her control over local law enforcement wasn't quite as absolute as she'd made it sound. Either way, I needed to vanish.

Now.

That was a little easier said than done. My altercation with the Russian hit team had been messy. In addition to the cuts and bruises I'd sustained in the car crash, I was now sporting the beginnings of a shiner underneath my left eye and covered in blood from at least three people.

I skulked into the semidarkness offered by an alley formed by another apartment building on one side and the teetering facade of a combination grocery store and electronics shop on the other. Peeling my long-sleeved shirt off, I wadded up the fabric, wiping the gore from my face and head as best as I could before stuffing the soiled garment into an overflowing trash can. The T-shirt I wore beneath the shirt was certainly cleaner, but still far from presentable.

I needed a wardrobe change.

I debated adding the Glock to the refuse pile, but didn't. The fiasco in the apartment marked the second time in less than six hours that someone had shoved a gun in my face. The lone Russian survivor, the beast of a man I had felled by beating him over the head with my Glock, was still out there.

After leaving Nolan's corpse, I'd stumbled out of the apartment only to find the doorway where the Russian assassin had been lying empty. The escaping tenants must have carried him to safety, which was good for him and bad for me. A possible encounter with the *Polizei* while I was carrying an illegal weapon paled in comparison with the fact that a Directorate V assassin knew my face.

The Glock was staying with me.

I moved deeper into the alley's welcoming darkness, weaving between overturned trash cans and urban debris. As the weak light streaming from the entrance began to fade, I removed the Glock from my waistband and combat-reloaded the pistol. The half-empty magazine went into my left pocket while the remaining full one stayed in my right. The Glock somehow felt more substantial when I holstered it. I'd operated on the pointy end of the spear long enough to know that a loaded pistol wasn't the solution to life's problems.

But in this case, it was a pretty good start.

The sirens climaxed, and I quickened my pace, thinking. There was no question about whether I'd honor Nolan's dying wish. The Irishman had now saved my life twice. If he had a daughter, I would do my best to find and help her. But I was also done with letting others dictate my next move.

It was time to go on the offensive.

At least, that was what I thought until a form materialized out of the darkness.

A form holding a pistol.

FOURTEEN

Facing down a pistol gets old.

Fast.

Don't get me wrong. Staring at the gaping maw of a 9mm was never a trivial matter. Though I couldn't see it, I knew that a 115-grain projectile was lurking just out of sight, ready to exert 368 pounds of force on my fragile body at a velocity of a hundred and fifty feet per second. Not trivial by any stretch of the imagination.

But certainly tiresome.

The person held the pistol in a two-handed grip at the high-ready position, tucked in close to the chest. Still able to fire but retracted enough to make disarming the weapon challenging.

Not that I wasn't up for a good challenge.

"Drake," the person with the gun said, my name more statement than question.

The voice caught me off guard for a couple of reasons.

One, it was feminine. In this part of town, women wore traditional Islamic garb and hurried from place to place as discreetly as possible even if they were accompanied by a male relative. They didn't skulk around in dark alleys with a pistol for company.

Two, the accent was strange but familiar. Not Austrian and probably not even European. But familiar all the same.

"Yep," I said, measuring distances and angles as I scooted half a step forward.

The pistol's muzzle reacted to my movement, angling downward with a quick dip like the end of a fishing pole with a bass on the line.

"Come with me," the woman said.

The pistol's muzzle was now centered on my right kneecap.

"Nope," I said. "You're the third person who's pointed a gun at me today. I'm not going anywhere unless you start talking. Fast. By the sound of those sirens, I'd say at least three *Polizei* cars are outside the apartment building."

"Four," the woman said. "Three *Polizei* and a fire engine."

"Just the tip of the iceberg," I said. "Once they find what's inside, every blue uniform in Austria will be canvassing this neighborhood. I'm not sticking around for that shit show. Talk or shoot, 'cause I'm outta here."

The pistol wiggled with indecision before drooping toward the pavement. I breathed a sigh of relief. Bravado aside, I didn't relish the thought of adding a third gunfight to the books in as many hours. That would have been a record, even for me.

"You owe a colleague of mine a favor," the woman said, stepping closer. "He's calling it in."

Light from a buzzing mercury lamp illuminated her features as she moved out of the shadows. Olive skin, brown eyes, and dark curly hair highlighted with streaks of brown. She could have passed for a dozen different nationalities. But I had a feeling I knew from which nation she hailed.

"Who's your colleague?" I said. "These days I seem to owe everyone favors."

"Benny," she said. "Benny Cohen."

"Let's go," I said.

FIFTEEN

Good to see you, Matthew."

"That's not what you said to me last time we talked," I said. "If I recall correctly, it was something about never wanting to hear the sound of my voice ever again."

"You Americans. So literal."

The nonchalance with which Benny spoke was somewhat at odds with our current situation. We were seated in the back of a silver Mercedes, which itself was part of a three-vehicle convoy weaving in and out of Vienna's streets. We were trying to put as much distance between ourselves and the gaggle in front of the Russian safe house as possible. The woman who'd accosted me in the alley was riding shotgun, while a man with broad shoulders and a thick neck was driving.

So far, he hadn't bothered to introduce himself.

Maybe he was the strong, silent type.

"You're looking well, Benny," I said. "Everything's healed up nicely."

Left unsaid was that if I hadn't rescued Benny from a Quds Force prison in Iraq, he would have died at the hands of his Iranian captors. Also unsaid was that I'd treated his wounds and kept him from succumbing to shock until his extraction team arrived. Contrary to popular belief, Israelis actually did understand subtle. But Benny was not just any Israeli. He was the Director of Operations for the Mossad—the most feared intelligence service on the planet.

Okay, maybe the second most feared. I'd wager that James Scott Glass still caused more jihadis to wet their man jammies than all of the Mossad operatives put together. After all, if you pissed off the Mossad, you wound up dead. But when James came for you, dying was the easy part.

"Quite so," Benny said. "My injuries have completely healed. As have your wife's."

Game, set, match. If Benny hadn't co-opted Israeli ISR assets and tasked them to locate a helicopter that was carrying Laila, my wife might have wound up in an Iranian prison. Or worse. Which all went to prove the point I already knew—when it came to negotiating, the only person capable of besting an Israeli was another Israeli.

Too bad I didn't have one on speed dial right about now.

"What can I do for you?" I said, shifting so that my right hip was free.

My last banal-seeming conversation in a speeding car

had been interrupted by a team of Russian hitters. As Mark Twain famously said, history doesn't repeat, but it does rhyme. If there was any rhyming this time, I wanted my Glock ready.

Benny's gaze flickered over my waist, but if me repositioning to better draw my pistol bothered him, he didn't show it. Instead, he took the conversation in an unexpected direction.

"We have common interests," Benny said.

"You think Van Halen was better with Sammy Hagar too?" I said. "Then let me save you some trouble—don't announce it on Twitter. David Lee Roth fans can be hurtful."

Benny attempted a smile, but the expression looked more grimace than grin. "I've forgotten how stimulating conversations with you can be."

"Sorry if I'm being a bit of a jackass," I said. "I come by it naturally. Also, getting taken off the street at gunpoint makes me grumpy. Cut the bullshit and get to the point. You're the Director of Operations, not some Vienna field hand. If you're here, something's gone sideways in a big way. Either give me the scoop or let me out. It's already been a long day."

Benny stared at me for a long moment before slowly nodding his head. "All right," Benny said, "we'll cut to the chase, as you Americans say. The Russian team in that apartment building was searching for something. We would like to find it before they do."

"Find what?" I said.

The woman interjected with a string of Hebrew, but Benny held up his hand.

"My colleague doesn't think I should be quite so forthright," Benny said. "I disagree. The truth is, we're not sure. Many years ago, when I was a young intelligence officer still earning my stripes, I recruited an asset who provided us with valuable intelligence for a time. Then the asset went dark."

"Why?" I said.

Benny shrugged. "Not sure, but I knew the asset's access would be temporary. Even so, I judged that, because of his placement, the risk of recruiting him was worth the reward."

I thought about what Benny was saying. It made sense after a fashion. An asset's ability to provide intelligence was predicated on their access to that information. In a perfect world, you recruited someone who would always have access. Someone like a fellow intelligence officer.

But this usually wasn't the case. Sometimes a person's normal career progression curtailed their access as they moved from job to job. Or maybe the asset simply got cold feet. Again, Benny's explanation was feasible, but I had a feeling I wasn't getting the entire story.

Imagine that.

"What changed?" I said.

"The asset resurfaced," Benny said.

"Why?" I said.

Benny shook his head. "We don't know. A Russian paramilitary team was operating in Vienna. Since we couldn't find the asset, we set up on them instead. Then this happened."

Benny waved his hand as if to encompass me, the speeding car, and his feisty colleague in the passenger seat.

"Sorry to be the bearer of bad news," I said, "but most of the Russian team is now out of action. Permanently."

"We know," Benny said. "We were listening."

At this, the woman in the passenger seat turned to steal a look at me. As if she couldn't believe the smart-ass in the backseat really was the same guy who'd decimated an entire Directorate V assassination team. Believe it, lady. I've been exceeding low expectations since fifth grade.

"Then I'm not sure why we're having this conversation," I said. "The Russian team is off the table."

"Not true."

The lady in the passenger seat jumped into the conversation. "One of them escaped."

She said *escaped* with a certain amount of distaste. As if I'd somehow left the job unfinished by allowing one of the six gunmen I'd bested to live. Her tone pissed me off. Or maybe I was pissed at myself for the way things had gone down at the apartment. Nolan had saved my life, and I hadn't been able to return the favor.

Either way, I was pissed.

"Sorry," I said, glaring at the nameless woman. "You're right. I misplaced a Russian. It must have been while I was busy killing the other *five*. Oh, yeah, but you already know that, since you had the flat under surveillance. Which means that if you'd gotten off your collective asses, my friend might still be alive. So please know that I mean this from the bottom of my heart: fuck off."

The last sentence came out more strongly than I'd intended. But far from being cowed, the Israeli leaned across the seat, jabbing her index finger at me. The image of a woman who was probably one hundred pounds soaking wet blowing up on me was too much. I started to laugh as the stress from the last several hours finally surfaced.

This did nothing for the woman's disposition. Her lips curled into a snarl as her pretty face constricted with anger. She spat something back at me that was a mixture of English and Hebrew. I laughed harder. By now I was wiping tears from my face, and the woman seemed to be on the verge of reintroducing me to her pistol.

Fortunately, Benny chose this moment to let loose a booming string of Hebrew. I couldn't understand his words, but their meaning seemed clear enough. *The two of you knock this shit off before I pull the car over and throw your asses into the street.* At the sound of Benny's outburst, the woman clamped her lips together and settled back in her seat. But her dark eyes bored holes into mine, promising me that this was far from over.

Whatever.

When it came to my current give-a-shit list, a wet-behind-the-ears Mossad officer ranked pretty low.

"Forgive me," Benny said as my laughter devolved into chuckles. "Perhaps I should have begun with introductions. Matthew Drake, I'd like you to meet Ella Al-fasi. Ella is my protégée."

Well, shit.

"Ella, Matthew is one of the most dangerous and re-sourceful men I know. Contrary to what you might have read in the official after-action report, Sayeret Matkal did not rescue me from the Iranians. Mr. Drake did."

"Alone?" Ella asked.

"Course not," I said. "What am I, Superman? I also had a Syrian smuggler and the stolen warhead from an American cruise missile."

The furrows that had faded from Ella's forehead dur-ing Benny's explanation returned with a vengeance as her lips twisted into a scowl. She still thought I was messing with her.

I have a way with women.

"Look, Benny," I said, glancing at my watch, "I do take my obligation to you seriously, but you're gonna have to get in line. Give me a couple of hours and I'll give you a ring. We can grab a falafel and reminisce about old times. Sound good?"

"No," Benny said. "It does not sound good. Much like when you needed my help to save your wife, this can-not wait. But I understand that my nation's interests won't supplant yours. Do what you need to do. I just ask that you bring us along for the ride."

"What exactly does that mean?" I said.

Benny gave a long sigh. I held my ground. Israelis viewed the world differently from Americans. Case in point, an Israeli friend of mine had said that when an American says no, they mean no. But when an Israeli uses the same word, they mean maybe. I figured that forcing Benny to state verbatim whatever it was he wanted was the best way to prevent any culturally based misunderstandings.

"It means that the Russians are our best link to our missing asset. You've just slapped them across the face. We'd like to be nearby when they return the favor."

"You want to run a joint operation?" I said.

Benny mumbled something in Hebrew before responding. "That's what I've been saying for the last thirty minutes."

I considered Benny's request as the city's blocks sped by. Though I hadn't operated with Benny long, I knew he was a professional. One doesn't rise to the post of Director of Operations in the Mossad otherwise. From a practical standpoint, joint operations with Israel weren't exactly the norm, but it was a friendly nation. Besides, I had a feeling he was right about the Russians. At the very least, partnering with Benny would give me someone to watch my back.

That was not insignificant.

"All right," I said, offering Benny my hand. "Partners."

"Mazel tov," Benny said with a smile. "I'm certain you and Ella will get along magnificently."

Fucking Israelis.

SIXTEEN

Peter continued his walk toward the Lincoln Memorial, but he no longer saw the crowd of fellow strollers or the beautiful weather. Instead, his thoughts centered on the encounter with the Russian woman and how he'd gotten into this mess in the first place.

During election week a year and a half ago, Jorge Gonzales's second term was far from a sure thing. In fact, polling had his Republican challenger rapidly closing the gap. That had been before disaster struck in the person of Beverly Castle, the Director of the Central Intelligence Agency. For reasons that had had more to do with her presidential ambitions than her concerns for the country, Beverly had authorized a covert operation into Syria. The raid hadn't gone well and the entire debacle had occurred in Russian-controlled territory.

So had begun the most tumultuous forty-eight hours of Peter's life.

Beverly had pushed for committing ground forces into Syria, a ploy Peter, and the majority of the American people, desperately opposed. In an attempt to defuse the situation, Peter had reached out to a diplomatic back channel he'd been carefully cultivating within the Russian consulate. He'd asked his contact to discourage American intervention by preventing the rescue force from transiting Russian airspace.

Once again, operational events hadn't transpired according to plan, but, politically, things couldn't have gone better. When word of the president's resolve leaked to the press, the administration had come out as heroes. Undecided voters broke almost uniformly for the president, and Beverly had resigned after the election and her successor owed his career to Peter and wouldn't soon forget it.

All in all, everything was perfect.

Everything but the debt Peter owed the Russians.

On election eve, Peter had been drinking in his favorite bar, watching the returns come in, when the woman had made her approach. The encounter had lasted less than a minute, but a lifetime's worth of information had been transferred in those scant sixty seconds.

The woman had made clear that Peter owed her government a favor, and when the time came, she would be the one to collect it. Now that his debt had finally come due, Peter felt something unexpected—relief.

One way or another, the waiting was over.

With a start, Peter found himself standing in front of a seated Lincoln. In times past, Peter often drew comfort while standing within the memorial, surrounded on two sides by Lincoln's immortal words—one section from his second inaugural speech, the other from his Gettysburg Address.

When the rough-and-tumble world of politics seemed too much to bear, Peter often sought solace in the company of the man who had given everything to see his beloved nation reunited. Over the course of his four years as president, Abraham Lincoln had lost a son to typhoid, his wife to grief, his wealth, and ultimately his very life. The difficulties Peter faced while trying to shepherd his ambitious agenda through the oversized personalities that dominated the legislative bodies paled in comparison.

Or perhaps not.

Peter regarded the sculpture of Lincoln, wondering what this great man would have done were he in Peter's situation. The answer came a heartbeat later. He would fight. The man who had given the last full measure to ensure his nation's survival would not back down from the embarrassment and attempted blackmail of a Russian agent. Besides, what had Peter done, exactly? Leaked nuclear secrets? Given away the identification of assets operating overseas?

No.

He'd made a phone call.

An ill-conceived phone call, to be sure, but a phone call all the same.

Hardly the stuff of spy novels.

Squaring his shoulders, Peter gave a small nod to his hero. Then he spun on his heel, leaving the place of reflection and solitude for the world beyond. The Russian and her demands would have to wait.

Peter had a speech to finish.

SEVENTEEN

OPISHNYA, UKRAINE

The sunlight played across the casket, warming the burnished wood. The box was piteously small for the two lives it represented, but Andriy Chura knew there was still room to spare within its walnut veneer and velvet-lined interior. Eschewing tradition, he'd served as one of the pallbearers, shepherding the remains of his grandson and son-in-law from the hearse to the grave.

The casket had been both unbearably light and intolerably heavy. Light because the separatist suicide drone that had stolen his progeny had also incinerated much of their bodies. Heavy because, though the doctors had tried to assure him otherwise, Andriy knew that the mind of his grief-stricken daughter resided next to the charred remains of her beloved.

His darling Nina had been sitting on her front porch, watching as her husband and only child played in the driveway. When the drone had streaked down from the heavens with its payload of high explosives and ball bearings, she'd had a front row seat to the carnage. Andriy had found her rocking back and forth on her hands and knees, surrounded by the human debris that had once been her beloved family. Her hair had stunk of burned flesh and her skin was covered in bitter ash. She'd fallen into a catatonic state shortly thereafter, one from which Andriy didn't expect her to emerge.

In a single heartbeat, Andriy had lost everything he held dear.

Well, almost everything.

"You must come home, Andriy Chura. By now Father Oleksiy will have found your store of horilka. If you're not there to stop him, he'll drink himself blind."

The voice came from his right and was as familiar as the words were soothing. Andriy wanted to smile at the image of the village's ninety-year-old priest putting away bottle after bottle of home-brewed liquor, but his lips seemed to have forgotten how. Or maybe it was just that the hollowness in his soul devoured everything but sorrow. Either way, he couldn't grasp the lifeline his friend had tossed him.

So he spoke his mind instead.

"My little Symon is in this wooden box," Andriy said, stroking the casket's polished finish with a trembling finger. "Once I leave, men with shovels will put him in a hole and cover him with dirt. I'll never be this close to him again. I can't leave him, Danilo. I just can't."

Without taking his eyes from the casket, Andriy stretched out his arm and draped it across the thin shoulders of his best friend. While Andriy had the stereotypical squat, heavy build of a former armor officer, Danilo Bagan was long and bony, more resembling a college professor than a spy. The two men had grown up together, coming of age at a time when the flag flying over their homeland bore the Soviet Union's hammer and sickle, not Ukraine's horizontal stripes of blue and yellow.

After university, the village boys had taken different paths. Andriy had become a tanker in the Ukrainian army, while Danilo had joined the SSR, or Committee for State Security, the Ukrainian intelligence service modeled on the KGB. After the fall of the Iron Curtain, both had continued their careers, working for their newly independent nation. Danilo took a position in the successor to the SSR, fittingly called the Secret Service of Ukraine, or SBU.

Andriy ascended through the ranks and helped to forge Ukraine's army into a cohesive fighting force, while Danilo faded from view, as was typical of those who practiced the profession of espionage. After decades of service, both men had eventually found their way back to their rural beginnings and each other, intending to live out their final days in peace.

But peace was not so easily found.

"The older I get, the less I think I really know," Danilo said, his soft voice matching the late-afternoon stillness. "But I do believe this—to survive a horrific loss, you must find a sense of purpose that is greater than the tragedy. We've prayed for peace, my friend. But God has given us war."

Andriy considered the man's words, knowing they were true but loathing them all the same. Crimea and much of eastern Ukraine were already in Russian hands. The Bear mounted exercise after exercise, moving men and equipment into invasion postures, a thinly veiled rehearsal for things to come.

Meanwhile, their supposed ally NATO dithered about extending Ukraine the umbrella of protection that came with full membership. The individual NATO countries were no better. Led by Germany, the Europeans signed energy deals with Moscow and looked the other way while corruption and graft kept the Ukrainian government from formulating a coherent response to Russia's aggression.

It was Ukraine's people who suffered as Kyiv and the rest of the world wavered. While pro-Russian separatists launched ever more brazen cease-fire violations with Moscow's implicit approval and sometimes outright participation, Ukraine's movie-star president gave impassioned speeches but did little.

As a result, Andriy's entire world had just been taken from him.

"What would you have me do?" Andriy said as the sun ducked behind a cloud, sending shadows crawling the length of the coffin. "Our nation is full of retired generals who pontificate from their comfortable armchairs. The same with our politicians. Why add one more voice to the raucous crowing?"

"First, you are not another general," Danilo said. "You single-handedly halted the Russian advance. People have not forgotten what you did, even if you pretend otherwise. Second, I don't want you to talk. I want you to act. Help me save our nation. This time for good."

Andriy shrugged. "This is me you're talking to, Danilo. Not some gullible village boy. As you say, I was there when the Russian advance ground to a halt. I know the truth. It wasn't our brilliant tactics or patriotism that thwarted their plans. It was international pressure and sanctions, plain and simple. The Russians tried to maintain the farce that it was volunteers, not their soldiers, who were fighting and they were caught in their lies. They won't make that mistake again."

"I agree that we can't resist the Bear with our own strength."

"So what, then?" Andriy said. "Beg NATO for help? Where was NATO when this happened?"

Andriy jabbed his finger at the coffin.

"If Russia invades tomorrow, do you think the western Europeans will even notice?" Andriy said. "The answer is no, Danilo Bagan. They did nothing when Moscow swallowed Crimea. Nothing. They will do nothing when the next attack comes."

"Which is why we must deter the Russians with something that drives fear into their Cossack hearts," Danilo said.

"There is just one thing the Russians fear," Andriy said. "We foolishly gave ours away thirty years ago."

"Not all of them," Danilo said.

Andriy's eyes snapped from the coffin to his friend's face. "Speak plainly, Danilo. I'm an old man with a broken heart. I don't have the stomach for intrigue or half-truths."

"Nor do I," Danilo said. "So here is the truth—unlike soldiers, spies never retire. From time to time, an asset still passes me information. Information that I make sure gets routed to the people who can use it. But this goes beyond just me. A device exists on Ukrainian soil. I can help you find it. But what to do with the weapon is beyond my expertise. For that, I need a soldier."

Andriy stood in silence for a long moment. When he finally spoke, his voice was that of a man confronting the inevitable.

"So be it."

EIGHTEEN

VIENNA, AUSTRIA

an I help you, *mein Herr*?"

C I looked at the eager salesman and considered my response. Ella stood beside me, blessedly quiet for once. But I could still feel displeasure radiating from her in waves. Our joint operation had been active for all of thirty minutes, and we already wanted to kill each other. To be fair, Ella had had about as much say in our arranged marriage as me. After Benny had announced his triumphant bait and switch, the car exploded with Hebrew as Ella voiced her displeasure. Vigorously. The two of them went back and forth for a good five minutes as I tried the door handle.

Locked.

In the end, Benny seemed to win the argument, which meant, in typical Israeli fashion, he yelled the loudest. At the conclusion of his diatribe, Ella gave a short nod, but the look she gave me wasn't inviting.

Right back at you, sister.

Benny then offered to take us to a Mossad safe house, and I promptly refused. Instead, I instructed him to drop us off at one of the premier fashion boutiques situated on Margaretenstrasse. I still needed a change of clothes for the poster-board session.

I also needed some time to myself.

Thanks to Benny's untimely interruption, I had yet to prep for the scientist bump or, more important, do anything with the phone number Nolan had given me. Running assets for the past six years had taught me a thing or two about mysterious phone numbers—you usually don't get a chance to call them more than once. I wanted to have a private conversation with Frodo before I potentially burned my one connection to Nolan's daughter. Though he clearly didn't understand why, Benny obliged my request. Working with foreign partners required some give-and-take. Benny was experienced enough to know that I probably had some cards I wasn't ready to show, so he didn't press.

The same could not be said for Ella.

"What are we doing?" Ella said as the trio of Mossad cars drove away.

Though she and I were notionally on the same team, we were far from being on the same sheet of music. Though only a foot of sidewalk separated us, she might as well have been peering at me from a bunker on the other side of the Maginot Line.

Time to start improving international relations.

"We're going shopping," I said, holding the door open for her. "My treat."

If this were Laila, those words would have swept away a history of wrongs while easing the chill in our relationship. This wasn't Laila. This was a senior Mossad operative who'd been foisted on a scruffy American. An American who could have been an extra in a Willie Nelson video.

The term *worlds apart* didn't begin to describe where we stood.

"I look fine," Ella said with a glare that dared me to say otherwise.

In my thirty-plus years on the planet, I'd like to think that I've plumbed the depths of a life mystery or two. I wasn't so much enlightened as smart enough to know what I didn't know. And while that list was fairly extensive, a woman's mind was still at the very top. But even a ranch hand like me could recognize the relational land mine that Ella had just laid in my path.

Fortunately, the charming salesman took that moment to throw open the door.

"Can I help you, *mein Herr*?"

"Yes, you can," I said, walking into the store. "The airline misplaced our suitcases and with it our formal attire. We need replacements. *Jetz*."

"Excellent," the salesman said. "And the Fräulein?"

"The Fräulein looks beautiful as always," I said. "She thinks her current outfit will suffice. I think that a Viennese party might require something more."

The salesman turned his critical eye on Ella, and to my surprise, she actually blushed.

"You're right, of course," the salesman said. "The

Fräulein is exquisite and would be welcome at any party in my city. That said, since you will be dressed in something fresh, maybe she should consider something new as well. Perhaps a dress by Emporio Armani?"

An expert on woman's fashion I was not, but the salesman seemed to have done this a time or two. Ella perked up at the designer's name, and I could see her mentally doing the math—play along and get a thousand-dollar dress, or stand by your principles and go home with nothing.

She chose the dress.

"What about Bottega Veneta or Dolce and Gabbana?" Ella said.

"But of course," the salesman said. "Which would you like to see?"

"All of them," Ella said, shooting another look at me.

Which was fine, because, in this case, the joke was on her. James was used to approving procurements for multimillion-dollar foreign weapons systems. A fancy dress or two wouldn't break the budget.

Or so I hoped.

"Very good," the salesman said. "And for you, sir?"

I gave my best imitation of a Gallic shrug. "I trust you. I need a coat, pants, and shirt. No tie. Everything needs to match my boots. I'd also like to make a phone call."

"Of course, of course," the salesman said. "Let me see to the lady, and I'll be back for you. In the meantime, please feel free to use the office in the back."

The salesman said something in German and a trio of

salespeople materialized from the shadows—two women and a man. All three went to work on Ella. In the blink of an eye, no fewer than five dresses with matching pairs of shoes and jewelry were headed Ella's way. Perhaps the hit to the DIA's procurement budget was going to be a bit larger than I'd anticipated. Still, if the gesture bought me some goodwill from the Israeli spitfire, it was money well spent.

Hopefully, James would feel the same way after seeing my expense report.

Moving past the cluster of salespeople, I found the closet-sized office the salesman had indicated and shut the door. A neatly arrayed desk with a small computer and a phone attached to an actual landline occupied the majority of the real estate, while a compact but functional wet bar ran along the wall.

The front portion of the office was made of glass and offered an unobstructed view of the showroom, while the rear walls were decorated with pictures of decked-out celebrities posing next to the salesman. I am not by any means a pop culture aficionado, but I still recognized three singers and a movie star from the dozens of photographs gracing the wall.

I may have underestimated my clothing budget.

Drastically.

Closing the office door, I shuttered the blinds over the glass wall and windows. Then I picked up the phone and dialed a series of numbers that connected me to a secure-communications node. I glanced at the digital clock mounted on the wall, did some math, and entered a second string of numbers, which authenticated my identity and, in turn, provided me with a onetime-use digital cipher.

Obviously, the store's phone wasn't secure—there was nothing I could do about that. But now, thanks to some IT magic and the algorithms developed by our friends at the NSA, the call from the communications node was encrypted. If one of the six thousand spies in residence in Vienna was interested in listening to my phone call, they'd have to tap the store's hard line itself. Not foolproof by any stretch, but—given the prodigious amount of other lucrative espionage opportunities in the City of Music—I was betting that an upscale clothing boutique ranked pretty low on a foreign intelligence service's target list.

The phone rang several times before a clear baritone answered.

"Matty—I was wondering when you'd call."

As always, the sound of Frodo's voice made me smile.

"Why?" I said. "Did ya hear about the Russian safe house?"

"Nope. But you've been operational for over three hours. That's more than enough time for you to get into trouble."

"Seriously?" I said. "You think I can't handle myself for three hours?"

"Chief had you down for two," Frodo said. "I gave you an extra hour because it's Vienna. What could go wrong there?"

"Plenty," I said. "I can't believe there's a pool on DIA officers running into trouble. That's just cold."

"Not officers, Matty. *Officer*. As in just you."

"Seriously?"

"Sorry, brother. Truth is truth. Before you get all sulky, tell Uncle Frodo what you've done did this time."

Okay, so first off, I do not sulk. Not usually, anyway. But Frodo had a point. I attracted trouble. Even before Frodo's life-altering injury, he and I had been in the shit a time or two. After he'd been relegated to a nonoperational role, my run-of-the-mill dumpster fires now more often resembled infernos. Maybe the way I did business could use improvement. I should probably devote time to pulling this thread a little further.

Sure.

Just as soon as I found Nolan's daughter, repaid my favor to the Mossad, and bumped a Chinese scientist who might be working on the next Terminator.

Yep, hours spent in personal reflection were definitely in my future.

"Matty? You still there?"

"Sorry," I said. "Just sulking. Here's what happened. . . ."

I spent the next several minutes bringing Frodo up to speed. Once I'd finished, he reacted with the heartfelt compassion to which I'd become accustomed.

"Good Lord," Frodo said. "The entire German Army rolled through Vienna without firing a shot. You, on the other hand, drop five bodies before lunch. Might want to pace yourself, brother."

"That would be funny," I said, "if the man I came here to save wasn't dead."

"Not this again," Frodo said. "Look, Matty, I don't pretend to understand what goes on in that thick skull of yours, but I do know this: You are not Superman. Never have been. Never will be. What you are is one of the bravest men I know. You breached an apartment packed with hitters. Solo. Why? Because Nolan's life was on the line. That took some big brass balls, my friend."

"Brass balls or not, Nolan is still dead."

"I get it, Matty," Frodo said, "but what we do is messy. The enemy gets a vote. Every time. But I'll tell it to you straight: If a bunch of shit bags had me, I'd take you stacked outside the door every day of the week and twice on Sundays. That's no bullshit."

It took me a moment to gather my composure before I could reply. Frodo was a veteran of the organization that defined the word *ninja*. Contrary to what you might see at the movie theater, no one rescued hostages better than Unit assaulters.

No one.

Frodo's comment wasn't just an offhand compliment. It was the kind of rare validation that could be offered only by a fellow professional. I treated it as such.

"Thanks, brother," I said, trying to keep the emotion from my voice. "That means a lot. But I'm still not mission complete with Nolan. He gave me a number. Said his daughter was at the other end. Could you—"

"Ask my fine-ass girlfriend to work her magic? I got you."

"When it comes to women, you do know how to pick them. How is Katherine?"

"I'll say it like this," Frodo said. "She's going on ten years with the NSA, but she told me that the off-the-books job she did for you was the most fun she's ever had."

"Nice of her to say," I said, "but it's me who owes her. Did she get the flowers?"

"I told you—just working on the op was thanks enough."

"Meaning you took credit for them," I said.

"Meaning my relationship with Katherine is none of your damn business. But on a totally unrelated note, she may be standing by to run a couple of phone numbers on the DL."

"Seriously?" I said.

"Son, this is not my first rodeo. I got her spooled up as soon as James told me he was sending you to Vienna. Though you're not her favorite person right now."

"Why not?" I said.

"She had you down for an hour."

"How big is your pool?"

"You can't handle the truth. Now, give Uncle Frodo the number. Time's a-wasting."

I rattled off the digits and Frodo repeated them.

"Okay, Matty," Frodo said, "I'll turn Katherine loose. Give her an hour or two to run the traps before you call Nolan's daughter. She'll want to do metadata queries and other nerd shit. If something hits, I'll call."

"How about an hour?" I said. "I'm sure Nolan had some kind of check-in procedure with his daughter. If we miss it and she thinks he's burned, the number's worthless."

"Roger that," Frodo said. "I'll tell my girl to be fast. Send more flowers. She likes the pink ones."

Frodo hung up before I could respond, which was probably good. I really was trying to be less of a smartass, but the whole office pool pissed me off. Not to mention that the pink flowers were not cheap. Fortunately, a knock at the door demanded my attention.

"Yep," I said, expecting to see the salesman and his entourage loaded down with suits. But it wasn't the Vienna salesman or even Ella who appeared. It was the blonde.

And this time she wasn't smiling.

NINETEEN

VIENNA, AUSTRIA

Say that again," Pyotr Sokolov said, eyeing the man standing in front of him.

"You heard me," Sergei Kuznetsov said. "They're dead. All of them."

Blood from a cut on Sergei's scalp seeped through his fingers, spiraling down his wrist and forearm in a thick crimson stream. Even so, Pyotr did not point the man toward the extensive medical kit he kept sequestered in the drawer of the desk behind which he was sitting or even offer Sergei a shop towel to stanch the bleeding. In Pyotr's experience, wounds resulting from stupidity were memorable in a way that stinging rebukes were not. If the undoubtedly sanitized account the man had just relayed was to be believed, the stupidity he'd exhibited had been monumental.

"Let me make sure I understand," Pyotr said, struggling to keep his voice calm. "You answered a knock at the safe house door only to be bludgeoned into unconsciousness. When you awoke, my men were dead, so you ran away. Do I have that right?"

Technically, the dead men did not belong to Pyotr. They were assassination specialists on loan from Directorate V of Russia's Federal Security Service, or FSB. The FSB was chartered with counterintelligence activity, while Pyotr was an employee of the motherland's Foreign Intelligence Service, or SVR.

Though both intelligence entities had once resided together under the umbrella of their Cold War predecessor, the KGB, they now pursued their mission sets independently. The two organizations rarely worked together, and when they did, it was only on extreme operations deemed to be so sensitive or so critical that the expertise of both services was required.

Operations like the one Pyotr was currently helming.

"I did not run away," Sergei said, taking a step closer.

Pyotr was not an imposing man. In fact, nothing about him was particularly memorable. He was of slightly less than average height and weight. He wore a loose-fitting button-down shirt that was functional but plain and overly large trousers that further emphasized his diminutive stature. His shoes were sturdy but worn, and his plain brown hair was styled in a cut that prioritized convenience over fashion.

A trained observer might have noted that Pyotr's features were European, but nothing more definitive. He had no arresting blue eyes, no square jaw, and no prominent nose. He was a ripple in an otherwise still pond, noticeable for a moment and then forgotten.

Which was exactly how Pyotr wanted it.

Unlike Pyotr, Sergei was both imposing and memorable. A military man to his core, Sergei hailed from an organization now called the Main Directorate of the General Staff of the Armed Forces of the Russian Federation. A long and banal-sounding title for the institution formerly known as the Main Intelligence Directorate, or by its Western acronym of GRU. All Russian military intelligence flowed through the GRU. In fact, the GRU was Russia's largest foreign intelligence service.

Sergei, like most GRU operatives, had begun his career elsewhere in the Russian military. Prior to making the switch to military intelligence, he'd commanded an infantry company in the Vozdushno-desantnye voyska Rossii, or VDV, the Russian Army's equivalent to the US Army's storied 82nd Airborne Division. Now he was a member of the GRU's First Directorate, charged with gathering intelligence across Europe.

Pyotr knew all this because he'd vigorously opposed the tasking to work with Sergei in the first place. In his opinion, the GRU's reputation for sloppiness was well deserved. Men whose formative years had been shaped by blunt-force organizations like the VDV didn't lose that mentality once they became intelligence officers. To the contrary, in Pyotr's experience, GRU members were like hammers who viewed every problem as a nail.

Sergei had proven to be no exception.

Though he'd given up his blue beret more than five years ago, Sergei still had a paratrooper's imposing physique. His towering frame showcased broad shoulders and a wide chest tapering to a narrow waist. His thick, calloused hands looked like they had been created solely for the purpose of squeezing the life from his enemies.

Judging by the way he was eyeing Pyotr's throat, Sergei was considering doing just that.

"Then how would you characterize what happened?" Pyotr said, deliberately keeping his face expressionless despite Sergei's provocation.

One step closer was all he'd need.

Just one small step.

Of the almost two million people who called Vienna home, almost thirty percent, or around six hundred thousand, were immigrants. The largest percentage of these noncitizens hailed from Serbia, a longtime Russian ally. This made Vienna, with its ready-made population of businesses, residences, and helpers, a perfect place for Pyotr to establish his European-based operational headquarters.

Case in point, Pyotr was meeting with the GRU officer in the back room of a sleepy Serbian-owned computer repair business. The shop's three outer rooms were stocked with laptops, tablets, and the usual accessories. Like the shop itself, the inventory was well-worn and not particularly appealing.

As a result, customers were rare.

Which was by design.

In a similar arrangement with half a dozen other businesses and flats scattered across Vienna, Pyotr paid the one-eyed Serbian proprietor handsomely for the right to come and go as he pleased through the store's rear exit, which emptied into a trash-strewn alley. As part of their agreement, Pyotr also maintained exclusive use of the small room in the back of the shop located closest to the exit. A room with a reinforced steel door and a surprisingly sophisticated cipher lock, given the rest of the store's dilapidated condition. It was within this soundproof room that Pyotr was debriefing the GRU soldier.

"I would characterize what happened as an operational failure," Sergei said. "Your operational failure. The SVR and Directorate V were charged with planning and execution. I was present in an advisory capacity only."

So this was how the GRU officer intended to spin the disaster. Pyotr was not surprised. After learning that the Directorate V team had tracked the Irishman to the American embassy, Sergei had insisted on triggering the snatch immediately—against Pyotr's explicit advice to the contrary. Any fool who'd operated clandestinely as an illegal knew it took time to establish a target's pattern of life and thereby determine the best operational window.

But that was the problem. Unlike Pyotr and his Directorate V compatriots, the GRU officer was not an illegal. As was the case for most GRU officials, Sergei was a declared member of the beautiful marble-and-granite Russian consulate located on a leafy section of Reisnerstrasse. The importance of this critical distinction couldn't be overemphasized. If he became compromised, Sergei had the protection of diplomatic immunity to fall back upon. In a worst-case scenario, Austria would declare him persona non grata and ship him back to Moscow.

If Pyotr or the Vympel operatives encountered similar difficulties, their collective outcome would be nowhere near as rosy. Rather than repatriation to Mother Russia, the illegals would face arrest, trial, and imprisonment.

Or worse.

With this in mind, illegals operated under the assumption that in all but the most urgent of cases, it was better to walk away with cover still intact than to push a bad situation and risk burning an entire team.

Or killing them outright.

This difference in operational philosophy was just one of the many chasms separating Pyotr and the GRU operative. Now Pyotr was paying the price for the division.

Although Directorate V notionally resided within the FSB, the reality of the situation was a bit different. An ex-KGB hand himself, the Russian president had decided to resurrect the functionality of the old Vympel Directorate originally manned with Spetsnaz commandos and charged with wreaking havoc overseas. Except that, rather than the irregular warfare and sabotage that were the trademarks of the earlier Special Operations Task Force, the Russian dictator had a different purpose in mind for his reconstituted Directorate V—assassinations. Assassinations of defectors, dissidents, journalists, and political enemies real and imagined.

A Russian surveillance team tasked with photographing all comers and goers at the US embassy had been the first ones to spot the Irishman. Running his image through facial-recognition protocols had yielded a startling discovery: He was known to Russian intelligence. His name was Nolan Burke—a wanted terrorist who'd monetized his IRA training and nationality by freelancing for the Russians.

Though Pyotr had no reason to connect Nolan to his ongoing operation, prudence was the name of the game. Besides, the traitorous Irishman was obviously offering something to the Americans. It was in Pyotr's best interest to determine what and mitigate any potential damage.

His course of action determined, Pyotr had turned to the closest available direct-action asset—Directorate V operatives already prepositioned in Vienna. Though kidnapping and interrogation went beyond their usual mission scope, Pyotr knew the team's reputation and operational track record. He was confident that they possessed the necessary expertise to deal with the traitorous Irishman.

And then Moscow had seen fit to add the arrogant GRU officer.

"That's an interesting assessment," Pyotr said, his voice absent the fury that burned within him. "Here's mine. Everyone in the safe house is dead. Everyone but you. This leads me to conclude that you cowardly traded the lives of those men for your own."

"You arrogant ass," Sergei said, taking the required final step closer. His hands shot forward, fingers grasping Pyotr's shirt in a breath-stealing cross-collar choke. "How dare you—"

The paratrooper broke off in midsentence, releasing Pyotr's shirt as he clawed at his own throat. He stumbled backward, face contorting with pain. His spasming lungs could no longer draw air past the blockage formed by his rapidly constricting trachea. Sergei's bulging eyes found Pyotr's and, for an instant, clarity seemed to replace the terror.

Then the instant was gone.

With a final gurgle, the GRU officer collapsed, pitching headlong onto the dirty carpeting.

Still seated behind his desk, Pyotr stared at the former paratrooper, waiting until the body spasmed a final time. Then he checked his watch. Fifteen seconds. Not bad. Not bad at all.

Opening his clenched fist, Pyotr examined the quarter-sized aerosol device he'd been palming, and nodded approvingly.

The instrument of death had been a gift from the now-deceased Vympel team leader. It consisted of a cartridge loaded with compressed air and an aerosolized compound. The weapon's range was limited, but it was easy to conceal, and it worked as promised. Should an autopsy ever be performed on the GRU man, the findings would list anaphylactic shock as the cause of death. But the compound responsible for inducing the shock was conveniently metabolized during the victim's death throes, rendering it undetectable.

A work of art, really.

Setting the device on the desk in front of him, Pyotr picked up a burner phone and placed a call to the one-eyed Serbian. A customer had tragically expired in his store. He needed to deal with the mess.

The Serbian readily agreed.

He always did.

The call complete, Pyotr leaned back in his chair, considering what to do next.

The operation he was overseeing went beyond a simple kidnapping and interrogation. In fact, it was not an exaggeration to say that if Pyotr was successful, his efforts would permanently alter Europe. This was why the GRU and the FSB had their fingers in Pyotr's pie. It was also why he was sitting in Vienna instead of in the operation's geographical center of gravity. Pyotr's presence was a testament to the risk posed by the Irishman.

And the problem was that he still wasn't able to quantify that risk.

Trading the burner for a smartphone, Pyotr brought up the video he'd already reviewed three times and pressed play. Unbeknownst to the now-deceased GRU officer, Pyotr knew exactly what had happened at the safe house because he'd had it wired for sight and sound. He watched again as a single man liquidated an entire Vympel team with the casual proficiency of a farmer threshing wheat. The video ended with the man crouched over the dying Irish traitor, speaking to him in American-accented English.

The Irishman had clearly offered something of value to the Americans, but what? And, more important, was the greater operation somehow at risk?

Pyotr played the last ten seconds of the video.

Find her. Before they do.

A string of digits.

Who? Who do I need to find?

My daughter. Call her. She'll answer.

The exchange was still as puzzling as it had been the first time Pyotr had viewed the video. No matter. He had two pieces of information that might unlock this puzzle— a phone number and the existence of a daughter.

Time to put both to use.

Grabbing the burner, Pyotr placed a final call.

TWENTY

VIENNA, AUSTRIA

Sorry," I said as the blonde strode into the room. "This changing room is occupied."

"Mein Gott," the blonde said, slamming the door behind her. "You are a wrecking ball. Five Russians are dead. Five! That's a quarter of Vienna's yearly homicide rate in one day."

"Would have been six," I said, "but that last Russian was slippery. And, yes, I'm fine. Thank you for asking."

What was said next was a bit hard for me to follow because, again, high school German. Even so, I caught enough *ficken* and *Scheisse* to understand that she wasn't reciting the rosary. Finally, the blonde ran out of steam and switched back to English.

"What did you do?" she said.

"Exactly what you asked," I said, raising my shirt to expose the Glock holstered at my waist. "Remember?"

The blonde leaned forward, her blue eyes predatory.

"Of course I remember. But I was expecting a bit more discretion. A body or two could be chalked up to the cost of doing business. But five? You've turned my peaceful city into Kabul."

"Discretion isn't really my thing," I said. "You wanted a message sent to the Russians. I think they received it."

"Tell me that you really aren't this stupid," the blonde said. "Those men you killed—do you know who they were?"

I did know who the men were, but did she?

Only one way to find out.

"GRU?"

"Nein."

The blonde began to pace as she spoke. "GRU operatives are brutes, but by and large they still adhere to the rules of espionage. Dirty deeds are rare. When such unpleasantness cannot be avoided, it is kept to the shadows. Especially here on neutral ground. But the men you killed do not subscribe to these beliefs. They are from Directorate V. You know it?"

"Yes," I said.

"Then you must also know that these assassins are the Russian president's international muscle," the blonde said, stopping to fix me with a glare. "The means by which he instills fear in those who seek to defy him. And you just killed a roomful of his enforcers."

"Again," I said, "you wanted me to send a message. Five dead Russians should do the trick."

The blonde looked at me, slowly shaking her head.

"I was thinking you'd be subtle," she said. "That

you'd adhere to the unwritten rules of my city. Instead, you've done the equivalent of slapping the Russian tyrant across the face and demanding satisfaction. If the Russian deaths go unanswered, the strongman's critics will begin to wonder whether he has lost his grip. His domestic enemies won't be far behind. I gave you the chance to save your friend. You repaid my kindness by turning Vienna into a war zone. I want you out of Austria. Immediately."

"Or what?" I said as my blood began to boil. "You'll sic the *Polizei* on me? That didn't go so well last time."

The blonde folded her arms beneath her breasts and stared down at me, a raptor eyeing a mouse.

"Just another American cowboy," she said, not bothering to hide her disgust. "You still don't know who I am, do you?"

"Nope," I said. "But I know what you are—a pain in my ass. A century ago your empire spanned half of Europe. Now you people are afraid to stand toe-to-toe with a two-bit dictator in charge of a nation with an economy on the brink of collapse. Pathetic."

Spots of color bloomed on the blonde's cheeks. She took a step closer. For a moment, I thought she was going to slap me. It wouldn't have been the first time a foreign intelligence officer had taken a dim view of my wit.

Or probably the last.

Instead, she jabbed an index finger into my chest.

"You have one hour to leave my country," the blonde said, anger making her accent more pronounced. "If you're still on Austrian soil sixty-one minutes from now, you'll see that we aren't so easily cowed."

So she did have a spine. I intended to compliment her newfound fortitude, but she had other plans. Spinning on her heel, the blonde yanked open the door and propelled herself through it.

I have a way with women.

TWENTY-ONE

OPISHNYA, UKRAINE

Andriy looked at the faces staring back at him from the semidarkness, trying to understand how this had become his life. Several of the countenances were old like his, dominated by eyes that had seen too much. Their expressions suggested that they wished for nothing more than the chance to live out their remaining lives in peace.

Two of the faces were young, barely more than boys.

One was in his thirties.

All of the men were old enough to know better, but they were here all the same.

When a national hero called a war council, honor demanded your attendance.

Andriy swallowed the bile that accompanied this thought. As Danilo had so aptly stated, knowing the device's location was only part of the equation. The intelligence operative had done his part to ensure his nation's survival.

Now it was Andriy's turn.

"Out with it, Andriy Chura. Some of us have important things yet to do tonight. Like sleep."

The comment caused a chuckle to ripple through the otherwise somber group. Andriy smiled along with them, the familiar gesture feeling strange on his lips. Only hours ago, he might have sworn that he'd never smile again. Now he was chuckling as if his grandson weren't lying in the earth's cold embrace.

As if his daughter weren't catatonic in her childhood bed.

This was life's cold reality. A reality that soldiers understood implicitly. No matter how grievous your loss, time refused to stand still. The world did not stop turning just because your lungs struggled to draw breath and your heart labored to beat. Eternity continued its endless march, dragging you with it. Fate had decreed that Andriy would go on living even though his soul had died.

He would play the cards he'd been dealt.

"Quite right, Olek," Andriy said, knocking the ash from his pipe into a soot-stained ceramic bowl. "As much as we all love hearing about your dreams, that isn't why I invited you here."

Olek was a fellow farmer who lived about five kilometers down the road. But he was also a legend. As one of the survivors of the Ilovaisk massacre, Olek was respected by the Ukrainian government and revered by the people. During the first Russian incursion in 2014, Olek's volunteer battalion had accomplished the impossible. The citizen soldiers had outpaced the Ukrainian army and secured the city of Ilovaisk ahead of the Russian advance. As the battalion commander, Olek had undertaken his lightning advance on the assurance that Ukrainian regular army units would reinforce and relieve his meager battalion.

The reinforcements had never come.

Undaunted, Olek fought on, blunting the Russian offensive and retaking the town from the separatists. With their nose bloodied and their reputation in tatters, the Russians had withdrawn, choosing to encircle the town and allow hunger and thirst to accomplish what bullets and artillery shells could not. After days with no resupply and zero assistance from the Ukrainian army, Olek had been forced to negotiate a withdrawal. The humiliation associated with his retreat would have been enough to savage Olek's reputation, rendering him ineffective as a future commander. But the Russians weren't content to savage just reputations. Waiting until the withdrawing citizen soldiers reached a prearranged kill zone, the Russians violated the terms of their own peace treaty by ambushing the defenseless fighters.

It was a slaughter.

But here again Olek rose to the occassion. Amidst a hail of machine-gun fire and swarms of sniper bullets, he escaped. But not just with his own life. The sinewy old farmer returned to the killing field three separate times to drag wounded men from the tattered remains of his battalion to safety. On the fourth trip, a sniper bullet hit home, shattering his leg.

But even this devastating wound hadn't been enough

to stop Olek. With a crippling injury that would have sent lesser men into shock, Olek had gritted his teeth and crawled from the ambush site, dragging a final comrade to safety.

To say that his veterans worshipped him was the worst sort of understatement. Olek's men and their families would lie down in traffic on his behalf. The rest of Ukraine wasn't far behind. Like Andriy, Olek had retired to his family farm after the armistice was signed, convinced that his sacrifice hadn't been in vain.

Now it was Andriy's job to convince him otherwise.

"We're gathered here tonight because I need your support," Andriy said.

"For what?" Olek said. "Are you finally giving Vasyl a run for his money?"

Vasyl was the village mayor, and though it was technically an elected position, he'd held the role for the last ten years. This was partly because, like in the rest of Ukraine, there was no small amount of corruption in the election process, but also because nobody else really wanted the large headaches and small compensation that went with the job.

"No," Andriy said, not smiling along with the rest of the men. "I'm asking for something more serious: I want your help reconstituting a volunteer battalion. A militia."

Like Olek's early comment, Andriy's statement also provoked a response. But this time, no one chuckled. The men's reactions largely broke down along generational fault lines. The boys who'd been too young to fight during the previous Russian war leaned forward with interest. The veterans backed away. Between the older men's crossed arms and hard looks, Andriy knew that he had his work cut out for him. This was why the business of fighting wars always fell to the young.

The old knew better.

"Ukraine has volunteer battalions galore," Olek said. "Why create another?"

"Because, like our current military, not one of the existing battalions is capable of stopping the coming Russian invasion," Andriy said.

"What do you mean, *coming*?" Olek said. "Do you know something Kyiv does not?"

"No. But, unlike Kyiv, Andriy isn't afraid to speak the truth."

The answer came from Danilo. It was both definitive and emotionless. The same matter-of-fact manner a weatherman might use when reporting the temperature. Unlike the chances of rain or whether the day would bring sun or clouds, the temperature wasn't open to interpretation.

It simply was.

"This buildup is different from the typical Russian posturing," Danilo said, pushing away from the wall he'd been leaning against. "I still have contacts in the Foreign Intelligence Service. The government won't announce it for fears of sparking a panic, but the Russians aren't just massing mechanized infantry and armor. They've pre-positioned logistical assets as well. Fuel tankers, ammunition trucks, and formations of second-echelon troops ready to exploit breaches in our lines. This is no rehearsal. No saber-rattling exercise to exact further concessions from the Europeans. The Russians are going to invade. Our response is the only thing left to decide."

"What would you have us do?" Olek said, thundering the question as his waxen cheeks flushed. "Send boys like these to grease the tracks of Russian tanks? The legend of our volunteer battalions is a source of national pride. Those of us who were there know the truth—we were lucky. Thanks to the excellent work of their Little Green Men, the Russians thought they would be able to roll across our border unmolested. We bloodied their noses, but we didn't stop them. Sanctions did. I hate the Russians as much as any man, but I won't allow stirring words or blind emotion to overwhelm common sense. If the Russians come again, there's nothing a bunch of farmers can do to stop them."

"That's where you're wrong, old friend," Andriy said, edging into the gap Danilo had so deftly opened. "There is one thing that gives even the Russian Bear pause. We once had bunkers full of these weapons, but we foolishly traded them away for promises and treaties. Words that weren't worth the paper they were written on. It's time we reclaimed our national heritage."

"How?" Olek said. "Do you think our fickle European friends will extend a protective umbrella? Even the Americans send us blankets instead of bullets. NATO, the supposed defender of freedom on European soil, won't even act on our application for full membership. We're on our own, Andriy. We're helpless."

"We are on our own," Andriy said, "but we are far from helpless."

Andriy paused even though he knew he had his audience on the edge of their seats. While he wholeheartedly believed that Danilo had discovered the one thing that just might hold back a Russian invasion, he also knew that the two of them could not exploit this advantage by themselves. To have any chance at succeeding, Andriy needed hard men. Soldiers who'd experienced combat and lived to tell the tale.

But more than that, he needed men he could trust.

Men from Opishnya.

But this was also his plan's greatest weakness. If a secret could be kept between two men only if one of them was dead, what chance did his have at staying hidden? Andriy looked above the heads of those seated closest to him, matching gazes with Danilo. While Andriy had been leading men from the turret of his T-72 tank, Danilo had been skulking in the shadows, convincing others to betray their countries. The spy's life had depended on his ability to judge the character of others.

Now Andriy's did as well.

The former intelligence operative met Andriy's questioning look and nodded.

"We won't be helpless," Andriy said, rushing through the words before he could take them back, "because we will have a weapon of our own."

"A nuclear weapon?" Olek said. "In Ukraine? Bah—I don't believe you."

"Then believe me," Danilo said. "I'm the one who found it."

This time even Olek was at a loss for words. His gaping mouth opened and closed twice before he remembered how to speak.

"You're telling me that you have a functioning weapon?" Olek said. "In your possession?"

"Not yet," Andriy said, "but it's on Ukrainian soil. I just need patriots to help me seize it. Patriots like the ones in this room."

"If you succeed, then what?" Olek whispered. "Will you use it against the Russians?"

"We won't have to," Andriy said. "Once we have the device, we will announce its existence to the world."

"The Europeans will demand you surrender it," Olek said.

"Which I will happily do in exchange for full and immediate membership in NATO. If they refuse, we're still better off than we are right now. Even a bear backs down from a cornered wolverine."

"You have been busy, Andriy," Olek said. "What do you expect from us?"

"The men in this room will lead our volunteer battalion. Boys from Opishnya. Men that we trust. They will secure and guard the weapon. Once we have it, other militia battalions will rally to our flag."

"And you will command them?" Olek said.

"No," Andriy said, "I would like you to have that honor."

"What about you? What will you lead?"

"The nation, if I must."

TWENTY-TWO

"Try the *tafelspitz* here. It's quite good."

Pyotr appeared to ponder his dinner guest's recommendation before nodding his assent to the hovering waiter. In reality, as with much of this meeting, Pyotr's hesitation was just an act. He'd been running this asset for almost two years, and, like any good handler, Pyotr had become attuned to his operative's idiosyncrasies.

For instance Myaso, or meat, as Pyotr had termed the asset, liked to think of himself as something of a gourmet. From what Pyotr could tell, the man's tastes were about as refined as a child's, but he didn't share his opinion with the heavyset bureaucrat sitting across the table from him.

Betraying one's country was hard on the soul. Part of the art of running assets was allowing them to live in a fantasy world of their own construction. A fairy tale to ease their ever-present guilt. In Myaso's make-believe world, he was a man of refinement and culture. A man whose prescient view of politics would be celebrated years from now when his fellow countrymen threw off the shackles binding them to the West and the European Union and their natural, preordained affinity for the East and Russia.

At least, that was what Myaso claimed. Whether or not the man actually believed this nonsense was immaterial. As long as he continued to provide valuable intelligence, Pyotr was more than happy to allow his asset to be the hero of his own story. Especially when the alternative was far less appetizing.

Pyotr played his role in this melodrama of sorts with relish. Not because he shared his asset's self-aggrandizing view of the future. No, Pyotr praised the man's palate and listened attentively to his dim-witted views on global politics for just one reason: The buffoon sitting across the linen tablecloth was a senior staff member in the Austrian BVT.

And Pyotr was the one who'd recruited him.

"Of course," Pyotr said, setting the menu aside with calm, practiced motions. "I'll defer to your culinary insight as always."

Though the words came out in a string of leisurely German, Pyotr struggled to contain his impatience. The operational clock was ticking. Pieces were moving into place across the battlefield while Pyotr was dithering over cuts of meat. Be that as it may, this was the way his asset operated. Pyotr needed to know if the Irishman had compromised the operation, and the man sitting across the table from him might just have the answer.

This insight was worth enduring mindless chatter about the state of beef in Austria.

"A bloodbath happened in my city today," Myaso said after taking a sip of Pichler Riesling. "Seven men dead. In a shoot-out."

"A mass shooting?" Pyotr said, reaching for his own glass of wine. "In Vienna? How very American of you. The migrant status in Vienna has become intolerable. You must get your immigration situation under control."

"I couldn't agree more," Myaso said. "But these particular immigrants weren't from the Middle East. In fact, they represent a collection of countries—Ukraine, Belarus, Russia, even Ireland."

"Very strange," Pyotr said, his fingers resting on the wineglass.

"Not just strange," Myaso said. "Illuminating. You and I have a mutually beneficial agreement. An arrangement, if you will. I allow you to conduct the occasional bit of unsavory business unmolested in exchange for your personal reassurance that this business will be conducted in a manner that is both professional and discreet. Today was neither."

Pyotr took another sip of wine, considering his response. Once again, he pushed aside the angry words he wanted to say—words that would have reminded Myaso of the nature of their relationship.

"I apologize for any inconvenience this incident has

caused you," Pyotr said, choosing his words carefully. "You will be compensated accordingly. That said, it's important that you understand that my men were the victims, not the perpetrators. They were taking care of a problem with the discretion for which we are known when they were unexpectedly interrupted by this man. Perhaps you could help me ascertain his identity and how he came to learn the location of my team's safe house."

Pyotr removed his phone from his suit pocket, scrolled through the pictures, and then messaged the appropriate one via an encrypted app designed to mimic a common social media program. The string of ones and zeroes surged through the Internet to the equivalent of a digital dead drop. From there, an invitation to view the image was embedded in an innocuous text to Myaso's phone. The entire interaction was untraceable and secure, and it required just seconds.

Pyotr slipped his phone back in his suit jacket and reached for the bread basket. A moment later Myaso's mobile pulsed. The faux aristocrat wiped his hands on a linen napkin before reaching for his own device.

"How did you get this?" Myaso said.

"A camera hidden at the residence," Pyotr said, tearing a roll in two. "I apologize for the poor quality. The subject wasn't one for standing still."

"Scheisse," Myaso said, looking at his phone. "Of course."

"You know him?" Pyotr said, fighting to contain his eagerness.

"Contrary to what you may think," Myaso said, shifting his attention from his phone to Pyotr, "my intelligence service is not some backwoods organization. I was aware of their presence the instant the six members of your assassination squad arrived in my country via three different airports. Nothing happens in Austria without my knowledge. Nothing. This man arrived at Vienna International Airport by private jet several hours ago. A BVT surveillance team picked him up, but lost him leaving the airport. We located him again as he was exiting the American embassy. He was present when your team kidnapped the Irish terrorist."

"Present where?" Pyotr said. "On the sidewalk?"

"No. In the target vehicle's passenger seat."

Pyotr's curled his fingers into fists beneath the table. Focusing on the pain of his fingernails burrowing into his palms allowed him to resist reaching across to Myaso and grabbing the incompetent fool by the throat. But just barely. Discretion was all well and good, but sometimes a situation really could be remedied only by blunt force trauma.

"If you knew this man was a problem," Pyotr said, enunciating each word as if he were speaking to a toddler, "why didn't you remove him from the equation?"

"I thought I did," Myaso said, frustration coloring his voice. "I gave explicit instructions to have him deported. Apparently, they weren't followed."

Pyotr slowly uncurled his fingers. He could feel the nail-shaped indentations in his skin, but the distraction offered by the pain was no longer necessary. This moment had just become an inflection point. In the espionage lexicon, Myaso had opened a gate.

Now it was up to Pyotr to walk through it.

"I think I have an idea that could solve both of our problems," Pyotr said. "Care to hear it?"

Myaso most certainly did.

TWENTY-THREE

VIENNA, AUSTRIA

A heads-up would have been nice," I said to Ella as we climbed out of the Volkswagen Uber that had ferried us from the boutique.

We could have easily walked to our destination. The Vienna University of Technology was a short five-minute stroll north down Operngasse to its iconic campus located off Resselgasse. But strolling was something you did for fun with a friend.

I didn't have time for fun, and Ella certainly wasn't a friend.

"About what?" Ella said, her thin smile at odds with the question.

"The blond woman. You know, the one you let burst into my dressing room unannounced?"

"You Americans are such prudes," Ella said, taking half a step closer to the street to make way for a trio of women. "Do you really think she's never seen a naked man?"

"I wasn't naked, not that it's any of your business. I was, however, in the middle of an important conversation. One I didn't intend to share with a member of the BVT. I thought we were partners."

"Sophie Gruber is not just a member of the BVT. She is its first female director. And we are not partners. Partners collaborate. We don't have a partnership or really any relationship at all. You tell me to do things without explaining why. I do them. Hence my new dress."

Ella punctuated her statement with a little twirl.

Technically speaking, her rejoinder was full of inaccuracies. First off, she hadn't purchased *a* dress. She'd bought a dress, heels, a purse, and a matching necklace-and-earrings set. The final bill had made me a bit woozy.

I'd armed an entire Iraqi militia for less.

This was not to say that the new wardrobe had in any way purchased the Mossad officer's goodwill. Just in case I'd somehow misinterpreted her less-than-subtle body language, Ella had told me as we were checking out that a closetful of Jimmy Choos wouldn't change her drastically low opinion of me. One of the wonderful benefits of working with Israelis was that you never had to guess their feelings.

Still, her change of clothes had the intended effect. In the no-nonsense pantsuit and sensible flats she'd been wearing earlier, Ella had been a pretty woman. Now, in a sleek one-shoulder silk-satin gown that complemented her dark complexion, Ella wasn't just pretty.

She was striking.

Which was exactly the look I was after.

Now it was time to explain why.

"All right," I said, guiding her to a quiet alcove in front of the university's iconic entrance, "here's the deal. I need your help."

"With what?" Ella said, touching the Valentino Garavani purse dangling from her wrist.

The boutique manager had been only too happy to hold Ella's pantsuit and other purchases until we returned from our engagement. Even so, I couldn't imagine that the Mossad officer had left behind her pistol.

"Not that kind," I said, lowering my voice as a pair of students wandered by. "At least, I hope not, anyway. You know about the academic conference?"

"Of course."

"I'm going to pitch someone at the poster-board session. You're the key to my approach."

"How so?"

I told her.

"We should get going," Ella said with a smile. "The session starts in five minutes."

I f you've never been to a poster-board session, you're missing out.

Said no one.

Ever.

Unless you're a tech nerd, poster-board sessions are an exercise in exhaustion. As the name suggests, these gatherings normally take place in a large open-air room in which scientists of all varieties man booths showcasing the results of their research. Since most hard science produces numbers and graphs rather than show-and-tell items, these equations and formulas are printed on large poster boards, which reside next to the scientist.

If you think that doesn't sound terribly interesting, you're right.

But it gets worse.

Much, much worse.

Scientists by and large have the social skills of a duck-billed platypus. If you can imagine attending a fifth-grade science fair in which all the fifth graders have been struck mute and are terrified to look you in the eye, you have the makings of a poster-board session. For the most part, the scientists hang out in their assigned stalls, hiding behind their posters. This is because the scientist is usually torn between two competing emotions.

On the one hand, they desperately hope that no one stops by so that they don't have to make conversation with a stranger. On the other, they desperately hope someone with an inordinate amount of money in the form of a grant or investment dollars does stop by and marvels at their astonishingly brilliant work. Preferably in silence, because, again, conversations aren't usually a scientist's forte.

Perhaps you're beginning to understand why these events are such a boatload of fun.

To make these academic Super Bowls even more interesting, there is often a darker underbelly at play. By their very nature, poster-board sessions are meant to showcase a scientist's work. This means that they are magnets for a certain type of predator.

Like me.

If you're an intelligence officer trying to determine what the good folks at XYZ University are working on, a poster-board session is a potential gold mine of information. Beyond that, these quasi-social events provide something every good agent runner dreams about when he falls asleep at night—access to potential assets. In other words, why settle for just gathering information about the university's work when you can recruit the scientist doing it instead?

Unfortunately, the countries from which the scientists doing the most defense-related work hailed weren't idiots. While grudgingly acknowledging the very real need for academics to socialize and exchange ideas with their peers, counterintelligence operatives did their best to ensure that wolves like me didn't mix with the sheep. This was why foreign scientists who engaged in particularly cutting-edge research often traveled with government minders. Sheepdogs, if you will, whose job it was to protect the livestock.

The trick was finding a way to separate the minder from his or her charge. This was where Ella would help immensely. Though undoubtedly a bit odd, my target scientist was male, and as long as he was straight, there wasn't a man on the planet capable of ignoring Ella in a figure-hugging dress.

At least, that was what I was hoping, anyway.

TWENTY-FOUR

ood afternoon, Herr and Fräulein. Could I please
have your names?"

"We're not on the list," I said, adopting my haughtiest
tone.

"No problem," the attendant said. "Registration is
the next table over."

"But this is the table with the badges," I said.

"I don't understand, sir," the attendant said, his smile
beginning to slip. "You must register in order to attend
the poster-board session."

"*Must* is such a strong word," I said with a smile of my
own. "Miss Bitton is a partner with the Freedom Foundation. She has several openings in the fellowship program for the next academic year and would like to
evaluate potential applicants. Discreetly. If news of our
attendance were to be made public, I'm afraid the ensu-

ing attention would distract from the attendees' excellent work. I'm sure you understand."

Judging by the confused look on the attendant's face, he didn't.

That was fine.

The attendant was slightly built with shaggy blond hair and the earnest eyes of an undergraduate who has yet to experience the cutthroat tyranny of egos that is higher education. I pegged him at about twenty-one— probably in his junior or senior year and volunteering today in the hopes of catching the eye of one of the more senior researchers on the hunt for laboratory assistants. He didn't have a clue at what I was hinting. No matter. Today I had a weapon much more potent than subter-fuge.

Ella.

"What was your name again?" the Israeli said, as if hearing my thoughts.

The attendant looked past me to my Mossad partner and swallowed.

Audibly.

"Lucas," he said, his voice cracking.

"Thank you for your help, Lucas," Ella said, smiling. "We very much appreciate it."

Just that quickly, another promising scientific mind was reduced to mush.

"Of course," Lucas said, nearly knocking over his wa-ter bottle as he reached for the stack of badges to his left. "I'll let the program director know you're here. I'm sure she won't mind. What was your organization again?"

"Freedom Foundation," Ella said, slipping the lanyard over her head. "We offer promising international students an all-expense-paid year of studying abroad at an American university. You should consider applying. Here's my card. Email me and my assistant will send you the details."

The business card was nothing special—just card stock we'd printed at the embassy. But Lucas accepted it with both hands as if it were made of gold instead of paper.

"Thank you," Lucas said. "I'll email you as soon as I get home. About the scholarship, I mean."

Ella favored him with another smile and handed me a badge, and just that easily, we were in.

I hope you're proud of yourself," I said as we followed the hustle of bodies heading toward the poster-board session.

"What do you mean?" Ella said.

"Lucas probably would have had a stellar career before he met you. Now he's brain-dead."

Ella didn't laugh, but she did smile.

Progress.

"Someone had to save us from your inept tradecraft."

Or maybe not.

"Inept? I had that little turd exactly where I wanted him."

"Five seconds," Ella said. "Maybe ten."

"Until what?"

"Until Lucas would have called security. You're really not very good at this."

The only reason we were here was because I was good at my job. Very good. But I was much too mature to point this out. Also, our entrance had caused quite the stir.

While a poster-board session is not exactly a cocktail party at the Met, this was Vienna. Accordingly, the university had done what it could to bring the gathering up to Viennese standards. Rather than a single campus sprawling hundreds of acres, the Vienna University of Technology had adopted a unique approach to managing its geographical footprint. As the city grew around the university's original location, the university had decided to expand via a number of subcampuses scattered throughout Vienna rather than tie up acres of valuable downtown real estate.

For this event, the administration had chosen well. The space we entered really could have passed for a ballroom. High vaulted ceilings were offset by sculpted crown molding and stone floors. Chandeliers provided glittering light while strategically placed tables offered chocolate, sparkling water, and of course a variety of Viennese coffees. But this was where the highbrow treatment ended.

Like most poster-board sessions sponsored by a university, the event's attendees were a mixture of students and established scientists. The participants were scattered throughout the grand space, their poster-board displays situated on circular high-top tables like forlorn islands adrift in a sea of majesty.

A scientist I was not, but sections of cardboard annotated with scrawling equations, indecipherable graphs, and indeterminate pictures were about as interesting as a treatise on eighteenth-century Russian literature. Judging by the lethargic crowd trudging from table to table, I was not alone in this assessment. If I had to guess, the majority of the attendees were either faculty or fellow students doing their level best to support their academic comrades during an ordeal considered a rite of passage in their community. Much like a trip to the dentist, everyone knew today was necessary, but no one wanted to be here.

And then there was Ella.

There are two schools of thought on how to employ tradecraft in events like this. The first is the more traditional. Be the gray man. Skulk from corner to corner, doing nothing to draw attention to yourself. Then, when the opportunity presents itself, intercept your quarry in a vulnerable moment away from his or her minders.

As you might imagine, I'm not really into skulking. To be fair, I don't think anyone paired with Ella could go unnoticed. Even without formal wear, Ella would have lit up the room. With her dark eyes and athletic figure, the Israeli could turn heads in a pair of sweatpants and a T-shirt. But in a curve-hugging Dolce & Gabbana gown, she could stop traffic.

Literally.

The room was constructed with an upper dais leading to the exits, which flowed down a set of steps to the lower section holding the poster-board exhibits. When her Louboutin heels began to click down the marble steps, every eye in the room tracked her progress.

Men wanted to know her.

Women wanted to be her.

There was no adopting the gray man persona with Ella, so we didn't try. Instead, we went with option two.

Own the room.

As per our play at the badging station, whispers announcing our presence had already spread through the crowd. Someone out of the ordinary was here. Someone important. And when that someone important had the looks and bearing of a socialite, so much the better.

In essence, Ella and I were hiding in plain sight. Our faux effort at being discreet had the opposite effect even as our ostentatious dress and mannerisms reinforced the audience's confirmation bias. We were movers and shakers because we looked and acted like movers and shakers. I wouldn't have to engineer a chance meeting with my target scientist.

He would come to me.

At least that was what I was hoping. If I didn't leave here with a successful bump, I was going to have to get a second job washing dishes to pay off my expense report.

Or should I say Ella's expense report.

A woman made a beeline for us as we reached the floor.

"Good afternoon," she said, extending her hand to Ella. "Thank you for joining us. I am Charlotte Bauer—"

"Dean of the school of engineering," Ella said as she shook the woman's hand with a radiant smile "Honored to meet you."

"The honor is all mine, Fräulein."

Apparently Ella's charm wasn't wasted on just men.

The dean of engineering was the antithesis of Ella's glamorous persona. She was late fifties or early sixties and looked the part of an academic. Her straight iron gray hair was styled in a pageboy cut, cropped close to the ears and off the neck. She wore a pantsuit that made no attempt to flatter her blocky body, and her wrinkled face bore not a trace of makeup. But her eyes lit up when Ella recognized her.

The Mossad operative still wasn't on my Christmas card list, but Ella had the goods.

"Pardon me for saying so," Charlotte said, "but we didn't know you were coming."

"Which is precisely the point," Ella said. "We understand how important events like this are for a budding scientist's career. The last thing we want to do is take attention away from the groundbreaking work on display."

"Nonsense," Charlotte said. "Your presence adds prestige to our little gathering. If you would do me the honor, I would be happy to serve as your escort. Was there anywhere in particular you wanted to start?"

Though she looked more schoolmarm than schmoozer, I could tell that Charlotte had done this a time or two. The key to getting people with money to attend events like these was to make them feel comfortable. Ella's protests aside, Charlotte knew those in Ella's position didn't waltz into an event intent on meeting everyone. Ella would have a list of students and scientists she wanted to see. Charlotte understood how the game was played. So while she would undoubtedly toss in a student or two of her own as she played tour guide, she would also let Ella set the agenda.

"Delightful," Ella said. "My assistant has the list."

That would be me.

Pulling a folded piece of paper from my suit coat's inner pocket, I made a show of scanning the blank lines even as I recalled the list of names I'd memorized from the program lying on Lucas's desk. Most of what you've seen or heard about spies is straight-up fabrication. I mean, I love a good Tom Cruise movie, but I have yet to free-fall into a room housing a single computer terminal with ropes hooked to my limbs.

Don't get me wrong: If the opportunity presented itself, I'd be all about a *Mission: Impossible*–type entrance. It's just that in the decade-plus I'd been a spy, my grand adventures tended to focus more on gunpowder and less on fantastical leaps of technology. That aside, there was one thing the movies got right about being a spy. You needed an excellent memory. This was the supernatural power I'd put to good use as I read off the imaginary list of names of the scientists Ella would like to see.

Charlotte listened with an engineer's precision and nodded her head.

"Excellent," Charlotte said. "We can start over here with Fräulein Moser."

While I was certain that Fräulein Moser was a masterful student, the tables and charts covering her poster board might as well have been Egyptian hieroglyphics for all the sense they made to me. I gathered that her thesis involved some sort of novel crystal lattice, but that was about as much as I could decipher.

Which was fine.

Of all the names I'd rattled off to the dean of engineering, Moser's was the most important. But not because of her research. No, Moser had the honor of sharing the end of the hall with Mr. Jianguo Liu, my Chinese target.

As the dutiful assistant, I stood back from the fray, jotting notes like crazy even as Ella carried the conversation. As I'd come to expect, the Israeli was charming but not patronizing. Judging by the questions she asked, Ella genuinely seemed to grasp the significance of Moser's research.

That made one of us.

I was much more focused on the three Chinese gentlemen standing to my left.

While Liu's poster board was no less understandable to farm boys from Utah, I felt an instant sort of kinship with the skinny kid standing next to his presentation. Dressed in stereotypical scientist attire of a plaid buttondown shirt that desperately needed ironing, khakis, and hiking boots, my target seemed a bit overwhelmed by Vienna's grandiosity.

His two friends probably were as well, but were much too cool to show it.

The Chinese student's minders looked straight out of central casting. Drab suits, short haircuts, and hard glares. Minder 1 had a linebacker's wide shoulders and a pugilist's flattened nose. Minder 2 had a slimmer build, but my intuition said he was the more dangerous of the pair. A wicked-looking scar bridged his eyebrows like a jagged lightning bolt.

But his eyes were what really pinged my radar. Not so much expressionless as dead. A corpse's eyes. Even Ella's appearance didn't do much to animate them. Muscles looked her over like she was something he planned to sample later. But Scar Face took the cake. His cold, dead eyes crawled across her body, and I felt my temper rise in response. I wanted to reach down his throat and yank out his spleen.

I didn't.

Instead, I used the time Ella had bought me to study their charge.

My target.

The Chinese scientist stared at Ella with an unabashed longing that even I could feel from across the room. In contrast to his two companions, the kid wasn't radiating lust or murderous intentions. His dumbstuck expression more mirrored what thirteen-year-old me felt the first time I saw Angie Albers in a skirt. Not so much sexual attraction as a deep appreciation for what the good Lord had created.

Which made sense.

According to the targeting package Frodo had put together, my scientist was all of nineteen. Since he'd already completed his undergraduate and master's degrees and was now a year from finishing his PhD, it was a safe bet that he probably hadn't gotten out of the house much. Now that he'd made his big breakthrough, he was in one of Europe's grandest cities in the presence of one of its most gorgeous residents.

No wonder he looked starstruck.

Ella favored Liu with a subdued smile as she swept by, but her attention was clearly focused on the earnest Fräulein Moser, she of mathematical symbols and nonsensical words. That didn't sit right with the Chinese version of Albert Einstein. Today's events would have felt overwhelming to a normal nineteen-year-old's male brain, and Liu's was hardly normal. Back home, he'd won three of the most prestigious academic awards by his eighteenth birthday. In short, he was a Big Deal.

In China, anyway.

And while Chinese university towns weren't exactly the City of Music, my scientist had spent his life in government-run schools drinking the indoctrination that proclaimed Chinese superiority in all things cultural, academic, and economic. A Big Deal in China should be a Huge Deal in the rest of the world. Yet the exotic woman who was handing out scholarship opportunities was about to pass him by.

This would not do.

I watched his face as prudence warred with indignation. Then his features hardened. A decision had been made. There was no way he was letting the pretty lady go without shooting his shot. As Ella finished her conversation with the earnest mathematician and prepared to transition to the chemist beside her, Liu made his move.

Or at least he tried to.

As he strode from his assigned circular table, he ran smack-dab into yours truly.

"Excuse me," I said, moving my finger down the blank page as if checking his name against my list. "Are you Liu?"

I adopted my best hurried-and-overworked-assistant persona, rushing out the words without bothering to make eye contact. The persona wasn't much of a stretch. Ella was already talking with the chemist. I needed to get a move on or risk losing her.

Liu looked from me to Ella and slowly nodded.

Across the room, the black heel to one of Ella's seven-hundred-fifty-dollar pumps snagged on the carpeting. She stumbled, revealing an exquisite length of leg in the process. Every male eye in the room tracked her progress, including those belonging to Liu's minders.

Every male eye but mine.

"Excellent," I said, fishing a business card from my pocket. "You were one of several students she wanted to meet with privately to discuss a fellowship in the United States. She has a break from nine to nine thirty tomorrow morning at Café Landtmann. Text the number on this card by three this afternoon to confirm. If we don't hear from you by then, your spot will be given to another researcher. Good day."

I pushed the card into his hands and turned away, darting over to where Ella was pulling herself together. From the corner of my eye, I saw Liu look from the card to his minders, once again his face a mask of indecision.

Then he tossed the card into the trash can at his feet.

A swing and a miss.

At least Ella and I both got new wardrobes out of the deal.

A moment later my phone vibrated—two long pulses followed by a short one.

Apparently, a computer scientist smart enough to build Skynet also possessed the mental acuity to memorize a phone number.

Who would have thought?

I kept my smile properly hidden as I gathered Ella's purse and endured her reproachful glare and chastising words. Everyone in her ever-expanding circle understood that though she was the one who tripped, I bore responsibility for the mishap. After all, what good was having an assistant if you couldn't publicly berate them every now and again?

I dutifully nodded in all the right places as I waited for a break in her tirade to insert the word *Mozart*. This was the brevity code word we'd agreed upon that would signify that I'd successfully bumped Liu. In other words, Ella's signal to wrap up her performance and collect her Oscar.

Then something odd happened.

My phone vibrated a second time. But not with the special ringtone I'd assigned to the digital in-box allocated for Liu. Though less than a handful of people on earth knew my cell's number, I'd still gone to the trouble of assigning one more custom ringtone. A short pulse followed by a long one bookended by another short one. The letter *F* in Morse code.

F as in Frodo.

Holding up a single index finger like a lonely light-house standing against the waves of Ella's displeasure, I pulled the phone from my pocket and turned away. A collective gasp sounded behind me. Who did I think I was to interrupt my well-deserved tongue-lashing?

Excellent question.

"Talk to me, Goose," I said.

Besides being my best friend, Frodo was also an afi-cionado of eighties and nineties movies. Especially those starring Tom Cruise. In fact, he'd once quoted the entire pivotal courtroom exchange between Tom and Jack Nicholson from *A Few Good Men* during a firefight. Granted, the firefight had been small as firefights went, but it was still an impressive feat.

With this in mind, *Top Gun* dialogue almost always elicited a chuckle.

Not this time.

"Cut the bullshit, Matty. This is serious. Katherine locked down the phone you were after. Then she dropped a proximity alert around it tied to your cell. It just pinged. The target phone is within seventy-five meters of you."

"Kudos to your girlfriend," I said, choosing to ignore the fact that my operational phone had been fed into the NSA's cavernous maw without my consent. "A truckload of those pink flowers is on the way. Can she give me a bearing?"

"Already asked. There's too much electronic interfer-ence."

I slowly turned as Frodo talked, surveying the room.

I was standing dead center in the ballroom. Everyone was within a seventy-five-meter radius. Nolan had said that the phone number belonged to his daughter, but that didn't mean she still had the device in her possession.

After the incident in Northern Ireland, Nolan had hidden from the very capable MI6, or British Secret Intelligence Service, for years. You didn't stay in the wind that long without learning a few operational tricks of the trade. Especially after the leaps and bounds in manhunting tactics, techniques, and procedures the US and our allies had perfected while tracking down terrorists in a post-9/11 world.

But even with his operational expertise, the Russians had still found Nolan. And if the Directorate V operatives could find him, they could certainly locate his daughter. I needed to proceed with caution.

"Is Katherine on the other line?" I said, walking to the southernmost part of the ballroom. "I'd like to try a couple things in real time."

"I'm gonna chalk that question up to jet lag. Of course she's on the other line."

"Sorry," I said, climbing the stairs to the upper dais. "I'm on a joint operation with a Mossad officer. My brain's a bit rattled."

"Apology accepted," Frodo said, "and whatever you do, don't argue with them. I once went to dinner with James and his Israeli counterpart. When the check came, they got into an argument over who was going to pay. It's the only time I've ever seen Chief cry."

The thought of fat crocodile tears draining from James's good eye was almost enough to put a smile on my face. Almost. From the center of the room, Ella was shooting me death glares even though I could read the operational intent behind her unkind looks. *Are we done here or not?* At the same time, I was surrounded by one hundred people, any one of whom could have been Nolan's daughter or part of the team sent to collect her.

Not ideal.

"Okay, stud," I said, installing myself in an alcove that provided the best vantage point of the circular room, "let's see if we can make something happen. Tell your girl to override the phone's operating system and give me its loudest ring. One. Ping. Only."

"Well played, Matty. Stand by."

There was a beat of silence as Frodo clicked over to the other line. Then: "Okay. The phone should be ringing . . . now."

An electronic chime sounded.

From two different phones.

Not good.

TWENTY-FIVE

I f I was surprised to hear two phones ring simultaneously, their owners seemed even more so. It didn't take more than a second to realize that the phones belonged to two completely different entities. Group number one consisted of a pair of Caucasian gentlemen in bad-fitting suits standing on the raised dais at the opposite end of the room.

Russians.

And then there was the final phone. While the Russians silenced their device after a ring or two, the second phone continued its shrill chime for an embarrassingly long time. After locating the phone's owner, I understood why. Three booths to my right, in the eastward corner of the room, stood a lonely-looking woman in front of an even lonelier-looking display.

The other students weren't exactly marketing majors, but the obligatory sections of cardboard were augmented with a number of more eye-catching paraphernalia. Most students had laptops set up on their tables displaying video clips of their experiments and the like. Some of the more enterprising academics had touchy-and-feelies—3D-printed models of their experiments or even some eye-catching lab ware.

One future entrepreneur even had gift cards to the local coffee shop emblazoned with a QR code that presumably directed the unsuspecting java lover to a website where you could view more of his sciencey stuff.

But not the lone academic in the corner.

Her display consisted of a single chart board with columns of meticulously written mathematical equations occupying the majority of the white space. The bottom third of the poster board had a number of graphs and charts no less ordered than the equations, but also hand generated. In fact, the only portion of her display that seemed custom produced was the prominent flag featured in the center of her table. A flag with blue borders, a red interior, and a single red star centered in a circle of white.

The flag of North Korea.

Huh.

Unlike some of her more flamboyant companions, the scientist wore a simple white laboratory coat on which her name was stitched in English and presumably Hangul above her right breast.

Choi.

Her raven-colored hair was done up in a bun and the formless brown dress she wore beneath her lab coat mirrored her simple flats. No Jimmy Choo heels for this re-searcher. In fact, a pair of stylish black glasses perched on the end of her nose was her only concession to fashion.

As with most of the displays, I hadn't the foggiest idea what she was presenting. Still, it didn't take a PhD to understand that her topic wasn't generating near the buzz of her contemporaries. She stood isolated in the corner, a drab island of solitude in a sea of chattering voices, flashy displays, and attempts at fashion.

But she wasn't alone.

At least not completely.

A single researcher was speaking to her. Judging by Choi's expression, it was the first person who'd stopped by since the event began. The rapturous expression on Choi's face seemed to indicate that she was just getting to the good part.

Whatever part that might be.

At first I thought she was going to ignore the ringing device. Then she seemed to hear her cell for the first time. Her countenance changed. With an upraised finger of apology to her visitor, Choi pulled the device from her pocket and stared at the screen.

Her face dropped.

I didn't know what she'd been expecting, but this wasn't it.

Then I understood.

I was looking at Nolan's half-Irish, half–North Korean daughter. She'd been anticipating a call from her father. Not from the number displayed on her cell's caller ID. A North Korean scientist at a Viennese academic conference probably didn't get a ton of personal calls. When the number didn't match the one her father had given her, Choi knew what had happened.

Or perhaps, more accurately, what wasn't going to happen.

Her dad wasn't coming.

She was on her own.

Except she wasn't. Nolan had saved my life. More important, he'd helped save Laila's. I'd been doing this long enough to understand that not every operation ended with the good guys hoisting pints back at the bar. In fact, many of them didn't. No matter. I'd sworn an oath to a dying man. I was going to honor it.

But first I needed another distraction.

Fortunately, I excelled at those.

Reaching into my pocket, I pulled out my phone and selected Ella's number. I texted her the brevity code word as well as the numbers 100, 101, and 102, each separated by commas. Unlike the US, Israel had separate extensions depending on the emergency.

I'd just texted her all of them.

Hopefully she'd get the message. If not, I'd have to do this the old-fashioned way.

As luck would have it, I was pretty good at that too.

TWENTY-SIX

Much to the Central Intelligence Agency's chagrin, the intelligence community now viewed DIA officers as the equivalent of their CIA counterparts. As you can imagine, this has done little to increase cooperation between the two agencies. Case in point, my relationships with CIA officers have not always been productive. In fact, I once planted my Glock's barrel in the back of the CIA Director's skull and thought long and hard about pulling the trigger.

Okay, so that might be a bit of an exaggeration. He wasn't the CIA Director just yet, but his Senate confirmation hearings had been proceeding swimmingly.

Anyway, what I'm trying to say is that even though I don't hold my Ivy League espionage contemporaries in the highest regard, I have to admit that the CIA-influenced training I received as a new DIA officer was superb. The majority of our time was devoted to the art and science of convincing a man or woman to betray their country, but we also studied a slew of other, no-less-important topics. Delightful classes on surreptitious entry, escape from restraint, and one of my favorites—border-crossing exercises.

While the Iron Curtain was nothing but a distant memory by the time I took up the espionage mantle, the lessons learned by the men and women who'd flitted between East and West Berlin while clandestinely running agents were passed to us in excruciating detail. I won't go into specifics, but suffice to say that I will never again view a German shepherd with anything that approachs affection.

At the time, I'd thought the extra precautions were overkill. Now I was thankful for my instructor's thoroughness. After all, if I'd executed the bump during training with four intelligence professionals monitoring my every move, how hard would it be to do the same thing with just two?

What was it with me and famous last words?

Squaring my shoulders, I moved toward Choi as I reviewed and discarded potential bump scenarios at an alarming rate. This was going to be challenging, no two ways about it. And while Ella was a great partner, I'd already used her with the Chinese scientist. People were suspicious by nature. Intelligence operatives doubly so. Ella as the center of attention would be written off once. Playing the same card twice wouldn't fly. Hopefully my Israeli friend had a few tricks of her own up her sleeve.

As if on cue, the building's power crashed, plunging the room into darkness.

Quickening my pace, I sliced through the room, threading between clumps of meandering scientists.

Here the university's odd choice in venues worked to my advantage. The ambience brought on by drawn shades and the recessed floor illumination that before felt forced was now an answer to prayer. While the room wasn't pitch-black, the lack of artificial lighting added a sense of confusion to the gathering as familiar landmarks became black silhouettes and people morphed into shadows.

Confusion was a spy's catnip.

Nervous murmurs in several languages provided a healthy amount of white noise, obscuring individual conversations. From somewhere to my left, the dean of engineering was calmly relaying instructions. The room's occupants had yet to heed them. This was partly due to the sense of disorder permeating the air and partly because the entire event had just become exponentially more interesting. For the same reasons a bar's dim lighting and loud music naturally lowered inhibitions, the ballroom's darkness and close confines added an edginess to what until now had been a predictably boring event. No one was in danger, but neither were they at just another stodgy academic event. The atmosphere felt spicy. The scientists were in no hurry to trade this newfound mystique for a discussion about molecular weights or the h-principle.

But I was on the clock all the same.

I covered the last two feet at a near run, knowing that my window of opportunity was closing. This was a nerd fest, not a rave. Our Viennese hostess would find a way to bring the shenanigans to a close shortly. Stepping between Choi and her female counterpart, I touched Nolan's daughter on the shoulder.

"Pardon the interruption, Dr. Choi," I said, "but I have a message for you. Could we speak outside?"

Choi's eyes met mine. Her gaze blazed through the dim light. She studied me for a long moment and then slowly nodded her head.

"Thank you," I said, transferring my touch from her shoulder to the natural handhold just above her elbow and below her triceps.

My time as a Ranger had taught me a number of valuable lessons. Not the least of these was that in a hostage-rescue scenario, the hostage was always the biggest wild card. While the actions of bad guys and good guys were usually pretty easy to predict, you could never count on a hostage acting rationally.

With this in mind, now that I had my hands on Nolan's daughter, I wasn't leaving the room without her. Ideally, she would take the hint and walk up the stairs to the safety offered by the corridor. But I was prepared to drag her kicking and screaming if necessary.

Fortunately for us both, Choi seemed ready to go. She gave a brief apologetic smile to her visitor and then started up the stairs, not exactly running but not dawdling either. As we reached the top of the dais, I edged past her, elbowing open the door for a quick peek.

Like the main room, the corridor's lighting was also extinguished, but emergency lamps mounted at intervals along the hallway cast ivory pools onto the tile floor. We seemed to be alone, but I still herded Choi to the left, in the direction opposite the building's entrance. My desire to conduct the next part of our encounter in private was at war with the clock ticking in my head. At its core, the espionage profession was a study in compromises, chief among them being speed and security.

"What is this about?" Choi said, speaking for the first time. Her English was accented but precise.

The diction of a scientist.

"Your father," I said, hustling her around a bend in the hallway.

We passed a set of bathrooms and a drinking fountain. I'd been hoping for a breakout room or, at the very least, a coat closet. I saw nothing but doors to my left leading back to the poster-board area. An oasis of silvery light revealed another set of doors at the end of the hall, but I was out of time.

A crash meeting was the contact method of last resort for a reason. With no way to survey the terrain ahead of time, you placed your bets and you took your chances. We would have to do this right here and right now or not at all.

"What about my father?" Choi said.

I'd expected the question, but not in the manner in which she'd asked it. As a rule, scientists weren't known for spontaneous outpourings of emotion. Even so, she'd phrased the question in an almost clinical manner. Something didn't feel right.

"He asked me to help you," I said.

Choi eyed me without speaking. After the silence began to stretch, she opened her mouth to speak. The *swish* of an opening door stopped her.

The bathroom door.

Which was behind me.

Damn it.

I turned to find myself facing a pistol.

A pistol held by a fit-looking man with Slavic features.

Yet another Russian.

He didn't look happy either.

TWENTY-SEVEN

nside," the man said, gesturing toward the bathroom with the pistol.

I turned, worried about Choi, but needn't have bothered. She was already walking toward the building's entrance and safety without a backward glance. When this was over, I was going to have a talk with my intuition. Every now and then, it would be great to know I was in over my head before the bad guy got the drop on me.

"Now," the man said.

His Russian accent was growing more pronounced, which suggested he was under stress. This encounter wasn't proceeding as he'd planned.

Welcome to the club.

With a sigh I held my hands at shoulder level, palms facing outward. I thought about protesting that he had the wrong guy, but didn't think it was worth the effort. Vienna was the city of spies for a reason. Besides, one of the keys to being a successful espionage professional was developing the ability to recognize a fellow practitioner.

He might not have known my name, but the Russian knew who I was.

Fast talking on my part wasn't going to convince him otherwise.

I moved toward the Russian and the bathroom only to watch as he slid to my left. He maintained a constant interval between us even as he cleared the way to the bathroom.

This guy knew what he was about.

Just my luck.

The bathroom was nothing special, even for Vienna. One urinal, a single stall, a sink with some fancy soap, and a stack of those linen hand towels Laila loved.

Oh, yeah, and a Russian with an SR-1 pistol and an attitude.

Following me inside, the Russian pushed the door closed with his foot. Then he reached into his pocket with one hand, keeping the pistol trained on me with the other.

The bathroom was about ten feet by five. Not exactly spacious but more than adequate for its intended purpose. Even so, it had promise. A pistol is best employed at ranges of ten to fifteen feet. Close enough so the shooter doesn't have to be a marksman while far enough away that his target can't get frisky. The space in which we were standing was right at the nexus between those two contingencies. Things weren't exactly rosy at the moment, but all hope was not lost.

Yet.

"Against the stall," the Russian said. "Move."

The problem about going up against another professional is that they tend to use the same tricks that you do. The distance separating us now made stripping my accoster's pistol from his one-handed grip impossible.

Time to start thinking about plan B.

I retreated until my back pressed against the stall's thin metal door even as the Russian withdrew a wedge-shaped length of rubber from his pocket. Dropping it to the tile, he drove it between the bathroom door and the floor with a practiced kick.

A doorstop.

The Russian carried a doorstop in his suit coat.

Why do I always get the Boy Scouts?

After a final strike with his heel to ensure that the rubber wedge was set, the Russian turned his attention back to me. Unlike the gorillas lurking in the posterboard session, this Russian had exceptional taste in clothing. Or at least access to a competent tailor. His suit's style was expensive but not ostentatious. A fabric and pattern that suggested class rather than flamboyance. A tightness across the man's back, shoulders, and biceps hinted at the athletic physique beneath, but didn't showcase it.

The man himself fit a similar mold. I put his age about equal with mine—early thirties. His hair was an unremarkable shade of brown, cut short but stylish. Long enough not to be confused with a military haircut, but also not the foppish length favored by those who pretended to be bohemians rather than intelligence professionals. Stubble that was something more than a five-o'clock shadow but less than a full beard covered a square jaw.

His face was intelligent and angular, with a web of fine wrinkles radiating from the corners of his blue eyes. I could imagine a scenario in which those eyes might sparkle with a good joke or fill with emotion at the sight of suffering.

Not today.

Today they radiated a chilling coldness.

"Where is my father?" the Russian said, again reaching into his coat pocket.

"Who?" I said with genuine confusion.

There were a number of different ways I'd imagined our conversation progressing. This hadn't been one of them.

"My father," the Russian repeated. His fingers reappeared from his jacket, this time with something long and cylindrical gripped between them. "You can tell me now or after I put a series of 9mm holes in your extremities. Your choice."

He threaded the suppressor onto the SR-1's barrel with quick, easy turns, keeping the pistol centered on my chest the entire time.

"Humor me," I said. "Who's your father?"

The pistol discharged in a blur of motion. One moment it had been sitting idly in the Russian's hands; the next the bathroom's tight confines were echoing with the pistol's report. Thanks to the suppressor, the muzzle blast was muted, but nothing short of Hollywood special effects would negate the sound in such a confined environment. On the positive side of the ledger, he'd angled the pistol downward. Other than the splintered slate, there was no permanent damage.

Well, almost no permanent damage.

"These boots were a gift from my wife," I said, reaching down to dust the stone shavings from what a moment ago had been a pristine section of glowing black toe. "Lucchese with ostrich skin. Handmade. If you've torn them, I will beat you senseless. Now, cut the tough-guy shit. Who is your father?"

The Russian stared at me, his eyes shards of ice. The sausage-shaped suppressor was still aimed at my kneecap, but the gunman's index finger was no longer resting on the trigger.

Progress.

"My father goes by many names," the Russian said. "I believe you know him as Nolan Burke."

Somehow, I'd figured that was what he was going to say. But for once I'd been hoping that my keen intellect had been mistaken. Besides, family trees weren't really my bag. I was the only six-year-old I knew who hadn't figured out Darth Vader's lineage ahead of time.

But here we were.

"Look," I said, lowering my hands, "I don't know who you are, but I'm on the clock, so I'll cut to the chase. Nolan is dead. Your countrymen killed him."

I've never been what you might term a sensitive guy, but in this case my directness was intentional. I'm good at reading people. The ability to crawl inside a potential asset's head is pretty much a job requirement. That said, the man I was sharing the bathroom with was also an intelligence professional. As my FBI friends liked to say, intelligence officers are professional liars. I needed to throw the Russian off-balance so I could judge his veracity. Nothing disturbs your sense of place in the world like unexpected news about your parents.

Just ask Luke Skywalker.

My words hit the Russian like a Joe Louis uppercut. He recoiled, sagging against the door as if to create distance between himself and what I'd just said. His physical reaction could very well have been fake, but the psychological one was much more telling. The tip of the suppressor wavered, drifting from the center of my chest to my toe. That simple gesture was more valuable than any polygraph.

If the Russian was acting, he could have given Mark Hamill a run for his money.

"How do you know?" the Russian said.

"I was there when it happened. For what it's worth, he went down fighting. Your comrades had roughed him up pretty good, but he still took one of them with him."

"Not comrades of mine," the Russian said. "They were FSB. Directorate V. You know it?"

I nodded.

"This is my fault," the Russian said. "I never should have used him."

The suppressor was now pointed at the floor, parallel with his leg.

"Used him for what?" I said.

"To pass a message. I needed a conduit to your government."

"Why?"

"To prevent World War Three."

TWENTY-EIGHT

So stopping a third world war hadn't been on the list of possible responses I'd expected. But the first rule of being an intelligence officer was to never act surprised by anything your asset told you. With that in mind, I responded accordingly.

"What the hell are you talking about?" I said.

All right, so probably not the best rejoinder, but I'd had a day. Besides, now that I'd finally cornered the person who could start connecting the operational dots, I intended to get some answers.

As the Russian began to speak, the bathroom's lights buzzed back to life.

Or maybe not.

"No time," the Russian said, unscrewing the suppressor. "I've got to get back before they notice my absence. You know the Prater?"

"Sure," I said.

"Good," the Russian said, slipping both the suppressor and SR-1 back into his suit pockets. "Meet me at the Giant Ferris Wheel in two hours. Coffee in your right hand if I'm clean. Left if I'm not. Got it?"

"Yep," I said.

"See you then."

The Russian scooped the doorstop from the floor, squirreled it away in yet another pocket, and was gone. As the door swung closed behind him, I had the disconcerting thought that I wasn't sure who was running whom. But before I could devote more energy to that particular rabbit hole, I needed to answer something more pressing.

What in the hell was the Prater?

Turns out, the Prater was one of the City of Spies' most famous landmarks. Or at least the Giant Ferris Wheel at its center certainly was. My CIA escort was kind enough to provide this information as he once again allowed me access to the secure conference room in the embassy's bowels. I'd thought not dripping water on his pretty conference table might thaw our frosty interservice relationship. But the sour look he was giving me from the opposite end of the room suggested that this was not the case.

Maybe that had something to do with the Mossad spy seated next to me.

"Let me get this straight," James said. "I send you out on a simple bump, and you come back with news that the world's gonna end?"

"Technically he was only talking about World War Three, Chief," Frodo said. His side of the VTC was still blank. "Though when Matty's on the job, Armageddon is always a possibility."

"Whose side you on?" I said.

"Sorry, brother," Frodo said, sounding nothing of the sort. "Gots to call 'em as I sees 'em."

"So besides ambushing a Russian hit team, getting your asset killed, and being declared persona non grata by the Director of the BVT, everything went exactly as briefed?" James said.

"Not entirely, Chief," I said, shifting in my seat. "I've also decided to run this as a joint operation."

"With who?" James said. "One of the Five Eyes?"

The term *Five Eyes* was intelligence shorthand for the US, Australia, Canada, New Zealand, and the United Kingdom. These five English-speaking countries shared reporting and findings transparently between their intelligence services. It was logical to assume that a joint operation would include one of our regular partners.

Unfortunately, logic and I had long ago parted ways.

"Nope," I said, fiddling with the VTC's remote control to widen the camera angle. "This is Ella Alfasi. Or at least I think that's her name. Mossad officers can be finicky about that sort of thing."

"Hello," Ella said, giving the camera an elegant wave. "And thank you for my new wardrobe. Dolce and Gabbana is notoriously hard to find in Tel Aviv."

Until that moment, I'd never really understood the

phrase *the silence was deafening*. But as I watched James's mouth open and close like a beached goldfish's, it finally made sense. If he'd screamed profanities or insulted my parentage, I'd have understood. As Mom liked to say, I can be an acquired taste. But the total silence coming from the other side of the world was terrifying in a way that was hard to describe.

"That's a very pretty dress," Frodo said, once again stepping into the breach on my behalf. "How much did it run?"

"Not sure," Ella said. "I stopped counting at three zeroes."

"A thousand bucks for a dress?"

"More like five," Ella said. "But don't forget the shoes, purse, and backup outfits."

"We've paid off Afghan warlords for less," Frodo said.

"But did they look this good?" Ella said with a smile.

Which left Frodo and me in a bit of a quandary. On the one hand, Ella really did look that good, so it seemed impolite not to tell her. On the other, I was married, and Frodo had a serious girlfriend. Complimenting an attractive Israeli spy's appearance didn't seem conducive to either of those relationships.

Fortunately, James saved the day.

"What in the actual fuck, Matthew?"

All right, so maybe that wasn't the segue I would have chosen, but his outburst did shift the conversation's focus away from Ella. Which meant that it was now fixated solely on me.

"Ella is Benny's protégée, Chief," I said, trying to ignore the fury radiating from James. "I owe Benny for the same reason I owed Nolan. I pay my debts."

"That's fan-fucking-tastic," James said, his booming voice eliciting a squeal of static from the overhead speakers. "You're a regular Knight of the Round Table. Are there any other boons or royal quests I should know about?"

"They saved my wife's life, Chief," I said, leaning forward in my chair. "Her life. If that makes things inconvenient for you, I'm happy to take a leave of absence."

"In case anyone's interested," Ella said, jumping in before James could reply, "I don't want to be here either. Unfortunately, my boss listens about as well as Mr. Drake. Which is to say not at all. So perhaps instead of shouting at one another, we could discuss what to do next. I'm not a fan of Matt's methods, but I can't argue with his results. Over the course of a single encounter, he managed to secure a second date with a GRU officer. That isn't exactly trivial."

Once again silence reigned from the opposite side of the Atlantic. But the ominous quality was gone. This time I felt an entirely different emotion radiating from the television—respect.

"Holy shit, Matty," Frodo said, amusement coloring his voice. "Talk about burying the lede."

"Is it true, Matthew?" James said. "Did you pitch the GRU officer in charge of safeguarding Russian scientists?"

Laila likes to say that I can snatch defeat from the jaws

of victory. At least I think that's what she says. When my wife gets good and truly pissed, she rants in a mixture of Pashtun and English. Pro tip: Do not correct your wife's pronunciation when she's simultaneously cursing you in two different languages.

Anyway, the point being I have a tendency toward brashness that sometimes can appear to be self-defeating. Or, in Frodo's terms, I can be a stubborn asshat. What I'm saying is that I've been known to let my own bull-headedness get in the way of my success from time to time.

Especially when someone is simultaneously cursing at me in two languages.

But since James was speaking in just one, I was ninety-nine percent sure everything was going to be fine.

"You bet your ass it's true," I said, matching his one-eyed death stare. "I'm a freaking spy. It's what I do."

Okay, so that last one percent could be tricky. Fortunately, James was so fixated on the shiny object represented by a potential GRU recruitment, he let my obvious show of disrespect slide.

Mostly.

"Boy, I know what you do and how you do it," James said. "That's why I hired you. Now tell me exactly what happened before I have to tune you up in front of your Israeli friend."

"Here's what I know," I said, parsing my story with an eye toward my Mossad counterpart. "After Frodo's NSA girlfriend pinged Nolan's phone number—"

"She what?" James said.

"Matty," Frodo said.

"Sorry, brother," I said. "I gots to call 'em as I sees 'em. Anyway, the phone was compromised or cloned. Frodo's ping rung two separate handsets. One belonged to a North Korean scientist named Choi. A couple of Russians had the other. Don't know who they were."

"Who's Choi?" James said.

"Not sure," I said. "Probably just a dangle. When I bumped her, the Russian was waiting. It was a crash meeting, so we didn't have much time together. He said that Nolan was his father. He wanted to use Nolan to establish a conduit so that the Russian could prevent World War Three."

"That's it?" James said. "Why didn't you get more?"

"Because that was when the distraction generated by my operational partner expired," I said.

"What distraction?" James said.

"The power grid," Ella said. "We took it down."

"Mother of God," James said, "you hacked into the university's power grid?"

"No," Ella said, shaking her head. "There wasn't time to be surgical. We blacked out the entire city."

"Hmm," Frodo said. "Pinging a single phone doesn't sound so terrible now, does it?"

The silence was again absolute, but for once James's disbelief was directed at a target other than yours truly. It was both a novel and exhilarating experience. One that I knew was altogether too good to last.

"What?" Ella said, folding her arms across her chest.

"Your operative needed a distraction. We provided it. You're welcome."

"Exactly," I said. "Though it would have been nice if y'all had held it for just a bit longer. But I guess even Israelis aren't perfect."

The look Ella gave me could be loosely termed as snide.

Loosely.

"Ms. Alfasi," James said, "we very much appreciate your nation's contribution to this operation. That said, I'm still not entirely clear why the Mossad's Director of Operations is nosing around Vienna. Please enlighten me."

That was a great question. In the craziness of the last several hours, I'd never really pinned Ella down in that regard. James might have been a hardheaded son of a bitch, but he hadn't risen to the rank of branch chief because he was stupid.

"You can take up the specifics with my director," Ella said.

Her answer came across as clean and practiced, but I could hear something in her tone.

So could James.

"I will," James said, "as soon as we're off this call. But since you're a participant in my operation, I think it's safe to assume your boss is comfortable with you sharing a bit more detail with your American partners."

"Okay," Ella said, after shooting me an unreadable look. "But it's going to cost you. Fortunately, the salesman was kind enough to give me his mobile number. You know, for contingencies."

"Chief," I said, "I—"

"Done," James said.

At this point we might as well have bought the clothing store.

"Excellent," Ella said with a smile. "I knew we could come to an arrangement."

"Wait," I said. "You don't have to check with Benny first?"

"Of course not," Ella said. "Director Cohen trusts my discretion in operational matters. Especially ones in which I'm the lead officer."

Well, son of a bitch. Ella's one-two combination had done little to assuage my hurt pride. First, she'd managed to belittle me in front of my boss. Second, she'd revealed that she'd had permission to share her intel all along.

Israelis.

Fortunately, my comrades in arms were much too polished to revel in the insult Ella had just lobbed my way.

"Damn, Matty," Frodo said. "I like this girl."

Or not.

"If everyone's about done establishing the pecking order and augmenting their wardrobes, I'd really like to get down to business," I said. "The clock's ticking."

"Here is what I'm willing to share," Ella said, leaning back in her chair and crossing her legs at the knee. A queen graciously granting an audience to the local riffraff. "A dormant asset established contact. He said he had information regarding a potential threat to European stability."

"Benny said that much already," I said, jumping in.

"He did," Ella said, "but if you'd allow me to finish, I'll tell you the rest. This asset is the man you know as Nolan."

"For the love . . . ," James said. "Was there anyone this guy wasn't talking to? Calling in favors is all well and good, Matthew. But this is feeling more about opportunism than honor."

I frowned, not liking where James was going, but that didn't mean he was wrong. An asset who wanted to sell information to the highest bidder might just exaggerate his reporting to drive up the asking price. That aside, there was something about what Ella had just said that pinged my radar.

Then I had it.

"Can you be more specific about the timeline?" I said. "When exactly did Nolan reach out to you?"

"Saturday," Ella said, giving me an unreadable look. "Fourteen hundred local time."

"Which would have been after he walked out of our embassy," Frodo said.

I nodded. "Exactly. Nolan might still have been shopping information, but that's not the only explanation. Judging by the attitude of my CIA friends here, I don't think he was given the warmest of welcomes. In fact, I wouldn't consider it a stretch to say the person who interviewed him didn't put much stock in his reporting. They didn't even offer Nolan sanctuary in the embassy as far as I could tell."

"So he hedged his bets by approaching an old handler?"

I shrugged. "Only Nolan can answer that. But it does make sense. And I wouldn't characterize it as hedging bets. I'd call it survival. If my life was at risk, I certainly wouldn't have put all my chips in the hands of a single inept bureaucrat."

"Or the life of someone you loved," Ella said.

I nodded again. "As he was dying, Nolan made me promise to help his daughter. That's who was supposed to be on the other end of the telephone number."

"Then how does a Russian GRU officer figure into this?" James said.

"Don't know," I said, glancing at the clock. "Maybe we should ask him."

TWENTY-NINE

Peter had left the Lincoln Memorial secure in the knowledge of what he must do. He would tell the president about his mistake and own up to the consequences. This millstone around his throat was affecting every aspect of his life, probably unnecessarily.

Besides, personal concerns aside, he owed it to Jorge to come clean.

From the day he'd first gone to work for the dynamic politician, Peter had had just one goal etched in his mind—seeing the country's first Hispanic president elected. Now Peter had doubled down on that goal by orchestrating Jorge's successful reelection. But all that would be for naught if the president's Republican adversaries caught wind of Peter's mistake.

He needed to bare his soul and throw himself at his friend's feet.

It was the right thing to do.

But the sight of the gates looming just ahead had a way of putting things into perspective. Yes, Peter *could* own up to his transgressions, but—like a wayward husband confessing his philandering ways—what would that really accomplish? Sure, Peter's conscience would be clear, but at what cost? In unburdening himself, he would merely be transferring responsibility for what he'd done onto Jorge's narrow shoulders. His friend was already carrying the weight of the entire nation. Would it really be fair to saddle him with this as well?

Besides, if Peter was going to come clean, shouldn't he do it in the most advantageous way possible? As of this moment, he knew next to nothing—a phone number for his contact at the Russian embassy, a description of the woman who'd twice approached him, and the place of their next meeting.

Of what practical use was this information? If Peter really wanted to atone for his sins, shouldn't he maintain this facade a little longer? At the very least, Peter could meet with the woman and determine her demands. Maybe he could even snap a clandestine picture or two or record their meeting with his cell. Then he would be able to present Jorge with something more valuable than just another adviser's admission of bad judgment.

By the time Peter had badged his way through security, his plan had solidified. He'd return to his office and review the president's speech with no one the wiser. Then, after Jorge finished his address to the nation, Peter would meet the woman at the bar as she'd requested. But this time Peter would be in the driver's seat. He'd probe her and collect as much information as possible.

After doing his homework, Peter would lay everything out for Jorge the next morning. Peter turned the plan around in his mind as he walked past the Cabinet Room and West Wing lobby, moving through the narrow hallways until he arrived at his office.

The space was small and Spartan. Peter's Harvard diploma and a single picture were the only personal touches Peter permitted himself. The diploma was there to remind him that, while he'd come from nothing, equal parts hard work, perseverance, and suffering had allowed him to achieve greatness. The photo embodied the reason for his sacrifices. Kristen—his kid sister. The blond-haired, blue-eyed beauty had been killed while deployed to yet another meaningless foreign war. She'd enlisted to pay for college, but ended her short life in a flag-draped coffin instead.

These two items were the touchstones that guided Peter's life and the lens through which he viewed the problem presented by the Russian woman. Satisfied that he'd examined the situation from every angle, Peter put the matter out of his mind. Instead, he logged on to his computer and brought up the latest version of the president's address.

Then his phone rang.

"Yes?" Peter said, holding the phone to his ear with one hand as he scrolled past the opening remarks with the other. The tone was good—vintage Jorge—but no one remembered good.

Peter needed great.

"The president would like to see you, sir," the president's personal secretary said.

"Sure," Peter said, snapping his laptop closed. "The Oval Office?"

"No, sir," the secretary said. "The Situation Room. And you'd better hurry."

THIRTY

Unlike many of the Oval Office's previous occupants, Jorge Gonzales hadn't allowed himself to become seduced by the trappings of power. He stilled poured his own coffee, and when outsiders weren't present, he encouraged his inner circle to call him by his first name. As Jorge was quick to remind anyone who'd listen, he might have the title Mr. President for life, but he was not a king and didn't want to be treated as such.

This same attitude applied to a different aspect of presidential powers. One that was every bit as seductive as the legion of staffers competing to address the commander in chief's every need. Many holders of the nation's highest office had arrived at 1600 Pennsylvania Avenue with a distrust if not outright aversion to the military.

This had a way of changing.

For instance, the first time a new president used kinetic, rather than diplomatic, means to solve an international problem was a significant milestone. Up until that point, the nation's chief executive usually resisted exercising the military option. Oftentimes they resented being forced down this path.

But the resistance didn't last long.

There was something seductive about playing God. About deciding who lived and who died while sitting in a leather chair as the operation transpired on high-definition televisions. Peter had heard whispers from his predecessors. Tales of past presidents who'd begun inventing reasons to spend more and more time in the Situation Room. Who began to take policy briefings from their seat at the head of the long wooden table even as the video feed of American enemies dying fiery deaths ran as a backdrop.

Fortunately, Jorge Gonzales had proven resistant to this siren's call. And this made Peter all the more worried as he wound down the narrow stairway leading to the basement vault door, slid his Blackberry into the wooden shelf next to the wall, and entered his security code into the cipher lock. Though he could stomach the use of military force when absolutely necessary, President Gonzales was still a pacificist at heart. He viewed the Situation Room and its enticing 4K monitors as a necessary evil and treated the place as such. If Peter's old friend was already ensconced in the underground tomb, it was for a serious reason.

The security door opened with an audible click, and Peter slipped inside, nodding to the obligatory Secret Service agent as he entered. The crowd of faces greeting him made his heart stutter even as he strode toward the empty seat beside the president. He slid into his chair as if this was just another day at the office.

It wasn't.

This was almost the exact cast of characters who had persuaded the president to illegally enter Russian-controlled Syrian airspace. The incursion had precipitated a near foreign-policy disaster. Relations with Russia had still yet to recover.

And here they were again.

"Sorry I'm late, sir," Peter said. "Got here as soon as I could."

"No problem, my friend," the president said with a tired smile. "I'm the one who insisted you take a break, remember? Unfortunately, my jest about the world not coming to an end might have been a bit premature. Jen, please continue."

"Yes, Mr. President."

Jen Brown was one of the two new faces in the group. She'd taken over as secretary of state shortly after Jorge had been sworn in for his second term. Short, with close-cropped black hair and a husky build, she reminded Peter of a collegiate wrestler gone to seed.

Still, in the short time they'd worked together, Peter had been impressed with her performance. Unlike her predecessor, Jen gave the president the lay of the land as it actually was, rather than interjecting rosy hopes of what it could or should be. On a team charged with navigating the travails of international relations, there was room for just once optimist—the president.

"As I was saying," Jen said, "due to the unprecedented Russian buildup along the border with Ukraine, Kyiv is pushing hard for full NATO membership effective immediately."

"Sorry to interrupt," Peter said, "but you said *unprecedented*. I understand that Russia massing troops on Ukraine's eastern border is disconcerting, but this is hardly the first time Moscow has flexed its muscles. What precisely about this is unprecedented?"

"I'll take that one."

The comment came from the group's second new member—Christina Sims, the interim CIA Director. The interim title wasn't so much a reflection on Christina's suitability for the job as it was the pall that still hung over the position. The previous director, Beverly Castle, had resigned under dubious circumstances while her successor, Charles Sinclair Robinson IV, was currently in prison awaiting trial for a litany of crimes. And to add insult to injury, Charles had been Peter's close friend. In the aftermath, Peter had offered his resignation.

Twice.

The first time, Jorge had turned Peter down immediately, saying that he never wanted to hear such foolishness again. Peter had offered the second time after the Senate Republicans had announced their intention to block any further nominee for the director's position until the administration provided a full accounting of what had transpired with Charles. Jorge had once again refused Peter's offer.

But he hadn't added the admonishment to never tender it again.

Peter could read between the lines.

His days in the White House were numbered.

"You are correct," Christina said, snapping Peter out of his musings. "Russia has certainly pre-positioned troops on its border with Ukraine before. But not like this."

She touched a button on her laptop computer, and the room's televisions sprang to life, revealing a slide emblazoned with the CIA's seal.

While Beverly and Charles had both been political animals, Christina Sims looked like the career CIA analyst she was. Though her brown hair was longer than the secretary of state's boxish cut, it still barely touched her collar. She was dressed appropriately for the gathering, but her plain slacks, blouse, and jacket were a far cry from the stylish dresses Beverly favored or the tailored suits Charles had enjoyed. Taken in sum, Christina gave off the persona of someone who was competent at her job, but who would much rather be laboring in anonymity at the CIA's sprawling headquarters in Langley, Virginia, than briefing the president and his staff.

Peter thought this made her perfect for the interim role.

"This is an image from one of our KH-11 reconnaissance satellites approximately three hours ago," Christina said, touching another button on her keyboard. In response, the CIA seal was replaced with imagery. "What you're seeing is a view from the Pogorovo training area in Russia. The military base is less than two hundred miles from the Ukrainian border. These are of particular interest."

Christina triggered a pencil-sized laser pointer and used the green spot to circle several vehicles in the center of the image. "In the past, the Russians have pre-positioned several brigades' worth of soldiers and equipment on the border as a show of force. But the logistical assets organic to a maneuver brigade would only support combat operations for about twenty-four hours. If the Russians were serious about invading Ukraine, they would need to pre-position fuel tankers and ammunition carriers, along with the other assets needed to service and recover the first echelon's armored vehicles. This is exactly what you see here."

Christina's proclamation sent a ripple of conversation through the room.

"What are you saying?" the secretary of defense said. "The Russians are going to invade Ukraine?"

"I'm saying that, unlike previous instances, today the Russians have both the means to stage an incursion into Ukraine and the logistical assets to support it."

"How long could the elements you've highlighted sustain combat operations?"

This time the question came from General Johnny Etzel, the chairman of the Joint Chiefs. The former Army aviator always brought to mind an academic with his lanky build and Buddy Holly–style reading glasses, but Peter wasn't taken in by appearances. He instinctively distrusted the West Pointer, as he did most members of the military, but Peter's dislike for Etzel ran beyond just his uniform. Etzel had lobbied hard for the rescue operation into Syria. He was to be watched.

Christina gave the slim general a quick nod before replying, acknowledging a fellow professional.

"You've cut to the heart of the matter, General," Christina said, folding her hands on the table. "As you know, resupply is a function of many things, including rate of march, combat losses, and the amount of ammunition expended. That said, if we assume that Russian expenditures would be on par with our own, the logistical tail they have pre-positioned would allow their ground forces to advance as far west as Kharkiv or potentially Kramatorsk."

The CIA Director again referenced her laptop, and this time a map of Ukraine replaced the satellite image. Red diamonds marked the location of Russian forces and a series of red arrows highlighted the proposed routes of advance.

"What's so important about Kramatorsk?" Peter asked.

He was certain he was butchering the city's name, but he could not have cared less. In just hours, the president was scheduled to give a national address, but, instead of refining the speech, they were discussing a potential Russian invasion of a country the average American couldn't find on a map.

A military tactician Peter was not, but his keen understanding of the American public had guided Jorge into the land's highest office not once but twice. While the concerns of Joe or Jill American were notoriously hard to predict, Peter could guarantee one thing: No one had the stomach for another foreign war.

The slide changed again. The map of Ukraine remained, but now the eastern side of the country was overlaid with red hash marks that culminated in a line running north to south just east of Kramatorsk.

A series of red dots marked cities immediately on the western side of the line.

"For all intents and purposes, the cities of Kharkiv and Kramatorsk represent Ukraine's eastern center of gravity," Christina said. "The crosshatches mark the territory Russia annexed during their last Ukrainian land grab back in 2014. The red dots designate cities with a good mix of pro-Russian Ukrainian separatists. In some of these cities, Russian is spoken by more than fifty percent of the population. As you can see, Kramatorsk forms a nexus of the territory currently under Ukrainian control but susceptible to Russian influence. If the Russian president intends to make another land grab, Kramatorsk is where he'd center his efforts."

"I appreciate your analysis," the president said, speaking for the first time, "but I need some help putting it into perspective. Is an invasion imminent or not?"

All eyes turned to the CIA Director. To her credit, the analyst turned leader of the nation's premier intelligence organization didn't shy away from the attention. Instead, she answered with an academic's slow, cautious diction.

"I defer to General Etzel on the topic of military tactics," Christina said, "but I will say this: These vehicles are the key to an invasion." The slide changed, returning to the original satellite imagery. Christina's green laser dot once again circled the parking lot full of tankers, trucks, and maintenance vehicles. "If these assets move from their staging area and start heading west, we've got a problem. Until then, we're just speculating."

The director's statement was exactly the opening Peter needed.

"Sir," Peter said, turning to the president, "I'll be the first to admit that Russia's military capabilities or intentions aren't my cup of tea. But I do know something about the anthill we'll kick over if we move on Ukraine's NATO membership. Even among the member nations, opinions are sharply divided. For all we know, addressing full membership now may spur Russia to action. At this moment, the Russians are still posturing. I think Christina has given us an excellent barometer to measure their intent. Let's use it."

"I'm inclined to agree with you," Jorge said, "but the presence of those vehicles is worrisome. General Etzel, is there a way to thread the needle? Something we can do to show our commitment to the people of Ukraine without escalating things with Russia in the process?"

Left unsaid was that relations with Russia, while not at a Cuban Missile Crisis level of frigidity, were at a dangerously low point. By ignoring Peter's advice on how to deal with the Syria situation, Jorge had been forced to call Russia's bluff.

Except Russia hadn't been bluffing.

The American incursion into Russian-controlled Syrian airspace had spawned an aerial engagement that had been both brief and deadly. A Russian jet had been downed, its pilot killed, and Russian airspace in Syria briefly put under American control. But the loss of life was trivial in comparison to the other loss.

A loss of face for the Russian president.

The Russian strongman stayed in power in part by the aura of invincibility surrounding him. In one form or fashion, he'd held the reins to his county since 1999. One did not rule with an iron fist for that long without accruing enemies. Enemies who lurked in the shadows, biding their time as they waited for the slightest indication that the tyrant's grip was weakening. For a politician in a Western democracy, the Syrian debacle would have been career ending.

For the leader of the modern state of Russia, it could have been terminal.

"I've got something that could fit the bill," General Etzel said, removing his black reading glasses and placing them on the table in front of him. "As part of Operation Inherent Resolve, we have a combined-arms task force executing a gunnery in Ukraine as we speak. It's more a confidence builder between NATO allies than a tactical deployment. That said, nothing demonstrates intent like an armored column with a squadron of Apaches providing overwatch. We could send them on a show-of-force movement into Kramatorsk if Kyiv is amenable."

"Sir," Peter said, already not liking where this was headed, "with all due respect to the general, I don't think we should do anything that might be considered provocative right now."

"I understand your concern, Peter," the president said, "but I'm reminded of something my high school history teacher used to say: *Si vis pacem, para bellum.* Do you know it?"

"'If you want peace, prepare for war,'" Christina said.

"Exactly," the president said, pointing a bony finger at the CIA Director. "I've never claimed to have stared into my Russian contemporary's soul, but I do know this: Nature abhors a vacuum. In this case, I'm afraid that if the Russian president believes we don't have the stomach to defend our Ukrainian allies, he'll fill the vacuum we've unintentionally created. If that happens, we'll be faced with a European war. Johnny, launch your spur ride."

"On it, sir," Etzel said.

As the meeting concluded, Peter couldn't help but think of another famous Latin quote, this one uttered by Julius Caesar as he crossed the Rubicon and started the war that would lead to the downfall of Roman democracy.

Alea iacta est.

The die is cast.

THIRTY-ONE

What is in this?" I said, taking another swallow of the beverage Ella had set on the table in front of me.

"You don't like it?" Ella said.

"On the contrary," I said. "If Turkish delight was drinkable, I think this is what it would taste like. Which makes it dangerous."

"Why?" Ella said. "Afraid that you're Edmund? Or more worried that I'm the White Witch?"

Once again I found myself reappraising my Israeli partner. In the short time we'd worked together, she'd shown three different versions of herself. An operative with a pistol pointed at my head, an espionage professional with an instinct for pitches that rivaled any DIA officer, and now an aficionado of Western literature. As much as I didn't want to admit it, I was slowly coming to enjoy working with the Mossad officer.

But that didn't make her question any less relevant.

"You're a C. S. Lewis fan?" I said.

Ella shrugged her slim shoulders. "I like *Narnia*, but as you might imagine, his Christian apologetics books don't do much for me. I'm a bigger fan of his fellow Inkling."

"Tolkien?"

Ella smiled. "All Israelis are born with wanderlust, so I guess it's no surprise that I wanted to be a hobbit. Our country is beautiful but small, and it lacks the security of the Shire. After my service in the IDF, I traveled extensively. But where most of my countrymen gravitated toward Europe or South America, I spent two years backpacking across New Zealand."

"Did you find what you were looking for?"

"No," Ella said, her expression now serious. "But remember: Not all who wander are lost. What about you? Why do you do this?"

I paused before answering, turning the Israeli spy's question over in my mind. I discarded the first couple of responses even though they undoubtedly contained grains of truth. The notions of good and evil weren't abstract concepts to me. I wasn't naive enough to believe that my nation was in the right all of the time, but I did believe that America had done more to lift humankind from suffering than any other nation in history.

But that wasn't all of it. At this moment I was in a Viennese park, prepared to meet a spy who might or might not have information that could stop a world-destabilizing war. The reason for doing that was far simpler and much more visceral.

"I do this because it needs to be done," I said, meeting Ella's dark eyes.

"Why you?" Ella said.

"Because I'm good at it."

The statement, while simplistic, was absolutely true. Even so, I mentally prepared for another verbal riposte from my reluctant comrade in arms. But rather than skewering me with her quick wit, Ella reached across the table and squeezed my forearm.

"I believe you," Ella said, her laughing eyes now serious. "Don't make me regret it. Our man just entered the park."

Standing, the Israeli spy gathered her affogato and carried it to the trash. As briefed, she took up a position at the far side of the outdoor seating area, joining the line of people waiting for a Ferris wheel ticket. Though we'd decided that I should meet the Russian alone, since that was what he expecting, I felt the sudden void of her absence.

This was partly because, even though ours was an arranged marriage, I'd come to rely on the Mossad officer's operational chops. Her performance at the poster-board session had been nothing short of masterful. While I hadn't had occasion to observe her martial prowess, I had to believe that the notoriously aggressive Israeli intelligence service didn't skimp when it came to paramilitary instruction.

But this was only part of the reason.

The easy way we'd taken to operating together served only to highlight the missing piece in my operational portfolio—Frodo.

Contrary to espionage novels, lone wolves do not survive long. As Frodo had driven home in spectacular fashion when I was a baby DIA officer, operations with the potential to go kinetic are no place for a single spy. As much as I wanted to pretend otherwise, I was finally coming to terms with the idea that Frodo was never again going to pick up his trusty HK and follow me into battle. Maybe it was time I finally talked with my best friend and our boss about getting a partner. Even though it hadn't been said, everyone on the secure VTC knew that a Mossad team was pulling surveillance for me for just one reason: I no longer had a crew of my own.

That had to change.

Otherwise I'd eventually find myself outmatched and outgunned. Again. Only pure dumb luck and good training had kept me from ending up in a body bag thus far, but my good fortune wouldn't last. As my boss in the Ranger Regiment had constantly reminded me, luck was not a method or a combat multiplier.

But that was a topic for later.

Probably much later.

I needed to get my head in the game. Ella had just transferred her purse from her right to her left hand. The Russian was entering our surveillance box.

It was go time.

THIRTY-TWO

The Russian ambled into the common area as if he didn't have a care in the world. Believe it or not, that was a skill. Anxious people walked faster, and nothing made a person more anxious than betraying their country. As such, surveillance teams were trained to key in on anxious people. My gait and posture were two things I had to continuously monitor every time I was heading for an asset meet.

Not so the Russian. His strides were long and even. Not fast enough to catch a watcher's eye, not slow enough to be obvious. He was what every intelligence operative aspired to be—smooth.

Me, not so much. At the exact moment the Russian GRU officer drew even with me, his meandering gaze centering on my coffee cup, Ella brushed her dark curly hair away from her face.

The wave-off signal.

The Russian was being followed.

The conservative play would have been to switch the coffee cup I was holding from one hand to the other and try again later. When an asset's life was in danger, I almost always defaulted to the conservative play.

Not today.

I'd already lost one asset, and I didn't plan on losing another. If the Russian was being followed, he was under suspicion. Under normal circumstances, a counterintelligence team surveilling a suspected asset would let the operative run for as long as possible in the hopes of identifying and targeting his handler and unmasking the rest of the network.

But when that asset was a potential mole, protocols changed. In that case, the surveillance team would be much more aggressive. The primary concern would be to limit the damage the double agent was doing to his service.

I expected this team to be aggressive. The GRU officer had news so dire that he'd sent his terrorist father on a quest for help. News about World War III. The Russians suspected they had a leak—that was why they had elected to torture Nolan instead of just killing him outright. But that ploy had backfired, and Nolan had taken his secret to the grave.

The Russians surveilling Nolan's son would give him a bit of line to see if they could identify his handler, but not much. If I aborted the meet and he returned to his hotel, they'd collapse on him. If that happened, the working over they had given Nolan would look like a bit of playground roughhousing compared to what they'd do to his son.

I couldn't let that happen.

Getting to my feet, I angled toward the Russian, coffee in my left hand.

Professional or not, my actions still gave him pause. He glanced from my hand to my face, a puzzled expression etched across his features. But I didn't have time to explain even if I could. Instead, I was looking over his shoulder.

At Ella.

Her eyes widened as she saw me move, her features twisting into a frown. Then she gave a quick nod, signifying that she got it.

At least I hoped that was what the gesture signified.

Either way, I was now committed.

The Giant Ferris Wheel formed the hub of the Prater. A large grassy area bounded by a network of walking trails lay to the west, while a roller coaster and additional carnival rides formed the eastern boundary. To the north sat a series of restaurants and cafés, while the south featured a mini-golf area and a planetarium beyond which the city reclaimed the real estate in the form of tree-lined walkways and eventually hotels, restaurants, and apartment buildings.

As I'd suspected he might, the GRU officer was approaching from the open area to the west. The route of travel from the wide unrestricted pedestrian area to the more constricted cobblestoned paths surrounding the Ferris wheel provided a series of natural choke points. Obstacles that funneled would-be watchers into several easily observable paths.

At the same time, the congested paths gave Nolan's son ample excuse to check for a tail while pausing for mothers pushing babies or oblivious children darting from attraction to attraction. This route also had the added advantage of permitting egress to the north, east, or south on the far side of the Ferris wheel. In the event of a wave off, the Russian could exit one direction while I went in another.

But that was no longer the plan. We didn't have time for whispered bathroom chats or half-understood signals. One way or another, the Russian was coming with me. How that happened was up to him.

Or perhaps not.

As I moved to intercept Nolan's son, a scrum of bodies rounded the tip of the Ferris wheel station to my right.

Bodies in blue uniforms with a single word in bright yellow script centered above their right breast pockets.

Polizei.

Maybe their appearance had nothing to do with me or the Russian intelligence officer standing feet away.

And maybe Frodo would take up ballet.

"Follow me," I said, my voice low but firm. "Now."

For a moment the Russian's pale blue eyes bored into mine; then they cut left. I followed his glance and saw a man with circular John Lennon sunglasses and a build that wasn't so much slim as anorexic. He was rock-star skinny, and his waxy skin and hunched stance suggested someone who exercised little and ate less. Someone who labored inside, whose work was all-consuming, who forgot about eating or sleeping. A scientist.

A Russian scientist.

The GRU officer was on the job.

The cluster of Vienna's finest spilled out of the sidewalk and flowed around the tables, moving toward a single target.

Me.

"You Russian?" I said, loud enough for my voice to carry across the small common area.

"*Kakoy?*" the Russian said, his thickening accent nicely conveying his confusion.

"Russki?" I said, pronouncing each syllable with a care that would have done Frodo proud.

And then I decked him.

Hard.

But in a purely professional manner.

I didn't put everything I had behind the jab, but I put enough. His head snapped back and he stumbled. But he kept his balance. This time when he looked at me, his blue eyes held something more than just confusion.

Anger.

Lots of it.

He came at me like Lawrence Taylor rolling up Joe Theismann, sinking his shoulder into my waist, wrapping his arms around my abdomen, and driving with his legs. I levitated. My feet flew out from under me as the

Russian smashed me into the concrete with a bit more force than was strictly necessary.

Apparently that professional-manner thing went both ways.

The cobblestones that had looked so aesthetically pleasing when I'd been upright were a whole lot less enjoyable once my noggin bounced off them. I was in la-la land, listening to Emma Stone sing for a moment or two.

Here again my time in the Ranger Regiment paid dividends. An officer could be challenged to an ad hoc combatives contest by any of his men at any time. These challenges weren't always delivered in the most sportsmanlike of manners.

Meaning they usually happened when I was looking the other way.

I'd become quite good at reacting after getting my bell rung. By the time the world swam back into focus, I was flat on my back. But I had the Russian in guard. With a grunt, I grabbed him by the back of the neck and cranked his face down until his ear was inches from my lips.

I'd intended to whisper an alternate meeting time and place, but Nolan's son had other ideas. Rocking forward, he speared his head into my jaw, snapping my teeth together. Or at least they would have snapped together if my pesky tongue hadn't been in the way.

There was selling a fight and then there was just being a complete asshole. This jack wagon had just crossed the line.

And that was when the boys and girls in blue joined the party.

I was in the middle of expressing my displeasure with the Russian's behavior in the form of an eye gouge when several pairs of hands relieved me of the required leverage. Several pairs of hands and at least one pair of feet to be precise. Apparently Austrian *Polizei* were big fans of steel-toed boots. The first kick to my ribs made me think that international détente was maybe the right way to go.

With the same precision and economical use of force that had once made Austria home of Europe's third-largest empire, the *Polizei* gang flipped me over to my stomach and snapped handcuffs on my wrists. The law enforcement officers weren't exactly gentle. I marked up their boorish behavior to simple immaturity. After all, who really thought it was a crime to punch a Russian intelligence officer in the face?

Then again, this was Vienna.

The local economy depended on spies plying their trade within the City of Music's welcoming embrace. There was probably a city ordinance prohibiting rival intelligence services from duking it out on the cobblestoned streets. Lurking in the shadows and subverting people were totally acceptable. But if things needed to get physical, best take that stuff somewhere more accustomed to violence.

Like Germany.

"You are an abomination."

The words were hissed into my ear by a feminine voice. A voice I'd heard only twice before, but had already come to recognize.

Miss Sophie Gruber. First female director of the BVT and a royal pain in the ass.

"That's what my fourth-grade teacher said," I said, turning in the direction of the voice. "But Miss Meyers could take away recess. You're just an empty suit."

A pair of incandescent blue eyes burned at me from just inches away.

"Better an empty suit than a fool," Sophie said, her words dripping with venom. "A fool about to spend time in an Austrian jail."

"Can't argue with your first comment," a familiar baritone voice said, "but I have to take issue with the second. That boy is a damn fool for sure. But he isn't going to jail. At least not today. Today, he's coming with me."

Scraping my cheek against the jagged cobblestones, I looked past Sophie's crouching form to the figure that stood behind her. Frodo. In the flesh. With two beefy dudes at his shoulders.

Hot damn.

"Hey, buddy," I said, making eye contact with my best friend. "When'd you get here?"

"About two minutes too late," Frodo said. "As usual."

I wanted to laugh, but didn't.

When we'd first met, Frodo had been one of the deadliest human beings I'd ever encountered. A soft-spoken black man with a physique skewed more toward endurance than strength. His ropy muscles and prominent tendons could have been crafted from steel cables and iron ingots rather than flesh and blood. But the man staring down at me was a caricature of the fearsome warrior I'd once known.

Earlier this year, Frodo had elected to have his mutilated leg amputated just below the knee so that he could be fitted with a prothesis. Rehab had gone well, and the combination of a prosthetic arm and leg had provided Frodo with an exponential improvement to his quality of life.

Even so, I still couldn't look at him without seeing the man he'd once been.

"Who are you?" Sophie said.

"Someone with diplomatic immunity," Frodo said, offering a reddish brown passport, "which I'm extending to that sorry sack you've just handcuffed. So please release him."

Sophie slowly stood, the fury blazing from her eyes now directed at Frodo. In my peripheral vision, I could see the *Polizei* helping Nolan's son to his feet even as his principal, the rock-star-skinny Russian scientist, continued to chat up the barista, oblivious to anything but her dimpled smile.

On the other side of the common area, Ella caught my eye. She shook her head, turned on her heel, and disappeared into the crowd. It wasn't often that I managed to anger two impressive women at the same time.

I was on a roll.

Sophie crossed her arms beneath her breasts, pointedly refusing to touch Frodo's passport. "Diplomatic immunity might protect him from being arrested, but it doesn't give either of you license to run roughshod over

Austrian law. I'm declaring you both persona non grata. Leave my country. Now."

"We'll head directly to the airport," Frodo said, sliding the passport back into his jacket pocket. "Our plane's waiting."

"I'll show you the way," Sophie said.

THIRTY-THREE

Persona non grata less than an hour after you landed," I said. "Is there an office pool for that?"

"You do have a way with people," Frodo said. "Maybe you should have been a pastor."

"Don't kid yourself," I said. "Pastors don't like people either. They just love Jesus."

"Boy, your issues might give even the world's most famous carpenter pause. Can you at least tell me why you were getting your ass beat?"

"That skinny Russian wasn't beating my ass," I said. "It was just an act."

"Looked pretty convincing to me. He was using your face as a punching bag."

"Had to sell it," I said, trying not to think about the puffy skin running the length of my cheekbone. "I needed to talk to Nolan's son, but he was on the job. So I improvised."

"Was that before or after the Austrian goon squad flex-cuffed your ankles to your wrists?" Frodo said.

"Before. Mostly. Though I guess after too. The Russian didn't get arrested. Neither did Ella. I'd call that success."

"Hmm," Frodo said, squirming as he tried to get comfortable in the sedan's cramped backseat. "That's an interesting take. Let me give you another. I've seen you at your finest, Matty. That wasn't it."

I looked out the window rather than answer.

True to his word, Frodo was taking us to the airport and the waiting Agency Gulfstream. Not that he'd had much choice. In a rather un-Austrian move, Sophie was deliberately disobeying traffic laws. Our "escort" consisted of BMWs to the front and rear of our sedan, their blue lights flashing. To my left, paralleling our progress, was the jet-black SUV carrying Sophie. She was staring at me.

I waved.

She did not.

Frodo was right about one thing: I did have a way with people.

"Why didn't you tell me you were coming?" I said, desperate to change the subject.

"Because when it comes to worrying, you're worse than my grandmother. And she's Catholic."

"What's her religion got to do with it?" I said.

Frodo rolled his eyes. "Guilt and worrying go hand in hand. Nobody does guilt better than Catholics."

I thought about exploring that statement further but

didn't. And not because I wasn't interested in the intricacies of the Catholic faith. My father constantly invoked nonsensical references to the pope. No, I was exercising restraint for a completely different reason: Frodo had just tried to change the subject.

"James doesn't know you're here, does he?"

"What kind of asinine question is that? He's my boss, Matty. Unlike some people, I actually tell my boss when I jaunt halfway across the world."

"Frodo."

"Okay, fine. I may not have provided him with an entirely accurate operational picture."

"Where's he think you are?" I said.

"Home with the flu."

"Seriously?"

"What?" Frodo said, shifting in his seat again. "Someone had to bail you out of trouble. If it weren't for me and these two fine gentlemen, you'd be sitting in an Austrian prison, recovering from your beatdown."

"I told you I had the Russian right where I wanted him," I said. "Hey, meatheads. How did it look to you?"

The meatheads in question, both junior DIA officers, were planted in the car's front seat. Though nothing but air separated us, they wisely kept their mouths shut and eyes focused straight ahead.

When Mom and Dad fought, the kids stayed out of the way.

"Well, I'm glad you're here," I said, squeezing Frodo's leg.

I'd spoken without thinking, but I was still surprised

by the sentiment accompanying my words. For too long Frodo had been home, manning the phones and radios while I'd been up to my eyeballs in trouble. With him seated next to me instead of thousands of miles away, I felt hopeful, even if the circumstances didn't warrant my optimism.

Frodo looked at me for a long moment, his eyes boring into mine.

Then he nodded.

"Thank you, brother," Frodo said. "That means a lot."

This time I was the one who nodded. Mainly because I didn't know what to say next. Frodo and I were crammed into the backseat of a sedan in the company of two dudes we didn't really know. Now we were talking about feelings and stuff. In that moment, I think we both would have rather faced a hillside full of pissed-off Taliban than the prospect of navigating this Hallmark moment.

A cell phone's shrill ring broke the spell.

Frodo and I looked at each other, each of us waiting for the other to answer.

Then Frodo helped with the obvious.

"It's in there," Frodo said, pointing at my coat pocket with the confidence of a JSOC-trained sniper.

He was right, as usual.

But there was just one problem.

It wasn't my phone.

THIRTY-FOUR

I removed the offending device gingerly, allowing it to dangle from my fingertips like it was a buzzing rattlesnake rather than a composition of plastic, metal, and silicon. I still had cause to be worried. A cell phone in the wrong hands was a thousand times more dangerous than a pit viper.

And much less discriminating.

"Not yours?" Frodo said.

"Never seen it before," I said. "I guess I wasn't the only one with a plan."

"The Russian?"

"He is Nolan's son," I said, replaying our tussle in my mind.

Once we hit the ground, our hands had been all over each other. Could he have slipped the phone into my pocket without me noticing? I'd like to think not, but, like his father, the GRU officer was a professional.

If Nolan really was his father.

"Sure about that?" Frodo said.

"Nope," I said. "You might want to give me some space. This thing could be packed with C-4 or something."

I meant the warning as a joke.

Mostly.

The Israelis were known for the ingenious methods they employed to knock off enemies. During the years of retribution following the Black September terrorist attacks, Mossad hit squads bagged more than one jihadi by adding a bit of plastic explosives to his telephone receiver.

But warning or joke, my words were wasted on Frodo.

"Answer the damn thing already," Frodo said, giving me the hurry-up gesture with his good arm.

His only arm.

The two of us breathed new life into the term *odd couple.*

Turning the phone over in my hands, I pressed the answer button and activated the speaker.

"You hit like a girl."

While I didn't recognize the voice on the phone, a Russian accent pointed me in the right direction. Not to mention his smart-ass comment.

"Bullshit," I said, massaging my bruised jaw. "I was trying to save your life, not shatter your nose. Next time we meet, I'll show you the difference."

"My father held you in high regard. I'm still not sure why. Either way, I'm now committed. It is you or nothing."

"Speak for yourself," I said. "I'm not committed to jack shit."

"You made my father a promise."

This gave me pause. I have a thing about debts. I pay them. Even if the person I owe is an asshat. Or even worse, a Russian asshat. Still, other than the intimate moment we'd shared in the men's bathroom and our scuffle near the Prater, I didn't know this dude from Adam.

Time to establish some bona fides.

"Your father said—"

"To look for a daughter," the Russian said, "correct?"

"Yes," I said, the word dragged from my lips.

I really wanted to be able to just hang up on this jack wagon and call it a day. Unfortunately, that was looking less and less likely.

"That's because he was a professional," the Russian said. "As you might imagine, a former member of the Real IRA doesn't stay operational for decades unless he's acquired a very particular set of skills. Skills that made him wise enough to convince my mother to hide his identity from both me and my stepfather. Be that as it may, his luck ran out. You and I are stuck with each other."

"The hell we are," I said. "I told your father that I would help his child. If that's really you and you want to come in from the cold, fine. Walk down to our embassy and ask for the military attaché. I'll make sure they're expecting you. Then we can talk about your options for defecting."

The laughter that echoed across the line had a condescending edge.

"Is that what you think?" the Russian said. "That I want to defect? You truly are underwhelming. I don't want to betray my country. I want to save it."

"From what?" I said.

"World War Three."

References to World War III aren't as common as one might think, even in my line of work. Especially when they're uttered by a spy. Frodo's eyes widened, and my DIA driver might have jerked the wheel just a hair.

Everyone seemed shaken by the Russian's answer.

Everyone but me.

I am after all an espionage professional.

"You said that in the bathroom," I said. "What else you got?"

"Ukraine is about to become ground zero in the next European conflict."

"No shit, Sherlock," I said. "Never would have figured that out from the mechanized armored brigade you chuckleheads have massed on the border."

"I really thought my father was a better judge of character."

"Listen up, shit bird," I said, "I convinced my wife to marry me. Everything else is gravy. If you've got something, say it. Otherwise quit wasting my time."

For a moment I was afraid I'd pushed things too far.

Then the Russian began to laugh.

"You are good," he said between chuckles. "Perhaps we stand a chance together after all."

I thought about pointing out that Laila had expressed similar thoughts, but I didn't. Contrary to popular belief, I could behave like an adult every now and then. So I waited for the GRU officer to continue.

"There's a Russian nuke loose in the Ukraine," the Russian said.

Okay, so that was news.

"What do you mean, *loose*?" I said.

"I mean that a refurbished tactical device is now in the hands of a Ukrainian arms dealer. His name is Bohdan Shevchenko. You may want to pay him a visit before he sells it to the wrong person and ignites a nuclear holocaust."

"How do you know this?" I said.

"Don't mistake the nature of this relationship," the Russian said, the previous traces of humor in his voice now gone. "I'm not your asset, and you're not my handler. I'm a fool whose attack of conscience cost him his father."

"Look," I said, "I'm sorry about Nolan, but he knew the rules of the game. If you want his sacrifice to mean something, give me more than just a wild-ass story and a name. I need concrete information. Details. How do you know about the nuke?"

Again silence was my answer.

Then the Russian spoke.

"Because I'm on intimate terms with the scientist who refurbished it. That is all I'll say. My father's blood has absolved me of my sins. What happens next is on your head."

He hung up.

THIRTY-FIVE

VIENNA, AUSTRIA

How is the City of Music?"

Pyotr frowned into the telephone, considering his answer. Like any discussion between covert operatives, there were layers to the conversation. Important subtext that would pass unnoticed by the casual observer and prove difficult for even a trained counterintelligence asset to intuit.

That said, Pyotr knew that his operation in Vienna was no longer the sterile undertaking he'd promised his superiors. If it hadn't been compromised outright, the plan was certainly exposed. Like bacteria, even the best-planned and -resourced espionage endeavor withered and died when exposed to sunlight.

"My business here is complete," Pyotr said.

Which was true, after a fashion. What was also true was that Pyotr's carefully crafted plan to use the resources of

Austria's Federal Police and intelligence service to flush out the American for his remaining Directorate V team to capture had not been successful.

That was troublesome for two reasons.

First, Pyotr did not believe that the American's arrest just as the Russian killers were closing in could have been attributed to poor luck. Either his BVT asset was compromised, or Myaso was playing both sides of the field. Regardless of which was true, the Austrian would have to be dealt with.

Second, and more important, the American was alive and now beyond Pyotr's reach. Pyotr still didn't have a handle on what the Irishman had known and what, if anything, he'd been able to communicate prior to his death. He'd planned on putting these questions to the American. Now he needed another plan.

"Then you've mitigated the potential risk?"

That was the million-dollar question.

Pyotr stared at the untouched stein of Gösser warming on the table in front of him. Allowing an alcoholic beverage to sit unmolested wasn't very Russian of him. Then again, he wasn't at an outdoor café on the northwest corner of Stephansplatz just for the libations or the view, though both were impressive.

To his front, two of the spires for which St. Stephen's Cathedral was famous soared heavenward, separated by the distinctive emerald-colored roof of one of the outbuildings. The courtyard of rectangular gray slate that surrounded the church was already crowded with people pouring in from adjacent streets and pedestrian walkways. The preponderance of storefront windows, readily available escape routes, natural choke points, and the constant flow of shoppers made this an ideal location to conduct a discreet conversation.

Pyotr just wished his report matched the genial feel of his surroundings.

"The source of the potential spill has been addressed," Pyotr said, "but the extent of the damage is still unknown. There's a new player. American and extremely capable. My intent was to continue my investigation with him. That is no longer possible."

Across the crowded square, a man and a woman walking hand in hand stopped in front of the cathedral's arched entrance. As if on cue, both pulled out their phones and began snapping pictures.

"What is your assessment of the Irishman's impact to the greater endeavor?"

Pyotr thought before responding. The Greater Endeavor, as the caller had so carelessly termed it, was the most audacious undertaking his country had embarked upon since the invasion of Afghanistan. Though the operation touched nearly every aspect of the Russian government, Pyotr was the man charged with setting the conditions for its execution.

To say that his career would rise or fall based on how the events of the next several days unfolded was to think too small. If he succeeded, Pyotr's reward would be lavish. When the favor of the Russian president shone upon you, it rivaled the brightness of the sun. Pyotr would very likely be the motherland's newest oligarch.

If he failed, his fall from grace would be both abrupt and terminal.

Everything came down to Nolan. What had he known and what had he passed to the Americans? Closing his eyes, Pyotr reviewed for the thousandth time the Irishman's operational placement. There was no reason to suspect that the former IRA member had known anything about the Greater Endeavor.

But thinking so wasn't the same as knowing so.

"I'm not sure," Pyotr finally said. The leaden words felt as if they'd been torn from his lips. "Based on what I've uncovered, I don't see any risk. But I can't be certain."

Not content with just selfies, the couple accosted a sharply dressed Viennese women obviously on her way elsewhere. Ignoring her thinly veiled look of annoyance, the pair thrust their cameras into her empty hands. As the couple repositioned themselves in front of the archway, the man dropped to one knee.

"That is exactly the right answer, comrade. If you had said differently, I would have been concerned that you weren't taking your responsibilities seriously enough. Proceed as planned. Trigger authority resides with you."

"Thank you for your faith in me," Pyotr said, hiding his relief. "But what about the American?"

"If you have the opportunity to pursue him again, do so. Otherwise, focus on the Greater Endeavor. We have a highly placed asset of our own. If the Americans intend to move, we'll know. Goodbye and good luck."

A shriek followed by peals of laughter echoed across

the courtyard. A small crowd had gathered around the couple. They began to cheer as the woman threw her arms around her new fiancé. Even the put-upon camerawoman was grinning. Though he didn't usually find joy in the happiness of strangers, Pyotr smiled as well.

It was a time for new beginnings.

THIRTY-SIX

OPISHNYA, UKRAINE

'm so sorry for your loss, my friend. Words alone cannot express my sadness."

Andriy dipped his head in acknowledgment rather than reply, not trusting himself to speak. The sorrow came in inexplicable waves, and he didn't have to fake the lump constricting his throat. But his reaction to Marko Yurchenko's offer of sympathy was a different matter.

Though they'd once been fellow Army officers, their paths had sharply diverged after the Soviet Union's collapse. Andriy had tried to continue to serve his country until the all-consuming corruption drove him back to the family farm. Marko had embraced the chaos and crony capitalism that was running rampant. He'd used the mayhem to enrich himself by lending his services to the region's arms dealers. The drone that had killed Andriy's family might have been of Russian design, but it had undoubtedly been trafficked to the separatists by one

of the people this human piece of filth called clients. Left
to his own devices, Andriy would have just as soon put a
bullet in the man's head as speak to him.

But he couldn't.

The nuclear weapon was too important. As promised,
Danilo had worked his magic. The former spy had called
in old debts and incurred new ones. At the end of the
day, the sum of his reporting pointed toward one man—
Marko.

Andriy wasn't surprised.

If there was an arms dealer in the Ukraine callous
enough to sell a nuclear weapon to the highest bidder,
Marko would know him. So, rather than express his true
feelings, Andriy adopted the same blank expression he'd
worn while ordering eighteen-year-old boys to their
deaths in the fight against the Russians.

Some facets of his old life returned easier than others.

"Thank you, my friend," Andriy said, forcing himself
to break the silence. The words tasted like vinegar, but
he spoke them all the same. "But as much as I value
them, I'm not here for your condolences. I wish to discuss business."

Here was a pub much more congruent with Andriy's
threadbare shirt and faded workingman's pants than his
companion's wardrobe. Marko had a carefully cultivated
persona beginning with his clothes. Even in a dingy establishment full of discolored wooden tables sticky with
beer, soot-stained ceilings, and an anemic fire flickering
in a rough stone fireplace, Marko dressed to impress. A
white shirt open at the collar paired with linen pants and

a sport coat. Not a single strand of gray desecrated his thick black hair. A jewel-encrusted watch glittered from his right wrist and a bracelet of white gold links hung from his left.

Even their choices in drinks announced the diverging paths the two men had chosen. A chipped mug beaded in condensation held a classic Ukrainian Lvivske next to Andriy's hand, the brew already decremented by several swallows. Marko had asked for a glass of Dom Pérignon, probably in an effort to embarrass the proprietor. The flute sat inches away from his buffed fingernails, untouched as the champagne's bubbles slowly escaped the liquor's grasp.

Andriy was already having trouble swallowing his distaste for this peacock of a man. Marko wasn't making his struggle any easier. But that was fine. As an armor officer who'd earned his spurs fighting alongside the Russians during the Afghan war, Andriy understood the importance of projecting a particular appearance just as well as his onetime companion.

He just had a different message to convey.

"Business?" Marko said, bushy eyebrows rising in mock surprise. "What sort of business would you have with me?"

The subtext in Marko's question was subtle, but noticeable all the same.

Shortly after he'd resigned his Army commission for his current, far more lucrative career, Marko had come to Andriy with a business proposition. At the time, Andriy had been overseeing the process of modernizing the

Ukrainian Army by procuring replacements for the aging Soviet-era T-64 main battle tank. While he hadn't yet realized the full extent of Marko's descent into depravity, Andriy knew that even meeting with his onetime comrade in arms risked a stain to his own reputation. Andriy had politely but firmly refused the invitation.

Now their roles were reversed.

"I've become something of an art collector in my old age," Andriy said, "old masters mainly. I understand that one of your clients might be in possession of a new piece of art. One with questionable provenance but of considerable value to the right collector. I'd like to submit a bid."

At this, Marko's eyes narrowed, all pretenses gone.

"What exactly are we talking about, Andriy Chura?" Marko said.

The pair of musclemen who'd accompanied the crook into the pub picked up on their boss's apprehension. Though, with the exception of the single bartender to Andriy's right, the room was empty, the bodyguards still reacted. One reached beneath his suit jacket while the other took a step forward, positioning himself within arm's reach of Andriy. The gray-haired, potbellied bartender didn't seem worried as he continued to dry the glasses arrayed on his wooden bar with a worn towel.

Andriy couldn't say the same.

"Call off your dogs," Andriy said, never breaking eye contact with the snake of a man on the other side of the table. "I'll speak plainly. One of your clients has a nuclear weapon. I want to purchase it."

Marko's lips pressed together, forming a thin line. Though he'd insisted that his bodyguards sweep Andriy and the room for bugs before the meeting had begun, suspicion was still written across his face. Marko didn't bring his men to heel, but neither did he get up from the table and end the meeting.

Or deny Andriy's statement.

Once again, Danilo's sources had proven correct.

"A purchase of this magnitude would require substantial funds," Marko said, his eyes traveling from Andriy's stubble-lined face to his worn jacket. "Forgive me for saying so, old friend, but you don't look like a man with the required means."

"Appearances can be deceiving," Andriy said. "You should know this better than anyone. Still, I take your point. I appreciate that you have better things to do than drink with a grieving old man. So let me set your mind at ease. A newfound spirit of patriotism has been rekindled in the ashes of my heart. To stand against the coming Russian horde, I've constituted a volunteer battalion. Like you, I still have friends from the old world. One of my former company commanders is now a general himself. He manages the foreign dollars that flow into Ukraine from the US and others. I gave him a call today. He agreed to provide the government funding needed to equip and train my new battalion. Substantial funding. Does that satisfy your misgivings?"

"Not by a long shot. But it does buy you five additional minutes of my very expensive time. Assuming one of my clients had such an item, how much would you be willing to pay for it?"

"What's the price?" Andriy said.

Marko slowly shook his head. "That isn't how this works. I'm already in talks with several interested parties. For the sake of our long friendship, I will allow you to submit a preemptive bid. One."

Reaching into his pocket, Andriy withdrew a pen and a scrap paper. With quick, practiced strokes, he wrote a series of numbers. Then he folded the stationery in half and slid it across the table.

Marko unfolded the note.

"You jest," Marko said. "Because of our shared history, I'll forget that this ridiculous conversation ever took place. I'm not sure whether your grief has driven you mad or you've truly lost your mind. Either way I—"

Andriy struck like a viper, his fist a blur. His top two knuckles buried themselves in the fleshy part of Marko's neck. The criminal's trachea spasmed in response, and Marko's mouth reflexively opened as he gasped for breath. From there, it was easy enough to snare the traitor's tongue with one hand even as Andriy unsheathed his knife with the other.

To their credit, Marko's bodyguards reacted quickly.

Just not quickly enough.

With the same nonchalant manner with which he'd been wiping down dirty glasses, the potbellied man drew a pistol from beneath the bar and fired twice. Both bodyguards dropped to the ground, each with a brand-new orifice in their skull.

Like Andriy, the bartender was an old man living in semiretirement. But also like Andriy, he'd once been a soldier, and he'd served his country with distinction. His final tour of duty had been as a marksmanship instructor. While he could no longer drop a running man with a single shot from a thousand yards, drilling two buffoons just five meters away was child's play.

Especially two distracted buffoons.

Now that he no longer required the bodyguards' attention, Andriy released Marko's tongue. But he kept the knife pressed against the man's throat.

"You're a dead man," Marko snarled. "A dead man."

"True enough," Andriy said, "but not today, I think. And certainly not by your hand. The blood of the four men you left outside has long since cooled. If you tell me who has the device voluntarily, you can leave this bar alive. Refuse, and you'll still tell me. But only after I've flayed the skin from your body and fed it to the dogs. It's a little trick I learned from the Afghans."

As if to punctuate Andriy's words, the pub's door swung open, admitting four men, each of them members of the newly formed Opishnya volunteer brigade.

"Dead man!" Marko screamed.

"As you wish," Andriy said before turning to his soldiers. "Hold him down. We'll do his right hand first."

Wordlessly, the men complied. Two of the boys from Opishnya restrained Marko while the remaining two pressed his palm flat on the wooden table's scarred surface. Marko yelled another stream of obscenities, but Andriy was no longer listening. The skin around the finger bones was tricky and he wanted to make sure he got it just right.

Attention to detail was yet another thing he'd learned from the Afghans.

THIRTY-SEVEN

UNDISCLOSED AIRSPACE

W here are you?"

"Right now?" I said, turning down the television's volume.

In a manner that clearly defied physics, James Glass could be equally loud in person or on a virtual call piped through three different satellites. Volume knobs had no power over a man who'd once broken a Taliban fighter's neck with his bare hands. The potency of James's presence was a gift.

But sometimes it was damned annoying.

"Yes, right now. In what grid coordinates are your ass cheeks parked?"

"Difficult to say, Chief," I said, glancing from the image of James on the wide-screen TV to the digital flight tracker mounted just below his scowling visage.

"Are you on a plane?" James said, his scowl turning murderous.

"Yes, sir."

"Is it heading toward me?"

"Absolutely, Chief."

I'd never before had cause to be grateful that the world was round.

I did now.

After an incident-free and remarkably speedy trip to Vienna International Airport, our two DIA babysitters delivered Frodo and me jet side to the Gulfstream Frodo had appropriated. It was a fine-looking aircraft, made even finer-looking by the fact that its staircase was extended and its engines were already roaring. Don't get me wrong. The City of Spies had a heck of a lot going for it, but Sophie and I were clearly never going to be besties.

No, that wasn't quite right. Professional disagreements I could live with, but my unpleasant feelings toward the blond lady with the expensive suit went beyond that. Asking someone else to do your dirty work and then acting pissy when the outcome wasn't what you had in mind was just bad form. This was no longer a professional squabble.

It was personal.

The feeling seemed to go both ways.

The two cars and Sophie's SUV escorted us all the way to the Gulfstream. As Frodo and I boarded the plane, the BMW's tinted window lowered. For a moment, I thought maybe Sophie wanted to make amends.

She didn't.

A slender arm slipped through the gap in the window and extended a certain finger.

It was still there when we taxied away.

Even so, when ranking the number of problems I was currently facing, an irate Austrian counterintelligence chief hardly rated honorable mention. A man who'd once saved my life was dead, and I was no closer to understanding why. I'd tried to carry out his dying wishes by helping his daughter, but I'd found a Russian GRU officer instead. An officer who might or might not have been Nolan's son and who claimed that a Russian nuclear weapon was now in the hands of a Ukrainian arms dealer.

My life was probably never in danger of becoming predictable, but this was a bit much. I have been known to engage in operations that some have charitably called questionable and others goat ropes. That said, I didn't make a habit of wading into potential world wars. Especially a conflict with Russia in one corner and NATO in the other. The smart play was to head west and let someone with actual European experience and expertise handle things.

Which was why we were rocketing east as fast as the jet could fly.

I wasn't much for passing the buck. About anything. Even though I would have rather been heading toward Austin and Laila's tank top, I couldn't do it. As Dad liked to say, there might not be an *I* in *team*, but there was a *me*. Not exactly sure what that had to do with the price of tea in China, but when Dad's voice intruded into my subconscious, I listened.

Usually.

"You're telling me that the Gulfstream Frodo stole and took to Vienna isn't actually crossing into Ukrainian airspace as we speak?"

People tended to lump James's impressive bulk together with his unconventional speech patterns and arrive at the conclusion that he was just another knuckle dragger. This mistaken assumption had proven to be fatal for more than one cocksure terrorist, not to mention the occasional DIA bureaucrat.

"The world is round, Chief," Frodo said, piping in from off camera.

Man, I'd missed that guy.

"I swear to God the two of you could find trouble in a nunnery," James said, shaking his stubbled head. "Where are you taking my airplane?"

"Ukraine, Chief," I said, resigned to telling the truth. Or at least a version of it.

"How did I know that?" James said.

"Because you used to date Miss Cleo?" Frodo said.

"I expect that kinda shit from Matthew," James said, aiming a stubby index finger at Frodo. "You are supposed to be the responsible one."

"Sorry, boss," Frodo said. "Matty's a bad influence."

"That's just hurtful," I said.

"If you two are through with the comedy routine, I might have something of interest to your pea-sized brains. I guessed you were headed for Ukraine because that's where the world's about to go up in smoke. Russian troops are massing, poised to invade, and the

Ukrainian president is formally asking NATO to invoke Article V."

"What, preemptively?" I said. "They can't do that. Besides, Ukraine isn't even a NATO member."

"Wouldn't bet on it," James said. "While you chuckle-heads were getting tossed out of Austria, the rest of Europe has been busy. The Baltic states and former Russian republics are pushing for immediate recognition of Ukraine as a full-fledged NATO member. A rift is forming between the legacy NATO countries and the newer ones who joined precisely so they'd have help keeping the Russian Bear at bay. If the legacy members don't rise to the occasion, there's a chance NATO might just cease to exist."

James's words rang with a dreadful finality through the cramped conference room. Although on the surface his warning about the alliance's future might have seemed alarmist, the North Atlantic Treaty Organization had been decaying from within since the Soviet Union had crumbled alongside the Berlin Wall. The majority of the member nations refused to contribute the mandatory two percent of GDP required for the common defense. Without the necessary funding, their military capabilities had atrophied along with their national will to employ what tactical resources remained.

That wasn't the worst of it.

Article V had been invoked after the September 11th attacks more than two decades ago. And while a large contingent of NATO countries had deployed to Afghanistan or Iraq, few had done actual fighting. Invoking something known as national caveats, countries like Germany that had enjoyed the blanket of protection afforded them by NATO for decades were content to sit behind a FOB's Hesco barrier while the brunt of the fighting was carried out by the Five Eye nations.

The split between the legacy and newer NATO members became readily apparent in the Global War on Terror's many battlefields. Small, economically depressed countries like Poland readily accepted the burdens of combat while their wealthier neighbors were happy to just watch the new guys carry the load.

When I was a Ranger Company commander, this had made me furious. Soldiers from nations we'd guarded during the Cold War and protected with our Pax Americana after the Soviet Union's fall lazed away the deployment while my men came home each night bruised and bloodied.

Or not at all.

Thanks to some stupendous damage control by the spin doctors in NATO's public relations' arm, the general populace hadn't really known how thoroughly their so-called allies had betrayed them. But the newer countries, countries that stood between Russia and the rest of Europe, certainly did.

And they weren't impressed.

After all, if a cash-flush Germany couldn't be bothered to fight Taliban cavemen who were armed with nothing more than small arms and RPGs, would they really stand against the Russian juggernaut if main battle tanks started rolling west? Until now this had been a largely theoretical question. But with Russia posturing to invade the Ukraine, theory had just become reality.

"Even if Ukraine is granted full NATO membership," I said, "how can they invoke Article V? They haven't been attacked."

"Depends on your point of view," James said. "The Russians are sneaky bastards. Crimea fell largely without a shot being fired, thanks to the work of Russian Little Green Men. Turns out, the Ukrainians have learned a thing or two since the last time Russia swallowed a large portion of their country in a single gulp. Photos depicting foreigners sighted in eastern Ukraine and Crimea are circulating through the international media. Cease-fire violations in some of the border cities are already occurring and the photographic evidence points to Russia. Several parliamentary hawks are citing this as a reason to invoke the mutual-defense clause. The sentiment is picking up steam among the other Baltic states. I think the balloon's about to go up."

"What's the official US position?" Frodo said.

As usual, the former sniper cut to the heart of the matter.

In theory, the NATO alliance was structured like the three musketeers—all for one and one for all. In reality, all musketeers were not created equal. The United States was the world's sole remaining superpower. Our military capacity exceeded that of all of the other NATO signatories put together. Posturing aside, if there was a war to be fought, American men and women would bear the brunt of it.

For the alliance's sake, we didn't throw our weight around often.

But when we did, the rest of the nation-states usually fell in line.

"At this point, it's anyone's guess," James said, his craggy face showing frustration. "The former Norwegian prime minister is currently the secretary-general of NATO, but the question of Ukraine's membership really comes down to us. If we give the thumbs-up, Ukraine's in. If we don't, their application is going to be kicked down the road at best or outright denied at worst."

"Any signals from the administration?" I said.

James shook his head. "Lots of hand-wringing and empty platitudes. The president's scheduled to give a speech to the nation tonight laying out his new domestic agenda. I'm sure he didn't plan to use this opportunity to talk about Ukraine, but at this point I don't see how he avoids it. Either way, Ukraine is a pool of gasoline looking for a match. Which brings me to the next obvious point: Why are you two headed there?"

"To stop the explosion," I said. "We made contact with the GRU officer. He laid a doozy on us. A Ukrainian arms dealer has gotten himself a tactical nuke. My Russian friend thinks we should do something about it."

I'd seen James Scott Glass speechless exactly twice.

As of today, that count extended to three.

"Say again, over," James said.

"You heard me," I said, "and before you ask, I don't know how to assess the accuracy of his reporting. Yet. He provided specifics about the device and the method by which he'd acquired his reporting. Everything is still circumspect."

"What's his status?" James said.

"In the wind," I said. "He passed along the info, but made it clear he had no intention of becoming my asset."

"He doesn't get to make that choice," James said. "You're supposed to run him, not the other way around."

"Thanks for the refresher course on asset handling, Chief," I said, feeling a flush building at the base of my neck. "He thinks he's a whistleblower, nothing more. I wasn't in a position to argue the point."

"Then get in one, Matthew," James thundered. "We're talking about nuclear weapons."

"Give me a little credit," I said, the rush of blood expanding from my neck to my ears. "Say the word and I'll turn this jet around. Frodo and I will crawl all over Vienna, trying to track down an uncooperative asset who's probably already back in Russia. Or we can try to validate his reporting and maybe stop World War Three in the process. Your call."

For the second time in the same conversation, I'd rendered James speechless. Maybe the world really was coming to an end.

"I think what Matty is trying to say, Chief," Frodo said, "is that we made the best decision possible with the information at our disposal. Sir."

Usually, Frodo had a knack for smoothing things over. Usually. But judging by the purple and crimson splotches coloring James's face, Frodo's magic wasn't going to do the trick today. I was bracing myself to eat a sabot round when something unexpected happened.

"Are those my boys?"

The female voice ringing from the speakers was unmistakably Southern and immediately soothing. At least to me. Judging by the change in James's expression, he found the interruption less so. In a millisecond's time, the former Green Beret went from looking like Moses about to close the Red Sea on the Egyptian Army to a boy caught with his hand in the cookie jar. A one-eyed boy with ham hocks for fists and a scar from a Taliban RPG running the length of his cheek, but a boy all the same.

"The door was locked," James thundered.

"Sure was. Thank goodness I have a key. Hello, dolls. I've missed you."

Technically, Ann Beaumont was James's secretary. But like most of the inhabitants of the chief's realm, Ann didn't much stand for technicalities. With shoulder-length brown hair that was still gracefully transitioning to silver, wrinkles that were more fine lines than furrows, and an elegant wardrobe that flattered her somewhat plump figure, Ann could have passed for someone's harmless aunt.

But there was nothing harmless about Ann Beaumont.

Rather than allow herself to be intimidated by the rough-and-tumble spies she counted as colleagues, Ann had appointed herself our collective den mother instead.

And woe to the uninformed outsider who tried to come between Ann and her *boys*. I'd once seen her dress down a DIA executive in a manner that would have made a Ranger School instructor proud. She was the one person at DIA, and maybe in the entire world, who was not intimidated by James's infamous reputation. On more than once occasion, Ann had put our boss back into his box with a deftness that defied description.

She was a honey badger.

If honey badgers wore Chanel perfume.

"Hi, Ann," I said. "You look nice this morning."

"Matthew Drake," Ann said, her drawl thickening, "flattery will get you nowhere."

Which might be true, but Ann's eyes sparkled all the same.

"Where are you boys off to now?" Ann said.

"Ukraine," Frodo said. "We're saving the world. Again."

"If the world needs saving," Ann said, leaning closer to the camera, "there's no doubt that you two are the ones for the job. It does this old girl's heart good to see my boys operational again. Take care of each other. I've got a bad feeling about this one."

This was unexpected. Though she worried incessantly when we were gone, Ann was normally a steady Eddy. The Ukraine situation must be more volatile than I realized. Which might also explain why James was ready to engage any target that had the misfortune of wandering into his gun line.

Except for Ann.

I scrambled for a one-liner to lighten the mood, but needn't have bothered. With a flourish of skirts, Ann vanished as suddenly as she'd come.

"What was that about?" Frodo said.

"You're asking me?" James said. "You don't know what she's like when the two of you are gone. If she thinks you're in danger, she goes full-on mama bear mode at the drop of a hat. The woman is insufferable."

I thought about pointing out someone else who also fit that description, but didn't. Contrary to what Laila might have thought, I did know how to build cultural bridges of understanding. Also, Ann's interlude had doused James's anger like a bucket of ice on a campfire. No doubt his eternal flame was still flickering in there somewhere, but only a fool poked a sleeping bear. Then again, Mama always claimed I didn't have the sense God had given a dish towel.

No reason to prove her wrong now.

"What's it going to be, Chief?" I said, folding my arms across my chest. "Ukraine or let the CIA handle things?"

"What's that mean?" James said, his eyebrows scrunching together like two furry caterpillars.

"Exactly what I said. If we're not gonna follow up on the Russian's reporting, we should turn it over to Langley. Our branch's charter is counterterrorism, not European shooting wars. The CIA's probably better equipped to handle this than us, anyway."

"Better equipped how?" James said.

"This is gonna get messy, boss," I said. "Real messy.

My initial plan was to ask for support from DIA's Kyiv Station. See what they could dig up on the arms dealer. That was before I knew that Russian tanks were about to roll into Ukraine. If the Russkies are following their Crimea playbook, eastern Ukraine is already lousy with Spetsnaz operatives. Anyone sailing into that shitstorm will need muscle. More than what just Frodo and I can bring to the table. The CIA has organic kinetic assets. They should handle this one."

"Who said anything about the CIA?" James thundered.

"Sorry, boss," I said. "Just trying to be proactive. Speaking of, I had Kyiv Station run this arms dealer through their database. Not only was he already on their radar, they're working a tech-procurement operation targeting him."

"For what?" James said.

"A Russian air defense system. The S-500, I believe."

Procuring military hardware was one of the missions of the intelligence community. These procurements ranged from relatively easy-to-obtain items, such as the newest sniper rifle, to a piece of hardware that had strategic implications to US foreign policy. In this case, we were after the algorithms that drove the friend-or-foe identification routines for the S-500. In typical digital fashion, the software was stored on the Russian equivalent of a little black box—something known as a line-replaceable unit, or LRU. While stealing the entire air defense system would be nice, the briefcase-sized LRU would give us access to the weapon's brain, allowing scientists to probe for vulnerabilities.

This target was much too enticing to pass up.

"Kyiv Station has been working this for months," I said. "They were in the process of requesting a fly team from DIA headquarters to act as the buyers. When I heard that, I figured that Frodo and I could fill the billet and investigate the nuke rumor at the same time."

"One shot, two kills," Frodo said.

I faked a cough as I tried to hide both a laugh and a smile of admiration. Frodo was a master at working movie dialogue into conversations with James.

"Then why do you need muscle?" James said, his frown mirroring the suspicion in his voice. "Procurement ops aren't kinetic."

Neither were asset meets at the Café Central. Or at least they weren't supposed to be. But rather than try to argue the point, I fell back on a source that James seldom disputed.

Himself.

"You said it, Chief," I said. "Ukraine is a tinderbox. Frodo and I will run this procurement by the book, but if the arms dealer really is holding a nuke, things are liable to get hairy. The best way to avoid a fight is to convince the other guy you're ready for one. Call me crazy, but it doesn't seem smart for us to roll into country with bags of money and no muscle."

With several mechanized brigades massing on the Ukraine border, Spetsnaz unconventional-warfare experts fomenting unrest, and the possibility of a nuclear weapon in the mix, I wanted my own quick reaction force.

"All right," James said. "I'll sign off on the procurement op and grease the skids with Kyiv Station. Your primary task is still to obtain the S-500's LRU, but if you can kill two birds with one stone, do it. I'll run the nuke angle by the director. If your Russian's reporting is corroborated by anything else, your primary tasking will shift to finding the nuke. Either way, be ready for an audible. I'm sticking my neck out on this one, Matthew. Don't screw this up."

I almost thanked James for the vote of confidence, but didn't.

It wasn't easy.

"Tracking, Chief," I said, smiling my most grateful smile. "I was thinking Unit guys for the muscle. Do we have any in theater?"

As a former Ranger, I'd worked alongside Delta Force operators on countless operations. While Rangers were hands down the best light infantry in the world, they were not what you would term a weapon of precision. For sexy stuff that required a light touch, Unit assaulters would always be my go-to.

That said, a team of snake-eating Green Berets in the form of the theater crisis response force, or CRF, would be a close second. While not on the same level as Delta Force assaulters, the handpicked Green Berets who manned this direct action entity were both top-shelf and possessed European-language capabilities Frodo and I lacked.

Either option would work just fine.

"The intel provided an overview of European Command's tactical footprint as part of this morning's battle update brief," James said. "The Russia buildup has the entire combatant command rattled. All army assets are currently spoken for."

"Then we're getting Raiders?" Frodo said, referring to the Marine Corps's special operations force. "Not as good, but I can work with those guys."

"Nope," James said. "Marines are busy too."

"You're saddling us with the Air Force?" I said. "That seems a little vindictive, Chief. But I guess combat controllers are better than nothing."

"You two shit birds talk more than my ex-wife. Wanna keep running your traps or listen for a change?" James said, his one-eyed glare bouncing between Frodo and me.

"I've met your ex-wife," I said. "That was below the belt."

Or at least that was what I intended to say until Frodo's pointy elbow caught me squarely in the diaphragm.

"Please continue, sir," Frodo said, ignoring my gasps for air.

"White SOF is the only asset available in-country," James said. "Navy SEALs, to be precise. A team from Group 2."

"That isn't funny, Chief," I said.

"A football team with guns," Frodo said, muttering under his breath.

"The team leader's call sign is Elvis," James said. "I'm sending you his contact info on high-side email. You wanted the shit sandwich, Matty. Now open wide and take a bite. Ranger up, boys."

James ended the call.

If I hadn't known better, I might have come away from the conversation with the distinct impression that James was enjoying the turd he'd just dropped in our operational punch bowl. But I'm sure I was just reading into his maniacal smile when the call dropped.

After all, there was really just one group of people who enjoyed working with SEALs.

Other SEALs.

THIRTY-EIGHT

KRAMATORSK, UKRAINE

Y ou two the intelligence cell?"

The questioner stood in a type of makeshift lobby just inside the safe house. If safe houses had lobbies. Then again, there wasn't much about the industrial structure Frodo and I found ourselves in that resembled any kind of safe house I'd ever used.

Viewed from the road, the structure looked like something from rust belt America. A sagging Cyclone fence encircling the skeletal remains of what had once been a factory or possibly an industrial warehouse. The decrepit building looked abandoned. I'd checked the address twice before following the pothole-marred private driveway into a crumbling parking lot crisscrossed with fissures. Weeds sprouted along the building's foundation, and the broken windows outnumbered those intact by at least ten to one.

But once I drove around to the rear of the building as instructed, things changed. A secondary fence with a gate boasting a new lock segregated the back of the building from the entrance. This combined with the parabolic-shaped antenna budding from the building's roof and the cluster of wireless cameras installed across the exterior confirmed that I'd come to the right place.

Now I just needed to convince the building's occupants.

"We're not the intelligence cell," I said, dropping my gear onto the scuffed linoleum floor.

"You're logistics? We're pretty well set on ammo and food, but we could use more beer."

I stifled a yawn while Frodo gave the speaker his best deadeye stare. Granted, in his current physical predicament, a look from Frodo wasn't all that worrisome. Then again, Frodo's physique had never been particularly intimidating. He did his best intimidation from behind a SIG Sauer optic. The SEAL asking the question didn't know that. In fact, there was a whole lot he didn't know.

Time to begin his education.

"My name's Matt," I said.

"Elvis," the speaker said. "I'm the team leader."

"Good to meet you, Elvis," I said, offering my hand. "Don't know what you've been briefed, but it's about to change. Give us thirty minutes to figure out what's what, and then wake up your swim buddies. I'm sorry about the early hour, but we've got work to do."

The SEAL shook my hand, taking my measure as he did. That was fine. If I'd been in his place, I would have been a bit suspicious if a scruffy pair of unknowns showed up at my front door only to claim they were now assuming control of my team.

Elvis had shaggy brown hair and a trademark bushy SEAL beard that framed intelligent gray eyes. He was leaner than the stereotypical frogman, but there was no hiding the tendons rippling across his muscular forearms like steel bands. He was a commando through and through, as much as his loose-fitting shirt and blue jeans tried to say otherwise.

But I wasn't sure he viewed me through the same lens.

There wasn't much about my appearance that inspired confidence. Access to a private jet was a pretty big perk, but the bird couldn't land where there wasn't a runway. We were in the small eastern city of Kramatorsk and the nearest airport was in Kharkiv, a three-hour drive to the northwest. Between the flight time from Vienna, getting sorted out at the airport, and the drive, it was now about three in the morning local time. I hadn't slept in an actual bed in almost two days.

I looked it.

To add insult to injury, since my departure from Austria had been, to put it kindly, abrupt, I was still wearing the remnants of the suit I'd purchased with Ella what seemed like a lifetime ago. In addition to the wrinkles and stains from hours of travel, my wardrobe was also somewhat worse for the wear, thanks to my scuffle with the Russian and Sophie's goons.

Hopefully one of the SEALs was my size and didn't mind sharing with a Ranger.

On the positive side, James had been hard at work while Frodo and I were transiting Austria and Ukraine. Since we were coming into country under nonofficial cover so that we could slide into the procurement legend Kyiv Station had already started putting together, we had to forgo the niceties associated with traveling under diplomatic immunity. What we got instead was a Range Rover pre-positioned in the long-term parking lot and the combination to the hidden compartment in the rear of the vehicle. Inside were new identities, money, and weapons.

For all his idiosyncrasies, James was hands down the best ops man in the business.

To be fair, the DIA folks at Kyiv Station had been working the procurement op plan for some time. While Frodo and I were new additions, the necessary coordination and planning in preparation for the arrival of the fly team from the States was largely already in place. Granted, the package had been primed for someone else, but I was an intelligence officer, which meant by default I was also a pretty good actor. I wasn't a European hand, but this certainly wasn't my first time procuring illicit weapons.

I felt confident that Frodo and I were in pretty good shape. Or at least we had been until I found myself at a safe house manned by frogmen. Frogmen who hadn't yet been told what they were doing or why.

Or maybe they'd just forgotten.

We were talking about SEALs.

We bumped into each other before?" the SEAL said, dropping my hand.

I didn't recognize him, but it wasn't a surprise that he thought I seemed familiar. Men who did what we did had a certain look. A hyperawareness that was difficult to hide. At least, that was how the Agency psychologists termed it. My explanation was a whole lot simpler.

One predator always recognizes another.

"Probably," I said. "It's been a long war. I've worked with your Dam Neck cousins a time or two when I was still in the Regiment. Maybe it's Frodo you know."

The SEAL's eyes had widened when I mentioned my time as a Ranger, but they almost popped out of his head when I referenced Frodo.

"Holy shit," the SEAL said, giving my bodyguard a head-to-toe appraisal. "You're Frodo?"

"The one and only," Frodo said. "We know each other?"

"By reputation only," the SEAL said. "I did a platoon with Kikki before he went over to Task Force Blue. My guys are going to be stoked to meet you."

Frodo waved away the comment with his good hand. "I was in the right place at the right time. Nothing more."

"Not from where I'm standing," the SEAL said. "And

I have a feeling the boys will feel the same way. Let me round them up. Follow me."

The SEAL grabbed Frodo's kit bag before turning on his heel and disappearing into the safe house, strangely not offering to give me a hand.

With anything.

"Kikki?" I said, gathering up our things. "That was you?"

"Like I said—right place at the right time."

I didn't press, because I could see the attention was making Frodo uncomfortable. But, uncomfortable or not, this would be a topic during our next beer summit. The Kikki operation was legendary. I was more than a little pissed I'd never put it together before now. During a mission gone horribly wrong, a SEAL recon element in Afghanistan had been compromised and one of its members, Kikki, grievously injured.

The ensuing firefight had pinned the SEALs in a bowl-shaped kill zone, preventing escape while at the same time rendering extraction by air impossible. The quick reaction force had been scrambled, but they were a half-hour flight away.

The SEALs had had just minutes.

But someone had been available to respond.

Actually, two someones.

A pair of Unit snipers had been orbiting in a Black Hawk a valley away, conducting a target interdiction mission, when they'd heard the radios light up with the SEALs' desperate pleas. To this day no one was willing to say exactly what had transpired between the Delta

Force operators and the 160th helicopter pilots. The official record reflected that, against orders to the contrary, Army aviators hovered above a ridgeline long enough for Frodo and his spotter to jump to the rocky soil.

What transpired next will forever live in the annals of special operations history. With the cold precision that's still a Unit hallmark, Frodo and his fellow sniper decimated the assaulting Taliban force. Together, the two shooters had an unofficial tally of thirty dead enemy fighters, several killed within yards of the SEALs' position.

Demoralized, and with their ranks significantly thinned, the Taliban retreated to lick their wounds, allowing the 160th aviators to work their magic. Once again, the world's finest pilots flew a helicopter into a place where helicopters weren't meant to go. The SEALs were airlifted to safety, Kikki's life was saved, and two more unnamed Delta operators made history.

And one of them just happened to be my best friend.

THIRTY-NINE

O kay," I said, looking at the mostly attentive faces
staring back at me. "I want to start by welcoming
you to the Defense Intelligence Agency. For the duration
of this operation, you've been sheep-dipped."

Mostly attentive because six of the faces in the audience belonged to SEALs. In my admittedly limited experience with naval commandos, I'd really seen them
attentive in only one scenario—a Call of Duty tourna-
ment. Okay, that wasn't quite fair. Coffee, energy drinks,
and liberal amounts of dip aside, it was still zero dark
thirty in the morning. Getting roused out of bed for an
update brief wasn't anybody's idea of fun. Also, if I was
being honest, I'd have to admit that when it came to
shooting bad guys in the face, SEALs were pretty on
point. It was just all the pesky planning and mission rehearsal stuff they didn't particularly enjoy.

To quote Frodo, a football team with guns.

"Does our temporary assignment come with a pay raise? These accommodations aren't exactly four-star."

The question came from a SEAL sitting to my right. He was early twenties with a mane of strawberry blond hair and a scraggly beard. Since he'd been in diapers when September 11th had kicked off, I was willing to bet his operational experience was probably limited. But he had a point. This portion of the industrial facility was certainly more structurally sound than the shell of a building facing the road, but it was not anything to write home about.

The logistics team who'd acquired the property had undoubtedly been looking for something that allowed us to stage, mission plan, and rehearse without attracting attention from pro-Russian locals, the arms dealer we were targeting, or even the corrupt Ukrainian government we were supposedly saving.

Viewed from this perspective, living rough in an abandoned warehouse offered us the two things most important to a safe house—security and anonymity.

Unfortunately, the trade-off meant dirty concrete floors, backed-up pipes, and bathroom amenities that were less than spectacular. Most of the team probably shared the SEALs' opinion of our living conditions, but they were professional enough not to voice it. Discipline among members of the special operations community might have been notoriously lax, but that came with an expectation of maturity. Right now the naval commando asking the question exuded the former in spades but not the latter.

As James would have said, it was time for a tune-up.

"No pay raise," I said with a forced smile, "but you do get your own parking spot."

This could have gone two ways. Way one, he laughed along with the group and let the matter drop, in which case all would be forgiven. Way two, he continued to be a jack wagon. If that happened, I'd need to deal with the situation immediately and in front of the team; otherwise his poor attitude would become infectious.

I was hoping for way one.

Mostly.

"I just want to start getting after it," the SEAL said, ignoring my olive branch. "You agency boys spend too much time planning and not enough actually doing."

Way two, here we come.

"What's your name, stud?" I said, zeroing in on the frogman's smirking face.

I could see Elvis shifting from where he'd been leaning against the wall, his lips pressed together as his eyes bored holes in the back of the SEAL's head. While I appreciated his help, I didn't need it. What happened next would be between the arrogant frogman and me.

"That there is Red. He's been on the team for about five seconds now. And unless he starts tightening up his shot group and easing way back on the attitude, he and his seabag will be heading back to the minesweeper that he came from. Minus his Trident. Feel me, Red?"

The comment had come from a man standing in the back of the room. He didn't look particularly intimidating. Though his physique mirrored a SEAL's athletic build, he was short and not nearly as muscled as the other commandos. His wardrobe of a faded Metallica T-shirt, board shorts, and flip-flops was also a bit non-standard. At first glance, he could have been mistaken for a roadie for the band emblazoned across his chest.

But first glances can be deceiving. His face reflected the hard, weather-beaten visage of a man who made his living in the elements, and his obligatory operator beard was a bit sparse on the right side of his face, revealing the shiny, puckered skin indicative of a burn.

SEAL or not, this was a man I could work with.

The change in Red's demeanor was both remarkable and instantaneous. One moment he'd been doing his best imitation of a special operator's I-don't-give-a-fuck slouch. The next, his feet were flat on the floor, his back ramrod straight, and his expression equal parts terror and contrition.

"Tracking, Senior," Red said, the flush on his face now mirroring his call sign.

"Good," the senior chief said, threading his way through the array of camp chairs, folding tables, and Pelican cases that littered the onetime cafeteria turned operations center. "The two men standing before you are worthy of your respect. You will give it to them. The one speaking is Matt Drake. He's a veteran of the Ranger Regiment and a DIA officer. He was putting bad guys in the dirt while most of you were still working up the courage to ask the pretty blonde in homeroom to prom. Standing next to him is Frodo. If you don't know Frodo's story, then ask a frogman whose Trident doesn't still have that fresh-from-the-BX gleam. Questions?"

The senior chief's raptorlike gaze moved from face to face before they settled on his team leader.

"Sorry about that, sir," the senior chief said. "Won't happen again."

"No worries, Axle," Elvis said, but his eyes hardened again when they centered on Red.

The team's newest member seemed to have a ways to go before he was one of the boys, which might account for his tough-guy attitude. Either way, I was more than happy to let bygones be bygones. Friendly interservice rivalries aside, the SEALs were my partners for this operation, and they'd be treated as such. Besides, though my Ranger heart hated to admit it, there was something comforting about having a squad of modern-day Vikings ready to wreak havoc on your behalf.

Sometimes a football team with guns wasn't such a bad thing.

"Thank you, Senior Chief," I said.

"It's Axle, sir."

"Then it's Matt or Matty, Axle."

"Unless his Mama's calling," Frodo said. "Then he goes by sweetie pie."

"Sweet it is," Axle said with a smile. "Now that we've got the formalities out of the way, how can my frogmen be of service, Sweet?"

I forced a smile even though I wanted to grimace. As call signs went, Sweet wasn't horrible, but it certainly wasn't what I would have chosen.

Then again, call signs seldom were.

"Here's what we've got, boys," I said, already feeling

a shift in the room's energy. "Frodo and I are on a mission to stop World War Three. I asked for the heaviest hitters special operations command had to offer. They must have all been busy, because I got you surfers instead."

Axle chuckled and the rest of the room keyed off him.

Just that quickly, the prior bullshit with Red was a thing of the past.

Now it was time to get down to business.

"This is Sam," I said, nodding to the man manning a laptop to my left. "He's a DIA all-source intelligence analyst. Your show, Sam."

Dressed in an outdoor shirt, jeans, and hiking boots, Sam's wardrobe shouted that he wasn't an operator. But that was fine, because he wasn't trying to be one. He had a runner's build and a quiet competence that was a welcome counterpoint to the safe house's testosterone-laced air. I'd never worked with Sam before, but he had a reputation for telling commanders what he thought rather than what they wanted to hear.

Sam was responsible for transforming the slew of raw intelligence flooding our operational cell into something usable. This was a critically important role—one in which there was no place for the analyst's ego to influence conclusions.

Fortunately, he seemed like the right man for the job.

When I'd first met him thirty minutes prior, Sam had introduced himself by providing an overview of the assets currently in place, the state of the enemy, and the conclusions he'd drawn thus far. Unlike with old Red, his assessment had been delivered with zero posturing, just the quiet competence of a professional who knew the organization and his place in it.

"Thank you, Sweet," Sam said with a half smile as he powered up the portable projector facing the wall. "Gentlemen, this is our target. His name is Bohdan Shevchenko. But since that's long and hard to understand we're assigning him the code name TARKA. He is a shit bird of the first order."

"Is that your professional assessment?" Elvis asked over the chuckles accompanying Sam's pronouncement.

"No," Sam replied, deadpan. "My professional assessment is that he's a homicidal asshat, but I didn't want to use foul language in mixed company."

Another round of laughter as the room's tension decreased yet another notch.

There was more to Sam than met the eye.

"TARKA became the focus of this operation thanks to an asset Matt and Frodo developed. Up until recently, TARKA had been content selling conventional weapons. Now he's got himself a tactical nuke."

Just that quickly the room turned serious. More than one of the SEALs traded glances while Red's jaw dropped, revealing a plug of chewing tobacco.

"Who's the asset?" Axle said.

I prepared to answer, but Sam beat me to the punch.

"Sorry, gentlemen," Sam said, all earlier traces of mirth gone. "Due to the asset's placement, we will not be divulging information about him or her. From here on, they will be referred to using the code name HEMINGWAY.

The DIA has assessed HEMINGWAY's reporting to be both accurate and reliable."

"I vouch for HEMINGWAY," I said. "If push comes to shove and we need to take action based on something HEMINGWAY says, my ass will be hanging in the breeze right next to y'all's."

Sam had done a fine job covering for me, but these guys were my team. I owed it to them to stand behind the Russian, especially since the SEALs could be going into harm's way based on his reporting. This was the true burden of command, and I did not take it lightly.

"Good enough for me," Elvis said, settling the issue for the team. "Who is this joker and where's he hiding?"

"As you might imagine, the *who* is a bit easier to answer than the *where*," Sam said, changing slides.

The new image showed TARKA in a much more formal setting. He was wearing a suit with his hands at his side and his chin thrust out.

"This is our guy about ten years ago," Sam said, his cadence taking on a professorial bearing as he warmed to the topic. "He was a member of the Ukrainian Verkhovna Rada, or parliament. An up-and-coming star until he abruptly resigned and disappeared from public view."

"To pursue more profitable endeavors?" Axle said.

"That's what we think," Sam said, nodding. "As I said earlier, we've had our eye on him for some time now. As a country, Ukraine could teach Afghan warlords a thing or two about corruption. To say it's systemic is a misrepresentation of the word. From members of parliament all the way down to local law enforcement, graft is rampant.

The miracle of Ukraine isn't that it's managed to avoid getting swallowed lock, stock, and barrel by Russia this long. It's that the country hasn't collapsed under the crippling weight of its own corruption. Unfortunately, this makes our friend TARKA more the rule than the exception."

"Why was he on the DIA's radar?" Elvis said.

"Because he's turned the sale of illicit weapons and goods into an art form," Sam said. "The Crimea annex briefed well and scored the Russian president major political points with the pro-Russian separatists in eastern Ukraine. But reality didn't play out quite so nicely. Only *after* he announced the seizure of the peninsula did the president's logisticians realize that the populace's natural resources all came from mainland Ukraine. Left to its own organic industry, Crimea doesn't even have the infrastructure to supply its population with fresh water, let alone day-to-day necessities. This gave rise to a thriving black market. Someone needed to protect the movement and distribution of those illegal goods."

"TARKA?" Frodo said.

Sam nodded again. "Over time, he migrated from basic foodstuffs to luxury items, and then to the ultimate commodity—weapons. But we're not talking about a couple of crates of rusted AK-47s and some recycled RPGs. Not our boy. When the Russians went through the last round of posturing, and the US refused to supply lethal aid, the Ukrainian government turned to TARKA for help."

"Seriously?" Axle said.

"'Fraid so," Sam said. "Look at the situation from their perspective. If your choice is between buying illegal weapons or become an unwitting Russian province, what are you going to choose?"

"Point taken," Axle said, scratching his scar. "But where did he get the weapons?"

Sam shrugged. "The usual places—South Africa, Israel, China. And one or two of the not so usual—like Russia."

"Come again?" Axle said.

"Ukraine doesn't have a lock on corruption," Sam said. "The current batch of billionaire Russian oligarchs has inspired strongmen the world over to greater heights of economic debauchery. Russia might be in a quasi-war with Ukraine, but patriotism doesn't pay the second mortgage on the summer dacha. For the right amount of money, Russian weapons flowed into Ukraine. TARKA was the man who guaranteed their delivery."

"And now he's progressed to nukes?" Elvis said. "Seems like an exponential leap with a serious downside to his livelihood, not to mention life. Countries might look the other way at the illegal sale of antitank missiles or drones, but trafficking nukes puts a nation-state-sized target on his back."

"Unless he's got protection," I said, jumping into the brief. "A man paid with his life to bring us this intel. He was murdered while being interrogated by his kidnappers. Russian kidnappers. Look, next to the Chinese, the Russians play the gray war game better than anyone else. The last time the Russians gobbled up a chunk of

Ukraine, the hard work had been done before a shot was even fired. Same with Georgia back in 2008. We know that Little Green Men are already in Ukraine setting the conditions for whatever the Russian president has up his sleeve. If there's a Russian nuke loose, I'm sure it's not a surprise to them."

"Then what's the play?" Axle said.

"As I said earlier, Kyiv Station has been on TARKA for quite some time," Sam said. "Several weeks ago, a local asset reported that TARKA was selling a Russian S-500."

"A what?" Axle said.

"It's an air defense system," I said. "One specifically designed to counter our fifth-generation stealth aircraft. The smart boys and girls at Redstone Arsenal need to get their hands on it so they can figure out what makes it tick and how to defeat it. We don't need the entire radar system. Just the LRU, or line-replaceable unit, housing the targeting algorithms. Think of it as a self-contained computer about the size of a small suitcase."

"How does this procurement tie into finding the nuke?" Elvis said.

"I'll take that," Sam said. He changed slides. Now a map of Kramatorsk appeared on the wall. "TARKA runs his entire operation from here, and we've been able to identify several key nodes."

Sam touched another button and red boxes highlighted three different areas on the map.

"These locations seem to be critical to TARKA's organization based on a combination of HUMINT and

SIGINT. The procurement meeting is supposed to take place here."

The slide changed again, this time showing the distinctive shape of an airfield. A single runway oriented west–east was bisected by a series of north–south-running taxiways. The typical hangars and maintenance buildings occupied the real estate to the south of the airstrip. To the north sat two more isolated structures. One of them stood to the northwest of the airstrip's center point and the other almost due north.

"This is Kramatorsk air force base," Sam said.

He then triggered a laser pointer and drew a lazy circle around the structure to the northwest of the runway.

"And this is where TARKA intends to meet the customers interested in acquiring the Russian air defense system. This warehouse is his main distribution center, and it's guarded by a combination of Ukrainian military assigned to the air force base and his private security team. If he's got a nuke, this is where we believe he'd keep it."

"That's gonna be a tough nut to crack," Axle said, walking to the front of the room for a better view. "Entry'll be a bitch, and the square footage under that roof is enormous. A target that big should have at least three teams plus an outer cordon."

"Couldn't agree more," I said, "which is why we're not going to breach the building. TARKA invited us to walk through the front door."

"I'm not a spook," Elvis said, scratching his beard, "but that sounds off. If TARKA's really got a nuke in there, why invite a bunch of strangers in for a gander?"

"Not a bunch," I said, gesturing to Frodo, "just me and my partner. But your point is well-taken. My guess is that he's holding the meeting in the warehouse because that's where he feels the safest. Either way, we're going to have a look courtesy of these."

I tossed Elvis a leather money clip.

"It's a new toy developed by the smart boys and girls at DIA's department of science and technology," I said. "My last chemistry class was somewhere south of tenth grade, but the layman's explanation is that nuclear weapons emit radiation at close distances. If that warehouse has a bomb, we'll know."

"And if it doesn't?" Axle said.

"That's where you boys come in," I said. "If the device isn't in the warehouse, we don't have time to play detective. Our next play will be kinetic. We'll conduct an extraordinary rendition of TARKA."

"I thought we didn't do those anymore," Elvis said.

"Loose nukes have a way of persuading the powers that be to bend the rules," I said. "The procurement meet is going down in a couple of hours, and I know everyone has mission prep to do before then. Any further questions?"

"Not a question as much as an *aw, shit*," Sam said. "Kyiv Station worked up the procurement op to be two people, but TARKA's expecting them to be a man and a woman. The ops coordinator just realized the mix-up. Since it's such short notice, Kyiv Station was prepared to loan us their female DIA officer, but she just went into emergency surgery for appendicitis. We're one teammate short."

"It has to be a woman?" I said.

Sam nodded. "The whole legend is built around her. Kyiv Station is shorthanded as it is, and she is their only female. We can find another female DIA officer, but it's gonna push the procurement window back. Should we start working a schedule slip?"

My thoughts turned to the situation update Sam had provided when we'd arrived at the safe house. Small skirmishes had already broken out in three of the contested towns in eastern Ukraine, undoubtedly proof that Russia's Little Green Men were already hard at work. The crisis was reaching critical mass.

A schedule slip wasn't an option.

"Nope," I said, taking my cell phone from my pocket. "I can get us a replacement."

Which was true.

What was also true was that I was already dreading the deal I'd have to broker to get her.

FORTY

Pyotr rubbed his tired eyes, gathering his thoughts. The last several hours had been a blur of activity. After receiving trigger authority, Pyotr had traveled east via a number of conveyances. He'd arrived as the sun was rising and was now safely ensconced in the command post he was using to supervise the Ukrainian operation, surrounded by able men. The end was near, but this was no time to become complacent. The Greater Endeavor, as Moscow had so casually termed the operation, was a complex tapestry in which the undoing of any single thread could unravel the entire undertaking.

"Where do we stand?" Pyotr said.

The question was directed to Dmitri Agapov, Pyotr's GRU liaison.

Unlike his now deceased comrade Sergei the paratrooper, the Army captain was an espionage professional. He had a compact, muscular frame that he hid beneath baggy clothes, dark eyes that sparkled when he laughed, and an open face. His hair was a dirty brown, while his neatly trimmed beard had hints of red. Taken in sum, the GRU operative's appearance lent itself to half a dozen European countries, and Dmitri had the language skills to match.

While Pyotr had been loath to involve anyone outside of the SVR for this phase of the operation, he had to admit that the military intelligence officer had proven to be a worthy addition to the team. An agent runner himself, Dmitri thought like a spy rather than the blunt-force object that had been Sergei. As such, Pyotr had begun to utilize the man as a second-in-command rather than just a conduit to the clandestine Spetsnaz operatives embedded throughout Ukraine.

While Pyotr had been in Vienna trying to lock down the Irishman and deal with the threat he represented, Dmitri had been running things in his absence. This would be Pyotr's first progress update since he'd handed the reins to his second-in-command.

"Everything is on track," Dmitri said. "Team Sierra has been equipped with Ukrainian militia uniforms and weapons. They are proceeding to target. Our cyber and social media campaigns are bearing fruit. People are responding. Phase one will commence momentarily."

"Excellent," Pyotr said. "Then we have nothing left to do but wait."

"Perhaps not," Dmitri said. "Team Tango sent flash traffic several hours ago. They're the Spetsnaz team assigned to monitor Kharkiv Airport. Unfortunately, their message wasn't flagged as high priority, so I didn't review it until just now. I take responsibility for the oversight, and I've rectified this shortcoming with our intelligence cell. In any case, you need to see this."

Dmitri slid the tablet he'd been holding across the table. The first image showed several people exiting a private jet. Pyotr swiped to the second snapshot as the GRU officer spoke.

"The aircraft is registered to a company that may or may not be legitimate. The intelligence cell is still working on penetrating the corporate filings. But based on Team Tango's reporting, this probably isn't important. According to our asset within air traffic control, the jet's flight plan originated in Vienna."

The words hit Pyotr like a physical blow. His gaze snapped from the tablet to Dmitri. The military man flinched.

"You're sure?" Pyotr said.

"Yes, comrade," Dmitri replied.

Shifting back to the tablet, Pyotr swiped through the pictures like a man possessed. Finally, after reaching the second image from the last, he found what he'd been dreading.

Dark, tousled hair, scruffy beard, and an athletic build.

The American intelligence operative who'd slaughtered the entire Vympel team.

Here.

"What is the status of our mobile SIGINT assets?" Pyotr said, his agile mind formulating a plan even as he spoke.

Taking a cue from their American counterparts, Russian special operations command now counted within its capabilities covert signals intelligence, or SIGINT, teams. These soldiers operated in the field, far behind enemy lines. The operatives specialized in clandestinely compromising an enemy's communications system and using it against them. The skill set offered by these teams ran the gamut from data theft, denial of service, virus introduction, clandestine voice and visual monitoring, and even locating and mapping individual communications nodes.

The Russians couldn't yet duplicate the full power of the American NSA, but the capability gap was closing a bit more every day.

"Our cyber penetration of Ukraine cell and data networks is complete," Dmitri said. "We own their entire communications infrastructure. Until phase two begins, our mobile SIGINT element is on standby."

"Excellent," Pyotr said. "Equip them with the reserve Spetsnaz team. This is what I want them to do."

For the next five minutes, Pyotr laid out the tasking in detail. The GRU officer listened attentively. At the end of the briefing, he had just one request.

"I'd like to lead the effort myself," Dmitri said.

"Granted," Pyotr said with a smile. "Good luck."

FORTY-ONE

Nina Aksamit jostled against the surging crowd as she looked for Hadeon. Though she was standing on the top step of the amphitheater-like staircase that flowed from the courtyard just outside the Palace of Culture's imposing white columns to the open pedestrian area below, she couldn't find what she was seeking. The dark-eyed boy with the shy smile she'd come to meet was nowhere in sight.

Not meet, Nina sternly corrected herself. *Demonstrate alongside.*

Like much of the rest of the murmuring crowd and twenty-five percent of Kramatorsk's population, Nina considered herself more Russian than Ukrainian. Russian was the language she and her family spoke at home, and the white, blue, and red Russian flag was what proudly flew outside her house.

Even so, Nina was acutely aware of the precarious spot

her nation occupied. At just fourteen, she was too young to remember the last time violence between pro-Russian separatists and Ukrainian nationals had engulfed her city, but like teenagers seemingly the world over, her life revolved around social media. To that end, the images of Ukrainian riot police beating pro-Russian demonstrators engulfed her WhatsApp and Instagram feeds.

While she'd never considered herself to be political, Nina was beginning to respond to the constant barrage of social media posts and blog entries from other pro-Russian Ukrainian youth. Without intending to, Nina had become active in the various communities that chronicled the abuses foisted upon her community.

And then there was Hadeon.

"Did you find them?"

The question came from her friend Olga, who was also fourteen. The girls had been best friends since second grade, and once Olga had started interacting with the separatist forums, it was inevitable that Nina would join her. Even so, it was Nina who'd discovered Hadeon and his handsome friend Faddei.

The pair was two years older than the girls, and while the age difference had concerned Nina, her rambunctious friend had assured her it wouldn't be a problem. To her credit, the spunky redhead had been right. Until now, communication between the four teenagers had taken the form of text messages or the occasional picture.

But today, that would change.

Assuming Nina ever found the boys amidst the massive crowd.

"Can you see them?" Olga said, squirming next to her.

"No," Nina said, stretching to her full height of just under 1.6 meters. "I don't know why they aren't here."

Half of Kramatorsk seemed to be taking part in the demonstration. Though it was only nine o'clock in the morning, a sea of people surged across the open space, converging at the base of the steps as even more demonstrators streamed in from the adjacent streets. The top of the stairs formed a natural stage, and several men were setting up a combination portable speaker and microphone. School had been canceled and many local businesses had temporarily shuttered as the crowds had continued to swell.

For the first time, Nina felt a flicker of unease at the countenance of some of her fellow protesters. Though the march had been billed as a peaceful show of solidarity for other pro-Russian teenagers, many of the faces Nina saw were older and harder.

This didn't feel right.

"Let's go over there," Olga said, pulling on Nina's sleeve. "If we climb the trees, maybe we can see better."

"Okay," Nina said, pushing through the crowd with her slighter friend following behind her.

The cluster of trees Olga had indicated was on the far side of the square. Nina's instant agreement to her friend's suggestion more reflected her sudden desire to distance herself from the swirling crowd than her hopes of spotting their cyber pals. If she saw the boys, fine. If she didn't, that was okay too. Thirty minutes earlier, the majority of demonstrators looked like the two young girls—young, happy, and female.

This was no longer true.

A sense of barely contained menace permeated the air. The children Nina's age had been herded to the center of the square by a second contingent of much older and predominantly male marchers.

Nina was worried.

"Hurry," Nina said, reaching behind her to grab her friend's hand.

The cluster of trees was now only twenty meters distant, but Nina was no longer focused on reaching their low-hanging limbs. Instead, she was pulling her friend toward the long stretch of pavement on the far side of the square. Pavement that led away from the palace and the churning demonstrators.

"Wait," Olga said. "Where are we going?"

The smaller girl stopped, yanking her hand free as she strained on tiptoes, trying to see above the jumble of heads.

"Olga," Nina said, turning back to her friend.

That was when she saw them. A formation of men on the opposite side of the square dressed in the piecemeal camouflage uniforms favored by militias.

Men with guns.

Nina stared as the dozen or so fighters lifted AK-74 rifles to their shoulders, her innocent mind still unable to comprehend what she was seeing.

Then she knew.

"Olga," Nina said again, this time screaming her friend's name.

She grabbed Olga's shoulder, intending to drag her slimmer friend to the concrete.

Olga turned to Nina, her green eyes questioning.

Then thunder rippled across the courtyard.

FORTY-TWO

Peter walked west on E Street NW, the Oval Office behind him and the unknown in front of him. This should have been a night for celebration. Indeed, several of the staffers had headed out en masse to a popular watering hole to the west of the White House, off G Street. One of the cluster of bars that officially closed at two a.m. but was known to bend the rules from time to time for West Wing employees, especially after a big night.

And tonight had been a big night. The president had crushed his prime-time address. Though he'd crafted most of Jorge Gonzales's big speeches, Peter remained his friend's biggest critic. While others saw rhetorical flourishes and inspirational anecdotes, Peter heard off-script messages and missed opportunities.

But not tonight.

Tonight, the president had stayed on message, hammering each point home like he was driving nails. Peter's secret polling group was already showing movement among independents, and the address was only hours old. Tomorrow, the hard work of converting this new-found political capital into forward momentum would begin.

But tonight was a night of celebration.

Except for Peter.

Peter was trudging west to take a meeting with a Russian spy.

The clarity of this thought took him by surprise. Since his previous encounter with the woman on the National Mall, Peter had been doing his best to recast their relationship in a more positive light. He'd begun his association with the Russians as a sort of back-channel communications conduit. A means to take the other nation's pulse in an informal manner.

For a period of time, Peter had convinced himself that this was all the Russian woman wanted.

The stark meeting he'd attended in the Situation Room exposed this thought for the fantasy that it was. As much as Peter inherently distrusted the military members of the president's cabinet, he couldn't fault their analysis. The Russians were moving on Ukraine, and the United States would set the tone for the world's response. Peter might be new to the game of cloak-and-dagger, but he was not naive enough to believe that the impending Russian invasion and his chance meeting with the Russian spy were unrelated.

That Peter was under a foreign government's thumb was no longer in question. What remained to be seen was how deep he'd inadvertently dug the hole in which he now found himself.

"Peter."

The sound of his name gave Peter a start. He instinctively stopped, turning toward the voice that had uttered it. Without realizing it, he'd drawn abreast of the eastern edge of Rawlins Park. The beautiful greenbelt featured a statue of General John A. Rawlins on the plot's eastern side, along with a reflecting pool bordered by benches shaded by leafy trees. Peering through the night, Peter could just make out a dark form sitting on the closest bench.

"Come here. I'm not going to bite."

The longer sentence gave voice to her accent. Not that Peter had any doubt who was speaking. Wise to the ways of espionage he might not be, but somehow Peter wasn't surprised to find the Russian operative lurking in an otherwise abandoned park. Taking a fortifying breath, Peter traded the sidewalk for the park's slate tile and sat down beside her.

"I thought we were meeting at the bar?" Peter said.

The reflecting pool was laid out like a long rectangle with the bench on which Peter was seated at its midpoint. To the left, the statue of the park's namesake kept watch, his indistinct outline shrouded by darkness. To the right, a second pool ran perpendicular to the first. A fountain throwing up bubbling streams of water made up its centerpiece.

"Change of plans," the woman said. "I wanted something a bit more . . . intimate."

She slid closer as she spoke, scooping up Peter's hand in hers even as her left leg pressed against his right. Peter stiffened in surprise and his heartbeat quickened. He could smell her perfume, the scent both exotic and spicy.

Then her head was resting on his shoulder.

"What are you doing?" Peter said, starting to pull away.

"Relax," the woman said with a throaty chuckle. "I'm not here to seduce you. But we are a man and a woman sitting alone in a park on a moonlit night. We should maintain appearances."

She threaded her arm through his, the length of her body pressed firmly against him.

"What's your name?" Peter said.

"You can call me . . . Rachel."

Her lips brushed his ear as she whispered the reply, and it took him a moment to recognize the significance.

Rachel.

The girl he'd wanted to marry after college.

The girl who'd broken his heart.

Peter turned toward the Russian only to find her face inches from his. Pale light spilled across her full lips, gathering in her eyes.

"I know everything about you, Peter. Everything."

Peter jerked his head away, taking refuge in the view of the fountain. Streams of water rocketed skyward before gravity exerted its pull, sending the droplets cascading back to earth.

"What do you want?" Peter said.

"To be your friend. Nothing more."

"I don't believe that."

"Why not?" the woman said, her tone sounding genuinely puzzled. "You don't think we could be friends, Peter?"

"I'm not an idiot."

"I wouldn't be here if I thought that," Rachel said, her breath tickling his neck. "Friends talk about a great many things, including work. I'd like to talk about your job. This is a pivotal moment in the relationship between our two nations. There's trouble in the Ukraine, Peter. Innocent people are being slaughtered. Boys and girls killed in the street."

"What are you talking about?" Peter said.

"Consider this my gift," Rachel said. "Something to help you understand the depth of my feelings toward you. A Ukrainian militia has gunned down a crowd full of peaceful demonstrators in Kramatorsk. Over fifty dead, most of them under the age of eighteen. These are our people, Peter. Russians who were murdered simply for exercising their God-given right to protest. We will not stand idly by as innocents die."

"Meaning what?"

"Meaning that we will protect the powerless just as you would if the situation were reversed. I'm telling you this as a friend. I'd like you to demonstrate your commitment to our friendship in return."

"How?" Peter said.

"By promoting understanding between our two nations. Help me see inside your president's head. I need to understand what he's thinking."

"That's it?" Peter said.

"That is much," Rachel said. "I don't take friendship lightly, Peter. If you have something urgent to tell me, make a reservation for a party of three at the bar where we were to meet tonight. Use the name Needing. If I need to speak with you, you'll get a text about your dry cleaning from Alamo Cleaners. We'll meet here, the site of our first date."

Without waiting for a reply, the woman leaned in and kissed Peter's cheek.

Then she stood and walked away without a backward glance.

Peter watched her shadowy form until she blended with the night, trying to ignore his thundering heart and the lines her soft lips had burned upon his skin.

His phone rang.

Pulling the device from his pocket, Peter managed a shaky "Hello."

"Peter Redman?"

"Yes," Peter said, sitting up a bit straighter.

"Sorry for calling so late, sir. This is the desk officer. The president has requested that all principals gather in the Situation Room. Immediately."

"On my way," Peter said, ending to the call.

Getting to his feet, Peter headed east, away from the moonlit park and the lingering scent of exotic perfume.

FORTY-THREE

A ndriy, a word."
Andriy looked from the militiaman he was inspecting to see Danilo standing to his left, worry etched across his face. This seemed to be his friend's permanent expression of late, but Andriy understood. The fate of a nation rested on their efforts.

"One moment," Andriy said, before turning back to the would-be soldier.

Andriy and the twelve armed men were gathered in the center of his hayfield. While the weather had been iffy all morning, the sun had made an appearance about an hour ago and the cloud cover had begun to lift. Conditions were far from optimal, but they were good enough to call in a favor with another former comrade in arms. This one was a commander in Ukraine's version of the National Guard, not the regular military.

But that was of no concern to Andriy. He was much

more interested in the assets under the commander's control. This was why he and his assault force were standing in a wet grassy field, hoping that the break in cloud cover held.

Like most militias, the new volunteer battalion was equipped with a hodgepodge of equipment and uniforms. Andriy was fine with this. His boys from Opishnya weren't going to be stalking Russians through the forest. No, this was a raid, plain and simple. As such, Andriy cared about two things—that his men looked enough alike to recognize one another and that their rifles fired.

Andriy worked the action on the man's AK-74, ensuring that the bolt cycled smoothly and was reasonably clear of dirt and grit before verifying that the empty magazine well was in a similar condition. The Russians might be murderous scum of the earth, but they designed amazing weapons. The AK variant of rifles was no exception. Unlike the more accurate American M4, an AK-74 would shoot under almost any condition without the need for constant and meticulous cleanings. For this operation, a steady volume of fire was far more important than pinpoint accuracy.

"You know how to use this?" Andriy said, handing the rifle back to its owner.

"I grew up hunting rabbits, Commander," the militiaman said. "I hit where I aim."

Andriy nodded, turning back to Danilo.

The intelligence operative was standing on the gravel path that led to the field, the cuffs of his trousers wet from walking through the grass. As Andriy drew closer, he noticed that Danilo made no move to meet him in the middle. Whatever news the former spy was bringing wasn't for everyone.

"How are they?" Danilo said.

Andriy looked at the group of men, mentally assessing their performance for the umpteenth time. They were a mixture of veterans who'd fought against the Russians in the previous war and untried boys like the one he'd just inspected. If he were being honest, Andriy would have had to admit that they weren't the most elite troops he'd ever led into battle. But the squad leaders commanding each five-man element had shed Russian blood before, and the rest were village boys.

Andriy knew he could trust them.

That would have to be enough.

"They'll do," Andriy said.

"I wish you'd reconsider leading the raid yourself."

Andriy shook his head. This was ground they'd covered several times before, and he had no intention of tilling it again.

"They need to have a commander with them, and Olek is too old. Besides, he's off gathering the other militia leaders for the war council. It has to be me."

Danilo nodded. "I understand why you feel that way. But I have news that might change your mind."

"Out with it, my friend," Andriy said. "We haven't much time."

In Andriy's mind, a clock had been ticking from the moment they'd gleaned the information regarding the nuke's location from Marko's tattered body. Each passing moment presented an opportunity for someone to stumble upon the weapon and move it. Andriy judged this likelihood to be very small, but he was a soldier, and soldiers knew that battles often turned on the unlikeliest of events.

"There's been a tragedy," Danilo said. "A Ukrainian militia in Kramatorsk opened fire on a peaceful crowd of pro-Russian demonstrators. Over ninety people were killed. Mostly teenagers."

"Which militia leader was responsible?" Andriy said. "Perhaps Olek can help bring him to justice."

"I don't think so," Danilo said. "In fact, I'd guess it wasn't the work of Ukrainians at all."

Andriy stared at his friend for a moment, not understanding.

Then he did.

"Russians?" Andriy said. "Could they be so callous? Yes, of course they could. These men killed their own countrymen to justify the Chechen War. What's a little Ukrainian blood?"

"It gets worse," Danilo said. "The Russians are demanding the right to move into Kramatorsk to secure the Russian-speaking populace. World opinion is divided, but Western Europe seems to be in favor of Russian intervention."

"What about Kyiv?" Andriy said.

Danilo shook his head. "What you'd expect. Their assurance of a swift and thorough investigation pales in comparison to the countless videos of masked Ukrainian militiamen gunning down teenagers. I'm sorry, my friend, but I no longer believe this will work. Even if we have the device, I don't think Europe will offer us protection."

Andriy ground his teeth even as he patted his pockets for the comforting shape of his pipe. He wanted to argue, wanted to protest that there was still a way, but in his heart, he knew his friend was right. Trying to force the Europeans to live up to their promises had always been a yeoman's task. Now, with the weight of public opinion stacked against Ukraine, it was impossible. The mere threat of a nuclear weapon was no longer enough.

Andriy pulled the pipe from his jacket and froze.

In an instant, he understood what needed to be done.

Only by destroying the Russians' means to invade could he protect his homeland.

The sound of mechanical thunder echoed through the air, underscoring his decision.

"Goodbye, my friend," Andriy said, grabbing the spy's hand. "Look after my daughter."

"Wait," Danilo said, realization dawning on his face. "What do you mean?"

"I'm doing what must be done," Andriy said.

"No," Danilo said, shaking his head. "We'll find another way."

"We both know there isn't one. Keep this for me. I can't take it where I'm going."

Andriy reverently handed his pipe to his oldest friend.

Then he ran toward the thunder and his destiny.

FORTY-FOUR

Nineteen-year-old Aleksandr Volkov felt sick to his stomach. Unfortunately, this feeling was an all-too-common occurrence since he'd joined the Desant, or Russian Paratroopers. There'd been the nausea he'd felt when reporting in for processing. The worry that had accompanied his first day of training after being roused from a fitful slumber by his instructors, hard-muscled men the size of gorillas. Then the nerves that had gone hand in hand with the first time Aleksandr had willingly hurled his body from a perfectly good aircraft.

After each first, he'd naively believed the sense of terror would fade. The first jump, the first time he'd been awarded his coveted paratrooper wings, and the first donning of his sky blue beret and blue-striped *telnyashka* undershirt. Each time, Aleksandr had done what was asked of him. Each time he'd thought that this would be the day he finally conquered his terror.

Now he was standing on the tarmac of Morozovsk airfield with kilos of gear strapped, buckled, and ratcheted to his thin frame. A million scattered thoughts fought for prominence in Aleksandr's distracted brain, but one kept the others at bay. Why had he ever thought volunteering for the VDV was a good idea?

Sure, the Airborne Assault Troops was a prestigious organization whose lineage stretched all the way back to the Great Patriotic War. But prestige only went so far. Aleksandr's village friends had elected to follow the normal conscription path for eighteen-year-old Russian males. They were almost done with their mandatory service, while Aleksandr was not even halfway through his. To make matters worse, in her last letter, Aleksandr's mother had let slip that Mikhail was already home—discharged early for an injury. The boy who had tormented Aleksandr from childhood was now free to pursue Polina's affections unmolested.

Why oh why hadn't he chosen the easy way and become a supply clerk?

Aleksandr tried not to dwell on that thought or the coincidence that Polina's perfume-scented letters had mysteriously stopped coming just about the time Mikhail had arrived back at the village. Aleksandr's first leave was coming up in two weeks. He would return home in his paratrooper uniform, beret perched jauntily on his head just like the way the veterans wore it. He would deal with Mikhail's treachery in person. But before he could do that, Aleksandr had one more hurdle to surpass—surviving the next twenty-four hours.

"It's quite a sight, isn't it, Comrade Volkov?"

Aleksandr jerked to attention at the sound of the familiar voice over his right shoulder. Or at least he tried to. The main and reserve parachutes constricted his frame, hunching him forward at the shoulders like an old man. Though he'd put on at least four kilos of muscle since joining the VDV, he was still slim by paratrooper standards. The parachute and associated kit almost doubled his body weight.

With a laugh that seemed more than a little out of character, Aleksandr's senior sergeant placed a hand on Aleksandr's narrow shoulder. "Relax, Private. It's normal to be nervous before a live-fire exercise. Trust in your training and listen to your leaders. We'll be loading in about five minutes. Until then, drink in the might of Mother Russia. Your sacrifices have earned you the right to be here. You're standing among the finest warriors the world has ever known. Be proud."

The sergeant moved on without waiting for a reply, laying a wide hand on the shoulder of the next paratrooper and undoubtedly giving another version of the same speech. Except, to Aleksandr, the senior sergeant's words weren't just a speech. He was proud. A single glance across the busy airfield convinced Aleksandr that his sergeant was correct: There wasn't a nation in the world that could stand up to this display of military might.

All around him, the airfield was a mass of activity.

The eight four-engine Il-76 transports squatted on the runway like bloated vultures. Men and equipment streamed up their open rear ramps, and the aircraft's blue-and-white paint schemes sparkled in the sun. Each plane weighed more than seventy-two thousand kilograms, more elephant than delicate bird of flight. Aleksandr often wondered how the massive aircraft could lumber down the runway and still climb so gracefully into the sky even with their cargo holds laden with thousands upon thousands of kilos' worth of men and equipment

Today was a perfect example.

To Aleksandr's right, a line of BMP-4 amphibious armored personnel carriers stretched down the tarmac, waiting their turn to enter the transports. As if the lead vehicle's driver could hear Aleksandr's thoughts, the BMP closest to him rumbled to life, its diesel engine belching black, stinging smoke from its exhaust manifold. With its rifled 100mm tank gun, 30mm autocannon, and 7.62mm coaxial mounted machine gun, the BMP was a tremendous asset on the battlefield. Line paratroopers like Aleksandr were lightly armed in comparison, carrying just their AK-74 rifle, a pistol, and perhaps an RPG or some other recoilless rifle.

Still, the BMP's firepower came with a price. Designed to be air-dropped, the BMP's hull was made of aluminum rather than the more robust but exponentially heavier steel. In yet another concession to speed and agility over safety, the BMP's three crew members and cargo of paratroopers rode inside the vehicle as it dropped from the transport rather than manning it after touchdown, as was the case with the American army.

Not for the first time, Aleksandr thanked St. Elijah, the patron saint of Russian paratroopers, that he hadn't been selected for one of the mechanized infantry spots. Hurtling from the open ramp of an Il-76 was terrifying but manageable. In addition to his main chute, Aleksandr carried a reserve parachute. Not only that, but he could see and avoid both obstacles on the ground, in the form of the earth rushing to meet him, and the potential hazards of his fellow paratroopers. If he'd been stuck in the vehicle's dark hull as the BMP swayed beneath a parachute during its rapid descent, Aleksandr knew he would have spent the drop vomiting in an airsickness bag. Or praying.

Or both.

"All right, men, it's our turn!"

The shouted command came from the senior sergeant, and the veterans to either side of Aleksandr gave the obligatory cheer as they helped one another to their feet. Then something truly unusual happened. As the lead paratrooper stepped off, guiding the column toward the Il-76's gaping cargo hold, he began to sing.

Here birds do not sing.
Trees do not grow.
And only we, shoulder to shoulder,
Grow into the ground here.

The words of "We Need One Victory" were quickly picked up by the rest of Aleksandr's platoon as one hundred hearty voices half sang, half shouted the paratrooper's song. Aleksandr added his voice to the chorus. Since arriving at the 98th Guards Airborne Division, Aleksandr had participated in countless field exercises and five jumps. But this was the first time the men had loaded their aircraft while singing. Aleksandr wondered if perhaps live-fire exercises might just be a bit more dangerous than the others let on.

This was the last straw for his troubled stomach. Turning to his right, Aleksandr stepped out of formation and vomited his meager breakfast on the pitted concrete, careful to ensure that the spray stayed clear of both his boots and his fellow paratroopers. Then, without missing a step, Aleksandr wiped his mouth with the back of his hand and slid back into formation. He prepared himself for the expected ridicule. Instead, he felt a comforting hand on his back and heard the senior sergeant's voice in his ear.

"Well done, Volkov. Better to get it out of your system now than on the plane. The first part of the flight will be nap of the earth. By the time the door opens over the drop zone, half the plane will be covered in puke."

Aleksandr turned, thinking that perhaps he'd misheard.

"Others throw up too?"

The veteran's hard face gave way to a rare smile. "Every paratrooper has thrown up, pissed himself, or worse. Fear is human. It's what you choose to do with that fear that separates a man from a paratrooper."

Aleksandr's stomach roiled again, but rather than vomit, he screamed out the song's last line with all his might. He might once have been a terrified kid, but that was true no longer. A blue-and-white *telnyashka* stretched across Aleksandr's chest.

He was a paratrooper.

FORTY-FIVE

KRAMATORSK, UKRAINE

've done many stupid things in my life," Ella said. "None so stupid as this."

"I get that a lot," I said, steering the Land Rover though the series of spiraling turns leading to the airfield's front gate.

"This is going to cost you."

"We've been over that," I said. "Benny gets everything from this mission. No redactions."

The surrounding countryside was disarmingly beautiful. Pastures of knee-high grass and wildflowers were interspersed with neatly tilled fields. The trees grew tall and in clumps, and the winding roads were gravel as often as pavement. Portions of our drive had brought to mind rural Ireland.

"I'm talking about the debt you owe me," Ella said, shifting in her seat.

"Get in line, sister," I said, slowing the SUV.

Soldiers who manned checkpoints took a dim view of fast-approaching vehicles.

"Oh, God," Ella said, shooting me a look of mock horror. "That's why you don't have a partner, isn't it? You get them all killed."

I'm sure the Mossad officer had made the statement in jest, but her comment hit a little too close to home. Once again, I saw a curtain of auburn hair splayed across a dirty concrete floor. Before Virginia, there'd been Frodo. He was still alive, but he could no longer use a knife and a fork. At least, not at the same time.

Maybe Ella was right.

Maybe the common denominator was me.

My right hand began to tremble.

"I'm sorry," Ella said, her mocking smile gone. "I didn't know. I—"

"Save it," I said, squeezing my fingers into a fist as we entered the final straightaway. "It's go time."

Go time had been a long while in coming. Getting Benny to sign off on Ella joining the team hadn't been as difficult as I'd feared, but covering the geography separating us had been a challenge. At first, we'd entertained the idea of putting her on a commercial flight from Vienna to Kharkiv, but one look at the available tickets showed that was a nonstarter. The quickest route took better than ten hours between connections and layovers.

I didn't have that kind of time.

Fortunately, there aren't too many problems that can't

be solved with enough money and the will to spend it. Well, that and James Scott Glass hell-bent on breaking through bureaucracies. Somehow, the good folks in logistics chartered a private jet from Vienna to Kharkiv. From there, James rustled up a helicopter to ferry Ella to a remote field just fifteen minutes from our safe house.

I was still a little iffy on where he'd found the helicopter. The pilot spoke English and gave me the covert-operative vibe, but I didn't know if he was CIA Air Branch, Army Flight Concepts, the latest incarnation of Blackwater, or maybe something else entirely. Nor did I really care. Through force of personality and truckloads of cash, Branch Chief Glass had moved Ella across two countries in three hours' less time than it had taken me to make the same journey.

When this was over, I owed my boss a beer.

Or even two.

The team had used the ensuing seven or so hours to prep, mission plan, eat, and rest. The junior SEALs checked gear, zeroed weapons, and, yes, played Call of Duty. Frodo, Elvis, Axle, Sam, and I walked through the concept of the operation.

Kramatorsk's resident warlord/arms dealer had made a brilliant decision when he'd chosen to safeguard his warehouse of trafficked weapons on an air force base. The installation had a history of violence, as it had been the site of a series of clashes between pro-Russian and pro-government forces a number of years ago. Back then, the local populace had come close to seizing the base before the Ukrainian government dispatched commandos to drive them out.

In the subsequent years, the base's security had been substantially upgraded. Access points now had antipersonnel barriers designed to prevent crowds from gathering, and the road leading to the checkpoint followed a series of serpentine curves interspersed with concrete obstacles. These obstructions forced approaching vehicles to reduce their speed as they navigated the hairpin turns.

The air base was modest in size, sporting only a single active runway, which ran from west to east. A large concrete apron and the typical administrative buildings paralleled the runway to the south with a series of three north-to-south taxiways connecting the two structures.

On the westmost end of the active runway, a single taxiway meandered north before bending back to the east and paralleling the runway for a third of its length. While not terribly stimulating on its own, the taxiway did make a couple of stops worth noting. A tributary broke off toward the northwest, ending in a cluster of buildings, revetments, and helipads separated by a seemingly random patch of woods.

But there was nothing random about the dense copse of a dozen tall, thickly leaved trees. They provided a perfect sight break for the single building at its center. A warehouse. A warehouse uniquely suited for the storage of black-market weapons or whatever else its owner wished to keep both secure and hidden from view.

Choosing to run his criminal enterprise from a military base really was a stroke of genius on TARKA's part. In addition to the roving guards and high fences, the land bordering the active runway was mostly grassy fields kept clear of obstructions that might hinder arriving or departing aircraft. This meant that a surreptitious approach to the airfield and TARKA's warehouse bordered on the impossible, hence my decision to locate the SEAL QRF outside of the airfield's perimeter.

But if things went sideways and I was no longer concerned with the SEALs being detected, the frogmen would still have to cover a significant amount of open terrain before they could add their guns to the fight. If Ella and I got into trouble, we'd be on our own for several minutes before Elvis's contingent of barrel-chested freedom fighters joined the party. For a critical period of time, I'd be both outmanned and outgunned.

Just like in Iraq.

All elements, this is Frodo. Sweet is Maverick. I say again, Sweet is Maverick."

Frodo's radio call announcing that Ella and I were approaching the airfield's gate snapped me back to the present. The transmission came from a tiny speaker wedged deep within my right ear canal. The device was linked via Bluetooth to my cell, which in turn was streaming the team's semisecure communications, even though my phone looked as if it was in standby mode. The earpiece could also transmit, since it picked up my voice as the sound waves traveled along my jawbone.

At the premission briefing, we'd decided to leave the device on continuous broadcast so that Ella and I wouldn't have to use a transmit button while meeting with TARKA. To keep the network chatter manageable, our coms gear broadcast on a separate frequency band from the team frequency we were monitoring. As control for the operation, Frodo would ride herd on both channels, relaying pertinent information to each party.

Or at least that was the way things were supposed to work. Coms gear was second only to Vegas roulette tables when it came to predictability. For all the high-tech gizmos and encrypted data streams, I often thought we were only a few steps removed from smoke signals and homing pigeons.

"Frodo, this is Axle. Charlie is green. I say again: Charlie is green."

As the one manning our tactical operations center, or TOC, back at the safe house, Frodo had the privilege of naming the checkpoints. Normally these followed some sort of theme, like hockey teams or beer brands.

Frodo had chosen *Top Gun* call signs.

He'd claimed it was to make our Navy teammates feel welcome. I didn't believe that for a second. In any case, the front gate was christened Maverick, while the warehouse, our ultimate destination, was dubbed Charlie after Kelly McGillis's iconic character.

Just goes to show that even Delta Force snipers were romantics at heart.

"Frodo, this is Elvis. QRF is ready to execute."

"This is Frodo, roger all."

Like most operators, I sometimes found radio chatter distracting. Not today. Hearing the SEALs chiming in was a tacit reminder that even though Ella and I were the Land Rover's only occupants, we weren't alone.

In a feat of ingenuity that had me rethinking my assessment of SEALs, Axle had come up with a workable sniper-hide site. Granted, he and his spotter, Slice, were hunkered down atop a sarcophagus in a cemetery due west of the runway. Still, after doing a test run, the senior chief had assured me that the position had line of sight to TARKA's warehouse.

I'd asked about the practicability of lying prone atop a concrete cairn, but Axle hadn't been worried. He'd said that after he'd spent half a day in triple-digit heat buried in trash during the Second Battle of Fallujah, a sarcophagus would be a walk in the park. I took him at his word, grateful that I'd never commanded a sniper section.

Elvis, Red, Happy, and Cajun had much nicer accommodations. They were staged in a two-vehicle element just to the northwest of the warehouse near a gas station and auto repair shop. Unlike Axle, Elvis and crew did not have line of sight to Charlie. Instead, their position provided the shortest straight-line distance to the warehouse through an identified breach point in the airfield's perimeter fence. If the operation went south, Elvis's element would serve as the QRF while Axle and Slice provided covering fire.

Frodo would coordinate the multiple moving pieces via the final bit of magic James had been able to conjure— an RQ-170 Sentinel UAV. The bat-shaped aircraft didn't carry ordnance but was stealthy and had an amazing suite of sensors. James had been able to finagle only a thirty-minute loiter time for the much-in-demand ISR asset, but that should be more than long enough. All in all, we'd pulled together a pretty decent operational plan, given the constraints and time.

Now it was time to go to work.

I brought the Range Rover to a stop, lining up the hood with the metal drop gate barring entrance to the airfield. To the left sat a sandbag-reinforced concrete bunker. A pair of soldiers exited the pillbox, ambling toward my side of the car.

"What's wrong with your hand?" Ella said.

"Too much caffeine," I said.

Ella was not Virginia, and this was not Iraq. I couldn't view every operation through the lens of that dark hallway. Down that path madness lay. Taking a deep breath, I lowered the SUV's tinted glass, giving the guard my best I-don't-talk-to-the-hired-help look.

The trembling ceased.

"I'm here for the potatoes," I said, relaying the agreed-upon code word.

"O-kay," the guard said, his accent playing havoc with the word. "You follow."

He gestured to a Škoda painted white with orange stripes that was idling beyond the gate.

I nodded and rolled the window back up. The guard stepped out of the way, and the steel vehicle barrier lifted. I pressed down on the gas, smoothly accelerating through the checkpoint.

"See," I said to Ella, "nothing to it."

"Sweet, this is Frodo. We've got trouble."

FORTY-SIX

UNDISCLOSED LOCATION, UKRAINE

Pyotr watched the video from the Orion-E drone with a feeling of anticipation. While not as stealthy or cutting-edge as the American Sentinel or Reaper aircraft, the Russian UAV was more than adequate for the mission at hand. In the annals of drone footage, the scene in the camera's crosshairs was depressingly unremarkable. An unremarkable city block located in an unremarkable city.

A scene that was instantly forgettable.

But that was about to change.

Glancing from the screen to his Vostok watch, Pyotr noted the time. Though he certainly had more accurate timepieces at his disposal, there was something inherently satisfying about tracking an operation with the watch he'd been given after graduating from the Academy of Foreign Intelligence years ago. He would never admit it to the legion of digital warriors who now composed much of Russia's intelligence services, but Pyotr preferred the springs and gears of an analog watch to the impersonality of electrons.

As the second hand swept across the top of the dial, Pyotr turned his attention to the black-and-white drone feed. For the space of a single heartbeat, nothing changed. Then a flash of light bloomed from the building, followed by a cloud of thick gray smoke.

Though Pyotr was far removed from the image, he could still taste the acrid fumes, smell the choking smoke, feel the grit and dust coating his skin, and hear the screams of the wounded. He was nowhere near the targeted pub, but Pyotr had earned his spurs in much the same way the members of his direct action Spetsnaz teams were earning theirs today. Pyotr's baptism by fire had come during the lead-up to the Chechen Wars, but years later the feeling was still the same. Fear as the backpack full of explosives was smuggled to its destination, anticipation while waiting for final confirmation, satisfaction when the device detonated, and then a final, unexpected emotion.

Remorse.

Then as now, the victims' deaths were necessary, but that didn't make the shedding of innocent Russian blood any easier. In Pyotr's day, it had been apartment buildings dropped to turn the populace's opinion against Chechen terrorists. Today it was a pub that served as a popular gathering place for pro-Russian separatists.

Then as now, the deaths weren't easy to bear, but like countless others who had served before him, Pyotr's allegiance would always be to the motherland first and above all else. Today, as had been the case three decades ago, the motherland was indistinguishable from the Russian president.

The former KGB officer turned dictator who ruled Russia with an iron fist had many shortcomings. Operational brilliance wasn't one of them. In 1999, he'd used his former service to engineer the war he wanted in Chechnya. Today he was doing the same in the Ukraine. What the Russian president wanted, he got. Pyotr could put aside his feelings and do his duty or follow the path taken by others who'd objected to the president of the Russian Federation's methods.

One path led to riches and glory.

The other a shallow unmarked grave.

It wasn't a difficult decision to make.

"Prepare flash traffic," Pyotr said to the young technician on duty. "Eyes only. Highest encryption."

The communications specialist, a portly man who looked barely old enough to shave, nodded even as he pushed his glasses against his nose. With a flurry of fingers, the technician carried out Pyotr's wishes, muttering to himself as he typed.

These were now the warriors who most often fought on the front lines on behalf of Matushka Rosa, Mother Russia. Cyber commandos who with a single keystroke brought a nation's infrastructure to its knees or hobbled its military command and control nodes. Men and women who would never smell blood or stare down the length of a Kalashnikov barrel at their enemy. Their skirmishes took place in the domain of ones and zeroes.

But they were deadly nonetheless.

"Flash traffic ready, comrade," the technician said. "What is the message?"

Pyotr paused for a moment with the brevity code word that would change his nation's history and reunite Ukraine with its sister people on the tip of his tongue.

"Ryazan," Pyotr said.

The analyst nodded, bent to his keyboard, and pressed the appropriate buttons.

A moment later it was done.

"Sent, sir," the technician said.

"Good," Pyotr said, but his thoughts were no longer with the encrypted message that had just leapt from technician's keyboard to the antenna mounted to the roof, to the cube sat in geosynchronous orbit, and from there to Moscow and beyond. Those feats, while impressive, were just nodes in the network, cogs in the machine. No, what Pyotr pictured were not ones and zeroes streaming back and forth but something with more substance.

More girth.

Though not a military man, even Pyotr could see the genius behind the operational plan he was enacting. For the second time in less than twenty-four hours, Ukrainians had seemingly visited violence upon their pro-Russian countrymen. First the shooting of peaceful protesters, now the bombing of a pub. A pub that Russian cyber warriors had specifically steered Ukrainian mourners toward through another brilliantly executed social media campaign. The gatherers thought they were attending a memorial. They were, after a fashion.

Their own.

As the tremendous death toll from the two events clearly demonstrated, the Russian-speaking people of eastern Ukraine could not rely on Kyiv for protection.

But salvation was coming.

"Sir," the technician said, his frantic tone snapping Pyotr out of his revelry, "you need to see this."

Pyotr looked from the center screen still showing the bombing's chaotic aftermath to an adjacent television. The one displaying imagery from his command post on Kramatorsk Air Base. For a moment, Pyotr couldn't quite grasp what he was seeing. Then his shocked brain fit the pieces together.

And he began to swear.

FORTY-SEVEN

KRAMATORSK, UKRAINE

"Frodo, Sweet. Send it," I said.

Ahead of us, the Škoda crossed from the road to the taxiway before swinging a hard left. A series of hangars and maintenance buildings loomed to our right along with several empty helipads.

"Roger that, Sweet," Frodo said. "You and Gal are gonna have company."

I wasn't thrilled with my call sign, but Ella absolutely hated hers. Still, for American movie buffs, there was just one Israeli worth remembering.

"Sentinel's side-looking radar array has two bogeys inbound from the west at a high rate of speed. ETA three mikes. Maybe less. Should have seen them before now, but they were hidden by ground clutter. The pilots must have some steady hands. Sensor operator is estimating the birds are less than fifty feet off the deck. The Sentinel's look-down angle is giving me a good Doppler return from the bogeys' rotor blades. The birds are almost two thousand feet below the airfield's traffic pattern."

"What does that mean?" Ella said, looking across the cabin at me.

"It means that the helicopters don't want the airfield to know they're coming," I said.

"Why?"

I shook my head, addressing my next statement to Frodo instead.

"Frodo, Sweet. Can you identify the targets?"

"Stand by—working it."

Up ahead, the Škoda continued north on the taxiway, oblivious to what was hurtling toward the airfield like a freight train.

For the first time since we'd arrived in Ukraine, the sun had made an appearance after near-constant storms. It still wasn't weather to write home about, but patches of golden light slitted through gaps in the clouds. The sunlight sparkled off the damp grass to my left. I'd always associated the calm after a storm with a turn for the better.

Not today.

I had a feeling the nearing helicopters were carrying a storm of their own.

"Sweet, Frodo. Best guess is that the bogeys are Mi-8 Hips. Pilots are still approaching the airfield using terrain-following flight. ETA one mike. Call the ball, Sweet."

"Call the what?" Ella said, a puzzled expression on her face.

"Inside joke," I said, even as my mind raced.

The follow-me Škoda was now on the north side of the runway, still tracking the taxiway due north. In about a hundred meters, the taxiway would split. One branch would turn northeast, while the other would continue north before doglegging to the northwest and our warehouse. Though I still couldn't see our target building, I could make out the copse of trees masking it along with several concrete revetments separating individual helipads.

Perhaps that was all this was—flyboys getting in a little nap-of-the-earth training before calling it a day and heading to the officers' club for a cold one.

Perhaps.

But I didn't think so. Flying a helicopter at treetop level took tremendous skill, even during the daytime. If the engine so much as coughed or the pilot misjudged a single gust of wind, the helo would hit the trees at better than one hundred and fifty miles per hour. At that speed, it made a Daytona 500 crash look like bumper cars. Pilots flew this way only when avoiding detection was a matter of life and death.

These weren't flyboys on a joyride.

"Frodo, Sweet. Bump me to the team internal frequency, over."

"Sweet, roger. Stand by."

We'd covered the potential need for me to jump to the SEALs' frequency during the contingencies portion of the premission brief. Frodo's instinct about keeping the nets separate had made sense. With Ella and me both on continuous broadcast, the SEALs would hear us every time we spoke, and that wouldn't do. The last thing any mission-focused operator needed was an endless stream of chatter in his ear.

Even so, operations that looked simple in a sterile team room had a way of evolving into something much more complex when the rubber met the road. Accordingly, I'd asked Frodo to engineer a work-around. Something that would allow me to talk directly to the shooters if the need arose. He'd promised to make it happen.

Now it was time to put that promise to the test.

"Sweet, this is Frodo. Go for the team."

"This is Sweet, roger. Break, break—Elvis, Axle, how do you read me?"

"Sweet, Elvis has you Lima Charlie."

"Sweet, Axle has you the same, over."

Frodo's bit of communications magic had actually worked. Score one for the good guys.

"Elvis and Axle, roger. Stand by for change of mission. Frodo has two Hips inbound flying nap of the earth. They're not coming just to say hello. Worst case— the birds are carrying shooters who intend to grab our package. We're not going to let that happen, over."

Even as the words left my mouth, I was still turning a single question over in my mind: Who was in the choppers? If I had to bet, the inbound shooters were either Russians or an interested buyer who thought that TARKA's asking price was a bit too steep. Either way, that nuke wasn't getting away.

"Roger that, Sweet. Elvis copies all. What's the play?"
What indeed?

FORTY-EIGHT

KRAMATORSK, UKRAINE

Andriy held on to his seat as the pilot in front of him yanked back on the stick between his legs, sending the Hip lurching skyward.

Andriy had become a tanker for a number of reasons, some profound and others silly. Even so, he'd been happy with his decision. He'd loved rolling to battle in the belly of a seventy-ton machine of war, dealing out death with cannon and machine gun. But occasionally he did wonder what it was like in the infantry. To move to battle on foot or under a parachute or by helicopter. Perhaps this could generate the same thrill as thundering across a field in a cloud of diesel smoke.

This helicopter ride had convinced him otherwise. The sharp banks to the left and right and the vertical climbs followed by equally steep dives had left his stomach in knots. Fortunately, the nap-of-the-earth portion of the flight was complete. Now it was time to do something with which Andriy was considerably more comfortable.

Killing.

"The taxiway," Andriy said, pointing over the pilot's shoulder, "there."

The aviator acknowledged the command with a nod, spinning the helicopter on its axis as he angled the bird's nose toward the concrete strip Andriy had indicated. The man in the seat next to Andriy stiffened, anticipating what was coming next.

As per the plan Andriy had developed with the veterans of his newly formed militia, his assault force was divided into two elements. The element with the lower number of experienced fighters would pull security while the assault force entered the building, subdued the occupants, and removed the weapon. Once Andriy had extracted the information he'd needed from Marko, it had been a simple matter to point Danilo in the right direction and turn him loose. Locating the facility where the weapon was stored hadn't been difficult.

Concocting a way to get at it had been much more so.

Thankfully, armor officers excelled at breaking through their enemies' defenses.

The bird touched down, slamming into the concrete with a spine-snapping jolt. But the rough landing was fine with Andriy. Speed was everything. Because the warehouse was located within the confines of a Ukrainian military base, security inside the building was expected to be sparse. Even so, these were militiamen, not commandos. Better to quickly overwhelm their adversaries than to engage in a protracted gunfight.

"Go, go, go!" Andriy screamed, but he needn't have bothered.

The assault force was already out of his helicopter, sprinting for the warehouse's door even as the security force from the second helicopter took up their positions. So far, everything was going to plan. But Andriy knew that wouldn't last, even if the operation went without a hitch. The moment the assault team returned with the weapon, he intended to direct them to the second helicopter. One Hip would easily hold twelve men in a pinch.

This would leave just Andriy, the pilots, and the weapon in the other helicopter.

He would not be heading home.

As per the revelation he'd had at the staging field, Andriy knew that this was his only opportunity to save his homeland. Once the birds were airborne, he would order his pilots to fly east, toward Russia and the lurking invasion force. There, Andriy would detonate the weapon, destroying the Russian army and rendering their invasion route radioactive.

It was the desperate plan of a desperate man, but sometimes those were the best kind. Just as three hundred Spartans had once sacrificed their lives to hold back the invading Persian Army, so too would Andriy make his death count.

But first he had to secure the device.

FORTY-NINE

KRAMATORSK AIR BASE, UKRAINE

The scene Pyotr was watching unfold on the TV screen could have been drawn from another world. An action movie with no bearing in reality. Or perhaps drone footage from an operation in Syria, twenty-four hundred kilometers away. Whatever the video's source, it certainly couldn't have been happening at Kramatorsk Air Base.

Because that was where Pyotr had his command post.

But it was.

The pole-mounted camera's field of view was centered on an unassuming building in a forgotten corner of the airfield surrounded by a grove of trees. But given the activity surrounding the structure, it was anything but forgotten. To the north of the building, a pair of Mi-8 helicopters was congregated on an adjacent taxiway, their gargantuan rotors still spinning as armed men ran from the open rear and side doors. At the same time, a pair of vehicles was converging on the building from the south via a taxiway.

For a split second, Pyotr entertained the hope that perhaps the intruders were customers. After all, despite being an integral part of Pyotr's plan, the building's owner was an infamous arms dealer. It certainly made sense that he would continue to traffic in the goods of his profession, as much for appearances' sake as for profit.

Then the armed men from the helicopter stacked on the warehouse's front door in a tactical formation. Pyotr's hopes turned to ash. Arms dealers didn't exactly offer their customers valet service, but neither did they require them to breach the building to gain entry.

Someone was hitting the warehouse of the region's most powerful weapons dealer in broad daylight, on a military installation no less. This wasn't the work of a customer upset with the smuggler's pricing. The operation was incredibly brazen, meaning that the attackers considered the extreme risk they were running worth the potential reward. There was just one item in the warehouse's inventory that fit this criterion.

An item that Pyotr desperately needed.

The carnage and murder in the streets of Kramatorsk would begin to sway world opinion toward the Russians. A nuclear weapon discovered in the hands of a notorious arms dealer would cement it. Especially if that arms dealer was being afforded protection by the Ukrainian military. For Pyotr's plan to come to fruition, the weapon had to stay exactly where it was.

Which meant that he had to protect it.

Leaping to his feet, Pyotr mentally inventoried the manpower at his disposal. Had he not sent his Spetsnaz security team on the mission with Dmitri, the equation would have been quite different. In place of the commandos, he had only lightly armed cyber warriors, communication technicians, and intelligence analysts.

He couldn't repel an assault with these resources.

"Comrade," the radio technician said, interrupting Pyotr's thoughts, "Moscow acknowledges your earlier transmission."

Earlier transmission?

Then the answer fell upon Pyotr like a stack of bricks.

He didn't need to repel the attackers.

He just needed to delay them.

"You," Pyotr said, pointing at the startled technician, "transmit brevity code Barbarossa. Barbarossa. Do you understand?"

"*Da*, comrade," the technician said, his already pasty skin turning an even more alarming shade of white. "Barbarossa. But where are you going?"

"To buy us time," Pyotr said, sprinting for the door.

FIFTY

ETA thirty seconds," Frodo said, talking over the SEAL.

I rolled down the Land Rover's window and was greeted by the smell of freshly cut grass and a spattering of rain as the weather took a turn for the worse. Ukraine really was a beautiful country. Maybe I'd have to come back here someday under slightly better circumstances.

The distinctive thunder of rotor blades churning the air underscored my thoughts. Craning my head out the window, I searched for the source of the sound, but found nothing. During true nap-of-the-earth terrain flight, pilots didn't just fly at treetop level.

They often flew below it.

A series of fields bordered the airfield to the west, each field bounded by a wood line. My guess was that the pilots were dropping below the height of the trees while traversing the fields and popping back up to canopy level when forced to do so. While difficult on the pilots, this was the most effective way to mask an aircraft's radar and visual signature.

It also explained why I could hear the helicopters but not see them.

"Elvis, Sweet. Prepare to breach. Initiate on my go."

"Elvis, roger."

"Axle, Sweet. I anticipate multiple targets. Prepare to engage with both guns. If I call weapons free, everyone other than me or Gal is a legitimate target. How copy, over?"

"Axle copies all. Standing by."

Our original assault plan had Axle and Slice working as a sniper-and-spotter duo. In this configuration, the sniper provided surgical precision shots and the spotter vectored him onto targets and helped adjust his fire. But that scenario had gone out the window as soon as the helicopters had entered the picture. Instead of single shots against decisive targets, I had a feeling I was going to need the snipers to thin the herd.

The two long guns would have to work in tandem.

I pictured the flurry of activity taking place atop the stone sarcophagus as Slice traded his tripod-mounted spotting scope for his rifle on the shooting platform's very tight confines. The orchestrated chaos wasn't difficult to imagine, since something very similar was happening in the Land Rover's cabin.

"Ben zona."

I wasn't sure if I was supposed to answer Ella's Hebrew muttering or just ignore it. I chose the latter. This wasn't just to keep the peace with the feisty Israeli. For the first time, I had a view of the front of the warehouse. Two helicopters were situated on the tarmac, blades spinning. Squabbling with Ella would have to wait.

At least, that was what I told myself.

Though it is hard to have a meaningful conversation with someone when you're staring at their backside.

The moment I'd announced the change in mission, Ella had slipped out of her seat belt and crawled into the Land Rover's backseat, ranting in Hebrew. At the sound of Velcro tearing away from the carpet, I risked a glance in the rearview mirror. My Mossad partner was sprawled over the rear seats, providing me with a perfect view of her . . .

Well.

"What's the combination again?" Ella said.

"1776," I said.

"Of course."

A series of electronic chimes sounded as she punched in the digits, followed by the comforting *chunk* of the concealed storage compartment unlocking. A moment later, Ella squirmed back to the front seat, her arms full of goodies. She continued her indecipherable soliloquy while slapping a magazine into the SIG Sauer Rattler lying across her lap.

The weapon looked like an AR variant, but with a 5.5-inch barrel and a folding extendable buttstock. Even better, it was chambered in a 5.56 NATO round, which packed a hell of a punch in a close fight.

And a close fight was where we were headed.

After checking to make sure the magazine was seated,

she yanked the weapon's charging handle to the rear with a bit more force than was strictly necessary.

At least in my humble opinion.

"Gal, this is Elvis. Our Hebrew isn't so good. Maybe switch to English?"

"You are all fucking insane," Ella said, flipping on the Rattler's Romeo4S Red Dot optic, before wedging the carbine between her leg and the door. "Insane."

"Roger that, Gal. Thanks for the translation."

Ella replied with a stream of curses that would have made even James blush while slipping a plate carrier over her head. She then adjusted the straps, cinching down the body armor with quick, practiced motions. Satisfied with the plate carrier's fit, she buckled her seat belt with a few more Hebrew words thrown in for good measure.

This time no one requested a translation.

"Sweet, this is Axle. I have eyes on both birds. They're disgorging troops—twelve shooters. Six are in a blocking position on the taxiway orienting to the southeast. The remainder are converging on the warehouse, over."

Ella readied the second Rattler before placing it on the console separating us. Then she dumped my plate carrier in my lap and reached across me to grab the steering wheel. To our front, the follow-me Škoda slammed on its brakes, apparently realizing that the way ahead was blocked by armed men.

"Roger that, Axle," I said, turning the steering wheel sharply left so that the Range Rover's hood pointed toward the southwest corner of the stand of trees concealing the warehouse.

"Hold it here," I said to Ella as I unclipped my seat belt. "Elvis, breach now. I say again, breach now. Move your element to checkpoint Ice and hold. Orient east toward Charlie and the dismounts. Gal and I will approach Charlie from the southwest, using the trees to hide us from the six-shooter blocking element. If you see the blocking element begin to reposition toward Charlie, you are cleared to interdict, over."

"Sweet, Elvis. Roger all."

"Break, break," I said. "Axle, Sweet. Do you have line of sight on both choppers?"

"Sweet, Axle. Affirmative."

"Roger," I said, shrugging into my plate carrier. "Can you take the pilots?"

"Stand by."

I cinched down the plate carrier's straps jostling the attachments. Whoever had kitted this thing out had spared no expense. In addition to magazine holders, the rig had a full med kit, flex ties, signal flares, spare batteries, and two knives. When this was over, I was going to have to buy all of Kyiv Station a beer.

Buckling my seat belt, I reclaimed driving duties from Ella.

"Sweet, Axle. Affirmative on pilots. Factoring in range to target and that we'll be shooting through cockpit's glass, I anticipate multiple shots to achieve target effect. We can do it, but it's gonna be messy, over."

Why was I not surprised?

FIFTY-ONE

"You aren't going to be able to get comfortable, Comrade Volkov. Might as well stop trying."

Aleksandr paused midsquirm, frowning at the smiling face across from him. His squad leader had been with the VDV for four years, which seemed like an eternity to young Aleksandr. In the strict hierarchy that was the rank structure of the Desant, Aleksandr's squad leader was the equivalent of an omnipotent being, while Aleksandr was a toddler still trying to master lacing his shoes.

But whether his squad leader was an omnipotent being or not, Aleksandr wasn't going to give up trying to situate the newest addition to his kit. The almost three-meter-long hardened case gave new meaning to the word *uncomfortable*.

"Here's the thing about being a paratrooper," Junior Sergeant Semenov said, his crooked nose and tobacco-stained teeth somehow making his words all the more compelling. "Most of it is *yerunda*. The training, the long waits, the uncomfortable plane rides, even the actual jumping. All *yerunda*."

"Then why are you still here, Comrade Semenov?" Aleksandr said.

Aleksandr wouldn't normally address his squad leader in such a brash manner, but waiting to leap into oblivion from a foul-smelling airplane tended to make one bolder.

"Ah," Semenov said, his smile returning, "because the one part of this job that isn't *yerunda* makes everything else worthwhile."

Aleksandr looked at the older soldier expectantly, waiting for the omnipotent being to reveal the secret to a paratrooper's happiness. But Semenov didn't dispense any mystical wisdom. Instead, he leaned forward, ignoring the pile of vomit in the aisle between them, and grabbed the case running up the left side of Aleksandr's body. With a grunt, the older man gave the softer canvas between the hard plastic end caps a yank, sliding the strap from the center of Aleksandr's back to his shoulder.

The relief was instantaneous. For the first time during the flight, Aleksandr could actually lean against the bulkhead and give the spasming muscles in his lower back a break. Suddenly the vomit on his uniform and boots, the stench of sweat, throw-up, and flatulence pervading the air, the groans of those still airsick, and even the bouncing turbulence and shrieking engines all faded to the background.

Aleksandr rested his helmet against the vibrating aluminum and closed his eyes.

This was heaven.

"Attention!"

The commanding voice came from the loudspeaker mounted just above Aleksandr's head, and he jerked in response. Not a big motion, but large enough for the dreaded strap to slip from his shoulder and return to its rightful place across his back. With a muttered curse, Aleksandr bent forward at the waist to relieve the strain as his cramped muscles announced their displeasure. Then the words the voice was saying registered, and his discomfort was a thing of the past.

"What was that?" Aleksandr said, staring at his squad leader.

"You heard him," Semenov said. "The ammunition we've been issued isn't for a live-fire exercise. We're on an actual mission."

"A mission to do what?" Aleksandr said.

"To do what paratroopers do," Semenov said, his smile again revealing brown teeth. "Jump over our enemy and bring their death and destruction with us. Remember your training, Aleksandr, and listen to your fire team leader. You'll do fine."

At that moment, the lumbering transport gave another stomach-clenching lurch, and Aleksandr found himself adding to the pile of vomit. He told himself that the turbulence was to blame.

It wasn't.

FIFTY-TWO

KRAMATORSK AIR BASE, UKRAINE

The view of the situation unfolding on the airfield that Pyotr had seen from the command center had been concerning, but not terrifying. Perhaps because the TV allowed Pyotr to distance himself from the significance of what he was observing. Or maybe the conference room's familiarity provided the illusion that this new development was just another operational setback. Whatever the psychology, Pyotr had gathered up his team of novice warriors with a sense of urgency girded by confidence.

This wasn't the end of the world. His forefathers had blunted the German advance on Moscow. Surely the dozen men staring back at him armed with AK-74s, RPGs, and a PK machine gun could do what needed to be done.

Pyotr continued to entertain this thought while he issued instructions, and then jumped into a Suzuki Vitara to lead their three-vehicle convoy. But this spirit of unbridled optimism died a violent and quick death once Pyotr got his first unfiltered view of the pandemonium enveloping the arms dealer's warehouse.

Because Pyotr didn't have a bird's-eye view of the entire building as perspective, the helicopters loomed like prehistoric insects. Their twin bulbous turbine intakes, which were situated just below the rotors, jutted out from above the cockpit like a swollen nose. Two pylons branched off from the fuselage like a tree trunk's limbs. The hard points closest to Pyotr featured an outboard rocket pod and an inboard cannon. Though he couldn't see it, Pyotr had to imagine the helicopter had similar armament on the opposite side. It didn't really matter either way. The weapons he could see were more than enough to turn his little convoy to dust.

The helicopters were key to everything.

Pyotr turned to his only hope.

The man with the RPG.

"How many times have you fired that weapon?" Pyotr said.

"Three times, comrade. But only once with a live warhead."

"No matter," Pyotr said with a confidence he no longer felt. "For your fourth time, you will have a very big target."

FIFTY-THREE

"Roger that," I said, wrenching the wheel farther to the left to put as much foliage between us and the dismounts on the tarmac as possible. "Stand by."

To my right, the follow-me Škoda was rapidly executing a three-point turn. Its occupants had apparently reached the conclusion that whatever was happening to the illicit weapons dealer was none of their business.

Wise decision.

Unfortunately for me, wise decisions weren't part of the job.

"Sweet, Frodo. First group of dismounts entering Charlie time now. I designate them Team Alpha. Second set of dismounts continuing to hold a blocking position on the taxiway. I designate them Team Bravo."

"Sweet, Elvis. We are at checkpoint Ice and holding. We have eyes on Team Bravo. They're facing away from us, and the noise from the helicopters seems to have masked our approach. I say again, we are undetected. For now."

"Sweet copies all," I said, flooring the pedal.

The Range Rover's V-8 engine roared in response, slamming me into the seat. Unlike some of the luxury faux off-road vehicles marketed to wealthy armchair adventurers, a Range Rover really could hold its own on an African safari. Which was good, because the rainy weather had done a number on the field we were bumping across. The last thing I needed was to get stuck in a mudhole. Though, from the way this operation was unfolding, it would certainly be par for the course.

We were in a precarious position—outmanned, outgunned, and without backup. As of this moment, we still had the element of surprise, but if I didn't give the SEALs clearance to execute soon, we'd lose that too.

The proverbial clock was ticking.

On the other hand, I knew precious little about what was actually happening. I was reasonably sure that an illicit nuclear weapon was in TARKA's warehouse. But once I moved past that assumption, my level of certainty fell off exponentially. I had an educated guess as to the identity of the shooters in the helicopters, but I was loath to start shedding blood on a guess.

Loss of innocent life aside, what if I was reading this wrong? What if the helicopters contained some variant of a Ukrainian quick reaction force sent to secure the weapon? I'd certainly screwed up an operation a time or two, but precipitating a shooting war between two notional allies would be a new one, even for me.

As a paramilitary operative, I lived in a gray zone in which the rules of engagement were malleable and alliances fluid. But we weren't in a dingy Aleppo safe house trying to ascertain whether the militant we were about to drop belonged to al-Qaeda, ISIS, or the Syrian army. A mistake on that scale meant potentially bagging the wrong guy and pissing off a warlord or two.

This decision had world-changing implications.

I couldn't just wing it.

"Axle, Sweet. Any identifiable markings on the helicopters?" I said.

"Sweet, stand by."

I could picture Axle swearing as he shifted his aimpoint from the cockpit to the aircraft themselves. There's nothing a sniper hates more than changing targets after they're already positioned to shoot.

But this wasn't a walk in the park for anyone.

As if to underscore my thoughts, the Range Rover's front wheels crunched into an unseen depression, smashing Ella and me into our seat belts. I added more gas and mentally chastised myself for not turning driving duties over to Ella. Coordinating the pieces of an ongoing operation while steering a moving vehicle was kind of like playing chess while skateboarding.

In other words, less than ideal.

"Right, right, right," Ella said, pointing to the gap in the trees we'd established as our landmark.

I cranked the Range Rover's wheel in response. According to our map recon, the gravel path wound through the woods and ended at the rear of the building.

The trees would give us cover for the time being, but once I hit that gap, we were committed.

"Sweet, Axle. I see yellow and blue circles on both birds. Looks like they're Ukrainian military, over."

Not good.

Axle's comment didn't clarify the tactical situation. In fact, it made everything even more nebulous. The birds weren't Russian, which was something, but the markings denoting them as Ukrainian military were hardly definitive. Sure, the Ukrainian Air Force used those symbols, but so did their National Guard, which was more closely tied to the militia brigades. In a country in which the majority of the politicians from the president on down were on the take, anyone could have rented those birds and their pilots.

Which gave me another idea.

"Axle, Sweet. How about Team Bravo? What are they wearing?"

"Sweet, Axle. Stand by."

I could feel Axle's frustration as he swung his optic to yet another target. Before his devastating injury, Frodo had been a JSOC sniper and my source of distance-shooting lore. He'd always claimed that pressing the trigger was the easiest part of the job.

I was beginning to understand why.

"Sweet, Axle. Dismounts are dressed in a collection of uniforms. Bits and pieces, but no real standardization. I'd say we're looking at a militia, over."

Axle's assessment made sense. A quick reaction force would presumably have come from one of Ukraine's elite units, such as 8th Special Purpose Regiment or Alpha Group. While they might not have nameplates and rank affixed to their shirts, the assaulters would be wearing a consistent uniform. Organizations that had to determine friend from foe in a split second under the stress of combat while looking through an optic were very particular about uniforms. I was still not in a position to make decisions with geopolitical ramifications, but I was pretty certain about one thing: A militia should not have a nuclear weapon.

Things were about to get loud.

"Axle, Sweet. Roger all. Take the pilots. Once pilots are down, shift to Team Bravo. Execute on my go."

"Axle copies all. Standing by."

"Elvis, Sweet. You're in overwatch. If Team Bravo flexes toward the building, intercept. Gal and I are going to kinetically breach the back side of Charlie. Intent is to drive squirters out the green side and into your kill zone. Once we breach, you are cleared hot, over."

"Elvis copies all. Standing by."

"What is a kinetic breach?" Ella said, gripping the dashboard as we careened toward the strand of trees and the warehouse.

"It's a technical term," I said, steering with both hands as the terrain grew rougher. "Two of us against six shooters plus however many are in the warehouse aren't great odds. We need to stack the deck in our favor."

"By flash-banging the room?" Ella said.

"I was thinking more bang and less flash," I said. "We're going to ram the building."

"Sweet Jesus," Ella said, bracing both feet against the floorboard.

"I didn't think Jesus was your kind of Jew," I said.

"Right now Buddha is my kind of Jew," Ella said, clutching the Rattler across her chest with both hands.

I thought Ella's reply was very witty, given the circumstances. I was going to compliment her on her gallows humor, but Frodo interrupted.

"Sweet, Frodo. You got company. Convoy of three vehicles heading west along the northern taxiway toward your location. ETA two mikes, over."

"Frodo, Sweet. Where did they originate, over?"

"Isolated structure at the northern most part of the airfield, over."

The more the merrier, I guess.

"Roger that, Frodo. Anything you can tell us about the occupants?"

"Sensor operator is reviewing the video now. I counted twelve individuals equipped with a mixture of small arms and RPGs. No uniforms, over."

I wrenched the wheel to the left as I threaded through the trees, only to see the building's sheet metal roll-up door just ahead.

The point of no return.

Time seemed to stand still as I thought through Frodo's report. Assuming TARKA had guards in the warehouse, there were three different armed groups converging on the same target. Four if you counted my team. This was now more shoot-out at the OK Corral than coordinated operation.

Aggression and violence of action were the calling cards of successful special operations missions. Even so, there was a fine line between initiative and blindly blundering into a numerically superior force. When that happened, things didn't work out so well for the attackers.

Just ask Custer.

That said, there were times when failure wasn't an option. When you pressed the attack no matter the odds because the idea of not succeeding was too catastrophic to contemplate. Some missions truly were no fail.

Preventing a nuclear war was one of them.

Shifting the Range Rover into neutral, I popped the truck into four-wheel drive and revved the engine. As the crimson rpm needle swung past seven thousand, I slammed the transmission into gear and made a single radio call.

"All elements, this is Sweet. Execute, execute, execute."

FIFTY-FOUR

As planned, the two trucks trailing Pyotr swung right and away from his SUV even as Pyotr slowed down. The pair sped along a path that took them perpendicular to the helicopters and directly in front of the six-man blocking position on the tarmac.

Then the Russians opened fire.

Even Pyotr was impressed with the intensity of the muzzle flashes emanating from the two vehicles. AK-74 barrels sprouted from every available orifice, and the soldier with the PK balanced the weapon on an open windowsill before letting loose. While the quantity of lead being launched into the air was mind-boggling, accuracy was not the group's strong point. In fact, from Pyotr's vantage point, the shooters didn't appear to have hit a thing.

But that was okay.

Pyotr was willing to go toe-to-toe with the invaders

to secure his nuke, but he also knew to temper his expectations. Brave men his impromptu defenders might be, but they were not Spetsnaz or even real soldiers. The chances of cyber warriors and electronic technicians inflicting real harm on the enemy force were close to nil.

In fact, Pyotr put better odds on the ragtag group accidentally shooting one another. This was why Pyotr had devised a role intentionally playing to their strengths. They were to be a distraction. A loud, bright, but mostly harmless distraction.

The real shooter was sitting behind Pyotr and cradling his rocket launcher.

Pyotr gave the pair of vehicles a several-second head start, then stomped on the gas. But where his comrades had turned right, Pyotr swung wide to the left, executing a pincer movement on the six men blocking the taxiway.

Except the shooters on the tarmac were not his target.

Once he'd judged the distance to be suitably close, he slammed on the brakes again.

"Out, out, out!" Pyotr shouted.

Distractions were all well and good, but even they worked for only a finite period of time. His was running out.

The rocketeer set up next to Pyotr, lining up the projectile's key with the launching tube as he mated the pair. Then he knelt, cocked the hammer, and took up a firing position. The closest Hip was turned broadside and only two hundred meters distant. The aircraft was well within the RPG's sighting range.

But was it within the gunner's?

———

The helicopter on the tarmac in front of him exploding was the first sign that the raid was no longer proceeding as Andriy had planned. As signs went, it was pretty powerful. For a moment he sat speechless, watching as flames engulfed his wingman.

Then the warrior in him reacted.

"Up," Andriy said to the pilots, "up, up, up."

To their credit, the aviators didn't question his orders. One moment they were sitting on the ground; the next, Andriy was on a rocket to the moon. The airfield fell away as the pilots turned the aircraft outbound.

"Where are you going?" Andriy said.

"We're leaving."

Unholstering his pistol, Andriy pressed it against the pilot's head.

"We're not leaving until I say we're leaving," Andriy snarled.

FIFTY-FIVE

As a company commander in the Ranger Regiment, I'd always hated giving the execute command. Doctrinally, infantry platoon leaders were expected to be in the thick of the fight, moving forward with the squad in contact while the platoon sergeant coordinated the supporting squads. When your men were in harm's way, you were never more than a step or two behind them.

This was no longer the case once I made captain and was given the opportunity to lead a company. Instead of thirty soldiers under my command, I'd had more than one hundred led by four platoon leaders. Where before I'd cleared a building on the heels of the entry team, I now watched the battle unfold from the sterility of an orbiting helicopter or the passenger seat of an armored all-terrain vehicle.

Listening to radio calls and watching disembodied thermal signatures writhe on the screen as the men entrusted to your care engaged in a visceral fight for survival felt wrong. A thousand times I'd wished that I could somehow be in the stack with them, convinced that I'd still be able to control the strategic battle while lending my own rifle to the tactical fight.

And a thousand times I'd been wrong.

As the Range Rover's black brush guard crunched into the roll-up door's thin aluminum, I realized the enormity of my oversight. Now that I was committed as a gunfighter, no one was controlling the battle.

"Frodo, Sweet," I said. "You have the fight. I say again, you have the fight."

"Sweet, Frodo—"

A high-pitched shriek drowned out Frodo's reply as metal tore from metal.

Then I was in the warehouse proper.

I've been a Dodge Ram man ever since the Hemi came back into production, but I had to admit the Range Rover was growing on me. If Laila ever suggested we get domesticated with a minivan, this little beauty was going to be my counteroffer. The V-8 engine thundered, generating 406 foot-pounds of torque, which powered me over the metal wreckage of the splintered door with admirable agility. Not only that, but the 8,400-candlepower LED-beam headlights snapped on, flooding the dimly lit warehouse with light.

Able to recognize a good idea when I saw one, I applauded the Land Rover's initiative by triggering the high beams, adding an additional 500 luminescence to the dimly lit interior. Still not quite as much candlepower as a flash-bang, but the fifty-five hundred pounds of steel more than made up for that shortcoming.

Time to put it to use.

I turned the wheel hard to the right, rolling off the metal shards and onto the warehouse's cement floor. The auto-leveling headlights compensated for the Range Rover's change in attitude, spotlighting a cluster of men near the exit on the north side of the building. Two of them had their rifles slung and were carrying a large Pelican-case-like trunk between them. The other four were arrayed to either side of the porters, rifles in the low-ready position. Along the edges of the beams, I could see several crumpled bodies, which I imagined had formerly been arms smugglers. But they were not my concern. As my Ranger Regiment first sergeant used to say, *Play stupid games, win stupid prizes.*

Instead, I was focused on the Pelican case.

Which might have been to my detriment.

"Contact right!" Ella screamed, punctuating her comment with a prolonged burst from her Rattler.

The SIG Sauer models we were using sported integrated suppressors, which made the weapon somewhat quieter. But in the Range Rover's tight confines and insulated cabin, the decrease in decibels didn't count for much. On the plus side, the Rattler's powerful report combined with the sound of shattering glass as Ella's rounds punched through the passenger window gave me an audible smack across the face.

Spinning the wheel farther to the right, I floored the gas pedal before steering back to the left. In another

positive for the Range Rover, the SUV cornered a hell of
a lot better than my Dodge Ram. The brush guard's
right edge dealt a glancing blow to a set of shelves, sending who knows what spilling across the floor.

But that was just collateral damage.

Like a bowling ball hooking toward the corner pins, I
swung the Range Rover left into the clump of men even
as I added more power.

The results were satisfactory.

Mostly.

One of the gunmen dodged right to avoid the scything
bumper and got a chest full of 5.56mm slugs, thanks to the
Israeli riding shotgun. His partner wasn't so quick. The
brush guard caught him in the knees, sending his crumpled
body spinning to the right. He wasn't going to be dancing
the flamenco anytime soon, but the force of the impact had
thrown him clear of the Range Rover's churning tires.

The two men carrying the Pelican case weren't so
lucky.

I'd straightened the wheel for a brief second during
my left turn and the Range Rover's bumper crunched
into the first man, throwing him onto the hood. His
partner fared even worse. The brush guard smashed his
hip and he dropped to the ground like a marionette with
its strings cut. The suddenness surprised even me, and
the tires *thump*ed over him before I could have stopped
even if that had been my intention.

It hadn't.

My intention was to grab the Pelican case and get the
hell out of the warehouse before anyone else showed up.

Unfortunately, someone else had the same plan.

"Contract front!" Ella shouted, firing her Rattler through the Range Rover's windshield.

I'd turned the SUV in a half circle so that the hood was now facing the gaping hole I'd created in the rear of the building even as the back end was oriented toward the structure's front door and the fallen Pelican case. Which turned out to be a good thing, since a pair of militia members was now closing on us. I swept my Rattler from the console, thumbed off the safety, centered the holographic crimson dot on a militia member's chest, and snapped off a quick pair even as Ella dropped his partner.

The shock and awe we'd generated with our unorthodox breach was rapidly fading.

Time to get the hell out of Dodge.

"Cover me," I said to Ella as I traded the Rattler for my Glock and bailed out of the SUV.

I skirted along the edge of the vehicle, leading with the pistol as I moved rearward. Rounding the back bumper, I triggered the hatchback with my left hand even as I kept the Glock's front sight post on the jumble of bodies. Three of the men were out of the fight, either dead or unconscious. One was lying on his back, a leg twisted at a grotesque angle. His eyes widened when he saw me, and he reached for his rifle.

My Glock barked three times.

Then it was just me and the Pelican case.

Until Ella's Rattler chattered again.

Sticking the Glock down the back of my pants, I

gripped the nearest hard plastic handle and dragged the case along the floor. As I did, the leather money clip in my right pocket began to vibrate.

I'd found the nuke.

Squatting, I grabbed either side of the case and tried to lift it into the Range Rover.

Mistake.

My back screamed.

Whatever was inside had to be made of dark matter.

Or uranium.

Perhaps the militia members hadn't allocated two men to carry the case just for convenience. I thought about asking Ella for help, but the sound of her Rattler rocking and rolling suggested that she was otherwise occupied. Threading my fingers beneath the corner of the case that was closest to the SUV, I deadlifted half the crate until the edge was even with the bumper. Then I dragged the container toward the Range Rover, my hamstrings burning and traps spasming.

The plastic began to slip through my sweat-soaked fingers just as I drew even with the bumper. With a grunt that would have done the Hulk proud, I slung the Pelican toward the SUV as my core howled. The hardened plastic edge caught on the bumper's lip, precariously balancing on a single scuffed corner.

Ignoring the waves of pain radiating from my lower back, I squatted again, grabbed the handle nearest to the floor, and began to push, driving with my legs. At first, the box refused to move. Then a volley of AK fire smashed into the Range Rover, spraying me with bits of glass and metal. While I wouldn't recommend the practice, getting shot at is a wonderful motivator. My muscles twitched in response to the adrenaline dump, and with another sound that was equal parts curse and scream, I shoved upward.

The box began to move.

For what seemed like an eternity, my world narrowed to just trembling muscles, shuddering breaths, and the crate's infinitesimal progress up the bumper. Inch by agonizing inch, I slid the Pelican up the ramp I'd formed with the bumper until the case's center of gravity shifted and the ramp became a fulcrum.

Then the front of the case swung down, crashing into the SUV's plush interior.

I gave the box a final shove before slamming the hatchback closed, nearly losing my footing in the process. I turned toward the driver's side, but a burst of rifle fire cratered the Range Rover's skin inches from my head. Ducking, I flowed up the opposite side of the SUV to where Ella stood crouching behind the passenger door as she worked her Rattler.

"Get in," I said, slapping her on the back. "You're driving."

In a sign of how far our relationship had progressed, the Mossad officer didn't argue.

Or maybe it was just indicative of how fearful she was for her life.

Either way, the Israeli dove into the Range Rover and wiggled across the seats.

My arms felt like spaghetti and my legs were columns

of jelly. Simply standing was a chore, but I grabbed Ella's Rattler all the same. Fitting the folding stock to my shoulder, I got my first view of the tactical situation through the holographic site.

It wasn't good.

Though Ella had neutralized the immediate threat, I could see two more vehicles approaching through the roll-up door's open frame. As I watched, the passenger in the lead car opened fire and the Range Rover's windshield spiderwebbed to the left of my head. Breaching the building from the rear might have been a grand idea, but we certainly weren't leaving the same way.

Time for an audible.

I slid into the passenger seat, resting the Rattler's short barrel in the gap between the SUV's open door and the doorframe, and began squeezing off aimed pairs at the approaching car.

"Reverse!" I shouted at Ella. "Reverse! Reverse!"

The Israeli slammed the transmission into reverse, spun in her seat, and stomped on the gas. As the Range Rover lurched into motion, I had two very important thoughts. One, popping out of the building unannounced was a good way to wind up in Elvis's or Axle's line of fire.

Two, it had been a very long time since I'd heard from Frodo.

With a start, I realized that I could no longer feel the transmitter nestled in my ear canal. Between me crashing through the building and rolling around on the ground with the Pelican case, the tiny device must have fallen out.

Fortunately, I'd kept better control of my phone.

Taking the cell from my pocket, I activated speaker mode.

"Sweet is exfilling Green side of Charlie, time now," I said. "I say again, two coming out Green side Charlie."

A rush of voices answered my transmission, but the squeal of buckling metal drowned them out for a second time as Ella crashed through the front door. Without the brush guard to distribute the impact's force, the vehicle's frame buckled, sending me smashing against the windshield even as a steel stud tore away my door. A foot more to the left and Ella would have T-boned the support structure, turning us into sitting ducks.

Maybe God really did protect fools, children, and Airborne Rangers.

Unfortunately, my newfound appreciation for the Almighty's benevolence was short-lived. On the positive side of the ledger, we were now clear of the building and relatively unhurt, and we had the nuke in our possession.

The negative side encompassed pretty much everything else.

FIFTY-SIX

I was in the Range Rover's passenger seat, so my first impression as we tore through the front of the building and onto the airfield was a positive one. Like all good commandos, Elvis had exercised a bit of initiative after losing radio coms with me. Rather than waiting at Ice as instructed, he'd moved his two-element team forward to the edge of Charlie, giving them an unobstructed line of sight to Team Bravo.

Judging by the muzzle flashes from his vehicles, he was putting this excellent field of fire to use by decimating what was left of the six-man blocking position still occupying that taxiway. It was exactly what I would have done in his position. If he and his team kept executing on this level, I might have to rethink my repertoire of SEAL jokes.

Or not.

As Frodo liked to remind me, life-altering decisions should never be made in the middle of a firefight. In any case, the good news was that the Team Alpha members in the warehouse were mostly out of commission, and Elvis and the boys had done a bang-up job with Team Bravo. Of the original six-man force, two were lying on the ground unmoving, and one was doing the funky chicken, which meant he was on his way to becoming unmoving. The remaining three were hunkered down on the pavement.

The SEALs had been busy.

Maybe a bit too busy.

After catching sight of Elvis and the boys, I noticed that a towering inferno had taken the place of one of the helicopters.

And we were barreling straight toward it.

"Stop," I said to Ella. "Stop, stop, stop."

She slammed on the brakes, bringing the Range Rover to a skidding halt closer to the helicopter-shaped fireball than I would have liked.

Then she looked at me.

Which was a problem.

Because she'd stopped neatly between the three remaining and rather pissed-off members of Team Bravo and our SEALs. Elvis and his fellow commandos no longer had clean shots at the bad guys.

The same couldn't be said of Team Bravo.

Rather than thanking us for saving them from the SEALs, Team Bravo's surviving members opened fire.

At us.

"Go, go, go!" I yelled, even as I leaned around Ella into the backseat, squeezing off rounds at the prone men.

"First stop, then go!" Ella yelled back. "Make up your mind."

I thought about reminding the Israeli that no one liked a smart-ass, but didn't. Mostly because all of my concentration was focused on the holographic sight.

Besides, Ella was doing fine without further encouragement from me. Wrenching the transmission into drive, she spun the wheel and hammered the gas. The SUV roared, and we shot toward the SEALs, though not quite as agilely as before. I'd like to believe this was because Ella was not near the wheelman I was, but it probably had something to do with the fact that at least one of our tires was flat and steam was venting through the SUV's perforated hood.

But that was okay.

Less than one hundred meters separated us from Elvis's overwatch position. We had it made in the shade. And that was about the time that the little voice that had been whispering in the back of my mind finally got my attention. I'd been so dumbfounded at the sight of a burning helicopter on the other side of the warehouse, I'd neglected to ask a fairly important question.

Where was the second helicopter?

Fortunately, I didn't have to devote a ton of brainpower to the answer. I caught motion in my peripheral vision and looked right. Streaking down from the heavens was a sight that had birthed fear into the hearts of many a battle-hardened mujahideen.

An angry Mi-8 Hip.

As I stared, the oblong canister mounted to the helicopter's inboard hard point began to flash.

"Swerve," I said, pointing at the diving gunship. "Swerve!"

Up until this point, Ella's language skills had been impeccable. Whether she had been verbally jousting with me during the poster-board session or precisely executing my tactical instructions during the warehouse breach, I never thought twice about her not being a native English speaker.

But that was then.

Now, with rifle rounds pinging off the Range Rover's frame, an aviation-gas-fueled fireball behind us, and Elvis and his fellow SEALs laying down suppressive fire in front of us, my command didn't seem to translate.

"Serve?" Ella said.

I reached across the cabin one-handed, stretching for the steering wheel.

I was too late.

Metal screamed and glass shattered as 20mm rounds tore into the vehicle like a Texas hailstorm, cratering the hood and destroying the windshield. The steam that had been escaping from the radiator in scattered wisps erupted into a full-fledged geyser, shrieking in a multihued cloud of engine oil, antifreeze, and good old-fashioned gasoline. The eight cylinders that had so faithfully powered us through muddy fields and building debris with equal vigor gave up the ghost in a spasm of metal grinding on metal like fingernails on a chalkboard.

But it was a much subtler sound that caused my heart to stutter.

The deep *thunk* of a bullet striking flesh.

Ella gurgled and limply slid down into her seat, hands falling from the steering wheel. Flecks of blood colored her lips as a tide of wetness spread across her blouse.

It was happening.

Again.

Dropping the Rattler, I leaned across the cabin to triage Ella, abandoning everything I'd ever been taught in the process. Or maybe not. In combat, wounded were never cared for until the enemy was subdued. To do otherwise was to put the mission at risk for the individual. But what if the mission was the individual? What if I had no intention of going home with another teammate's death on my conscience?

What then?

My probing fingers found puckered flesh just below Ella's right shoulder. She screamed when I touched the bullet wound, but I let out a cry for a different reason. The projectile had entered below the shoulder bone but above the chest cavity. I couldn't be sure of the trajectory, but my preliminary assessment was that the injury was survivable.

If she received medical attention in time.

Reaching for the med kit attached to her plate carrier, I ripped it open, found the Celox applicator, and shoved it into the entry wound. Ella cried out, her hands flailing against my arm as she tried to push away the pain. I tucked my chin to my chest, weathering the storm while injecting six grams of quick-clotting granules directly into the bullet channel.

Ella's body went rigid, and her teeth snapped together like she'd grabbed hold of a live wire. The pain had to be god-awful, but the miracle bandage would expand into the wound and stop the bleeding.

Mostly.

In a perfect world, I'd check her for exit wounds and administer the same treatment.

There wasn't time.

A shadow fell across Ella's face. Turning, I saw the Mi-8 banking steeply to the right as it thundered overhead. Its spindly landing gear and bulky exterior stores still brought to mind a poorly constructed child's toy, but after Ella's injury I didn't need further convincing of the aircraft's deadly nature. Undoubtedly, the pilots were lining up for another gun run to finish what they'd started.

I didn't intend to give them the chance.

Sliding into Ella's seat, I shouldered the driver's door, doing my best to keep my weight off her broken body. In a first, the door glided open as if on well-oiled hinges, sending me tumbling to the tarmac. I turned as I fell, landing on my back instead of on my head, but my relief was still short-lived.

In keeping with today's events, the overcast sky had cleared slightly, but it was enough. Four winged shapes broke through the cloud cover, their gray color and fuzzy outlines reminding me of a school of whales moving just below the ocean's surface. I had about a second to wonder why a formation of transports would be overflying the airfield. Then the airplanes began disgorging tiny shapes, like bits of fluff blowing from a dandelion.

Fluff attached to a silk canopy.

Paratroopers.

The gray sky was filling with paratroopers.

For fuck's sake.

FIFTY-SEVEN

The Il-76's rear clamshell doors opened with a metallic whine that Aleksandr had always associated with the sound of a closing coffin. A blast of fresh air filled the cargo area, stirring up the smell of vomit and other less savory items. Though Aleksandr had jumped only a handful of times, he'd already concluded that the pilots and crew conspired to make the aircraft as inhospitable as possible during the flight to the drop zone. What better way to ensure that the paratroopers were eager to exit when the time came? Though Aleksandr wasn't so sure this axiom held true when exiting the beckoning doors meant entering combat.

Either way, he was about to find out.

Suddenly Aleksandr had thousands of questions about details he should have clarified. Did he remember the rally point's location? Should he lower the case with his weapon or ride it to the ground as the veterans suggested? Had he remembered to check his reserve?

Panic gripped Aleksandr's chest with icy fingers. He leaned forward, intending to blast his questions at his squad leader in rapid fire, but the lamps mounted to the bulkhead turned green and the horn sounded.

Aleksandr stood with the rest of his stick, the motions coming automatically.

Hook up to the static line.

Check the static line.

Check your equipment.

Check your helmet.

Then the column was moving.

Like a stack of dominoes dropping one by one, each paratrooper shuffled toward the gaping opening at the rear of the plane before disappearing into the void. Aleksandr thought about his mother and Polina's perfume-scented letters. Then the slipstream's hungry fingers curled around him, flapping his trousers and threatening to strip his gear from his body.

He looked at the static line above him a final time.

Everything seemed in order.

Almost everything.

The case. In the adrenaline-soaked excitement, he'd completely forgotten about the case. He'd never jumped with one before. Was there something special he needed to do prior to exiting the aircraft? What if it came loose or, worse, got tangled in his chute?

Aleksandr frantically tried to recall the ten-minute

block of instruction his squad leader had given him before they'd boarded the plane, but the sight of open sky and the sound of the howling wind overwhelmed his senses.

The paratrooper in front of Aleksandr disappeared into the void.

Now it was his turn.

Frantic with terror, Aleksandr turned toward the jumpmaster standing at the door's threshold. Surely he could ask just one question. One tiny clarification on the case's placement before jumping.

Two seconds was all that he needed.

Three tops.

But if time and tide waited for no man, neither did a jumpmaster supervising a combat jump. Aleksandr hesitated at the door's threshold, turning toward the veteran's grizzled face, a question on his lips. The jumpmaster had other ideas. Grabbing Aleksandr by the harness, the giant yanked the reluctant paratrooper forward and the hungry slipstream did the rest.

One second, Aleksandr was in the IL-76's metal confines.

The next, his knees were in the breeze.

Aleksandr always found the sudden quiet surprising. The constant roar of the IL-76's four Soloviev D-30 engines, the curses and groans as the paratroopers exited the aircraft, the thundering wind during the brief seconds of free fall, and the *snap* of the canopy inflating all made parachuting a noisy business. But once his parachute fully inflated, a blissful silence enveloped Aleksandr. Though the creaking of gear and the occasional curses from fellow sky soldiers still carried through the air, they came as though from a great distance. If he closed his eyes, Aleksandr could pretend that the breeze in his face and the crackling white nylon above him were the sole components of his solitary universe.

Usually.

But apparently combat jumps were different.

The lack of soothing quiet was the first difference. Rather than the familiar but soft sounds of chutes snapping in the wind and the murmur of voices, something much less pastoral demanded his attention.

Gunfire.

Lots of it.

Looking past his scuffed boots, Aleksandr surveyed the scene beneath him for the first time. Like in the rehearsal brief for what was supposed to be a live-fire exercise, the drop zone was an airfield. But this was where the similarities ended. Rather than movable wooden buildings that contained shoot houses populated by inanimate targets, Aleksandr saw significant activity on the western side of the airfield.

The side his platoon was assigned to secure.

The cluster of buildings and taxiways was as they'd been depicted in the terrain model his squad had studied, which led Aleksandr to believe that perhaps this mission had been planned for a bit longer than his squad leader had led on. But rather than empty tarmac, the concrete was swarming with groups of men doing their best to kill one another.

As Aleksandr watched, two vehicles moved from the west, taking a team of dismounted troops on the east under fire. Between them stood a roiling wall of flames consuming what had once been a helicopter.

To the south, vehicles were maneuvering around the target building just as a truck crashed through the building's northern wall to the sound of bending metal and breaking glass. Though Aleksandr was far from a tactician, even with his short time in the military, he could tell that the scene below was a giant free-for-all in which bullets were indiscriminately flying in every direction.

And he was drifting right toward the thick of it.

Hauling on his risers, Aleksandr steered his chute away from the chaos and sheets of flame, aiming for the hard-packed dirt to the north of the active runway and southeast of the target building. Landing there would give him more ground to cover to reach the rally point, but it would also keep him clear of the fire's grasping fingers or the swarms of unseen bullets filleting the air.

He was partially successful.

A more experienced paratrooper would have known the effect thermals exerted on men falling from the sky under nylon canopies. In the same way that rising hot air allowed a hawk to circle a parking lot for hours without flapping its wings, invisible pockets of unstable air meant that Aleksandr had less control over his descent than he thought.

One instant, he was on a stable glide path to the inviting field.

The next, he was in a free-falling elevator.

Aleksandr had just enough time to voice one of the more inventive expletives he'd learned from Junior Sergeant Semenov.

Then his boots met pavement at 5.8 meters per second.

FIFTY-EIGHT

As a rule, military parachute jumps do not end with pleasant landings. This was because, unlike civilian canopies, which were designed to reintroduce their passengers to Mother Earth with the softest of kisses, military chutes were built with something else in mind.

Time.

Or, more accurately, minimizing the amount of time a paratrooper hung helplessly from his parachute while drifting through enemy-controlled airspace. A paratrooper on the ground, united with his brothers and equipment, was a fearsome weapon to behold.

A paratrooper dangling from a wind-filled silk sheet was good for just one thing—target practice.

To reduce a paratrooper's exposure to ground and air fire, military chutes were meant to safely transition a soldier through the period of vulnerability as quickly as possible. For a Russian sky soldier, this meant that landing was the equivalent of jumping from a 3.5-meter platform while loaded with equipment.

By anyone's measure, the deceleration that occurred when an object traveling at this not-insubstantial velocity met the unforgiving ground was significant. The resulting collision generated more than enough force to break bones. To help mitigate this physics problem, paratroopers the world over used two techniques: one, some version of a parachute landing fall designed to distribute the force generated by impact across the soldier's entire body instead of just his feet; two, target a landing zone that was soft enough to offer some cushion of its own.

In other words, not concrete.

Aleksandr piled into the ground with the finesse of a bowling ball rolling off of a table. To his instructor's credit, Aleksandr executed the Russian version of a parachute-landing fall perfectly. Maybe a bit too perfectly. Keeping his knees together, Aleksandr hit feetfirst before flopping backward, taking the brunt of the impact along the thicker muscles of his thighs, buttocks, and back.

Unfortunately, he forgot about the newly added canvas-and-plastic case.

Instead of slapping the ground and dissipating the energy as he'd been taught, Aleksandr pivoted across the case, whiplashing his head against the concrete. His helmet kept Aleksandr from splitting his skull, but the collision still rung his bell. For a long moment, Aleksandr lay sprawled against the cement, contemplating the sky.

Then a helicopter thundered overhead.

A helicopter spitting rockets and cannon fire from its stubby pylons.

Suddenly Aleksandr's pounding head wasn't such a concern.

Getting unsteadily to his feet, Aleksandr popped his chute loose and then unslung the case. Undoing the closest zipper, Aleksandr dug his folding-stock AK-74 free. Racking the bolt to chamber a round, Aleksandr took a moment to survey the situation.

Unlike the majority of his stick, Aleksandr's last-minute course change had landed him about two hundred meters away from the intended point of impact. This meant that he had a clear view of his comrades forming up into fire teams as they prepared to move toward the rally point.

And an even clearer view of the helicopter banking over as it pointed its bulbous nose at the little formation. For a moment, Aleksandr held out hope that the Mi-8 was a friendly. Then he saw the Ukrainian markings at about the same time the pilot launched another salvo of rockets targeting the clumped paratroopers.

The projectiles detonated in clusters of fire, throwing soil and bodies skyward with equal vigor. The concussions hammered against Aleksandr's chest, staggering him even as the stinging acrid smoke brought tears to his eyes.

Whipping away the grit and grime, Aleksandr got his first look at the aftermath.

No one was still upright. As Aleksandr watched, Junior Sergeant Semenov and another comrade staggered unsteadily to their feet. Two more paratroopers were on the ground thrashing, while the remaining four were sprawled lifelessly across the concrete. In that moment, a rage engulfed Aleksandr, making the anger he'd felt for Mikhail seem like a candle next to a bonfire. His squad mates, his fellow paratroopers, his . . . brothers . . . were dying, and there was nothing Aleksandr could do.

Or was there?

As the helicopter pirouetted overhead, lining up for another gun run, Aleksandr remembered the source of his aching head.

The canvas case.

But more than that, Aleksandr recalled the case's purpose.

Unzipping the larger compartment, Aleksandr withdrew the contents and rendered the device operational with quick, efficient motions, hearing Semenov's booming voice reciting the instructions in his head. As the lumbering bird of prey settled into its attack trajectory, Aleksandr elevated the tube, centered the sight on the helicopter, heard the tone, and squeezed the trigger.

For a moment, nothing happened.

Then the tube belched a Strela missile in a puff of smoke.

Andriy watched the chaos unfolding outside the Hip's bullet-pockmarked cockpit, still trying to understand what exactly was happening. Russian paratroopers were landing at the airfield. How could this be?

"What now, Comrade General?" the pilot said, his voice shaking.

What indeed?

His boys from Opishnya were on the ground fighting and dying. The nuke was beyond his reach. Everything Andriy had set out to do was turning to ash before his eyes.

He was helpless.

No, that wasn't true.

Andriy was in a command of a helicopter that still had ammunition. What was it that the famous American general had said? When in doubt, attack.

Andriy intended to do just that.

"Turn back inbound and target that group," Andriy said to the pilot, indicating a cluster of paratroopers massing next to the warehouse.

"Comrade, we cannot stop this many soldiers!" the pilot yelled. "We must break contact!"

The pistol's report was surprisingly loud, given the ambient noise flooding the cabin. One moment, the pilot had been screaming at Andriy. The next, he was slumped in his seat, his previously indignant face now splattered across the glass.

Turning, Andriy pointed his pistol at the copilot.

"We will break contact when I say we will break contact. Questions?"

"No, Comrade General," the copilot said.

"Excellent," Andriy said. "Now turn inbound and strafe those paratroopers."

The copilot readily complied, banking the helicopter

over on its side. The aviator began firing salvos of rockets as soon as his wings rolled level. Andriy smiled in spite of himself, taking joy from the smoke trails streaking from his aircraft like death's sooty fingers.

Then a sooty finger was pointing back at him.

The missile streaked toward the helicopter, a hound chasing a rabbit. The pilot must have seen the threat, because the Mi-8 nosed over while turning to the left, perhaps attempting to hide the hot gases exhausting from the aircraft's twin-turbine engines.

The maneuver didn't work.

Like a sprinter approaching the finish line, the missile seemed to gather itself in midflight before snapping to the left, its hungry seeker head adjusting for the helicopter's changing course at mind-numbing speed. One moment, the Strela was angling toward the Hip.

The next, the missile detonated in a flash of orange fire just beneath the rotor.

No sooner had the thunderclap from the exploding missile reached Aleksandr than he saw a second, much larger flash. This time the explosion enveloped the entire aircraft. The helicopter shuddered once, then dropped from the sky like a stone, trailing flames all the way to the ground. The Hip impacted the earth with a horrible finality. An undulating sea of fire washed over the helicopter until only clouds of thick, greasy smoke remained.

With a start, Aleksandr realized he was still holding the empty launcher. Dropping the tube, he turned back to the rally point only to see Sergeant Semenov on his feet, beckoning. Unshouldering his rifle, Aleksandr snapped the folding stock into place and ran toward his brothers.

For the first time, Aleksandr understood exactly why he'd joined the paratroopers.

FIFTY-NINE

Russian paratroopers were jumping onto an airfield overrun with Russian and Ukrainian shooters, and an Mi-8 gunship had just been blown out of the sky. My Israeli counterpart was grievously wounded, and my SEAL QRF was decisively engaged and probably running low on ammunition. Oh, yeah, and I had a nuclear bomb stuck in a truck that wouldn't run.

This was a low point, to be sure.

In fact, unless the bomb spontaneously detonated, I didn't see how things could get any worse.

"Matt, Frodo. The safe house is under attack. I say again, safe house is under attack."

Oh, sweet Jesus.

"Frodo, hold on, brother. We're coming."

"Hurry, Matty."

I tried to reply, but a burst of automatic weapons fire came across the line. Then nothing but silence. Digging the phone out of my pocket, I looked at the screen only to have my fears confirmed.

The connection had dropped.

The enormity of what that signified crashed over me in a wave of emotion. I wanted to tear out my hair, pound the pavement, or howl at the moon.

I did none of those things.

Instead, I got to my feet, pulled Ella from the Range Rover, and threw her limp body over my shoulder. Then I stripped a signal flare from my vest and ignited it one-handed.

A red flame shot from the stick like a miniature Roman candle.

Turning, I tossed the flare onto the SUV's fuel-soaked hood.

The gas caught with a *whoosh* that singed my arm hair.

Stumbling away, I made for Elvis and the SEALs with a blast furnace at my back. Understanding my intent, Elvis's SUV surged forward even as Happy, Cajun, and Red poured on covering fire. I sprinted for the oncoming vehicle with more than just the fear of rifle rounds driving me forward. I was about as far from being a nuclear weapons expert as possible, but I did understand one critical piece of information. Nukes rely on conventional explosives to generate the shock wave necessary to compress the fissile material into achieving critical mass. Take away the explosives, and you take away the bomb's ability to detonate.

As I'd once tried to explain to my mother, sometimes fire really was the answer to life's problems.

Of course, the fly in the ointment was that fire affects explosives in one of two ways. The flame can either consume the energetics or ignite them. I was praying for consume. If we went the ignite route, there was a chance radioactive material would be blown all over the runway.

And me.

Then again, no plan was perfect.

In another bit of luck, the flaming pyre that had once been my trusty Land Rover seemed to be a magnet for the rest of the airfield's combatants.

Not to mention the hundreds of paratroopers landing across the runway.

Elvis's SUV roared up beside me, both doors opening before the vehicle stopped. Cajun leapt from the driver's seat, helping me get Ella in the rear cabin as Elvis stood tall at the front of the SUV, shielding me with his own body. The SEAL team leader smoothly executed a magazine change and continued to lay down suppressive fire, alternating between the remains of Team Bravo and the Russian SUVs rounding the side of the warehouse.

"Got her," Cajun said, following Ella into the Range Rover.

I slapped Elvis on the shoulder and jumped into the front passenger seat as he slid across to the driver's seat. A shadow passed overhead as I was closing the passenger door. Looking up, I saw several BRDM fighting vehicles floating down under multiple parachutes.

The Russians had come ready for a fight—that was for damn sure.

But the airfield was no longer my problem.

I'd done what I could to save Ukraine and the rest of Europe. I was now focused on just two things: the Israeli gasping for breath in the seat behind me, and the phone in my pocket. The phone linking me to my best friend.

"Go, go, go," I said, slamming my door. "Head for the rally point. Elvis, tell Axle we're egressing. I'm gonna try to reestablish coms with Frodo."

Digging out the cell, I hit redial and held the mobile to my ear.

Elvis floored the accelerator even as he relayed my instructions to Happy and Red as well as to Axle and his spotter, Slice. Behind me, Cajun was frantically triaging Ella. He'd already torn away her plate carrier and most of her shirt and was in the process of running his hands down her back, presumably searching for an exit wound.

I wanted to ask if she was all right.

I wanted to see what was going on behind us.

I wanted to strategize with Elvis.

I couldn't do any of those things.

Instead, I listened to the sound of a ringing phone.

Once.

Twice.

Three times.

On the sixth ring, someone picked up.

Frodo's voice mail.

"Fuck," I said, pounding my fist against the Range Rover's roof. "Fuck, fuck, fuck."

"What now?" Elvis said.

We were bouncing across the field bordering the western edge of the airfield, retracing the route Elvis had used to enter the air base. The perimeter fence loomed just ahead. Once through, we'd link up with Axle and Slice and our convoy would number three.

Then I'd have to make a decision.

The safe house was on the other side of town, but the DIA logisticians had chosen the industrial complex for more than just its remote location. In addition to its isolation, the safe house could be accessed by only a single west–east-running road that was more potholes than pavement. The road's disrepair necessitated a slower rate of travel, meaning that it would take double the usual time to cover the five-kilometer stretch leading to a larger north–south-running thoroughfare that in turn eventually spilled into one of the main traffic arteries.

The choice before me was simple.

If I thought Frodo was still at the safe house, we needed to turn left at the next intersection. But if I believed he'd been taken by the assaulters, I could turn right and exploit the road's poor condition by paralleling it at a much faster pace. In theory, this might allow me to get ahead of Frodo's kidnappers and stage an interdiction before they hit the larger thoroughfare and vanished.

I closed my eyes, blocking out everything as I thought. Frodo hadn't answered his phone, which meant he was in trouble. But that trouble could equate to a wide range of scenarios. In one possible outcome, Frodo had held his own against the attackers, but had been gravely wounded during the fight. If that was the case and I turned right, he might succumb to his injuries before I realized my mistake and doubled back.

But if I turned left and he'd been captured, I'd lose my one chance at saving him, no matter how remote. The Russians had just staged an airborne operation undoubtedly to establish a bridgehead for a larger follow-on invasion force. I might have dealt with the nuclear weapon, but this country was still a powder keg.

If Frodo's attackers were a Spetsnaz squad and they were able to link up with either the paratroopers occupying the air base or the main body of the Russian invasion force, it would take more than just a handful of SEALs and an ex-Ranger to get him back.

In fact, capture by Russian commandos was probably just a delayed death sentence. Once the Spetsnaz extracted whatever they were after from Frodo, he'd instantly become a liability. Russia had gone to great lengths to ensure that their invasion looked like a reaction to the chaos enveloping Ukraine instead of its cause. This narrative would go up in smoke if an American operative was allowed to tell the story of his capture and torture at the hands of Russian Little Green Men.

My decision was life or death no matter how I viewed it.

Frodo's life or death.

"Which way?" Elvis said. "Left or right?"

"How's Gal?" I said to Cajun.

"Stable," he said, even as he hung an IV from the handle above the door, "but critical. The round that got her must have been a fragment or ricochet. A direct hit from that gunship's cannon would have torn her arm clean off. She's got time, but not much."

I welcomed the good news, but it didn't make my choice any easier.

Left or right?

Heaven or hell?

Live or die?

Why did everything in my life always seem to come down to a coin toss?

"Right," I said to Elvis. "Tell your boys to reload and refit. We're going to war."

SIXTY

"Where we setting up?" Elvis said, yelling over the Range Rover's roar.

In another revelation that made me reassess my view of the universe and everything in it, SEALs were apparently good at more than just playing Call of Duty and drinking beer. For instance, Elvis was driving the shit out of our SUV.

Once I'd explained my plan, he'd dropped the hammer and not let up yet. Since turning right, I hadn't seen the speedometer drop below one hundred and fifty kilometers per hour. And that was saying something on these half-assed Ukrainian roads. But our speed came at a price. The time I had to figure out where we were going to interdict the Russian kill team was rapidly diminishing.

"Head east for at least another five klicks," I said, doing the time-distance math in my head. "Then look for a spot to stage. I need to make a call."

While I was ever so cautiously arriving at a new appreciation for my naval brethren's skills, I would rather have surrendered my Ranger tab than delegated responsibility for picking a kill zone to a frogman. Sure, Elvis could swim and grow a great beard, but he wasn't an infantryman. My forefathers had been laying out L-shaped ambushes while his had still been snorting helium and making funny voices.

Or whatever it was tadpoles did for fun.

The point was that just because I was beginning to think that Elvis and his boys were fairly competent commandos did not mean I was ready to hand them the keys to the kingdom. Unfortunately, I didn't have a whole lot of choice. My assertions to the contrary, the sum of my plan could not be to set up an ambush and hope that Frodo and his Russian kidnappers stumbled into it. For this to work, I needed intelligence.

The actionable kind.

Staring at my cell, I thought about who to call. The Russian whose conscience had cost him his father? As much as I hated to admit it, James was half right about Nolan's son. An asset doesn't get to dictate the terms of the relationship with their handler.

Not ever.

Now that the shock of Nolan's death had worn off, I had to imagine that there was hate smoldering inside his son. A hate I could stoke into an open flame. Given enough time, I'd worm my way into the GRU officer's head and make him my asset.

It was what I did.

But while I was damn good at my job, I also had a realistic assessment of my abilities. Recruiting an asset was a courtship that took finesse and guile.

I had time for neither.

Besides, what if against all odds I somehow recruited him with a single phone call? How could a GRU officer who protected scientists for a living provide me with the location of a Spetsnaz kill team in Ukraine or the means to track them? The GRU officer was worth revisiting at a later date, but he wasn't going to help me in the next ten minutes.

Which was to say he was useless.

My second choice had all kinds of assets as his disposal. And what James Scott Glass didn't have, he was more than willing to steal. But again, the clock was ticking. Though the chief was a force to be reckoned with, man tracking was not his expertise. He'd need time to work the telephone, twisting arms and calling in markers.

Time that Frodo didn't have.

Which left my third choice.

In some ways it was the most obvious option, but also the most horrific. No one in their position should ever receive the call I was about to place. But I was out of alternatives, and we were running out of road.

It was now or never.

I looked at the clock and did the time conversion. Probably still at the office, which meant their cell would be tucked in a wooden shelf somewhere outside the SCIF. Which was a problem, because I didn't have an office number, and their place of employment wasn't the kind of organization that published a phone directory.

Or maybe it did.

James had made a promise to stand up a fusion cell for the duration of this mission. One operating continuously, twenty-four hours a day, seven days a week. Except that government employees sometimes took a dim view of the words *continuous operation*. Especially employees who worked in massive cubical farms for sprawling bureaucracies. Folks who'd never served on the pointy end of the spear and for whom a bad day at the office meant that the in-house Starbucks was out of pumpkin spice.

While the person I intended to call didn't fall into this bucket, the folks manning the phones very well might. Here's to hoping that, in this instance, a career civil service employee would match the dedication of his private sector comrade.

I keyed a DIA telephone number and pressed send.

The phone rang.

Once.

Twice.

Three times.

I was revising the definition of *continuous operation* when the call was abruptly answered.

"Hello."

I said a name.

"Just a minute."

A moment later, a familiar voice came on the line.

"Katherine speaking."

"Katherine, it's Matt," I said. "Frodo's in trouble."

SIXTY-ONE

A sharp intake of breath greeted my proclamation.

I pictured Katherine on the other end of the phone, hearing the news that every significant other dreads. After meeting her just once, I'd understood why Frodo had been taken with her. A slim African American woman with warm eyes, shoulder-length hair, and a contagious laugh, Katherine was both smart and pretty. But more than that, she projected a sense of calm steadiness. Like Laila, Katherine seemed to understand that her man's past had shaped him, and she accepted it all—both the good and the bad.

Now I was about to put that acceptance to the test.

"How can I help?" Katherine said.

Her voice was a bit shaky, but I could hear the resolve in her tone.

Frodo had chosen well.

Or maybe it was the other way around.

"I think a Spetsnaz direct action team has Frodo. I need to be able to track them so we can interdict. Lock down this phone so you know where we are. Then find the Russians and vector me to them."

"Okay," Katherine said, her voice a little less steady, "give me a sec."

I could hear the questions lurking behind her words. Lots of them. Questions she desperately wanted to ask, but knew she couldn't. Or perhaps she was terrified I might actually answer them. Either way, the sound of clicking filled the line as she pounded at her keyboard.

"Next exit is just ahead," Elvis said. "We staying or going?"

The road we were following had been steadily winding up a series of foothills. As we came around the final S-turn, the pavement straightened for a fifty-meter west–east-running stretch before emptying into a two-lane bridge spanning a river several hundred feet below. The south side of the road had a rest area featuring several picnic tables, a couple of benches, and restrooms—all of which abutted a scenic overlook just west of the bridge.

To the north was a sheer drop-off bounded by flimsy-looking guardrails. The exit Elvis was referencing sat on the far, eastern side of the bridge. I knew from my map recon that the off-ramp led back to the valley floor and a traffic artery that serviced three major thoroughfares.

If the Russians made it to the off-ramp, they were gone.

"Pull into the rest area," I said, putting Katherine on mute as a plan came together. "We'll take 'em here. Send

Axle and Slice to high ground. Have Red and Happy follow us into the pull-off. We're going to need to cross-load vehicles and brief the plan."

"Tracking," Elvis said. He steered into the rest area as he issued instructions to the team, never letting up on the gas.

Taking the phone off mute, I put the handset back to my ear.

"Katherine? Where are we?"

"Sorry," Katherine said. "I was running the raw SIGINT data I've been collecting from your area of operations through a couple of machine-learning algorithms. Russian cyber teams have completely compromised Ukraine's communications infrastructure. The Spetsnaz operatives can mask their digital footprints by routing everything through Ukrainian servers and cell hubs. I've got some promising anomalies, but it's going to take the computers a bit to churn through the background noise. I can probably have something in thirty minutes."

"Katherine," I said tempering my voice to keep the message as emotionless as possible, "I have maybe five minutes. Probably less. If you can't give me something before then, Frodo's gone."

"Okay, okay. Give me a minute."

"One minute," I said, and then put the phone on mute.

As I'd been talking with Katherine, Happy and Red had pulled up beside me and hopped out of their vehicle. Elvis was standing to my right with his phone on speaker to loop Axle and Slice in.

"Cajun," I said to the medic behind me, "what's Gal's status?"

"Stable," Cajun said. "But she's gonna need a surgeon. Soon."

"Good," I said. "Then hop out. I need your rifle."

The SEAL obliged. Then there were four frogmen staring at me. Between us we had had three M4s, my Rattler, and Red's belt-fed M249 Squad Automatic Weapon, or SAW, plus the snipers' long guns. As ambush firepower went, it wasn't a lot.

It would have to do.

"Okay," I said, "who's done a vehicle interdiction before?"

The SEALs looked uneasily at one another for a beat before Axle chimed in from the phone.

"We know the basics," Axle said. "But it's not one of our normal mission sets. Maybe you could give us a quick refresher?"

I smiled even as my stomach sank.

Vehicle interdictions were one of the most difficult battle drills to execute. Back in the nineties, Delta Force operators had practiced them extensively before deploying to Bosnia. Even so, I'd heard from veterans who'd been there that the tactics had failed more times than they'd succeeded. Frodo's generation of warriors had improved upon those early tactics, techniques, and procedures, or TTPs, as part of the Unit's never-ending deployments to Iraq, but a successful interdiction still took detailed planning and dozens of rehearsals.

We had time for neither.

"No worries," I said. "Here's how it's gonna go. We'll be broken down into three elements. Snipers, assault team, and support team. Assault team will be me, Elvis, Red, and Happy. Cajun, you're going solo in the vehicle with Gal. Tracking?"

"Shouldn't Cajun have another shooter for security?" Elvis said.

"Absolutely," I said. "But we don't have the bodies. It's gonna take you, me, and Happy to clear the target vehicle."

"What about Red?" Elvis said.

"Red here is the linchpin to the whole operation," I said with an even wider smile. "His ass is gonna be right next to mine. Okay?"

I could tell from Elvis's expression it wasn't okay.

Too damned bad.

If we were about to go swimming, I'd defer to the frogmen. But we were in my world, and I was calling the shots. To his credit, Elvis nodded, keeping his thoughts to himself just like a good leader should.

If I wasn't careful, I might start to like this guy.

"Okay," I said, "we'll assume the Russians are traveling in a multivehicle convoy. If that's the case, the precious cargo will always be in the rear seat of the second vehicle. Probably that right rear passenger seat. Tracking?"

The SEALs nodded.

"Good," I said. "The key to pulling this off is to slow or stop the lead vehicle."

"With the snipers?" Elvis said.

I shook my head. "Axle and Slice are hell on wheels, but trying to shoot through a vehicle's windshield at sixty miles an hour is a nonstarter."

"He's right," Axle said. "The bullets will fracture as they pass through the glass. We'd need to put five or six rounds into each occupant just to achieve target effect. Won't work."

"Then how?" Elvis said.

"Whatcha shooting in that SAW?" I said, turning to Red.

"Green tips," Red said.

"My man," I said, squeezing Red's shoulder.

Green-tipped 5.56 rounds had a steel core designed to penetrate light armor.

Perfect for what I had in mind.

"Red's going to initiate on my mark," I said, turning to the team's most junior member. "Hose the shit out of that lead vehicle. Start with the engine block and work your way back through the passenger cabin. Everyone in the lead vehicle dies. Everyone. Got it?"

Red gave a quick nod. His bravado from our first interaction was long gone.

Combat had a way of doing that.

"Good," I said. "After that, transition to any vehicles behind number two. Everyone dies in those as well. Cajun, any squirters from the rear vehicles are your responsibility. Put them down hard and fast. Otherwise, the Russians will flank us. If that happens, we'll be up shit's creek without a paddle. Tracking?"

"Like a bloodhound," Cajun said. His words came

out long and slow, revealing the accent for which he was named.

"Final piece is us," I said, looking between Elvis and Happy. "We're gonna execute as the lead vehicle comes out of that hairpin turn. The curve in the road will slow it down some. Before he accelerates again, Red'll light him up. If we're lucky, we'll get a collision between the first and second vehicles. Either way, the second vehicle has to slow down to avoid hitting the first. When that happens, we ram the son of a bitch with our SUV. Elvis drives, Happy in the right front passenger seat. I'll be in the left rear passenger seat. Elvis and Happy have the front half of the number two car, the target car. I've got the rear. Angle your shots accordingly. If we accidentally kill the precious cargo, this is all for nothing. Okay?"

Elvis and Happy nodded.

"Red," I said, transitioning back to the SAW gunner, "make sure you shift to the rear vehicle on my mark. Otherwise, you risk hitting us as we assault through the kill zone. Axle and Slice, y'all need to finish what Red starts on the front car once he shifts fire. Then you've got squirters and targets of opportunity. Questions?"

"Not a question," Axle said. "Just a little something for my fellow frogmen. Boys, the man in that car saved Kikki. We are not going to be the frogmen who let him get killed. Clear?"

"Hooyah, Senior Chief," Elvis said.

"That's all, Sweet," Axle said.

Which was good, because at that moment Katherine's voice crackled from my phone.

"Matt, I . . . I can't. There's just too much data. I'm sorry."

For the first time, I heard the strain break through her composure. Not only was an operator in the field asking for the impossible, but if Katherine didn't deliver, the man she loved would die. I'd put her in an unimaginable situation. One in which she couldn't divorce herself from the potential consequences. I needed to help Katherine think of alternatives.

Fast.

"Okay," I said, climbing into the SUV's left rear passenger seat as the SEALs cross-loaded vehicles and prepared for the coming assault. "Let's try this a different way. Forget about the Russians. Focus on Frodo. Can you lock down his phone?"

"Of course, of course," Katherine said, keyboard singing. "It's off-line, but the last ping was from an industrial complex west of the city proper."

Elvis climbed into the driver's position as Happy jumped into the front passenger seat. Cajun loaded a sedated Ella into the second SUV and repositioned to the west. To my left, Red took up a seated firing position at a picnic bench, extending the SAW's bipod legs as he checked sight lines.

"That's our safe house," I said. "The Russians probably killed his phone when they grabbed him. Can you power it back on?"

"No," Katherine said, her voice wavering. "They must have disconnected the battery."

Or dropped it into a Faraday bag or taken any number

of other precautions. For the first time in my operational career, I was up against a near-peer nation-state. I had to assume that the usual tricks weren't going to work because the Russians knew them too.

"Axle's got three vehicles coming up the hill to the west," Elvis said, interrupting my thoughts. "SUVs with tinted windows. This could be them."

It could also be a businessman and his entourage or any other of the millions who called Ukraine home. If I initiated, people were going to die. I couldn't start killing on a hunch.

"Stand by," I said to Elvis.

"What's that?" Katherine said.

"Nothing," I said. "Good job with the phone, but that's a dead end. Is there anything else that Frodo wears we could track? An Apple watch, a Garmin, a Fitbit? Anything?"

I pictured my friend as I spoke, already knowing the answer. Frodo was an operator through and through. He knew the dangers posed by the plethora of seemingly innocuous digital devices. Even if he used them in his personal life, which I was fairly certain he didn't, he would have sanitized himself before traveling overseas.

This was going to be another dry hole.

"No," Katherine said, "I can't think of—Wait. WAIT!"

"Climbing the final hill now," Elvis said. "They'll be in the kill zone in forty-five seconds."

"Hang on," I said to Katherine before pressing the phone against my chest and addressing Elvis. "Confirm everybody's ready. You've got to drill that second vehicle no matter what. Timing's gonna be a bitch, but you've got the skills. Red, you ready?"

"Ready," the frogman said.

Red had his SAW oriented to the left, buttstock snugged into his shoulder, waiting for the lead vehicle's appearance. I could hear the stress in his voice, but that was good. If he wasn't at least a little stressed right now, I'd be worried.

"Katherine," I said, wedging the cell between my cheek and shoulder as I readied my Rattler, "we're out of time."

"I gave Frodo something to help us stay connected," Katherine said. "It's like a bracelet. It doesn't message or anything, but the newer model has cell, Wi-Fi, and satellite connectivity. When I touch mine, his vibrates. Like a hug from me. He wears it on his leg instead of his arm, just above his prothesis. NSA's already developed a hack for it. Maybe I can—"

"Katherine," I said, "if you can ping the bracelet, do it now. This exact second."

"Give me a—"

"Fifteen seconds," Elvis said.

"Here we go," Katherine said. "I'm pinging it—"

"Ten," Elvis said.

"Oh, my God, oh, my God," Katherine said, "it's right—"

"Now or never," Elvis said.

"Hit it, Red!" I said.

SIXTY-TWO

The tracers from Red's SAW seemed to hover in mid-
air. Like an incandescent swarm of sparkling crimson
fireflies. For a moment, nothing felt real. The black SUV
on the road to our left, the floating tracer rounds, even
my Rattler's plastic grip were all ethereal.

Disconnected.

Then the SUV swept past us and swerved left, piling
into the guardrail as Red's 5.56 green tips took the vehicle apart. That boy could shoot a SAW like nobody's
business. With a precision that would have matched my
best gunner in the Ranger Regiment, Red walked the
rounds past the engine block and into the passenger
cabin, decimating everything in his path.

Tires exploded, steam vented, metal screamed, and
glass shattered.

It was fucking awesome.

But it was taking too long.

"Shift," I screamed.

The second vehicle in the convoy swerved out of the turn.

Frodo's vehicle.

We had to trigger.

"Red, shift," I yelled again.

But Red kept rocking the SAW, spent brass casings cascading onto the picnic bench like a golden waterfall.

He couldn't hear me.

Rookie mistake.

My rookie mistake.

"Go," I said, slapping Elvis on the back.

This was the part of special operations that never made the recruiting video. The moment where your life hung by a thread because the mission unfolded differently than planned. The instant when you had to blindly trust your teammate to do the right thing or you'd die and the mission would fail.

To his credit, Elvis punched the gas.

I held my breath as we shot into the road, waiting to be torn in two by a buzzsaw of green tips.

But that didn't happen.

Instead, we T-boned the front passenger door of the second SUV. The collision bounced me into the driver's seat, but that was to be expected.

Speed was the name of the game.

I wasn't wearing my seat belt.

Yanking open the door handle, I flowed to the left, Rattler tucked into my shoulder even as Elvis fired a burst from his M4 through our windshield straight into the stricken SUV.

That hadn't been part of the plan either.

But the plan was no longer my concern.

Red and Cajun working the rear vehicle, Axle and Slice picking up squirters, even Elvis and Happy neutralizing the front two passengers weren't my concern. Those tasks were either going to happen or not.

I'd set the operation in motion.

Now I was a gunfighter just like everyone else.

My universe shrank to the holographic red dot hovering in front of my right eyeball. I covered the distance to the SUV in two strides, rolling my feet from heel to toe in the tactical walk I'd practiced thousands of times on the range.

But this wasn't the range, and the people inside weren't target dummies.

I drew even with the door.

Saw Frodo slumped on the other side of the glass.

Saw a figure beyond him.

A figure with a gun.

I fired the Rattler, continuously pulling the trigger as I moved closer. The rounds punched through the glass, but either the angle was wrong or the window was shattering or deflecting my bullets.

I was getting hits, but not target effect.

The gunman was still moving.

I surged forward, driving the Rattler's muzzle through the shattered window and following my weapon into the car. Glass tore at my hands and my forearms, cutting at my face and neck, but the pain was something secondary.

Something far away.

I leaned over Frodo, covering his body with my own. The holographic dot landed on the man's shoulder. Rather than shift to his chest, I pressed the trigger three times.

The Russian gasped, the pistol he'd been holding tumbling from his fingers.

I panned the red dot to his forehead, taking the slack out of the trigger.

Then I had an idea.

Lunging, I cracked the Russian in the temple with the Rattler's stubby barrel.

His eyes rolled back into his head, and he slumped against the door.

"*Moskva rulit*, motherfucker," I said.

"Matty? Is that you?"

With a start, I realized I was still stretched across Frodo.

"Yeah, brother," I said, wiggling out of the window. "I'm here."

"I don't feel so good," Frodo said.

"You look like shit," I said with a smile. "You hit?"

"In the shoulder," Frodo said. "My good shoulder. But the Russians bandaged it."

"Hang tight," I said. "We'll have you out in a minute. Elvis?"

"Here," Elvis said, slapping me on my back.

"How we looking?"

"Pretty damn good. Russians are down, and the team is green. We're ready to evac."

"Okay," I said. "Have Cajun see to Frodo and that Russian in the backseat."

"Why the Russian?"

"We're taking him with us."

SIXTY-THREE

C hief, it's Matty. I need help."

"Matthew—thank God, son. Katherine's here. She's brought me up to speed. Tell me what you need. I will make it happen."

I took a second to swallow before answering. I'd known James for a long time. I'd seen him happy, and I'd seen him ready to rend human flesh with his bare hands. But I'd never seen him paternal. I'd thought I'd lived through the entire Glass experience.

I'd been wrong.

"Roger that, Chief," I said, clearing my throat. "I'm in a convoy of three vehicles en route to the safe house. We're about ten minutes out. I have two WIA in need of urgent surgical. One of them is Frodo. I also believe there are several KIA at the safe house. Maybe some wounded there as well, but I doubt it. I think everyone else is dead."

"Jesus. What happened?"

"Russians, Chief. A Spetsnaz team hit the safe house. They snatched Frodo. We snatched him back."

"Listen to me, Matthew," James said. "The Russians are going to follow up the airfield seizure at Kramatorsk with a full-on ground invasion. Between the pro-Russian separatists that have been murdered and rumors of that loose nuke, world opinion is swinging in their direction. A US mechanized infantry brigade with an aviation package is close by. They're in Ukraine for a show-of-force mission, but my guess is the president's going to pull them back."

"It's bullshit, Chief," I said. "All of it."

"I know it's a sour pill to swallow," James said, "but it is what it is. Get to the safe house. I've had birds in the air looking for you for the last twenty minutes. They'll meet you there with medical assets and infantrymen. We're going to secure our fallen and get the hell out of Dodge. This is bigger than us, Matthew."

"I've got a GRU captain who says otherwise," I said.

"Speak."

"His name is Dmitri Agapov," I said. "He's the sole survivor of the direct action team that hit the safe house. I asked him some questions. He gave me some answers."

"What kind of answers?"

"Like I said, Chief, this whole thing is bullshit. The Russians planted that nuke on the airfield precisely for the airborne unit to discover. Not only that, but the supposed militiamen who shot those teenagers were actually a Spetsnaz detachment. This is all a Russian setup."

"What's the condition of the GRU officer?" James said.

"He's got three 5.56 holes in his right arm and shoulder," I said, "so he's been better. But he speaks excellent English."

"You know what I mean, goddamn it."

There was the James Glass I knew and loved.

"No, I don't," I said, "so if you want to spell it out, feel free. If not, then back the fuck off. What I will say is that our prisoner was the leader of a unit that killed several Americans while operating illegally in Ukraine. Oh, and they weren't wearing uniforms, so I don't think they give two shits about the Geneva convention. I sure don't."

"Okay, okay. You've made your point, Matthew. Get your asses back to the safe house and, for Christ's sake, keep the GRU officer alive. He might be the key to all of this."

"Roger that, Chief," I said. "Thanks for the help."

"Matthew?"

"Yes, Chief?"

"Good job, son."

The call ended.

"Is that how you and your boss always talk?" Elvis said from the driver's seat next to me.

"No," I said, "sometimes we get angry."

He gave me an incredulous look.

"What?" I said. "Your boss talks are all rainbows and unicorns?"

Shaking his head, Elvis changed topics.

"What about the other thing he said? You think that GRU dude really is the ticket out of this mess?"

"I don't know," I said. "Could be, I guess. But I'm a firm believer in the adage that anything worth shooting once is worth shooting twice."

Elvis shot me another look, but this time I didn't try to explain.

I was too busy dialing.

SIXTY-FOUR

thought I made it clear that I never wanted to talk with you again."

"Yes, I'm doing fine," I said. "Thank you for asking."

I really didn't like this guy. Maybe it was because I wasn't having the best of days, or maybe we just didn't have compatible astrological signs. Or it could have been my newly developed hatred for Russian accents. Either way, I was ready to be done with this douchebag.

Almost.

"I don't know why I answered, but it was obviously a mistake. Goodbye."

"The last time we talked, you said that whatever happened next was on my head," I said. "Remember?"

Nolan's son didn't answer, but he didn't hang up either. I let the silence build, determined to make him be the one to break it. I looked through my window, watching as countryside gave way to city as we drew ever closer to the safe house. I tried not to think about Frodo and Ella in the vehicle behind me. Cajun said they were both stable, but he was going to need more saline pronto.

The trail vehicle held the wounded GRU officer. It wasn't hard not to think about him. I'd let Cajun bandage his gunshot wounds and give him a hit of morphine.

That was it.

Contrary to what I'd promised James, I couldn't care less whether the Russian lived or died. On the one hand, a confession provided in real time would make for powerful TV. Good thing I'd recorded his earlier admission with my phone. That way I wouldn't lose any sleep if something terrible happened to him.

Kind of like another Russian I knew.

"I remember," Nolan's son said.

"Good," I said, "because I'm about to toss that ball back into your court."

"What do you mean?"

"The name of the man who had your father tortured and killed. Want it?"

Another long pause.

The sound of helicopters echoed through the car. I rolled down the window and stuck out my head. A Chinook and a pair of Black Hawks trailed by two Apache gunships screamed by.

The medics and the cavalry were on their way.

Hallelujah.

"Why would you give this to me?"

"Because I pay my debts. Especially the ones I owe in blood. Do you want it or not?"

Elvis made the final turn onto the gravel road leading to the safe house and floored the accelerator. The Chinook and two Black Hawks touched down in a cloud of grit. The Apaches were circling overhead. The 30mm cannons hanging from beneath the gunships' noses swiveled in all directions, hunting for something that needed shooting.

I knew how they felt.

"Tell me."

I relayed the name the GRU officer had given me. The SVR piece of shit who'd run the whole operation. To think he and I had been within shooting distance back at the air base. It was almost enough to make me want to take a little detour before I left Ukraine for good. Unfortunately, I'd have to get through a battalion's worth of Russian paratroopers first.

That made him a little harder to reach.

But not impossible.

Like me, Nolan's son was an intelligence officer. A professional. As such, I wasn't expecting a reaction when I said the name. But I got one. A single sharply drawn breath. Not much. But it was enough.

"This still doesn't change—"

I hung up.

If I never heard another Russian voice, it would be too soon.

Elvis stopped the truck and I jumped out, waving down the flood of uniforms pouring from the Chinook.

Then I sprinted over to the second truck and opened the door. Ella was still sedated, but Frodo was very much awake.

"How you doing, buddy?" I said, grabbing his hand.

"Been better," Frodo said, his eyes glassy from pain medicine. "What now?"

"Now we go home."

SIXTY-FIVE

WASHINGTON, DC

The Situation Room was located in the West Wing's basement. Untold layers of insulating dirt, concrete, and rebar separated the crown molding, ceiling tiles, and rows of harsh fluorescent lighting above Peter's head from the outside world. The temperature was kept at a constant seventy-five degrees and the humidity pegged at fifty-one percent. There was absolutely no way to know the actual time of day from the room's antiseptic furnishings.

But Peter knew.

So did the rest of the room's occupants.

The White House steward had already set the conditions for the group's arrival with towering carafes of coffee and hot water. An assortment of teas, cream, and condiments lined the coffee service station along the back wall, along with a heaping plate of pastries. White ceramic mugs emblazoned with the presidential seal sat pre-positioned in front of black place mats, which in turn were perfectly aligned with the matching black leather chairs surrounding the conference table. All in all, the scene could have been mistaken for an early-morning celebratory breakfast with the president after the previous night's national address.

It wasn't.

It was a council of war.

"Shall we begin?" President Gonzales said.

Since he'd called the meeting and had the shortest commute, the president was dressed more formally than most of his principals. He was wearing a button-down shirt, slacks, and loafers. In a nod to the early-morning hour, he'd forgone a jacket or tie. The other cabinet members had on a mixture of jeans, slacks, and the like, the one exception being Peter.

He'd never gone home, and he was still in last night's suit.

The secretary of defense, a balding middle-aged man from Ohio named Jason Billings, had kidded Peter about a hot date. Peter smiled along with the joke while inwardly shuddering.

If only Billings knew.

"Yes, Mr. President," Christina Sims said. "I'll start if that's okay?"

The president nodded, and the interim CIA Director cleared her throat.

It wasn't lost on Peter that the newest addition to this quorum had chosen the seat directly beside Christina. Jeremy Thompson was the Director of National Intelligence, or DNI. The portly man was notionally the CIA Director's boss, since in accordance with post-9/11 recommendations, all of the intelligence community's many members fell under the DNI's purview.

As was often the case with Washington fiefdoms, reality played out a little differently.

"At our last gathering, you asked me a single question, Mr. President: Is a Russian invasion of Ukraine imminent? I can now definitively answer that it is."

Christina touched a button on her ever-present laptop. The earlier map of Ukraine appeared on half of the flat-screen with an overhead shot of an airfield taking up the second half.

"This is the Kramatorsk Air Base. As we speak, the Russians are in the process of consolidating their hold on the airfield following an airborne operation they executed to seize it."

"How did this happen?" the president said. "I thought you said that the Russian logistic vehicles were the key indicator?"

"I did," Christina said, "and I was wrong."

Peter's weren't the only set of eyebrows that rose. Politics was a full-contact sport, and even the most novice players learned the game's most important lesson early: Never admit you were wrong.

"With all due respect to the interim Director," General Etzel said, leaning forward in his seat, "the Russians got one past us, sir. We're still deconstructing what happened, but early indications are that they used commercial flight routes and had their birds squawking airline transponder codes. This was a preplanned airfield seizure, plain and simple."

"Which goes against the official Russian narrative," Christina said. "Ostensibly, this is a peacekeeping operation designed to protect the pro-Russian population of Kramatorsk from further violence. In reality, it's nothing of the sort."

"We have some further reporting that corroborates this," Jeremy Thompson said.

Judging by the look that Christina shot her counterpart, the DNI hadn't bothered to share this information with the interim CIA Director.

Unlike the career CIA intelligence analyst, Peter didn't find this surprising at all. A Senate seat was rumored to be opening up in Jeremy's home state. Serving on the president's cabinet was all well and good, but nothing beat the prestige of wearing a blue-and-white Senate lapel pin.

"What specifically do you know, Jeremy?" the president said.

"Sir," the DNI said, "DIA assesses with high confidence that the violence in Kramatorsk has actually been perpetrated by Spetsnaz teams posing as pro-Ukrainian militia members. This includes the shooting at the Palace of Culture, the pub bombing, and the nuclear weapon discovered on Kramatorsk Air Base."

Peter had made the mistake of taking a swallow of coffee during the DNI's update. Now he almost spat it across the table.

"The Russians found a nuclear weapon?" Peter said.

"Actually, we found it first," Jeremy said.

"Who is *we*?" Peter said.

"A paramilitary team. They were on the airfield prior to the invasion, conducting a procurement operation. They validated the nuclear weapon's presence before rendering it inoperable."

"How?" Peter said.

"By setting it on fire."

"Holy shit," Peter said. "Who authorized that operation?"

"I did," the president said. "Due to its sensitivity, I compartmentalized the DIA's activity in Ukraine. Sorry, Peter. Please continue, Jeremy."

Only his decades as a political operative allowed Peter to maintain a blank expression as he nodded in acknowledgment. In Peter's years of service with the president, Jorge Gonzales had never hidden anything from him. Not once. And now he'd been excluded from the decision-making process for one of the most consequential events of Jorge's administration.

Why?

Then he knew.

This was his friend's gentle way of letting Peter know that his time had come. There would be no anonymous leaks to reporters, no scurrilous talk about the office, no public demands for his resignation. Just a gradual diminishment of Peter's responsibilities until he took the hint. To the end, his friend was doing everything in his power to ensure Peter's transition was made with honor and on his own terms.

And how was Peter repaying the president's discretion?

By covertly meeting with a Russian intelligence officer.

"Mr. President," Jeremy said, "our DIA team has the leader of one of the direct action teams in custody. A Russian GRU officer. This reporting comes directly from him."

"How do we use the Russian?" the president said.

"Sir, I would recommend doing this delicately," Christina said. "The Russian president is already on television building the case for a much larger peacekeeping operation in Ukraine. The logistical assets I highlighted during our last meeting are moving west. To get him to back down, you'll have to provide the president with an opportunity to save face."

"I understand," the president said. "Get me the transcript from the GRU officer. I'll call the Russian president directly."

"I don't believe that's wise, sir," the secretary of state said. "It's not a case of you just picking up the phone. Your calls to the Russian president are widely publicized on their side. My counterpart will know about the conversation, as will their press and countless others. We need something subtle. A back channel."

In that moment Peter pictured Jorge Gonzales as he'd first seen him—the mayor of a Texas city that had just been devastated by back-to-back hurricanes. Jorge had been detailing his recovery plan during an impromptu press conference even as rain streamed from the bill of his faded Astros ballcap. That had been the instant when Peter had known that this plainspoken son of Mexican immigrants was destined for greatness.

Like then, Peter knew now exactly what he needed to do.

"Mr. President," Peter said, his voice a little shaky, "I think I can help."

SIXTY-SIX

WASHINGTON, DC

Inessa Petrova did not easily scare. This was not so much a boast as it was a statement of fact. The auburn-haired, caramel-eyed woman was an illegal. An undocumented Russian spy who ran and recruited high-profile assets deemed too sensitive for Washington, DC's acknowledged SVR officers. She lived in the precarious space between success and an American jail cell. She was good at her job.

Or at least she had been.

Her current circumstances put her earlier assessment of both her bravery and competence in jeopardy.

The car slowed, making another right-hand turn.

Inessa had tried to keep track of the vehicle's changes in direction and speed, but the hood and earmuffs she was wearing made that impossible. She'd also tried to engage her captors in conversation, but those efforts had also proven less than fruitful. Inessa had managed a single glimpse of two burly men and a woman before she'd been face-planted on the ground, flex-cuffed, hooded, and thrown into the back of the car. Her attempt at conversation had garnered her a warning, delivered in a woman's voice. If she spoke again, she'd be gagged as well.

Then the sound-blocking earmuffs were strapped to her head.

The sensory deprivation left Inessa with only her thoughts for company, and they were not encouraging. In the span of just hours she'd gone from the high of a successful recruitment to the low of capture. In hindsight, she should have been more suspicious of the request for a crash meeting so soon after her last engagement with the American.

Then again, she hadn't had a choice. Her instructions on this matter from Moscow had been clear. Until the operation in Ukraine was complete, she was her nation's window into the American decision-making process. If her asset requested her presence day or night, she would accommodate him.

So she had.

The car slowed and then stopped.

Inessa tensed, trying to prepare for whatever was coming. Had this been a Russian operation, the beatings would now begin. Blows to the head, face, and body designed not to inflict damage as much as to reinforce the prisoner's helplessness. A precursor for things to come if the detainee didn't answer the interrogators' questions satisfactorily.

Fortunately, she was in America, not Russia. The Americans did not torture prisoners while interrogating them. But that didn't make the solitary confinement cells in their super-max prison any more hospitable.

The car doors opened, then closed.

Inessa held her breath, trying to determine if she was alone.

She was not.

Hands tore the earmuffs and hood from her face.

She blinked away the tears brought about by the sudden flood of light. Then her blurry vision cleared as she saw who was sitting across from her.

She gasped.

"You know who I am?"

Inessa nodded.

"Good. I'm told that spies have excellent memories. Is that true?"

"I'm not a—"

"Stop," the man said, holding up a brown hand. "We don't have time for this nonsense. I know exactly who and what you are. You know the same about me. I need you to deliver a message to your president. Immediately and word for word. If you do, you will be permitted to leave my country unmolested. If you do not, you will spend the rest of your days in an American prison. Understood?"

Inessa nodded again.

"Excellent," the man said with a smile. "This is what I want you to say."

SIXTY-SEVEN

MOSCOW, RUSSIA

Rain slashed down from a dark, unforgiving Moscow sky. Pyotr huddled against the downpour, waiting his turn in the taxi queue at Moscow Domodedovo Airport. This was not at all how he'd pictured his triumphant homecoming.

Probably because there was nothing triumphant about it.

For reasons Pyotr still didn't understand, the Russian president had not authorized a follow-on Russian ground invasion of Ukraine. Or even subsequent airlifts to bolster the troop presence at Kramatorsk. Instead, an American mechanized infantry brigade had arrived to conduct joint peacekeeping patrols with the Russian paratroopers.

At least, this was what Pyotr had gathered while monitoring the news feeds during his flight back to Moscow.

Shortly after the airfield had been secured, a business jet had touched down.

A business jet for Pyotr.

He was to return to Moscow.

Immediately.

Pyotr had gratefully complied, convinced that this was the president's way of congratulating him for a job well done.

Now he was less sure.

He'd been dropped off at the terminal with instructions to take a cab to Moscow Center. There was no waiting limousine. No congratulatory phone call. No gathering of his peers.

Just cold Moscow rain and a line of cranky passengers.

"Excuse me, *ser*. Is this yours?"

Pyotr glaced at the questioner, intending to vent the day's frustrations.

He didn't get the chance.

As Pyotr turned, a blast of aerosolized mist caught him full in the face.

The results were instantaneous.

His trachea constricted even as his lungs began to spasm. Clawing at his throat, Pyotr looked from the quarter-sized device that was his undoing to the person holding it. He saw a fit man with an angular face.

And something more.

Another intelligence professional.

Pyotr couldn't put into words how he knew, but he was certain all the same.

One predator always recognized another.

The man caught Pyotr as his knees buckled, gently lowering him to the wet cement even as he shouted for a doctor. As his world faded to black, Pyotr heard just three words.

For my father.

EPILOGUE

AUSTIN, TEXAS

I followed the crowd out of the Jetway and into the airport proper, glad to be home. Funny how that worked. I'd spent the majority of my life in places other than this, but somehow Austin had earned the coveted title of *home*. Knots I didn't realize were still there loosened in my shoulders and neck as the airport's unique ambience embraced me.

To the left, a faux food truck sold breakfast tacos of the brisket or spicy-chorizo-sausage variety. On the right, a quartet of musicians strummed through a Stevie Ray Vaughan number while a life-sized cardboard cutout of Willie Nelson looked on approvingly. The crowd ebbed and flowed around me. Cowboys in dusty boots, skintight jeans, and pearly-snap shirts mixed with tech gurus in ball-caps, T-shirts, and the obligatory Chuck Taylor high-tops.

This place was part Texas, part California, and part something else hard to define.

Maybe that was why the vibe here resonated so much

with Laila and me. Individually, the two of us were pieces of many things. Together, our jagged edges formed a beautiful mosaic. I followed the crowd down the escalator to baggage claim, the thought of Laila bringing a smile to my face.

The trip had already kept us apart far longer than I'd expected, but there was no way I was leaving Frodo in Landstuhl, Germany. Along with Ella, he'd been evaced to the military hospital after Army medics had stabilized them both. Ella's countrymen had quickly arranged a transfer for her, but Frodo's underlying medical condition had necessitated a longer stay. I'd let James know in no uncertain terms that I wasn't coming back to the States without Frodo. For all his faults, our boss had an uncanny way of sensing the rare times when he was on the losing end of an argument. Rather than press me and suffer the consequences, James did what he always did in unwinnable scenarios—changed the rules of the game.

In this case, his pseudo victory took the form of a pair of men with serious faces and credentials to a mysterious government agency who arrived while I was keeping watch from Frodo's bedside. The medical center at Wilson Barracks had certainly seen its share of craziness in the two-plus decades it had cared for men and women injured in the exhaustive war on terror. Still, I was willing to bet that this was the first time a patient recovery room had been magically transformed into a SCIF for a three-hour classified debrief.

If that hadn't been interesting enough, Benny had ghosted through the door with an American escort just as the mystery men were leaving. In typical Israeli fashion, after assuring me that Ella was fine, he'd let me know that my debt to him had not yet been paid.

I politely told him to take that up with my boss.

He politely assured me that he already had.

The DIA's head shed was seriously considering accepting a liaison officer from the Mossad.

Ella.

For some reason, I wasn't surprised.

But while I wasn't certain if or when this mythical joint assignment would ever come to fruition, I was fairly confident about one thing. If Ella made the jump across the pond to Washington, a sizable wardrobe would travel with her.

After Benny's departure, Frodo and I had our third visitor.

Though, to be fair, she hadn't come to see me.

Katherine had traveled at her agency's expense with a set of temporary duty orders stating that her place of business was at Frodo's side until he was well enough to travel. It was obvious that her presence was doing much more to aid Frodo's convalescence than mine.

After giving my best friend a handshake and his girlfriend a hug, I gathered my things and made the call to James I'd been dreading. Purposely speaking from an unsecure line, I let the chief know that I was taking my vacation.

Period.

In a first, James did me one better. He gave me permission to power down my phone for exactly fourteen days. He also sprang for first-class travel all the way from Frankfurt to Austin, which I gratefully accepted. I should have viewed his generosity with more suspicion. The flight just so happened to have a two-hour layover in Washington. In another unforeseen turn of events, my branch chief was waiting to greet me when the plane deboarded.

Like the dutiful DIA officer I was, I followed him through an unmarked airport door leading to a small room with comfortable furniture and stale coffee. There, we debriefed the mission.

Again.

At the one-hour-and-fifty-eight-minute mark, James told me that I needed to keep better track of the time. My plane was already boarding.

I made the flight.

Barely.

In a petty act of revenge, I might have also powered down my phone and removed the battery. Strictly speaking, my vacation wasn't supposed to start until the following day.

But as James so often reminded me, rules were for suckers.

M att."
The voice I loved above all others jolted me from my thoughts.

My wife was an exquisitely beautiful woman, but tonight she positively glowed. In a nod to the summer heat, she was wearing an off-the-shoulder emerald dress that matched her sparkling eyes and showcased miles of smooth brown skin.

God bless Texas.

"What are you doing here?" I said, bounding down the steps.

"We wanted to welcome you home."

I dropped my bag, kissed her soft lips, and wrapped my arms around her. For a long moment, I just held my wife, breathing in her warm vanilla scent and savoring the feel of her body through the dress's thin fabric.

Then her comment registered.

"We?" I said, pulling away. "Who's *we*? I only see you."

We'd gone round and round about getting a dog.

Maybe she'd gotten tired of waiting.

"That's because you're not looking hard enough."

Laila opened her left hand, revealing a stick.

A stick with two horizontal pink lines.

My mouth dropped open.

"You're . . . you're . . . ," I said.

"Yes!"

I crushed Laila to my chest, swinging her in a circle. Her shoes went tumbling even as her thick, fragrant hair billowed into a raven halo. She let out a silvery laugh and laced her fingers across the back of my neck.

I'd been wrong earlier.

Austin wasn't home.

This was.

"Say something," Laila said from the circle of my

arms, pounding her fists against my chest. "Say something!"

"I can't believe it," I said, laughing as I kissed the top of her head. "I just can't believe it."

"I think it's a girl," Laila said, pushing back so that she could see my face. "I really do. What should we name her?"

I didn't have a clue.

Then I did.

"How about Virginia?"

ACKNOWLEDGMENTS

Once again, I find myself in debt to a number of fantastic folks who helped take *Hostile Intent* from mindless scribblings to the book you've just read. There are too many to thank, but I'll give it my best shot.

If you loved this book, a monstrous amount of credit belongs to my incredible team at Berkley Publishing. I've now had the pleasure of working with editor extraordinaire Tom Colgan on four novels. He makes me a better writer and my books better stories. Thank you, Tom. Marketing rock star Jin Yu is hell on wheels in all the best ways, and Danielle Keir is the publicist by which all others should be measured. Thank you to you both.

Many of you have asked me about my incredible covers, and I realized I was remiss in not thanking the Berkley art team of Anthony Ramondo and Steve Meditz in the acknowledgments sections of *Without Sanction* and *The Outside Man*. Once again, these gentlemen reached into my head and pulled out a breathtaking image of Matt doing what Matt does. Thank you both for bringing my favorite protagonist to life in such a heartstopping manner.

But art isn't just confined to the covers. Jaime Mendola-Hobbie and Allison Prince have produced a staggering number of amazing marketing images. I can't thank them enough for spreading the word about Matt Drake to every corner of social media.

If, like me, you thought that writing novels would get easier with time, you're wrong. Terribly wrong. Writing is hard, but my personal support crew of Nick Petrie, Bill Schweigart, and Graham Brown makes it easier. In addition to being fantastic writers in their own right, this trio of malcontents encouraged me in ways too numerous to count. Everyone needs a crew, and these gents, along with our fearless agent, Barbara Poelle, are mine.

Speaking of crews, I'd like to thank the reviewers and podcasters who have graciously helped me along my writer's journey. Chief among these are the three amigos from the *Crew Reviews* podcast—Chris Albanese, Sean Cameron, and Mike Houtz. Thank you so much for having me on twice in the same year. If I'm lucky enough to grace your show again, I'll try not to tell the same boring stories. But no guarantees.

As with my other novels, I received stellar feedback from my gang of beta readers. Thank you, Erica Nichols, Tommy Ledbetter, and Bill Schweigart for your time and insightful comments. You make me a better storyteller.

Like I'm prone to do, I often painted myself into technical corners during the writing of *Hostile Intent*. Fortunately, my cadre of subject matter experts once again rode to my rescue. Jason Beighley, retired Army Sergeant Major and Special Mission Unit veteran, helped me keep my tactics straight and my powder dry. Retired Army Colonel Kelsey Smith gave me an invaluable tutorial on the situation in Ukraine and the menace its eastern neighbor represents. Former Army Ranger Brandon Cates explained the finer points of airfield seizures for the low cost of a single cup of coffee. His colleague former Army Ranger Greg Glass provided invaluable help with a weapons system for the slightly higher cost of a beer. Or three. Unfortunately, this weapons system didn't make *Hostile Intent*, but it did grace the pages of *Tom Clancy Target Acquired*. If you haven't already read that one, give it a look and see if you can guess which system!

While we're talking about *Target Acquired*, I need to thank a couple more people, as Tom Clancy books don't contain acknowledgments sections. Retired Army Master Sergeant and former Green Beret Dave Marks was kind enough to let me pick his brain about Iraq, a compound of Shia cultists, and a day he'll never forget. Retired Air Force Lieutenant Colonel and former F-16 fighter jock Eric Fagerland graciously whipped my air-to-air sequences into shape. Thank you all.

On the topic of great guys, I'd like to thank my writing comrades in arms who have made this genre such a welcoming place. Jack Carr, Chris Hauty, Joshua Hood, Jeffrey Wilson, Brian Andrews, and Kyle Mills have all been incredibly generous with their time and advice. Fellow Tom Clancy writers Marc Cameron, Mike Maden, and Mark Greaney were exceptionally helpful as I navigated the daunting process of joining the Clancy Universe. In particular, Mark Greaney fielded more than one terrified text or phone call in which he patiently shared his experience and wisdom while reassuring me that I did in fact have what it takes to write with the big dogs. If you've never had the pleasure of meeting them, Mark and his wife, Allison, are kind and generous people who make this world a better place.

Brad and Elaine Taylor fall into this same category. As with my previous books, Brad went out of his way to help me in any way he could, even agreeing to back-to-back interviews for *Target Acquired* and *The Outside Man* without TOO much grumbling. In the same vein, Elaine Taylor allowed me to peek behind the writing curtain by selflessly sharing the highs and lows of their stellar career along with her extraordinary marketing prowess. And she made sure Brad showed up to our interviews on time. Mostly. Thank you to you both. I'm honored to call you friends.

I'm also incredibly grateful for you, my reader. Because of your loyalty, I've achieved my childhood dream of telling stories for a living. Thank you. If you want to see more of Matt and Frodo in action, please consider leaving five-star reviews for this and my other books on Amazon. I can't overemphasize the importance of these reviews. If you want to keep abreast of everything I'm writing, including my work in the Tom Clancy Universe and beyond, please consider heading over to my website at donbentley-books.com and signing up for my newsletter. I always love hearing from readers, so please feel free to drop me a line while you're there or at donbentleybooks@gmail.com.

Finally, I'd like to thank my family. My wife, Angela, is a constant source of encouragement and my first, and most important, reader. During the revising of *Hostile Intent*, she graduated to research assistant and copy editor. Without her tireless efforts, this book would not exist. Her love and support gave me a reason to write novels in the first place, and I'm a better man for knowing her. Thank you, baby. For everything.

To my three kids, Will, Faith, and Kelia—I'm so very proud of the people you've become, and I love being your dad.

—DON

Matt Drake returns in

FORGOTTEN WAR

Turn the page for a sample of this captivating thriller

PROLOGUE

BAGRAM, AFGHANISTAN

Brother—you are free."

Mullah Qari Wasiq blinked in the bright sunlight, his tired eyes watering as they struggled to adjust to the unexpected brilliance. Ten years. He'd waited ten years to hear those words, but at the moment when his freedom was finally realized, Qari found himself consumed with thoughts of something else.

The will of Allah.

Qari looked from the cloudless blue sky to the five mountaintops that surrounded Bagram Air Base. Though Bāgh Darē Ghar stood the highest at nearly twenty-four hundred meters, Kōh-e Tōp was by far the most prominent. These two peaks had kept Qari company for almost a decade, but the glimpses he'd stolen from the tiny window in his cell had not done them justice. Seeing the summits in their full unfiltered glory took his breath away.

"Brother?"

With a sigh, Qari turned from the mountains to the man standing before him.

The young man standing before him.

Ten years ago, Qari had been young too. But captivity in Parwan Detention Facility, Afghanistan's most notorious prison, had aged him. His once luxurious beard was scraggly and streaked with gray. His hair was a patchy mess, his back feeble, and his eyesight poor, but Qari now had strength in a place that had once been a dwelling for weakness.

His spirit.

"What is the time?" Qari said, his voice raspy from disuse.

"Brother?"

"The time, boy," Qari said. "What is the time?"

The fighter shook his head, but he pulled out a cell phone all the same.

"Ten a.m., brother."

"Thank you," Qari said with a nod.

Two hours before *Dhuhr*, or noon, prayers.

That was fine.

With a groan, Qari removed his outer tunic, revealing the emaciated flesh beneath.

The fighter sucked in a breath.

Qari wondered which affliction had caused the young Talib the greatest surprise—Qari's protruding ribs or the puckered flesh from the gunshot wound sustained during his capture? Or perhaps it was the faint web of lines that spidered across his abdomen? Maybe even the collection of shiny burns on his forearm. Scars delivered by guards who'd used his body as an ashtray.

Qari could mark the passage of time by the scars that now dotted his body.

Bending on wobbly knees, Qari arranged his tunic on the ground facing west, brushing away the dirt as he fashioned a makeshift *sajjada*, or prayer rug. Then he lowered himself to the fabric and began to pray. Each time his forehead brushed the cloth, he praised Allah for granting him a second chance. For purging his soul. For burning away his pride. For giving him new purpose in his humility. In many ways, Qari considered himself fortunate. Historically, Allah often used periods of isolation to shape his followers. Qari could have spent forty years wandering the desert like Moses, but he had not.

After the final *salat*, Qari stood and reclaimed his tunic.

Where there once had been but a single fighter, now a gaggle of ten stood. Ten warriors, one for each year of his imprisonment.

Allah was faithful and merciful.

"Are you Mullah Wasiq?"

This time the question came from one of the new arrivals. Unlike his boyish companions, the speaker had an air of gravitas. His beard was thick and stretched to the middle of his chest. His face was weather-beaten and his dark eyes glowed with intelligence.

This was a commander, not just another foot soldier.

"I am," Qari said, his voice already stronger.

"Praise Allah," the commander said. "I am called Abdul. We've been searching for you."

Qari nodded.

The guard had told him the truth.

Like all nonbelievers, the man had been weak, but as Qari had learned the hard way, Allah transformed weakness into strength. Many of the prison guards had grown friendlier as the fighting between the Taliban and progovernment forces drifted ever closer to Kabul. But this man had shown mercy long before his brethren. When the sound of artillery fire had rolled over the jail's walls, Qari had taken the man into his confidence and given him a message.

A message for his Talib brethren who, Allah willing, would be his liberators.

"The guard found you?" Qari said.

"He did," Abdul said. "We discovered the building just as you described."

The commander pointed toward one of the men, and for the first time, Qari realized that his former captor was standing among his liberators.

Qari stared at the man, taking in his frightened features and lack of a weapon.

"Did they mistreat you?" Qari said.

The jailer shook his head. "No, sir," the man said. "They honored our agreement."

"Good," Qari said. "And the technician . . . he is still here?"

"Yes, brother," the jailer said.

"Find this man and bring him to me," Qari said, turning his attention back to Taliban commander. "The knowledge he carries in his head is vital."

Already his confidence was returning as the crushing helplessness of the last ten years faded like a mist burned away by the rising sun. Qari pushed back against this feeling. He was no longer the arrogant commander he'd once been. Allah had reformed him, reshaped his life's purpose.

He would not forget his transformation so quickly.

"The brothers have finished loading the equipment," the commander said. "We took appropriate precautions, but you may inspect our work if you please."

Qari shook his head.

He was probably the least qualified to judge the quality of their work. Qari hadn't been the most technologically savvy before his imprisonment. He could only imagine how much things had changed since. While he understood the value of the information housed in the building, the electronic medium on which it was stored might as well have been taken from another planet. This was why he needed the technician. Besides, Qari's faith did not rest with electronic boxes or flashing lights. Allah had brought this moment to fruition. Surely he would not let it be undone by the very men he'd enlisted to his purpose.

"No," Qari said, "but I require a phone."

The commander reached into his pocket, withdrew his cell, and handed it to Qari.

"Thank you," Qari said, even as he began punching

in the number he'd carefully memorized. He'd recited the digits daily, each time he finished his prayers. He'd been uncertain that he'd ever have the opportunity to dial them, but neither could he abandon the hope they'd represented.

No, Qari mentally corrected himself. That wasn't right. His hope, like his salvation, was in Allah. The phone number, as with the computers in the building, was a tool.

Nothing more.

Victory did not reside in flesh and blood or the things they created.

"Pardon, brother," the commander said, interrupting Qari's efforts. "What should be done with him?"

He pointed a dirty fingernail at the cowering jailer.

Qari studied the man's face even as he hit the dial button.

"Kill him," Qari said.

"Wait," the jailer said, his voice pitiful. "You said you'd be merciful."

"Mercy belongs to Allah," Qari said, "not men. But you are correct. Allah has seen fit to grant you mercy. Your family will not also bear the cost of your sins, unlike your fellow jailers."

The man let loose with a pitiful scream, which was quickly silenced by a gunshot.

Qari didn't pay attention to either sound.

He was too busy listening to the ringing phone.

ONE

AUSTIN, TEXAS

Today was supposed to be a good day.

A day for celebrating new beginnings and old friendships. Few places in the world were better suited for celebration than my home city of Austin, Texas. While the self-proclaimed home of the weird wasn't anyone's idea of paradise in August, the city offered many ways to mitigate the stifling heat and suffocating humidity. It was four o'clock in the afternoon on a Thursday, and by now the three-acre Barton Springs Pool was undoubtedly crammed full of swimmers. The spring-fed water offered both refuge from the sun and a chance to meet the elusive and federally protected Barton Springs salamander, which lived in the pool's rock-lined bottom.

If the spring's year-round sixty-eight-degree water wasn't your cup of tea, the good folks over at Deep Eddy Pool would probably let you in a little early while they prepared for another nightly showing of *Jaws*. You read that right. Hundreds of people would soon be floating in inner tubes as they watched the scariest shark movie ever made. If experience was any guide, an illicit flask or two filled to the brim with the Austin-based Deep Eddy Vodka would be circulating among the audience.

I was partial to the Ruby Red variant.

This was Austin at her eccentric finest.

Though I loved my home city's eclectic summer offerings, I was seeking sanctuary somewhere more befitting a man of my low stature.

A bar.

But not just any bar.

The establishment in which my two companions and I found ourselves had no equal.

At least no modern equal.

The bar was small, dimly lit, and adhered to strict rules. Rule number one—booths must be reserved. Reservations were for a minimum of one hour and a maximum of three. Rule number two—no mobile devices and no obnoxious behavior. Despite, or perhaps maybe because of, its prime location, the bar's capacity probably topped out at about fifty. The customers sat in a row of booths that flanked a single walkway that led from the entrance to the employee area in the rear. Obnoxious behavior in the form of drunken carousing or endless electronic scrolling detracted from the bar's atmosphere.

And atmosphere was king.

The bar's history was both sordid and long. At different points it had served as a brothel and a speakeasy among other equally less reputable businesses. Now the establishment was a fixture on Austin's infamous Sixth Street. An island of calm in which the Austinites who actually paid for the city's expenses via ever-increasing property taxes could enjoy an evening apart from the throngs of college students who regularly mobbed the street. If there was an establishment in Austin custom-made for private celebrations, the Twilight Wrangler was it.

And we were here to celebrate.

Assuming our missing party eventually joined us.

"You sure you told her the right place?"

The question came from a slightly built African American man seated across the table from me. When we'd first met, he'd been one of the deadliest human beings I'd ever encountered. His physique had always skewed more toward endurance than strength, but his ropy muscles and prominent tendons could have been crafted from steel cables and iron ingots rather than flesh and blood.

Now he was a shadow of the fearsome warrior he'd once been. While we were operating together in Syria, an explosively formed penetrator had sheared off his left arm at the elbow and ruined his left leg. He'd recently had the mutilated leg amputated just below the knee so that he could be fitted with a prothesis. Rehab had gone well, and the procedure had given him an exponential quality-of-life improvement.

Even so, I couldn't look at him without seeing the man he'd once been.

Though his given name was Frederick Tyler Cates, everyone called him Frodo, including his fiancée, Katherine, who was seated beside him. Their recently announced engagement was one of the reasons we were here to celebrate. I was ecstatically happy for the couple. I knew Katherine well, but my relationship with Frodo ran much deeper. He was my confidant, coworker, and, most important, best friend.

I treated him accordingly.

"Of course I'm sure, ya jack wagon," I said. "She's my wife."

While the girl in question was most assuredly my wife, I was less certain about the first part of my statement. My wife wasn't late. Ever. Since it was now fifteen minutes past the time we'd agreed to meet, there was a better-than-even chance I'd given her the wrong address.

But I wasn't about to admit this to Frodo.

"Maybe she's looking for parking." Katherine's statement was infinitely reasonable.

Like Frodo and me, Katherine had spent time in the military before taking her current role in the NSA, but she'd inhabited an utterly different world. The slim African American woman with warm eyes, shoulder-length hair, and a contagious laugh had been an aviator—a Black Hawk pilot, to be precise. And while helicopter pilots were a breed unto themselves, Katherine and her fellow aviators could on occasion admit when they were wrong.

This was not the case for men like Frodo and me. We hailed from organizations within Special Operations Command that viewed being wrong as only slightly better than being last.

Or maybe that was just me.

In any case, there was no way I could acknowledge the

slim possibility that I'd texted my wife the address of our favorite watering hole on Rainey Street rather than that of the Twilight Wrangler. But I was beginning to get worried. Laila was not looking for parking because she wasn't driving. My wife excelled at a good many things. Battling Austin's homicidal motorists for the one remaining parking spot this side of Lady Bird Lake was not one of them. Laila was Ubering, which meant that her tardiness was not due to parking.

This was concerning.

"Everything okay, Matty?" Frodo said.

His earlier levity had vanished.

I'd organized this meeting at Laila's request, and she'd been adamant that its true purpose remain a secret. Katherine had taken this condition in stride, but Frodo had done everything he could to worm the topic of discussion out of me ahead of time. He'd grown more and more annoyed the closer we'd come to the appointed hour as his attempts to interrogate me continued to fail. Now his concern had a different target. Unlike our fellow patrons, Frodo and I did not have vocations in which a wife's absence could be taken lightly.

Frodo had not earned his nickname because he resembled a hobbit or had a penchant for second breakfasts. Prior to becoming a double amputee, Frodo had been a member of an organization known as the Unit to the special operators skillful enough to be listed among its members. As was the custom with newly minted assaulters, Frodo had been awarded a call sign.

Whether or not he liked it was immaterial.

I, on the other hand, had spent my last military assignment as a company commander in the vaunted Ranger Regiment. Jumping out of airplanes and kicking in doors alongside the finest infantrymen God had ever created had been a fine way to earn a paycheck. Those years did not hold a candle to my current vocation. Case in point, I'd once engaged in a shoot-out with a team of Iraqi hitters just a few blocks from where we currently sat.

Unexplained absences made me nervous.

"She's Ubering," I said, fishing my phone from my pocket. "Should be here by now."

The change in Frodo was subtle but recognizable. At least to me. One moment the fingertips of his remaining hand were resting on the stem of his fancy cocktail glass. The next, the calloused brown digits were nowhere to be seen, which probably meant they were hovering in the vicinity of his concealed SIG Sauer.

But it was more than just the location of his hand that signified a change in my best friend. Frodo's narrow shoulders now presented sharp edges against his button-down shirt, and his eyes projected hyperalertness. Frodo might have been a double amputee who walked with the aid of a cane, but dismissing him because of his injuries would have been a mistake.

A lamed wolf did not somehow become a sheep.

"Y'all need something?"

Our waitress had approached with a broad smile—after all, who wasn't happy to be working at a gourmet cocktail bar—but her grin had steadily evaporated the closer she came to our table. She had the bleached blond hair and requisite septum ring and sleeve tattoo required of a hip Austin waitress, but now her laughing eyes communicated something else.

Concern.

"We're fine," Katherine said, trying to warm up the sudden chill. "Right, guys?"

I was about to agree when my phone vibrated.

After reaching into my pocket, I pulled out the offending device.

The waitress took a step backward.

Maybe Frodo wasn't the only one who looked ready to brawl.

At six feet and one hundred eighty-five pounds, I wasn't physically insignificant, but neither did I inspire an automatic *Oh, shit* when someone drunkenly spilled beer on my boots. This was by intention. In my line of work, it was better to go unnoticed. To be the proverbial gray man. Accordingly, I was sporting what Laila playfully termed my ragamuffin look.

At least I hoped it was playfully.

My hair was long and my beard scruffy, but my Wrangler pearly-snap shirt framed the wide shoulders and broad back of a person for whom physical fitness was more than just a passing fancy. Even so, I still worked to project the just-another-guy-enjoying-a-drink vibe.

Except that, like Frodo, sometimes the real me peeked through.

"Right," I said, trying to add a reassurance to my voice I didn't feel.

The Glock 23 tucked into my Don Hume waistband

holster pressed comfortingly against my right hip even as the pulsing phone reminded me that there were some problems that a trusty .40-caliber pistol couldn't solve. Yet another reason I missed having Frodo watching my back with his eye pressed to a SIG Sauer TANGO6T optic mounted to his HK 417. A 7.62mm projectile traveling at a speed of twenty-six hundred feet per second wasn't the answer to all of life's problems, but it certainly solved many of them.

I unlocked the phone to see a text message. The originating number consisted of the digits 911 repeated over and over. The person responsible for sending the text was a former master sergeant from 10th Special Forces Group named James Scott Glass. He was also my boss. Subtlety wasn't his thing. Across the table, Frodo reached for his own phone. I had a feeling that not all was well in our world.

The text confirmed my suspicion.

CHECK OUT THE NEWS. NOW.

"Can you turn that to a news station?" I said to the waitress, pointing at the flat-screen mounted to the wall above the bar.

She slowly shook her head.

"I'm sorry," the waitress said. "The manager says it ruins the ambience."

"Please," I said even as I peeled a couple of twenties from my money clip. "It's important."

"No need for that," the waitress said, refusing the offered bills. "I'll see if I can find the remote. But only for a minute or two. Okay?"

"Sure," I said.

"What's this mean?" Frodo said, flashing me his phone. The same message glared from his screen.

"We're about to find out," I said.

The waitress pointed a black remote at the TV and the display glowed to life. It was tuned to MSNBC—we were in Austin—but I didn't care about the station's political leanings. I was too busy focused on the video playing over the anchor's shoulder.

"Holy shit," Frodo said.

"Can you turn it up?" I said. "Please."

The waitress shot me a look but obliged.

A moment later, a cultured voice flooded the room.

"This is unprecedented," the newscaster said. "The Taliban now control Bagram Air Base."

"Holy shit," Frodo said again.

Mom loved to remind me that foul language was evidence of low intelligence. That might be true, but in this case I didn't agree. Though he'd joined the Army straight out of high school and had never darkened the doorway of an institution of higher learning, Frodo was one of the most intelligent people I knew and he had a vocabulary to match. He wasn't swearing because he was too lazy to think of better words. He was cursing because he was shell-shocked.

So was I.

"Why is that on, Hannah?"

The tone carried just enough indignation to indicate

that the man asking the question was the bar's manager. He was standing at the far end of the room, hands on his hips and glaring at our waitress. Like Hannah, the manager was dressed in black slacks and a white dress shirt. The top several buttons were undone and his shirtsleeves were rolled, exposing portions of a tattoo that seemed to traverse his entire torso. While Hannah's nose ring and ink seemed somehow charming, the effect wasn't nearly so endearing on this joker. My assessment probably had something to do with the tone of voice he was using with Hannah.

"Hey," I said, waving to get his attention, "my fault. I asked her to turn it on."

The manager could have taken the off-ramp I'd provided.

He didn't.

"Thank you for apologizing, sir," the manager said, "but Hannah should have known better."

Crossing the bar in three quick strides, the manager snatched the remote from Hannah and pointed it at the TV.

"Stop," Frodo said.

My commando friend didn't shout, but the manager still jerked.

I understood why.

Authority radiated from Frodo's voice.

"I'm sorry?" the manager said, turning toward Frodo.

"Don't be sorry," Frodo said, speaking with a drill sergeant's crisp cadence. "Just leave it on."

"Until the station break," I said. "Please. We're Afghanistan vets."

"I'm grateful for your service," the manager said in a tone suggesting otherwise, "but our policy is clear."

He extended the remote toward the TV.

"Don't. Touch. It."

Frodo's words cracked through the air, each one landing like Rocky Marciano's mighty right hand. Images of carnage and rioting shone from the screen, but at that moment, Afghanistan didn't have anything on the violence Frodo's tone promised.

"We don't mind if you leave it on."

The comment came from a couple seated at the table catty-corner to ours. The man was the one who spoke, but his date vigorously nodded. The man's earnest expression suggested that he genuinely wanted to help, but I was betting he would have the opposite effect. Maybe the manager might have backed down before, but now his face-saving off-ramp was gone. Petty tyrants are the same the world over whether they run a bar or a country. A man who isn't secure in his own authority will always view differing opinions as attacks.

"Sorry," the manager said, stabbing the remote.

The TV winked off.

The manager turned from the TV to Frodo, a self-satisfied smirk stretched across his face. Like the television, the manager's smile died a quick death. The average person's concept of violence is formed by action movies or schoolyard shoving matches. This naivety leaves them wholly unprepared for the visceral nature of actual combat.

To be fair, few human beings have meted out violence on the scale practiced by Frodo. Comparing the squabbles of day-to-day American life with the world that Frodo and I inhabited was the equivalent of calling a house cat a mountain lion. Sure, the two felines shared similar qualities, but someone who'd seen both would never confuse one for the other. The look on the manager's face suggested that he'd just stumbled upon his first lion.

I made a grab for my best friend but needn't have bothered. A half second earlier, I'd been convinced that Frodo was a heartbeat away from thrashing the arrogant manager with his prosthesis. Now something else demanded our collective attention.

The door to the bar slammed open, and two people entered.

People with guns.